SINISTER ASCENSION

MARC L. ABBOTT

COPYRIGHT NOTICE

OTHER TITLES BY MARC L. ABBOTT

DEDICATION

In Memory of Martina Carrill

REVIEWS FOR SINISTER ASCENSION

"Sinister Ascension starts with a bang, and explosion really, and never lets up from there. Propulsive and agile, Marc Abbott writes horror but combines it with a compelling, appealingly grounded feel."

— VICTOR LAVALLE, AWARD-WINNING
AUTHOR OF *LONE WOMEN*

"Sinister Ascension's fast action opening puts us in the middle of the battle between good/evil and immediately invests us in the characters' struggle. Abbott sustains high energy from page one to the end as supernatural beings, not all bad, work with an against humans who have their own surprise abilities to prevent death and possession of friends by a vengeful demon. The effortless, engaging storytelling style of Abbott's writing takes us on a journey worth every moment spent in this thrilling novel."

— LINDA D. ADDISON, AWARD-WINNING
AUTHOR, HWA LIFETIME ACHIEVEMENT
AWARD RECIPIENT AND SFPA GRAND
MASTER

"Gruesome, contemporary, and chilling, *Sinister Ascension* delivers a frighteningly original take on vampire mythologies from one of the most imaginative speculative fiction writers of our time. Marc Abbott plumbs the darkest depths of the undead to deliver an intimate and unsettling tale of life, death, and everything in between. Not to be missed!"

— JAMES CHAMBERS, BRAM STOKER AWARD® -WINNING AUTHOR OF *A BRIGHT AND BEAUTIFUL ETERNAL WORLD* AND *ON THE NIGHT BORDER*

CHAPTER ONE

Dwain Rucker swung the axe in a hard arc, splitting the wooden cover of the six-foot crate. The wood crackled and moaned as he wrenched it out. He grunted and swung again. This time, it broke the top open. He tossed the tool aside and wrenched the planks away.

"Hurry up." Dwain's brother, Robert, stared nervously at the door to the dorm room. "Todd might be back at any minute."

"Let him come back. I'll take this ax and bury it deep into his chest," Dwain said.

"I don't like this plan. Too many people will get hurt."

"And if we don't stop Todd and this experiment of his, thousands will die."

Robert peered through the window to the science building and then at his watch. He bumped his foot against a gasoline canister he had brought with him.

"We only have a few minutes before that bomb goes off," Robert said.

"Excellent. By the time security responds, they won't make it back here in time to put out the fire I'm going to set to this crate. Then we go after Todd and end all this."

"The bomb? It's only going to destroy the crate in there?" Robert asked.

Dwain didn't respond. He turned his attention back to the crate before him and continued to rip the planks off until he could peer inside.

"What do you see?" Robert said.

"Nothing. I–"

"It's not a decoy, is it?"

"I'm sure it isn't." Dwain delved in and halfway down, he touched moist dirt. He scooped up a handful and raised his hand to the light. Pushing bits of it away with his fingertips, Dwain exposed a large, squirming black leech. "Filthy."

Dwain dropped the leech and stomped on it. Blood gushed from its body and spattered across the floor. Robert gagged.

"Gimmie the canister." Dwain walked over to a bed and wiped the bottom of his shoe on the sheets.

Robert handed the canister to Dwain, then hurried to the door. He placed his ear against it and listened.

"Hallway's quiet. We're going to get expelled for this, you know."

"I'll take expulsion over death," Dwain said. "No one wanted to listen to me. I told them about what Todd was doing with the leeches. They accused me of being jealous because he tried to woo Crystal. Neither of us got help." He waved his finger, pointing from himself to Robert. "I don't care if this whole school burns to the ground. If this is what it will take to stop him, then this is how it's going to go down."

Dwain unscrewed the top of the canister and poured the contents onto the soil. As it absorbed the liquid, the crate trembled.

Gasoline leaked from below, causing a trail. The strong odor burned Dwain's nostrils while Robert covered his nose.

"My God, is that smell coming from the leeches?" Robert said.

Dwain tossed the canister aside, lifted his shirt, and removed a road flare he had tucked into his pants. He stepped back from the crate and glanced at his watch.

"Three, two. . ."

Dwain turned to the window. The sun had set, giving off a midnight blue hue to the twilight sky.

Then a bright flash came from one of the science building's upper floor lab windows. An earth-trembling explosion followed. A huge fireball lit up the winter evening sky.

Dwain placed his hand over his heart and sighed with relief.

"Beautiful," he whispered.

"Dear God, what did we do?" Robert watched the fire consume part of the building. "Dwain, what did you put in that pipe bomb? It wasn't supposed to–"

A loud banging on the door caught their attention.

"Open up." A voice from the other side said. "Let me in or so help me."

"It's Todd," Robert said.

"Open the door," Dwain said.

"Are you crazy?"

The door buckled after a loud thud.

"I got this. Go out the window."

"He's going to kill you."

"He's–"

The frame splintered and broke as the door was kicked open. A tall African American man dressed in jeans and a winter coat stood before them. He eyed the burning science building out the window, then gazed at the crate and the canister.

Dwain struck the flare. It lit up like a candle, sizzling and glowing red. He held it tight as he drew his arm back, readying to throw it into the crate.

"What are you going to do with that?" Todd said in a deep voice.

"Your little experiment is over. You've got nothing," Dwain said. "I'm gonna light this crate up."

Todd seemed unfazed. "You didn't think these were the only two crates I had, did you?"

"I already know where the other one is, and it's not as important as these two," Dwain said.

"These two are not *that* important," Todd said.

"Nice try. But you wouldn't be here if they weren't."

Todd stared at the flare before turning his attention to Robert. "Your brother is crazy; you know? He's been running all over campus with these silly rumors about my experiments and me. Now he's dragged you into this, too. Robert, you're a reasonable man."

"Stop it," Robert said. "I trust my brother. After the atrocities I've seen, I know he's sane."

"Dwain, c'mon, my brotha–"

"I'm not your brotha. We both happen to be black. It doesn't make us down in any way."

Todd's eyebrows sank to form a frown. "Okay, it's like that then. If I were you, I'd put the flare out before you get your feelings hurt."

"Really?" Dwain said.

"Isn't it bad enough Crystal left you for being a fool? Now you want to go and do this?" Todd said.

Dwain's body warmed with rage. He gripped the flare tighter as his breathing increased.

"Don't you dare speak her name," Dwain said through clenched teeth.

"Where is Crystal?" Robert said. "We know you did something with her."

"Me?" Todd shook his head. "I didn't do a thing to her. If you can't find her, it's because she doesn't want to have anything to do with you."

"I'm done dealing with you." Dwain tossed the flare into the crate.

"No!" Todd screamed.

The flare touched the dirt, and the entire contents went up in flames. Todd watched in shock while the fire consumed it. He pointed a threatening finger at Dwain.

"This is on your hands."

"Go–"

A bloodcurdling scream erupted from inside the crate. Dwain and Robert turned and watched in horror as Dwain's girlfriend, Crystal, jumped out of the burning crate. Waving her hands around wildly, she attempted to put the fire out, but the more she flailed, the higher the flames.

"Crystal! No. No," Dwain screamed.

Robert wrenched the sheets off the bed. He rushed to her, covered her, and tried to put the fire out. Carefully he withdrew the sheet off her burned body; she let out a final cry, fell to the floor, and died.

Dwain stared at her body. Tears streamed down his face while Todd laughed at him.

Moving faster than Dwain could see, Todd rushed to the crate and flipped it over. Burning wood and soil spilled all over. He picked up a piece of burning wood and threw it onto the bed, setting it ablaze. Dwain tried to lunge at Todd through the fire, but Robert held him back.

Todd retreated through the door into the hall, stopped, and turned to them.

"Now you can burn together." Todd removed the door from the hinges and set it in place within the frame.

Dwain and Robert backed away from the fire as thick smoke filled the room. Robert leaped over the bed. He landed but slipped and fell onto the floor.

"I'm okay."

"Get the door down," Dwain called out. He started coughing uncontrollably.

Robert got to his feet. The smoke stung his eyes as it penetrated his shirt. He yanked the door. It fell back toward him. He dodged it. A blast of cool air entered the room.

The fire burst up and out, engulfing Dwain as he jumped forward. He screamed in agony as he fell forward, ablaze.

Robert started to go back, but Dwain's cries of pain slowly silenced. The fire destroyed the room and his body with it.

———

Robert started sprinting away from the room but became overwhelmed with grief. At the end of the hall, he leaned against the wall, tears streaming from his eyes. Through a window in the hall, he saw Todd running away from the dorm to a Mustang parked across the street.

Robert bolted for the stairs and up to the emergency exit, crashing through it just in time to see Todd speeding away. He started to chase after him but realized he would never catch up. His cell phone went off in his pocket. He removed it and answered.

"Todd's escaped. We missed our opportunity." He paused. "Dwain's dead."

"This is unfortunate," the voice on the other end said. "I suggest you go gather up all the paperwork I gave you on what

Todd is and get over to Bruckner. Todd's headed there. Get a hotel room in town. I'll be in touch."

"What about—"

"Every moment you spend questioning me is time you're giving him to get away."

The caller hung up.

Robert glanced back at the burning science building, then at the dorm fire. Crowds of students rushed toward the quad, screaming, putting distance between them and the fires. Robert went in the opposite direction. He had to hurry before they locked down the campus.

CHAPTER TWO

*D*on't forget to ask her about speaking to the dead before you hang up.

The thought went through Carmen Guerra's mind as she sat cross-legged on the floor of her dorm room, her phone tucked securely between her shoulder and ear. She smiled as she brushed back a strand of her ebony hair and tucked it behind her free ear. On the floor before her sat an old photo album. Protected by a thin, clear sheet of cellophane were four 3 x 5 pictures, each with fading corners, on a thick card stock page. She turned the page to look at the next four directly on the backside.

"I'm on page five. I think this is the old fort in San Juan." She leaned in as she spoke into the receiver, "It's you and three men."

"Does it say what jear on the page?" the gentle voice of her grandmother, Maria Guerra, said. Despite all the years she had been in America, she had never fully grasped how to phonetically say any word that began with the letter Y, so it always came out sounding like a hard J.

Carmen scanned the page for the year. In the top right-hand corner, she found it written in black ink. "It says 1957."

"Ah, that was the summer before we moved to New Jork."

"You have your arm around one guy with a white straw hat. Is that Abuelo?"

"Jes, it's him. The other two in the picture were his brothers, Ernesto and George. Jou would have loved them. They were so full of life."

"Thank you so much for giving this to me."

"Family is important. It's about time jou got to see and know more about everyone. Jou have any questions about anyone in the album; call me and we can talk. I know it like the back of my hand," Maria said.

"I will." Carmen closed the album and placed it on her bed behind her. She grunted as she got to her feet. "How's your knee?"

"Hay Dios Mio, it's been acting up all morning."

"Make sure you soak in the tub later. Don't let it get stiff on you."

"Hey, who's the abuela around here? Jou worry about you. I'll be fine." Maria's voice changed into a serious tone. "And speaking of jou."

"Abuela, no."

"What?"

"I know where this is going. My major again, isn't it?"

"I just don't understand why jou're taking a major that's not going to lead anywhere. Why math? Why not, psychology or one of the sciences."

"You're sounding like mom. She put you up to this, didn't she?"

"We feel jou're wasting jour time with that degree. Jou're a smart girl and I don't want to see jou waste jour time getting something jou're not going to use. What about psychology? Jou said jou liked that elective you took."

Carmen sighed so hard her breath sounded like a gust of wind through the receiver. "I'm sorry I said it now. It was one class."

"Jou need to take life seriously, Carmencita. Jou keep fooling around, taking the easy way out."

"How am I taking the easy road out?"

"The only reason jou're going for that degree is because the subject comes easy for jou."

"The only thing that matters is I get a college degree, Abuela. That's what everyone wants from me. I'm not going to put myself in a difficult position for no reason."

"Jou cannot dodge difficult things your entire life. Eventually, jou're going to come across something jou have no choice but to face, and then what? Will jou be ready?"

Carmen got quiet as she crossed the room to her desk and sat at it. She took a pencil from a cup of pens and pencils and began to doodle on the surface. It was her way of zoning out of a conversation.

"Carmen, stop doodling and listen to me."

She stopped. "How did you...

"Listen to jour abuela. Stop fooling around. It's time to get serious!"

"I take a lot of things seriously."

"Like that boyfriend of jours? The two of jou wouldn't stay off the phone half the time we were in Puerto Rico."

A knock at the door caught her attention and before Carmen could respond, it opened, and the R.A. looked in. She adjusted her glasses as she scanned the room.

"Hey, what's up?"

"Just doing a quick assessment of the rooms. Any repairs needed?"

"Not on my side of the room."

The R.A. marked on a piece of paper she had with her on a clipboard. "What about your roommate?"

"Kim's not back yet, so I don't know."

"You happen to know when she's coming back?"

"Later today."

"Have her come see me then. Oh, let her know someone found her keys in the bathroom the day you all were leaving for break. I'm sure she'll want them back."

"I'll tell her," Carmen said. The R.A. nodded and closed the door as she slipped back out. "Sorry. R.A. was looking for Kim."

"I'll go then."

"No, Abuela, it can wait. I need to talk to you about something, anyway."

"Si?

"I wanted to revisit a conversation we had at Aunt Angela's house?"

"We had so many at her house. Jou have to refresh my memory."

"At Aunt Angela's house, we were on the porch, and you told me about the time you and she were younger, could talk to. . ."

"Oh, that conversation," Maria interrupted. "That was a long time ago."

"But you said it runs in the family."

"I know what I told jou, and I also said not everyone exhibits it. Where is this going?"

"How come I don't have it? The ability?"

"Who said jou don't? I never said jou don't have the ability. I said it's sometimes more prominent with some than others. And it can also skip a generation or two."

"Okay, who's not being serious now?"

"Many of the women in our family were mediums. A lot of them served the communities they lived in. Jour aunt still does from time to time. It's a gift and a blessing."

"So special, no one but you and Aunt Angela have it," Carmen scoffed.

"Why are jou getting upset about this?"

"I just feel like I'm . . . I don't know . . . You guys come down on me about my major. You make me feel like I'm wasting my life. Then you brag about speaking to the dead like it's some badge of honor, but of course, I have to be the skipped generation, which makes me no more important than my degree goals."

"Jou cannot compare the two."

"Well, with neither a good degree nor a special ability, how will I be able to make a living?"

"Jou think bein' a medium is a way to make a living? Our ability allows us to be a link between the living and the dead. To allow loved ones, friends, and familia, to connect one last time."

Carmen looked at the album. "You ever talk to Abuelo?"

For a moment, Carmen thought Maria had hung up on her as she had gone silent. Her stomach dropped like on the first dip on a roller coaster as she heard Maria praying in Spanish for God to forgive her. Guilt set in.

"How could jou say such an awful thing to me? How could jou, Carmencita? All I have ever done is loved and supported jou and jou say such a cruel thing!"

"I'm sorry, Abuela. I didn't mean it to be cruel. I'm honestly asking." Carmen said sincerely as a lump formed in her throat. "Do you? Have you? I mean, how would I know if I even had the ability?"

"For starters, jou don't just talk to the dead like jou're picking up the phone." Maria sighed, then said, "Jou'll feel it, physically at first. As time goes on, you get used to it, you can sense the presence. If the presence is strong enough, it will feel like a–"

A knock at Carmen's room door caught her attention. "Hey, someone's at the door. I'll call you soon and we can talk more, okay? And Abuela, Te Amo."

"I know, my dear. Don't call too late. I may be out on a date," Maria said.

"Abuela!" Carmen laughed, and they hung up at the same time. She placed the phone back on its base. As she walked to the door, she adjusted her sweatpants and tugged the bottom of her form fitting sleeveless top over her waist.

Upon opening the door, a tall white boy with long dirty blonde hair seized her around the waist, drew her into him, leaned down, and kissed her. Carmen struck his shoulder with her fist, but gave in as his arms tightened around her waist. He lifted her off the floor and carried her back into the room. She heard the door shut behind him; she cupped his face in her hands and kissed him back deeply. She controlled the rhythm, making him slow down while keeping the passion.

Gently, she put her hand around the back of his head and wrapped her arms around his neck. Then she wrapped her legs around his waist, locking them in an X.

The door suddenly opened behind them.

"Dayton Connors, you know better!" the voice of the R.A. bellowed. "You being on the floor means doors stay open."

Carmen broke the kiss and laughed. Dayton winked at her as he lowered her back to the floor. He turned and smiled at the R.A..

"It won't happen again."

"I did you a favor letting you up here unannounced. Don't make me regret it." She glanced at Carmen. "Put a sweatshirt on. We don't need him any more excited than he already is." She turned and left the room with the door open.

Carmen dragged him back to her and kissed him once more.

"God, I have missed you," he said.

They held one another. She placed her head on his chest.

"I've missed you too." She looked up at him. "I was wondering where you were."

"Eric got a new tv for Christmas and we were setting up the gaming system. We're going to have a Madden tournament in a few minutes. But I had to come and see you."

"How come you didn't call me?"

"Your line was busy."

"You could have called my cell."

"But then I couldn't do my little surprise on you."

She playfully struck his shoulder again. "You're lucky I didn't knock the crap outta you."

"Yeah, how did you even know it was me? I could have been some stranger."

"I know my boyfriend's lips." She stepped away to her dresser, opened the drawer, and grabbed a sweatshirt. She smiled as she watched Dayton's face droop slightly from disappointment as she covered herself. "Madden, huh?"

"Yeah. I got it for Christmas. Can't wait to try it out with the guys. How was PR?"

"Nice. Got to see family. I found out…" Carmen stopped short of telling him about the medium lineage. She wasn't sure how he would react and preferred not to find out just yet. "Never mind. I'll walk you back. I need some air anyway."

"Sure."

Carmen went to her closet and got her coat. She slipped it on, checked to make sure she had her keys, took her cell phone off the bed, then took Dayton by the hand and led him out, closing the door behind her.

The moment they stepped outside, she jumped on his back. Dayton took hold of her legs and gave her a piggyback ride across the quad.

"I should have gone to school down south, like Florida or Texas," Dayton said. "Even after four years of being up here, I can't get used to this New England cold."

"It's not too bad. You should try a winter in New York City. You're from the Midwest and you're complaining?"

"Different kinda cold out there." Dayton stopped, and she slid off his back. He took her hand, and they started walking. She grew quiet. "What's wrong?"

"Argued with my abuela. Another one of her you don't take things seriously speech."

"Ah, one of those speeches. I got one too at home. Graduation looming and I have no plans for the immediate future."

"I want to do a little traveling. Maybe spend some time in PR. Who knows, I might go back to school for a master's after a year off and then go from there."

"I never heard you mention getting a masters."

"I don't know. Maybe. But who cares right now?" They stopped, and she embraced Dayton and nuzzled into his chest. "Right now, it's all about you and me."

"No other place I'd rather be." He kissed the top of her forehead.

"Yo, Dayton! The crews here. Come on in so you can get your ass kicked," someone from Chambers Hall yelled out across campus.

"Is that Eric screaming?"

"Yeah. Lemme go on over here and handle this." He kissed her. "This won't take long."

"Go get 'em, babe." She watched Dayton jog back to Chambers Hall.

Carmen continued across campus with no destination in mind. She looked up at the grey sky as her thoughts turned to what it would be like to speak to the dead. Her aunt never described how conversations sounded, just that the spirits would talk to her. She imagined they were soft-spoken, gentle, and kind. What would they say to her? How would she respond?

Her thoughts turned to her grandfather and how he sounded. His deep but smooth voice always made her smile. Imagining she could hear him again made her eyes well up. She dabbed them with her sleeve as an elated feeling swept over her. How wonderful to know there stood a chance she could one day hear him again. She started to make her way toward the lake behind her dorm, then an idea came to her.

"I wonder." She turned in the direction of where the campus founders were buried and walked to the markers.

In an area surrounded by a seven-inch-high wall that formed a square, four long marble markers sat on the surface of the lawn. Etched into the top of each of them were the founders' names, birth and death dates and their years of service to the university.

Carmen stepped over the wall, stood in front of one of the markers, and closed her eyes. "If you can hear me, tap me on the shoulder," she said aloud. She waited to feel something. A tap. A whisper in the ear. A gut punch. After waiting a full minute, and nothing happened, she opened her eyes, sucked her teeth, and headed to the lake. "Some ability."

She walked a path between two dorms towards the lake. The ripples of the water caused by a gentle breeze and the vacant bench where Dayton had first asked her out made her smile.

Her cell phone buzzed. She took it out and on the screen were two semicolons and a right parenthesis from Dayton. A happy face. Carmen started to text him back, staring down as she walked. She heard a male voice with a southern accent coming toward her.

"Todd, I got everythin' in place. We're in Chambers Hall. Make sure you see the R.A. for your room key. I also did my usual sweep of the campus as well. An if ya want my advice, you should get outta where you are t'night." The young man's voice stopped.

Carmen looked up.

A tall, muscular white guy in cargo pants and a down coat stood in the middle of the walkway. He watched her as she approached. "I'm pickin' up the van this afternoon for trans-porting the crates as well. We're good to go. I'll be in touch." The young man ended the call.

Their eyes locked. She watched the expression on his face go from admiration to nervousness. He fixed his lips as though he were about to speak. Instead, he took his phone and made another call while making a quick left and heading across the quad, never looking back.

Carmen turned her attention back to her phone, sent a reply text, then turned to see the young man disappear between the two buildings. After a moment, a headache began to grow in her skull.

Carmen touched the side of her head with the palm of her hand. It subsided a bit. She took another step, and a loud pop went off in both ears. She dropped her cell as she put her hands up to her ears. The agony crept into her teeth.

"Hay Dios Mio!" She pressed her fingertips into her upper lip, pushing down on her gums. Then the discomfort started to subside. She clenched her teeth and groaned as she stood. Dizziness caused her to wobble a bit.

"Ahh, damn migraines," she whispered. She looked up her roommate's number and called her. It rang four times, then went to voicemail. "Hey, Kim, it's Carmen. Call me back and let me know what time you're coming in. Don't forget we have plans. And the R.A. found your keys in case you were wondering where they were."

She hung up, then decided to go back to her room to lay down.

CHAPTER THREE

Kim Morris adjusted her earphones as she waited for her boyfriend, Eric Tucker, to answer his phone. As she listened to it ring, her call waiting beeped. She glanced at the screen, saw Carmen's name on the screen above Eric's, and ignored it. She continued to wait for Eric to answer as she unfolded the first letter he had ever written her. The paper had turned yellow, but Kim could make out the semi-faded words as she read it to herself.

Dear Kim,

Words cannot describe how you make me feel. From the moment I saw you, I knew in my heart we were meant to be together. The deep brown of your eyes captivates my soul. No woman has ever made me feel alive before. I wanted you to know not a moment goes by that I don't think about you, and I get excited thinking about the next time we meet.

The other night we kissed for the first time; I don't even know how to explain it. It was perfect.

I know this is sudden and after one kiss, you probably think I'm crazy. But I'm willing to take it slow. I'm feeling you and if you give me the chance, I can show you that a good man isn't hard to find.

Trust in your heart. Trust in me.

Eric

"Hello," Eric answered.

"Don't be late," Kim said into the microphone piece on the headphone wire. She folded the letter and put it back in her purse.

"I'm not."

"I mean it. I need you to be at the station by the time I arrive. Carmen and I have plans tonight, and I don't want us to be late."

"I know. I have your info written down; Amtrak at one-thirty. I'll be at the station on time."

"Okay." Kim glanced at her watch. "Feels like I've been on this train forever."

"You left at, what, six this morning?"

"Five thirty."

"Can't wait to see you. I've missed you."

"I missed you too. I had hoped you were going to visit me more over the break."

"I tried, but after that first trip to see you, I got back home and had a lot of family come in over the holiday and I couldn't get away."

"I understand," she said. "It's just–"

"Huntington. Next stop, Huntington," the conductor shouted as he walked through the car.

The train horn blew and the couple sitting across from Kim stood and gathered their bags.

"You okay?" Eric said.

"Yeah, we're about to pull into Huntington."

"Huntington, that's where Stafford College is. They were on

the news this afternoon about those two terrible fires. They're
saying now one of them might have been arson."

"I heard someone bombed the science building. They still
haven't found the person?"

"Nope. Their president was on talkin' 'bout holding off the
start of the semester until February. But the seniors are protestin'
his idea. They want to graduate on time."

"I can understand that. But I'd rather know my campus is safe
than come back and have my life at risk."

"Like my grandma would say, 'It's always something.' Dayton
is on his way back now, so I'll get the keys to the car from him.
He's been a ghost for most of the day," Eric said.

"He's probably with Carmen."

"Of course, he's with Carmen. I have never seen him into a girl
like he is with your roommate."

"I'm glad the two of them hooked up."

"I'm happy for Dayton, too. He was so nervous about even
approaching her after the whole thing with Curtis. Glad Carmen
decided to give him a chance. Anyway, I'll see you in an hour. I
love you."

"I love you too, baby," Kim said. "Be on time."

"Yeah, yeah, see you soon."

Kim ended the call. She plugged her phone into the outlet
under the window to charge it. She went back to check her voicemail for Carmen's message.

The conductor appeared at the far end of the car and announced,
"Huntington, five minutes away." This time, more people stood.
"Passengers will be exiting through the door at the far end of the car."

Kim texted Carmen rather than call her, letting her know
what time she would be in and to thank her for the information
on her keys. Then she put her earphones into her book bag before
removing her science textbook to read.

They arrived at Huntington, and people shuffled toward the exit with their coats zipped up to their chins.

"Huntington. Watch your step as you exit the train."

As new passengers boarded, Kim glanced over at the seat next to her and placed her book bag in it. The seat had been vacant for the past hour. She had been able to spread out, a rarity on the ride back to school.

"All aboooard!" the conductor said. The horn blared, and the train moved. The conductor started to close the door.

"Wait! Wait!" a man called out.

The conductor reopened the door, and the running man jumped up into the car and stumbled.

"Watch yourself," the conductor said.

"Thanks." He boarded the car and walked up to Kim. "Excuse me? Is someone sitting here?"

Kim raised her head. A strikingly handsome man stood before her, smartly dressed, which she found favorable. People who appeared as they slept in their clothes tended to be talkers. He smiled at her, then adjusted his book bag on his shoulder. She couldn't help but smile back.

"No." She reached for her book bag.

"Hand me your bag. You're settled in there," he said. He took her book bag and held it up to the overhead compartment. "Okay if I put it up here?"

"Sure."

The man put Kim's book bag up in the overhead, then placed his bag on the seat. Kim's eyes widened. She had seen the bag once in a Louis Vuitton ad.

"Thanks." He placed his bag on the floor and settled in.

"No problem."

He glanced at the book cover. "Microbiology. You studying for a class?"

"Biology is my major," Kim said over the top of the book. "I'm trying to prepare for my new class this semester."

"You should check out a book by Lawrence Mesker. It simplifies a lot of what you're reading now."

Kim lowered the book. "You study microbiology?"

"In undergrad I did. I'm now working on my Ph.D. in Oligochaetology. I'm headed to another school to finish it. The school I attended lost its program funding. I had to transfer."

"What school are you going to?" Kim said.

"Bruckner University."

"I go to Bruckner. They have a great science program."

"That's why I chose it."

"How long will it take for you to complete the program?" Kim said.

"I'll be done by June," he said.

"Oligochaetology, isn't that the study of like snakes or something?"

"It's worms. It's complex. I'm not sure if I could fully explain it properly. I would have to show you my notes, which, unfortunately, I don't have with me now."

"Oh," Kim said.

"But," he raised a finger, "I can tell you this: it deals with the physiology and life of annelids."

"I have never heard of someone going for their Ph.D. in a study of worms," Kim said.

"They're quite fascinating. But I don't want to bore you with those details. You need to study," he said.

"It's not boring." Kim's cell phone rang. She glanced at the screen and saw Carmen's name. "Hey, roomie. Yes, my train is on time. Eric is picking me up. Yes, I told him to be on time. Did you decide where we're going to eat?" She held a single finger up to the man. "Okay. What happened?" She listened. "Well, let's save it for later. I can't wait either. See you later." Kim pressed the end button on the screen, then set her phone to the side. "My roommate."

"I see. You two close?"

"Yeah, we're good friends."

"I've never cared for roommates. I like my privacy," he said.

"Getting a single room on campus is impossible."

"I heard. Um, do you know how long until we get to Bruckner?"

"Little less than an hour."

"Thanks." He took out his phone and typed a text message. He hit send and then waited for the response. His phone chimed within seconds. He read the reply. "Excuse me, I need to make a call. Hold my seat?"

"Sure."

"Todd. Todd Anderson."

"Kim Morris."

"Nice to meet you, Kim." Todd stood and walked toward the end of the car.

Kim returned to reading the textbook.

———

Todd stepped into the bathroom at the end of the car. He locked the door before dialing his cousin Zeborah's number.

"Todd, where tha hell are you?"

"I left my car at Huntington Station's Park and lock. I'll have to pick it up later," he said. "I'm currently on a train headed to Bruckner."

"What'd you do, try ta burn tha whole campus down?"

"The damn Rucker brothers. Someone tipped them off to my leaving, and all hell broke loose."

"What about the items in the crates?" Zeborah said.

"Other than a small consignment of the annelids with me, the crate in my room was destroyed. The one in the lab I had already cleared out and relocated all the contents to the backup crate in the storage area in the basement of the science building. It should still be there, and you should be able to get it. The last one is in our off-campus storage facility. But the one at Stafford is the most important one to get."

"Damn it, man. This changes all my plans. Ima have to go now and git that crate from Stafford. You betta pray I don't get stopped by tha police. I was your roommate there."

"You transferred out two weeks ago. We took care of the paperwork, so there would be no reason for anyone to question you other than where you think I may have gone."

Zeborah grew quiet. After a moment he said, "What if tha Rucker's—?"

"Okay, you know what, I don't want to hear about the Rucker's anymore. They're no longer a factor in any of this. Just get the crates to Bruckner University, then contact Kevin and get him to retrieve my car. Once he has it, tell him to contact me."

"Why don't you contact him yourself?"

"Zeborah, I'm not in the mood for this. Just do what I tell you."

"I shoulda never got involved in this."

"And yet you did. This train gets into Bruckner around one-thirty. I'll meet you on campus at two-thirty. Should give you plenty of time between now and then to get everything finished. We're done."

Todd ended the call, buried his phone deep in his pocket, and headed back to his seat.

"My cousin," he said as he slid into his seat.

"Not my business."

"It's a force of habit. I'm used to feeding people information. Sometimes I forget to keep information to myself."

"Hmm. Kind of strange for a person who likes their privacy to tell all their personal information."

"You're an exceptional listener."

"I'm a woman," Kim chuckled.

"Ah-ha. Okay. Whatever. Men are superb listeners too."

"Not true," she said. "Men have selective hearing; bad selective hearing."

"What about male psychologists? Huh?"

"Uh-uh, you can't use the medical profession for your basis. I'm speaking in general. Most men I know are terrible listeners. You tell them something and they either do the opposite or forget."

"You keep some bad company then," Todd said.

"That's rude," Kim said.

"I didn't mean to offend you, but you said most men. You're generalizing."

"I said most men *I* know. See, right there, you weren't listening."

Todd laughed. "Okay, you got me there."

"That's what Eric says when he knows I caught him in something."

"Who's he, your brother?"

"Eric's my. . ." Kim stopped short. "He's a great friend."

"Great, as in a classmate or as in boyfriend?" She didn't answer immediately. Todd understood what she meant. "Well, we got that out in the open. I would have hated to try to put the moves on you and get my feelings hurt."

Todd made a silly grin and Kim laughed. He closed his eyes while Kim laughed even louder.

"It wasn't *that* funny," Todd said.

CHAPTER FOUR

The train arrived at a crowded Bruckner Station at 1:35 PM. Kim pushed her way through the sea of people as she made it across the large hall, through the waiting area, toward the doors leading out to the street. She must have repeated the words "excuse me" at least a dozen times.

A row of anxious taxi drivers hollered to get her attention. She blew past them and out the double doors to the curbside pickup. The frigid air caused her to pull the zipper of her coat up to her chin as she sucked her teeth out of frustration. She scanned the line of parked yellow cabs for Dayton's car. It was nowhere in sight.

"Damn it, Eric, running late, as usual."

"Maybe you should wait inside. It's cold out here." Todd stepped up next to her, staring.

She could feel his eyes on her but ignored him. She glanced at him and said, "I'll be fine." Kim turned her attention back to the parking lot.

Cracking a smile, he adjusted his bag on his shoulder. "Well, I guess I will see you around on campus."

"Maybe."

"My invitation is open to you to come to see my experiment. Just look for me in the science labs."

"I'll keep it in mind," Kim said.

Todd put his hand out, reaching for her. Kim faced him abruptly as his fingertips grasped her winter hat and tugged it down over her ears. He withdrew his hand, and his fingertips grazed her cheek.

Kim shuddered.

"Sorry, my hands get cold fast." Todd stared into her eyes and smirked. She stared back, mesmerized. She fixed her mouth to say something, then Todd said, "Take care, Kim."

He walked down the row of cabs and waved to the driver standing by the first one. The driver opened the door, took his bag as he got into the back seat, and closed the door.

Kim watched as the cab drove off. She put her hand to the part of her cheek where Todd had touched her. She started to smile but wasn't sure why. Thunder rumbled in the distance as she wiped the spot. She gazed out beyond the parking lot and saw darker clouds coming in over the already grey sky. Gradually, she came back to reality. Kim took her cell phone out and called Eric.

"Hello, Eric's phone."

Kim paused; her mouth dropped open in shock. "Dayton?"

"Yeah, who's this?"

Kim didn't respond. She listened to the artificial cheering in the background from a television. Louder cheers erupted over it from actual people in the room.

"This is Kim, Dayton."

"Kim?"

"Yes, your girlfriend's roommate."

A loud chime blared and the cheering from the television stopped. Kim knew the sound. Someone put a video game on pause. The entire room went quiet.

"Hey, Kim, what's up?" Dayton said.

"What's up with you answering Eric's phone?"

"Huh? Why am I answering his phone? Well, I–"

"Put Eric on the phone now."

She heard whispering. Then Eric answered. "Hey, baby."

"Tell me you are in the car and not playing video games with the guys. You're on your way here to pick me up."

Something fell and shattered in the background. Voices murmured; then someone let out a loud laugh. Kim closed her eyes and shook her head in disgust.

"I'm in the car now," Eric lied. "I'm stuck in traffic."

"Uh-huh. Well, get clear of the traffic of people moving back into the dorm, then let me know so I can gauge what time you will be here for real."

"Baby, my bad, I lost track of time."

"Whatever Eric, hurry up." She hung up before he could respond. "Men."

CHAPTER FIVE

The cab headed up Main Avenue through the small town of Bruckner, made up of rows of mom-and-pop stores, a general store, and a post office. At an intersection was a small strip mall with an electronics store on the left-hand side of the street and on the right side, a large coffee house with a bookstore attached to it. The cab made a right turn off the main street and onto a road, cutting through woodland.

The cab stopped at a light. Todd snapped out of his thoughts. He looked to his right. A two-lane road led to a diner. Its neon sign that read Cory's Diner faced him. The parking lot adjacent to the structure was filled with cars. He smiled at the liveliness of the place before settling back in his seat.

The driver continued along the winding road for a mile until they arrived at a guard booth with a raised arm. The security guard inside waved to the cab as they drove past. Todd peered out the opposite window at a brick wall with a marble plaque in the center which had BRUCKNER UNIVERSITY EST. 1891 carved into it.

"What hall you in?" Larry, the driver, asked.

"Chambers Hall."

"It's down here." They drove toward a large, old brick dormitory with a tower and steeple at the top. In front, students were unloading their gear. "You'd think it's the first day of school."

"For some of us, it is."

Todd peered out the other side of the car and saw a row of older dorms across the campus. He remembered those were the female dorms. At the center of the quadrangle stood a large fountain, currently turned off due to the winter weather. Diagonal to that were basketball courts. He turned around to the front window. He could see the administration to the far left, the bursar and library were to the right. A building, shaped like a donut, sat forefront of the library. A crowd had gathered in front of it.

"What's the funny round building?" Todd said.

"Oh, the university commons. Students spend time together there between classes and get food after dinner."

"You know your way around this campus."

"I better, I used to go here."

"I see. You know where the science building is?"

"Sure do." Larry pointed to a five-story black glass building towering over the others. "The science center is there. The only modern one on this entire campus."

They coasted to a stop behind the last car in front of Chambers Hall, parked, and Larry turned to collect his money. Todd gave him enough with a tip, thanked him, then got out. He glanced again at the science building and scratched his chin.

"That's going to be a problem." He took out his phone and called Zeborah. "I'm at the dorm. The science building is on the other side of the campus."

"I know," Zeborah said.

"Well, thanks for telling me."

"I did tell ya."

"Well, you know what this means. I'm going to have to set a lab up in the room," Todd said.

"Not a choice idea. Old buildings like Chambers have limits on how much power you can run, ya know. Mess around and blow a fuse and they'll start searchin' the rooms."

"Let me worry if that happens," Todd said. "You'll bring the crate from the storage facility to me here at the dorm. Take the other one and put it into the reserved lab in the science building."

"You still in tha basement, right?" Zeborah said.

"If they tell me differently at check in, I'll call you. And I want the crate for my room brought to me tonight. We can wait until Monday for the other."

"We agreed to transfer everythin' at once."

"I'm running against a clock. My experiment was at a crucial stage, and now, thanks to Dwain's stunt, I must wait a month. Luckily, I have enough leeches to sustain me. But now I must find a new Crystal. The key to my final step," Todd said.

"Not on campus. Ya have tha whole town to search through for a woman."

"Hearing you talk like that sickens me. Worry about getting my stuff to me. I will be waiting for you to arrive, then we'll head out to survey the town."

"Eat from one of ya pre-packed meals. Don't try anythin' on campus."

"I'll be fine. Listen." He took the phone from his ear and turned it to face the storm clouds. The sound of a low roar of thunder sent students crossing campus running toward their destinations.

"Storm's coming."

Zeborah hung up. Todd grinned as he headed inside the dorm.

———

"Uh, ladies? You know the rules. Wait for your friends here in the lobby, not the lounge," Resident Assistant David Yanolatos said. "We're not starting this second semester on the wrong foot. You don't want to follow my rules. There's the door."

Todd looked up from the paperwork David had given him and observed him escort a pair of girls back to the door. He stood with his chest out, making his already bulky frame appear bigger. One of them, a brunette with a ponytail, approached him.

"You only work here, you don't own the building, David," Michelle said

"Uh, no, Michelle, I'm in charge. Nothing happens without my say and I'll enforce the rules how I see fit." He turned to Todd. "Excuse me, ladies."

David returned to Todd's side and went over simple guidelines with him while fielding questions from incoming students who were bringing in appliances for their rooms. He then turned back to Todd and gestured for the paperwork.

"If you're done?"

"Hmm? Oh, go ahead." Todd handed them over.

David reviewed them, then walked to the copier. While he waited for his copies, Todd caught Michelle and her friend checking him out. He gave them a dazzling smile, showing off his pearly white teeth.

"Hello," he said, adding bass to his voice.

The girls smiled back with a dreamy gaze.

"Hi," Michelle said. "You're new here?"

"Yes, I'm transferring in for the semester." Todd strode over to her and shook her hand while he stared into her eyes. "I'm Todd."

Todd glanced at her chest and watched it rise and fall from her quickened breathing. She instinctively covered her heart with her hand.

"Michelle," she said. "This is my roommate, Debra."

"Michelle? It's nice to meet you." He nodded to Debra. "You too, as well. What year are you?"

Todd fixed his gaze on her dry lips and watched as she licked them.

"I'm a . . ."

"You're what?" Now his pulse quickened. He stared into her hazel eyes, then down at her wet lips. "What are you, Michelle?"

"I'm. . ."

Todd leaned forward as though he were about to kiss her. He touched the side of her face.

Can you hear me? Do you hear my voice in your head?

Michelle nodded.

Todd inched closer to Michelle as she stood on her toes. Out the corner of his eye, he saw Debra reach out and grab her roommate's arm.

"Michelle," she said.

"I hear you." Michelle's eyes remained fixed on Todd.

"Hey, what're you doing?" Carson Philips called out.

Carson rushed over, clutched Todd's arm, and yanked him away from Michelle. Immediately, the trance severed.

Todd's head pounded. He could hear screaming, but it sounded as though he were underwater. He shut his eyes, then opened them. The voices returned to normal, and he lost his link with Michelle. He saw David had Carson in a bear hug.

"He tried to kiss my girl," Carson yelled.

"Kick his ass," his friend, Earnest Collier, said.

"Everyone needs to take a chill pill," David said.

Carson calmed down and he let him go.

"Now what happened here?" David asked.

"It's my mistake. I couldn't help it," Todd said.

"Couldn't help what?" David said.

"Well, in my spare time, I study magic. I have been trying to perfect this hypnotic act. I accidentally tried to hypnotize her," Todd said.

"You hypnotized her for what? So, she would kiss you?" Carson said.

"No. Wow, the power of suggestion. Here's what happened. I stared into her eyes. I must have thought about kissing my ex-girlfriend." Todd turned to Michelle. "It wasn't intentional."

"It's fine. I just need fresh air." Michelle turned and stumbled out the door.

Carson and Earnest sized Todd up. They whispered to one another and stood in front of Debra to block his view of her.

"It won't happen again." Todd extended his hand as a gesture of peace.

Carson shook it weakly, then headed out with the girls and Earnest in tow.

"The females around here are attractive," Todd said.

"Yeah, well, visitation is reserved to the lounge during the week," David said. "No visitors of the opposite sex in your room until the weekend."

"You won't have any issues with me. I'm a strictly stick-to-the-rules kind of man."

"Mmhmm. Well, no more magic tricks around here, either. Here's your key. Go through those doors and downstairs. There are only two rooms down there and a storage closet, which is off-limits for personal use. Understand?"

"Got it."

"There's also no bathroom down there. You'll have to use the one on this floor at the far end of the hall. Oh, and about your car, see me later for a temporary sticker so you can park in the lot. You'll have to wait until the office opens Tuesday to get a perma-nent parking sticker." David signed off on the paperwork, then handed him the copy. "Here's a list of stuff you can't have in your room. Failure to comply will lead to disciplinary action. Got it?"

Todd nodded. "No problem."

"Welcome to Bruckner University." David shook Todd's hand and turned to go back into the office.

———

Todd rushed into his room, threw his bag on the bed, and slammed the door. He leaned against it, closed his eyes, and breathed heavily, his head swimming. He wanted to fall on the bed, but he couldn't bring his legs to move.

"Damn it!"

He opened his eyes. The room had a small window which barely brought in light. He patted alongside the wall, found the switch, and flicked it up.

A soft white bulb gave off a warm glow. The large room had a stuffy smell and appeared as though it hadn't been occupied for some time. A desk with a shelf, lamp, and backboard sat against the wall to his right. Next to it stood two large wardrobes whose doors were open and empty inside. A dresser sat against the far wall, the bed on the left jetting out from the wall. The cold off-white color paint on the cinderblock walls was depressing. But the heat coming from the radiator made it cozy.

Todd's lightheadedness transferred to his stomach, causing it to churn and bubble. Then it rapidly spread throughout his abdomen. Todd lurched forward and struck the mattress. Clutching his stomach with one hand, he frantically reached for his bag. He dragged it over, opened the top flap, and dug inside. It took him a moment to find a Ziploc bag filled with dirt.

Sliding down to the floor in a sitting position, he leaned against the bed and held the bag close to his body. His hands shook as he did his best to concentrate on trying to open it. He closed his eyes, undid the seal, and fished around inside it.

"Come on, where are you?" He fisted a clump of dirt, and something started squirming within it. "There you are."

Todd extracted his hand, cupping a large, writhing black leech. He brushed the excess dirt off it, smiled, and then took it by the tail end with two fingers. He tilted his head back, opened his mouth, and dropped it in. As he bit down hard on the leech, blood exploded in his mouth. He swallowed the entire thing, savoring the taste of blood as it trickled down his throat.

Todd's head stopped swimming. The pains and aches subsided. He closed the bag and placed it next to him. He sat for a moment, allowing the blood to do its work. After a minute, he noticed it didn't restore his strength as fast as it should. He realized the issue. The host's blood that the leeches fed off had lost its potency. The leeches were no longer getting nutrition from it. He'd have to find a new host for the current leeches being brought to him to feed on until he was ready for the ascension. He made a mental note to tell Zeborah to find him a victim soon.

He slid onto the bed and lay on his back. He focused his attention on the bulb and put himself into a deep sleep.

CHAPTER SIX

The Camry's rear tires skidded across the asphalt, kicking up slush as it drifted across Main Avenue. Upon straightening out, a car behind it slammed on the brakes and blared its horn.

"Sorry," Eric yelled at the closed window.

"Hey, I still have payments left on this car." Dayton's face turned slightly pink from yelling. "Slow it down. Driving like a maniac isn't going to make up for how long Kim has been waiting."

"I can't believe I lost track of time." Eric sped down Main Avenue, then mashed on the horn as he crossed lanes. "C'mon. Move it."

"Maybe you should have driven, Dayton," Carmen said softly from the back seat.

"You think? Eric, Jesus Christ, will you slow down! You're gonna kill us all. Watch the truck."

"Carmen, can I get over?" Eric said.

"You got it," she said.

Eric cut the wheel, and the Camry slid into the right lane. Eric pressed on the gas and the car sped up.

"Ease up," Dayton said. "Train station's up there."

"Man, you should've warned me about the time."

"I told you don't start playing *Madden* against Curtis, but you wouldn't listen to me. This is all on you, man." Dayton's Midwestern twang resounded when he said, "man."

"Man," Carmen said, copying his twang.

"I don't sound like that."

"Yes, you do. It's cute."

Eric pushed his foot down on the brake at a red light. He glimpsed Dayton, who turned to face Carmen. They stared at one another, and he raised his eyebrows up and down.

"You're the cute one," Dayton said.

"Stop flirting." Carmen smiled from ear to ear.

"You know I wanna do more than flirt with you."

Eric watched Carmen as she leaned forward and kissed Dayton on the lips. She tucked her hair back, exposing her full face. Dayton caressed her.

"*Que Lindö.*" Carmen's Spanish accent came out. She kissed Dayton again.

"Are you two serious?"

"You worry about the road," Dayton said.

"You should've sat in the back," Eric said. The light turned green, and he began driving again.

"You'll be thankful I'm here in a minute," Dayton said. "Make a right. A right."

Eric cut the wheel hard. The Camry skidded and turned into the parking lot of the train station. People scattered to avoid being run over. He honked the horn as he circled and made his way to the entrance.

He spotted Kim standing in front of the last door at the far end. She didn't move from her spot. She had a blank expression on her face, which made it hard to determine her emotions. Eric stared back, breathing heavily, his bottom lip quivering.

"Carmen?" Eric said.

"She's pissed," Carmen said. "Let me handle this."

"Thank you."

"Don't thank me. I'm pissed at you, too." Carmen got out of the car and slammed the door. "Hey, roomie."

Eric watched as Kim's expression changed to delight. Screaming with joy, she dashed to meet Carmen halfway.

They turned and walked back to get Kim's bag. Eric fumbled for the door, but Dayton stopped him.

"Wait a minute. Let Carmen soften her up a little," Dayton said.

"But her bags."

"I can handle it. With any luck, not getting her bag will be the only thing she ends up mad at you for." Dayton opened the car door.

"I have to apologize."

"Keep your mouth shut and let her bring it up." Dayton got out of the car. "Kim. Hey, you."

"Uh-uh, don't "hey you" me," Kim said. "I–"

"Lemme get your bag for you. You know how lazy Eric can be," Dayton said.

Eric frowned as Dayton took Kim's bag and motioned for him to open the trunk. As he did, Carmen left Kim's side and joined Dayton in the back of the car. Kim stopped at the passenger side door and stared coldly at him.

Eric opened his door and stepped out. He and Kim stared at one another for a moment, then he walked around and opened her door. She slowly shook her head.

"I can explain," he said.

"Eric, shut up," Dayton said.

"Let's go." Kim got into the car, slammed the door, and slapped the lock down. Eric caught Dayton shaking his head at him.

"What'd I say?"

Eric walked back around and got in. The second he left the station and headed down Main Street, Kim turned on him.

"Video games? Really, Eric?"

"I thought I had time for a quick game," he said.

"Why can't you be where I ask?"

"Why are you making it sound like I deliberately abandoned you?"

Eric and Kim yelled over one another, neither giving the other a chance to speak.

————

E ric stopped the car in front of Wakeford Hall, the third oldest female dorm on campus. Kim exited quickly. He started to open his door, but Dayton put his hand on his shoulder, signaling him to stay. Then he and Carmen got out and helped Kim get her bags. Eric watched from the rear-view mirror as Kim walked away, angry.

"I'll see you later?" Dayton said.

"We'll see." Carmen kissed him. "What a way to start the final semester, huh?"

Dayton stepped up to the passenger side, waited for the girls to be out of earshot, Dayton tapped on the roof. "Okay, let's go. Out."

Eric opened the door and exited the car. Dayton held his hand out as Eric tossed him the key.

"I should've–"

"Uh-uh, nope. Don't say you should have listened to me. You never do," Dayton said.

They walked to the front of the car and leaned against the hood.

"I don't know what's happening, Dayton," Eric said. "I should be more attentive than this."

"Don't beat yourself up. She's not as angry as you think. I have seen her go supernova, and this is a pebble in a stream."

"I know, it's just I don't do it on purpose."

"You know perfectly well why you do what you do, and it's not for lack of caring."

"Why do you think I do it?"

"Honestly?" Dayton dug the nail of his pinky into his gum and scratched. "I think you've gotten too comfortable with her and don't feel like you have to try."

"Try what?"

"Being her boyfriend. You two have been together since freshman year; you're like an old married couple now. You take what you have with her for granted."

"Wow, this coming from someone who has just started a relationship."

"No, this is coming from your roommate and friend since the day you and Kim hooked up. I've been living through your arguments and missteps for years. I know more about the two of you than you two do."

Eric processed his words. "I–"

"Listen, take me and Carmen. I know this thing between us is new, but we try to live as if tomorrow is the last day of school. Who knows what may happen? Think of your relationship as being on the cusp of something greater and you're trying to reach for that wonderful thing. Stop being a slacker and do right by her. You know plenty of guys on this campus will swoop in if you don't."

"You're right. I'll try harder," Eric said.

"Nice."

Eric raised an eyebrow. "'On the cusp of something greater?'

Are you kidding me? Chapter six of Mrs. Keller's psychology class last semester. You're quoting the textbook."

"Now, now, my man," Dayton spoke in a phony British accent. "'Tis, after all, my major." He and Eric laughed together. "But seriously, I love you two. Get your act together. Get in, I'll drive us back. Carmen wants the car later, so I have to come back for her."

Eric glanced at Wakeford Hall as they traded places, and he got in.

"You want to get in a game on the court tomorrow morning?" Eric said.

"Uh, don't you have something to do tomorrow?"

"No, I got the whole day."

"That's funny because I know Carmen wanted me to take her to the store after you and Kim—"

"Aw, damn. Kim and I are supposed to be running errands tomorrow," Eric moaned.

"You need to pay me to be your personal assistant."

"What is wrong with me?"

They grew quiet as they drove and parked in the parking lot alongside Chambers Hall. As they left the car, Eric was in deep thought. His entire world used to revolve around Kim, but in the last two semesters, he didn't see the need to run to her the second she called him. Should she end up stranded somewhere or hurt, he would be there immediately. Dayton had a point. He'd taken their relationship for granted.

"Listen, if we get up early and they cleared off the court, I'm down," Dayton said. "Make sure you keep track of time."

"I can do that." Eric glimpsed at the sky. "I think it's going to rain."

"It's been thundering, but nothing's happened yet. You want to ask the fellas to play as well?"

"Sure. I get tired of beating you one-on-one."

"What? You must be thinking of someone else. You have never beaten me in basketball."

"C'mon man, I'm like old school Michael Jordan on the court." Eric showed off a fake-out, then a jump shot.

"You mean Michael 'You're Done.' You need a ladder to make a layup," Dayton joked.

"Ha, ha, hilarious. Keep talkin.' Tomorrow you'll be eating those words."

They continued to tease one another as they neared the entrance. Outside, a small group had gathered around Carson and Earnest.

"Hey man, what's going on?" Eric said.

"You should have been here earlier." Carson told Eric about Todd and the hypnosis trick.

"What? He tried to kiss Michelle?" Eric said.

"If I hadn't come along, he would have. I'd keep a watch out for him. Don't let him near your girl," Carson said.

"Thanks for the heads up." Eric turned to Dayton. "Every semester we get one clown in here. Now we got one doing magic."

"A regular smooth operator, huh?" Dayton said.

They entered the dorm. As they made their way past the main office, Todd stepped out of the stairwell, walking straight for them. His phone chimed. He took it out and read a text message. Instead of stopping to respond to it, he started typing as he walked.

David called to Eric, who turned to say hello. He stepped in Todd's path. With neither of them watching where they were going, they collided.

Todd fumbled with the phone. He tried to catch it, but it slipped off his fingertips and hit the floor. He immediately picked it up to check it for damage.

"My bad," Eric said. "I wasn't paying attention."

"No kidding." Todd brushed himself off. "You nearly broke my phone, jackass."

"What?" Eric said.

"Hey, there's no cause for the attitude," Dayton said. "Accidents happen."

"Fine, it is what it is," Todd said. "Watch where you're going next time."

"Hey Todd, I need to see you for a minute," David said.

"Can't it wait? I'm in a bit of a hurry."

"No, it can't. I need your signature on this. It will only take a second. Unless, of course, you have a magic pen that can float over here and sign it."

Todd frowned at him and approached the office. Eric tapped Dayton and pointed to Todd.

"The magician," Eric said.

Todd stopped and glared back at Eric.

"Is there a problem?" Todd said.

"Nope, no problem at all," Eric said.

Todd walked to David and signed the form without reading it. He tossed the pen across the counter. He eyeballed Eric as he left the office.

Eric made a quick observation of Todd's casual wear. It screamed player on the prowl.

"Nice getup." Eric said condescendingly.

"You got a problem with the way I dress?"

"Just making an observation."

"I see. Well, the thing here is I like to dress like a man, you know. Have some semblance of style. I mean, I guess I could rock jeans and sneakers." Todd fixed his gaze on Eric's pants and sneakers. "Just not too sure anything off the clearance rack would fit me nicely."

"What the hell is that supposed to mean?" Eric started to approach him, but Dayton grasped his arm.

"You take it easy . . . brotha." Todd turned and put his phone to his ear. "Yeah, I'm on my way to meet you now." Then he went out the front door.

Eric turned to David and shook his head.

"A player if I ever saw one," David said.

"Him right there. I'm gonna have to keep an eye on," Eric said.

CHAPTER SEVEN

Todd walked to the main gate where Zeborah sat waiting for him in a cargo van. He signed him in, got into the passenger side, and they rode toward Chambers Hall. Todd looked in the back and saw a brown wood crate.

"There's only one here."

"Tha one from Stafford. Lucky for us, they weren't keeping anyone from doin' pickups from storage. Cops and fire department are all over the dorm, though," Zeborah said.

"Listen, I'm going to need you to find me a host for this batch of leeches to feed off. The ones I have are losing their potency and I have a feeling these will, too."

"I'll have to search tha town for someone who won't go unnoticed if they're missin'."

"Fine. Make a left up here. The parking lot goes around to the back."

Zeborah took the turn into the lot, parking the van at the farthest end by the entrance to the basement. Todd got out, hurried to the door, and propped it open with a brick.

Zeborah, dressed in jeans and a down coat, got out of his seat and slipped into the rear area of the van. He opened the doors from the inside, then started to push the crate out. Todd ran up and took hold of the other end and together they carried it into Todd's room.

After setting it in a corner, they returned to the van, shut the doors, and walked to the entrance of the parking lot.

"Kevin picked up ya car at tha Huntington Station parkin' lot and brought it over," Zeborah said. "It's at tha train station."

"What possessed him to move it? I specifically said keep an eye on it. I didn't say bring it here."

"You can't leave ya car abandoned in anotha town's parkin' lot. After twenty-four hours it'll git towed and then what? Kevin thought it best since you're movin' everythin' now to bring it to Bruckner. He took the proper precautions. You needn't worry."

"So, what, I'm supposed to go get the car tonight by myself?" Todd said.

Thunder resounded above them, followed by a streak of lightning. The harder Todd breathed, the louder the thunder. Zeborah raised his hand.

"Ya need ta calm down. No need ta git worked up. I'm gonna take you to git your car." Zeborah started the van. "By tha way, Monday I'll bring tha otha crate."

Todd breathed easy. "I'll deal with Kevin tonight. Let's take a walk. I need to get better acquainted with this place."

They walked from Chambers Hall and made their way around the entire campus. They spent much of their time at the science building, circling it twice while memorizing the exits. From there, they headed to the far end of the campus, where they discovered a second entrance. Two guards stationed in a security booth were attending to a passenger van. They gave the van permission to enter, then a car, filled with students waiting patiently to exit, went through. Todd motioned with his head for Zeborah to follow him.

"Afternoon." Todd waved to the guards in the booth.

"Afternoon," one guard said back. "Can I help you?"

"We're new here. Where does this exit go?"

The guard stepped out of the booth and pointed down the road leading away from them.

"This leads out to I-95. There's an exit from the south. Lets you off on a connecting road about a mile and a half down."

"It cuts through the woods?" Todd said. "How come I don't see a lot of people using this way?"

"There's no town along this road. It's all woodland area. Mostly everyone comes through the main. You can use this road if you want, it's safe, but wild animals cross the road quite a bit. That's why we close this by eight. Wouldn't want anyone to hit a deer traveling through there at night."

"We can use it like tha front entrance?" Zeborah said.

"Up until eight," the guard said.

"Thank you." Todd and Zeborah turned and headed back to Chambers Hall. "This is good. We can use this gate to bring the other crate in and take it to the science building. I also think you should park the van in the woods back there, too. Keep it where no one can see it. If we need to make a quick exit, we're not stuck trying to drive off campus."

"Want me to do it now?" Zeborah said.

"No. Do it Monday after you bring in the second crate. This is excellent; two ways in and two ways out."

Todd and Zeborah walked to the quadrangle and stood in the center of it. Todd observed the students walking to and from their destinations, laughing and enjoying life. He focused his attention on a group of girls talking just feet from him and Zeborah. One of the girls smiled at him. He smiled back and winked. She giggled and tossed her hair before leaning to her friends and whispering. The others then started to laugh.

"Hey," Zeborah said.

"Hmm?"

"Damn it, look at me."

Todd turned to him. "Yes?"

"Don't mess with the women on this campus, ya hear me?"

"I wasn't–"

"This isn't a joke, Todd. It's bad enough you got me involved in this experiment of yours. I won't become an accessory to your demented mind games against women as well. It's immoral."

"Oh? And exactly at what point did you become the moral one? Hmm? You, who have discarded women over the years?"

"Don't lecture me on women."

"I wouldn't dare lecture a master of nocturnal and carnal appetites."

Zeborah grasped Todd by his collar and drew him close. Todd's eyes moved down to Zeborah's hands and, still with a smile on his face, he calmly sucked his teeth and spoke.

"Tsk-tsk-tsk. Shame on you, cousin, such a temper. Now take your hands off me," Todd said. "No unnecessary attention, remember?"

Zeborah let him go. "I have given all that up since–"

"Still pining for your blonde-haired love? What a waste." He turned his attention back to the campus. "Maybe you got a point about the women here. I'm going downtown for a while."

"You do that."

Zeborah watched Todd head back towards Chambers Hall. He stood alone for a moment before deciding to take a stroll to clear his head.

———

Zeborah headed past one of the girl's dormitories, down a small cobblestone path that snaked around the back of Wakeford Hall and ended at the bank of Duvall Lake. He recalled seeing it marked on one of the campus maps. Bodies of water always soothed him.

At the bank, while staring out across its surface, a light breeze had started, causing waves to ripple across. Zeborah closed his eyes and breathed easy, feeling his anger leave him.

A blonde-haired woman appeared in his thoughts. She stood in the lake before him, up to her knees. The hem of her yellow sundress spread out on the surface. Her hair blew in the wind; she tucked it back behind her ear as she smiled at him.

"The water is cold," he said to her. "You'll freeze. Come out of there."

The woman waded further out and spun slowly, with her arms extended. She then finished, turned to Zeborah and blew him a kiss.

"I love you," she whispered.

Zeborah opened his eyes. The woman disappeared. A tear went down his cheek as anger rushed through him.

"Why did you leave me?" Zeborah said.

The wind answered with a howl as the waves on the surface picked up. Zeborah wiped his eyes before turning and walking away.

He made his way back between the dormitories. He saw the same Hispanic girl he had seen the day before, on her phone, again texting. It was like déjà vu. This time, they would pass one another. She lifted her head, and their eyes met briefly. He couldn't tell if she remembered him or not. But he could sense her aura. This wasn't an ordinary girl. He couldn't put a finger on why, and he didn't want to stop to talk to her, so he nodded, grinned, and kept walking.

Zeborah's stomach churned. A pain shot up into his throat. He stopped and turned to see the girl facing him. He turned away from her and doubled over. The excruciating pain went around to his back; like a thousand tiny needles had penetrated his skin. He stumbled away as fast as he could and, in the process, tripped over a bush and slid four feet until he stopped himself with his elbow. It hurt too much to stand. He crawled on all fours as far as he could before he collapsed out of breath.

Zeborah lay on the ground like a fish out of water, gasping for air until he could breathe better.

"What the hell?" he whispered as he flexed his gut.

After a few minutes, the agony subsided. Zeborah rose to his feet and breathed deep. While the chilly air stung his throat, only for a moment, then it, too, subsided.

He looked back and caught a glimpse of her running into Wakeford Hall.

Once well enough to walk, he headed back to Chambers Hall. He went straight to Todd's room and collapsed on the bed. He closed his eyes and rubbed the bridge of his nose for a moment as his gut grumbled.

"I haven't felt anything like that since. . ." Zeborah stopped short and sat up. The memory of the same excruciating pain returned. "*No*. There can't be one here."

CHAPTER EIGHT

Carmen had always been prone to stress headaches. Migraines were her worst enemy and whenever she got mentally overwhelmed, it would hit her like a sledgehammer.

This, however, felt one thousand times worse.

Unlike the day before, this one didn't build up. It struck with no warning. As she passed the tall white guy, she remembered seeing him the day before. She didn't have time to even register it. The headache happened right after seeing him. The pain even went into her gums, causing her teeth to hurt. He fell over the bush writhing in pain. She ran. Something inside told her to get away from him.

She didn't know why.

She burst through the dorm's door, stumbled across the foyer, and ran into the lounge, where she collapsed on a sofa. The migraine had made her dizzy. She feared if she tried to go back to her room, she would fall down the stairs. As she lay on her back, the whole room spun. The last time she had that symptom, she had the flu.

She shut her eyes as her head swam and caused nausea. She

took a series of deep breaths. It started to go away and now she could think.

Carmen retraced her step in her mind. She remembered passing the guy, then the pain came. Maybe he had on cheap cologne, and it caused her headache. The only thing worse than stress is a bad fragrance. She didn't remember smelling anything.

Her head still throbbed, but she carefully sat up, got her bearings, and left the lounge.

As she approached the foyer, her headache returned, but not as intense as before. She paused to rub her temples.

"'Scuse me," a female voice said.

Carmen turned and saw an attractive, blonde-haired girl in a yellow sundress carrying a small white purse and smiling at her. "Can you tell me what buildin' this is?" She spoke with a heavy Southern accent.

"The name of the building?" Carmen said.

"No, I know the name. I saw it outside. What kinda building,' is it?"

"What kind?" Carmen rolled her eyes up. "*Hay Dios mío.* It's a dorm. The female dorm."

"A dorm?"

"A dormitory. You lost?"

"I don't know. I mean, I think I know where I am." The girl appeared confused. "This is all new to me."

Carmen approached her. "You new here?"

"This is a school, right?" she said.

"Yes. This is Bruckner University."

"Bruckner." The girl walked to the front door and peered out at the campus. "Wow, it sure is big." She turned to Carmen with a big smile. "I have to find somebody who will listen ta me. Ya know?"

Carmen shook her head. "I'm not sure what you mean."

"Yeah, it's a little complicated to explain." She glanced at the floor, and then at Carmen. "Do you live here?"

"Yes," Carmen said.

"Like you stay here full time?"

"I am a student here. I have a room here and I sleep here until the end of the semester, then I go home." Carmen spoke as clearly as she could for fear the girl wouldn't understand.

"You do? Well, bless your heart. You might be the person I can talk to," she said.

The girl started to walk back toward her as the R.A. turned the corner, startling Carmen.

"Hey girl, what's going on?" she said.

"I'm trying to help this student here." Carmen pointed in the girl's direction.

"What student?"

Carmen turned. "This one over–" She stopped short. The girl had disappeared. "That's funny. She was right here. A girl in a yellow sundress with a Southern accent."

"A sundress in this weather? She must have been a transfer student. You know they get on campus and get all turned around," the R.A. said.

"Yeah, maybe." Carmen rubbed her temple as she headed for her room.

She walked in and found Kim putting away the rest of her clothes. From the looks of it, she appeared to have calmed down from the argument with Eric.

"Hey, they ran out of hamburgers at the Commons. I guess we can run to the diner unless you want to wait until we go out tonight." Carmen pressed the side of her head as she sat on her bed.

"I can wait. You okay?"

"Just got a splitting headache on the way back. It's nothing. I'll be fine. I think the question of the hour is, how are you doing?"

"I'm better. Just had to calm down and let it go. I swear Eric works my last nerve sometimes." She picked up a shirt, shook it, then proceeded to switch it for the one she had on.

"Men are like cats," Carmen said.

"What?"

"Men, they're like cats. They warm up to you, then you take them in, and they get set in their ways and don't change."

"Where did you hear that?"

"My *abuela*," Carmen said. "I told her about Dayton and me, and she warned me to watch out because men are like cats. All sweet and loving until they get you."

"Your abuela is funny." Kim checked herself in the mirror and adjusted the new shirt she put on. Satisfied with the outfit, she let out a big sigh. "Why does everyone like to make excuses for him?"

"Eric loves you."

"This isn't about love. It's about respect. He takes our relationship for granted and I'm getting tired of it. I'm going to have to nip this in the bud."

"Well, can it wait until tomorrow? I don't want it to interfere with our night," Carmen said.

"Oh, it will wait. Tonight, we're hanging," Kim said. "Just us girls."

"Dayton's loaning us the car, so we don't have to take the school shuttle."

"So, what happened over the holiday with your grandma?"

"Remember, I told you we were going down to Puerto Rico for a week? While at my aunt Angela's my abuela drops this bomb and tells me on her side of the family, the women were mediums."

"Mediums?" Kim glanced at the floor. "Wait, that's the ability to talk to the dead, isn't it? Wow, seriously?"

"As a heart attack."

"This is your father's mother or your mom's?"

"My mother's mother. Can you believe it? My mother never told me there were mediums in my family."

"What caused that to come up in a conversation?"

"One of the neighbors came by one night to see her. We're all sitting around, and she mentions this incident where her family couldn't find the deed to her uncle's house. Turns out the family had been fighting over whom he'd left it to because shortly before he passed, he had signed it over to someone, but he didn't say whom. And of course, they couldn't ask him, so they called my aunt to see if she could reach him to ask about it. While trying to commune with him, he appeared to my abuela and told her. She said he walked up to her while they were sitting there in the living room and started talking."

"Wow, was it, like, a surprise to her?"

"Until then, she hadn't participated in a séance. She knew her mother and my aunt did those things, but, yeah, she was shocked."

"She wasn't scared?"

"No. She said he wasn't like all decayed or anything. He looked like how he did when he was alive."

"Where was it?"

"The séance?"

"The deed?"

"In a family bible he had stored away in his den."

"Certainly not what I thought you were going to tell me." Kim raised her eyebrow. "Are you about to tell me you can see dead people?"

Carmen shook her head. "No, I can't. Well, I don't know if I can. It's possible, but nothing has happened since they told me about it."

"Your mom doesn't have the ability?"

"If she did, she would have said something, I'm sure. I don't know. Maybe, maybe not."

"Did you ask her?"

"Well, my mom didn't seem too enthused that it came up, so I didn't press her about it."

"After your grandmother, no one else in the family could do this. How come?" Kim waved her hand at her question. "I'm sorry to ask all these questions."

"It's okay. She told me the ability skips a generation or two. I mean, if I have kids, they might have the power."

"You better tell Dayton."

"Shut up." Carmen smiled.

"That's fascinating. You should look into it on your own. I'm sure the library has books on the subject." Kim got her coat and tried it on over her outfit. "How would you know if the dead did come to speak with you? I mean, like, if it were a physical, what's it called, an apparition? Would you know the difference?"

"Good question. My aunt mentioned something about symptoms, but my abuela explained it as being more like a feeling. I still have a lot of questions we're going to go over."

"Are you scared about it?"

"Hm, not really. Honestly, I would love to talk to my Abuelo if I did have the ability." They both grew silent for a moment. "Family, I tell you."

Kim took off the coat. "I'll be back in a few. I'll see if the vending machine down the hall has anything."

Carmen walked to the window and looked down at the front of the dorm. She spotted the girl in yellow, walking back and forth in a confused manner.

"Let me go help this poor girl."

She hurried from the room, down the stairs, and out the front door, but the girl had disappeared. Carmen stepped close to where she thought the girl had been and an uneasiness came over her, followed by a chill. She took another step into her space and started to feel wobbly. She put her hands out to steady herself, but then stepped back.

"No, Carmen," she said to herself. "They never mentioned chills or dizziness. It's the weather. You're coming down with something." She thought about the incident of her passing the tall white guy. "The guy you saw was real. You saw him twice already. You're not seeing ghosts."

She went back inside to her room. She struggled with calling Maria and telling her what had just happened, and finally she decided to let it go and lie down.

CHAPTER NINE

Curtis Sterling slammed on the brakes, put his car in park, and stepped out of it, staring at the large cargo van sitting in his parking spot behind Chambers Hall. He tilted his head back and yelled in frustration before walking to the van to look for a parking sticker in the window.

"Who the hell is this?" He stood on his toes and looked in the front window. He didn't see one. He walked to the rear and looked at the bumper. "Every semester I have to deal with some fool in my spot." He took a step back and started to memorize the license plate number.

"Can I help you?" Todd called out.

"Is this your van?"

"It is."

"You're parked in my spot."

Todd looked at the three empty spots preceding the van. "And you can't park in any of these here?"

"This is my assigned spot I paid for at the start of the year. You need to get a parking pass to park back here," Curtis said. "You mind moving your van over so I can get in my spot?"

Todd looked at the van again as he approached Curtis. He stepped before him, grinning. "I do mind. You can have the spot after I leave. Until then, you can park your happy ass in one of these empty ones."

Curtis, taken aback, started to speak then stopped to consider what his next choice of words should be.

"What did you just say?"

"I'm not moving the van."

"Okay, you do know I can have it moved, right?"

Todd closed the space between them. "Is that right?"

"You gonna wanna take two steps back, bro," Curtis warned.

"Or what? What're you gonna do?"

"What's your problem?"

"You're my problem, mister 'You're parked in my spot'. I catch you near my van again," he stepped closer, "I'm . . ."

Curtis shoved Todd, putting distance between them. Todd balled his fists and Curtis backed up.

"I warned you to step back from me," Curtis said.

Todd moved in and grasped Curtis by his collar, jerked him forward, then tossed him to the ground. Curtis scrambled to his feet and prepared to fight back. Zeborah ran up and put himself between the two of them.

"Hey now, what's all this?"

"Who are you?" Curtis asked.

"I'm his cousin. What's the problem?"

"Your cousin is parked in my spot. I asked him to move it and he got violent. He's supposed to have a parking pass to be back here." Curtis pointed at Todd. He's asking for an ass-kicking," Curtis said.

Zeborah calmly approached Curtis; his hand raised as a gesture of peace. "Listen, he's been on edge. We just got here, had a rough time on the road. We didn't know about the parking situation. I parked tha van there. I'll move it right now. Just gimme a second." Zeborah went back to Todd and whispered something to him. Todd glanced at Zeborah, then walked to the passenger side of the van. Zeborah returned. "Can we let this go?"

Curtis looked him up and down, and back at the van. "Get your boy under control. He put a hand on me again. We're gonna have problems."

Zeborah walked away without speaking and got into the van. He and Todd drove off as Curtis got back in his car and put into the parking space.

Curtis hurried from his car into the dorm. Climbing the stairs two at a time, he stepped out onto the third floor and made a beeline for the last room at the far end. He pounded on the door multiple times.

"Okay, okay, I'm coming. Why you knocking on my door like the cops?" Eric opened the door. "Hey, Curtis, what's up?"

Curtis pushed his way into the room. "It's about to be on in this place. I almost got into a fight in the parking lot."

"What?" Dayton said as he paused his video game. "What happened?"

"This new cat parked his van in my spot. I told him to move it, and he put hands on me," Curtis said.

"Who?" Eric said.

"I don't know who he was. He dressed like he lived in the Men's casual section at Macy's."

"Oh, hell no. Not that fool. I had a run-in with him in the lobby."

"He got up in my face, so I had to push him back."

"I'm telling you, Dayton. We're gonna have to keep a close eye on him. He's starting crap with everybody he crosses in this dorm," Eric said.

"Yeah, I don't get it. He just got here and already making enemies. I suggest staying away from him," Dayton said.

"You gonna report this?"

Curtis shook his head. "Na, I just into the work-study program, and I don't need them hearin' I got into a fight. I might get kicked out."

"That's great, man. Where are you working?" Eric asked.

"The library. They got me working with the returns and general fiction. I want to see if they are going to let me work in archives where all the cool, rare stuff is."

"Nice. I'm happy for you. At least now I got a hookup. If I need something, I know who to go to," Eric said. "You up for a game?"

"Na, I just came to vent. You got Kim?"

"Yeah, and she's heated," Dayton said.

"Damn, son."

"Let it go, Curtis," Eric said.

"Okay, I'm out. Dayton, say hi to Carmen for me," Curtis said.

Dayton nodded as Curtis left the room.

CHAPTER TEN

Zeborah exited the electronics store with three bags full of wires and power cords. He tossed them into the back of the van before climbing into the cab. He sat silent as Todd meditated next to him. Seconds passed before he decided to break the uneasy quietness between them.

"How many people you plan on pissin' off b'fore this is all over?"

Todd opened his eyes. "It's necessary to build animosity around me. The more hatred brewing around me, the stronger the darkness inside me grows. It feeds off it." He turned to Zeborah and smiled. "Besides, it's fun."

"I'm glad you think this is fun."

"I don't want any of these clowns trying to get friendly with me. I don't want nor do I need that. I only need one thing, and I will find it on my own."

"We can't afford ta run again. You miss this next phase, ya not gonna be able to come back from tha results."

"Then we better make sure I get through this. No more

unforeseen interruptions." Todd closed his eyes. "You get every-thing we need for the setup?"

"We're good to go."

"Wake me when we're ready to meet Kevin."

Zeborah looked out the window. His thoughts lingered on the medium.

———

They left the store lot at 9 PM. Zeborah took Main Avenue and headed in the direction of the train station. Just before they reached the parking lot, he made a hard right down a side street.

The scene melted from small-town America to an abandoned steel mill town. An industrial side of Bruckner, tucked away behind trees and overgrowth, appeared before them. The decrepit shells of once-thriving businesses made the area look like a ghost town.

Zeborah made another turn that took them down a row of warehouses. Todd could see the different names in faded paint gracing their walls. Hat makers, fabric distributors, and an appli-ance store servicing commercial business were all shuttered. In front stood derelicts, gathered around empty drums with a fire burning inside them. They watched Zeborah and Todd as they drove by.

Zeborah broke the silence. "While you rested, I calculated tha time from now until you'll be done with this experiment. By tha time their spring break begins. Which is perfect cause we can slip away without any problems. We can bring the host you'll need for tha ascension here."

"Could work. It's out of the way."

They started on a slight decline toward an abandoned railroad trestle. He saw Kevin standing next to Todd's Mustang, his hands deep in his trench coat pockets. On the other side of the street, two men huddled around a fire burning in a large metal drum.

Zeborah drove past Kevin, parked at the curb, and killed the engine. Todd got out and hurried to the car.

"You brought my car here. Why?" Todd said.

"Good place for an ambush if needed. The Rucker brothers might still be out there." Kevin smirked. "You been on the hunt yet for a new Crystal?"

"I just got here, Kevin. Don't you think I should be patient and settle in first? Isn't that what you're always telling me?" Todd said.

"Well, at least you're taking my advice for once. Especially given the fact we need a full lay of the land. I need to find a place to hold Rakim."

"Where's he now?" Zeborah asked as he joined them.

"He's around. I have control over him. There shouldn't be any concerns."

"How did you get him here?" Todd said.

Kevin pointed to the Mustang. "I transported him here in your trunk."

"You did what?! His body could have tainted the soil I have in there. Do you know how much of a setback that would cause?"

"As if the hell you caused back in Stafford isn't a big enough setback already?" Kevin removed the Mustang keys from his pocket and handed them to Todd. Before he could move to it, Kevin held him by the arm. They exchanged hard glares at one another. "Why don't you finish what you need to with those vile worms and let me find you a host for this experiment? We don't need any more accidental deaths on our hands."

"I will find the one who is perfect to help finish this *experiment*...as you call it. I know exactly the type I need to link with. You don't. What I do need is for you and Zeborah to follow my directions and keep your nose out of the direct ascension business." Todd yanked his arm away from Kevin's grip. "And keep a leash on Rakim."

Todd moved to the Mustang, got in, and slammed the door. After turning over the engine, he put the car in gear and sped off from under the trestle, did a U-turn, then drove back the opposite way at high speed.

————

They watched as the Mustang's taillights grew faint. Kevin turned to Zeborah.

"I'm going to need you and the van in a moment. Things are about to get messy." Kevin glanced up at one of the beams shrouded in darkness.

Two red eyes stared back at him. Kevin turned his attention to the two homeless men across the street by the fire. He raised two fingers, pointed to them, and said, "Go feed."

————

The homeless men were sharing a bottle of whiskey and talking as Rakim crawled above them. He made a low growl, extended his clawed hand while stretching his body as he decided who he would attack first.

He watched the man to the right tilt his head back to get the last drop. Their eyes locked as the homeless man let go of the bottle, and it shattered on the ground.

"Bobby, is that a bat?" the man pointed at Rakim.

Rakim dropped down on him and sank his teeth into his shoulder. Blood spurted from the wound. The man screamed as he fell over and struck his head on the concrete, knocking himself out.

Rakim let out an inhuman scream, jumped over the fire, and

grabbed the other man by the throat. He choked him, leaned in, sank teeth into his jugular, and drank. The man went limp as he sucked hard.

With his hunger satisfied, Rakim let him go and returned to the other homeless man. He crawled over to his still body and sniffed him from head to toe. He let out another inhuman howl that echoed throughout the underpass. He took the man's body and dragged him out of the fire's light and into darkness.

Kevin could never get used to how vicious their cousin had become. He listened to Rakim slash into the homeless man's body. Blood flowed down the sidewalk and into the light, collecting around the barrel's base.

"He's almost done," Kevin said. "I need you to take the body and drop it off at this address." Kevin dug into his pocket, took out a small piece of paper and handed it to Zeborah.

Zeborah unfolded it and read the name and address on it. "LaChard?"

"Maurice LaChard. He is the head of the Coven that governs this territory."

"Why we doin' a body dump on his doorstep? Why don't we go see him?"

"I need his undivided attention. The condition of this body will pique his curiosity as to what kind of vampire would inflict this type of damage. He's going to want answers. It opens the door for me to tell him everything I need him to know," Kevin said

Zeborah put the address away and watched Rakim finish feeding. "What exactly do you need to see him for?"

"I need to get permission to operate in his territory. I don't want to have any bad blood brewing over any miscommunication." Kevin looked at him and saw the blank expression on his face. "You with me?"

"Hm?" Zeborah looked at him. "I heard you. Sorry, I zoned out."

"What's wrong?"

"I don't know yet. Somethin' happened on tha campus earlier... if it's anything important I'll let you know."

"With Todd?"

"No."

Kevin nodded, and walked away, leaving Zeborah alone with Rakim to finish feeding.

CHAPTER ELEVEN

Carmen dropped Kim off before driving to Chambers Hall to return Dayton's car. As they agreed, she left the keys with David, the R.A. She stepped out of the dorm just as Todd drove past.

She looked at the Mustang with an overwhelming sense of dread. Her joy seeped out of her as the hairs on her arm and neck rose. Her breathing became labored, followed by an icy chill. It crawled along her skin, between the hairs, and down to her hands, making them clammy.

Todd stared at her. A sinister grin gradually began to form on his face, causing him to look like a demented clown with no makeup on. A voice inside told her to run.

She darted across the road, making a beeline for Wakeford on the other side of campus. Once she had distanced herself, she glanced back and saw the girl in yellow standing at the curb yelling at Todd's car.

"You leave her alone!" she screamed.

"Hey!" Carmen called out.

The girl turned and waved. "I got him," she said before chasing after him.

Carmen crossed her arms as she walked the rest of the way. The dread melted away the closer she got to her dorm. But at the front door, she heard the faint scream, "Leave her alone" in the distance. She closed her eyes and took a deep breath.

"Keep it together, Carmen. If this happens again, call Abuela."

CHAPTER TWELVE

Grey clouds started to roll in at 9 AM as students began showing up at the main gate to grab the first shuttles headed into town. The sky drew curious glances because the local weather reports had called for sun.

Kim eyeballed the clouds at the thunder rumbling in the distance. She hadn't taken her umbrella, and she didn't have any intentions of walking back to get it. Her concern was getting to the fountain on the quad to meet Eric.

"Kim!" Carmen called out as she walked up to her, waving a set of keys. "You forgot these again."

"Girl, I don't know where my head is. Thanks," she said as she took them from her, "Sorry you had to leave the room."

"It's cool. I needed to get some air, anyway." Carmen glanced up at the sky and frowned.

"You okay?"

"Yeah. Just don't like the look of the clouds. They don't feel right."

"Hey, thanks again for last night. I needed it."

Carmen perked up. "What are roommates for? We need to make the burger spot a regular. They got good food there."

"Whenever you want to go, I'm down and, hey, I meant to ask, you gonna tell Dayton about the medium thing? I bet he'd get a real kick out of it." Kim sounded eager.

Carmen gave her a pensive look. "Kim, I appreciate you took what I said seriously about my family, but it's not something I'm anxious to tell a lot of people about, you know?"

"Oh my God, I'm so sorry." Kim put a comforting hand on Carmen's shoulder. "I wasn't trying to—"

"No, I understand what you're saying. It's just I need time."

"My lips are sealed. But if you need my help or anything, you know you can come to me."

"Thanks." Carmen looked at her watch. "Speaking of time, where is Eric? Weren't you two supposed to meet to go to the mall?"

"You noticed it too. I'm going over to Chambers and see what's going on."

"That's all you, amiga. I'll catch you later."

The clock on the administration building chimed to mark nine-fifteen. Kim began her walk across the campus to Chambers Hall. She took out her cell phone and called Eric's room but got no answer. She hung up and called his cell phone. It went to voice-mail. Kim dialed him again. She heard Eric's voice carry from a distance. She stopped and listened. He yelled, "Post up," followed by Dayton saying, "Pass it here!" She turned in the direction of the basketball court.

"Oh no," Kim whispered to herself. "I swear he'd better not be playing ball."

Kim furiously marched toward the basketball court as she put her cell phone in her purse. The closer she got, the louder the voices from the court became. She saw four guys playing. Dayton stuck out like a sore thumb. She watched him jump up for a rebound, turn and pass the ball to Eric, who had his back to her.

"Shoot it, E," Dayton yelled.

Eric made a jump shot, and the ball sailed through the hoop.

Kim walked up to the fence; her mouth open in shock as she watched Eric and Dayton scream with delight and rushed to each other to give a high five. She gripped the fence as her anger built up in the back of her throat. Her breath shot out of her mouth against the cold like a dragon blowing fire.

"Eric!"

Players on the court stopped moving. Eric, still smiling from his shot, followed their gaze.

"Oh-oh," Dayton said softly.

Eric stared at her. She held up her wrist and tapped her watch.

"Aw, shit," he said.

"Eric, you're playing *ball?*" Before he could respond, Kim walked onto the court and approached him. "Thanks a lot, Dayton," she said without looking at him.

"What? I–"

"Are you ready, Eric?"

"I need to run back to the room to...ow." He rubbed his shin as he noticed Dayton's foot sliding from behind his leg. "Yeah, I'm ready to go."

"You're all sweaty. The sale ends at one o'clock."

"I'll only be a minute. I'll change quick." He turned to Dayton. "Lemme get the keys to the car?"

"They're in the room on my desk. Just go."

"Thanks, bro."

"No, thank you . . . idiot," Dayton said under his breath.

Eric hurried off the court, with Kim following him.

———

Dayton put on his jacket and waved goodbye to the opposing team. He took his cellphone out of his pocket and called Carmen.

"Just wanted to give you a heads up. They're running late. She caught us playing ball."

"Estupido! What is up with Eric this year?"

"I'm thinking we should tread lightly with them. Unless they come to us for help, we need to not get involved."

"Might be easier for you. I can't stand to see Kim miserable."

"Trust me, a depressed Eric isn't pleasant to be around either. I'm going to have a lot on my plate this semester and the last thing I need is someone's personal issues getting in the way." Carmen grew quiet and didn't respond. "You still there?"

"I'm here." Her voice sounded like she'd become depressed. "I see your point, Dayton, but please keep an eye on him. I understand someone's personal issues can be hard to deal with, and it's not on your list of top priorities . . ."

"Hey, what's wrong?"

"What?"

"I can hear it in your voice. You're getting upset with me. I wasn't trying to be cruel with what I said." Dayton took a seat on the bench. "It's just with this being our senior year, you know."

"I know. Listen, I'll call you later, okay?"

"You don't have to hang up."

"Call you later." Carmen ended the call.

Dayton sat back and let out a sigh of frustration. He put his phone back in his pocket and went over the conversation in his head. Of all the things to make her cross with him, not wanting to get into Eric's love life made no sense. Was it a case of not what he said but the way he said it? He started to replay the tone of his conversation over in his mind.

"Already in deep thought?" Dayton looked up to see Curtis. "Classes start on Monday, you know."

"Girlfriend issues, that's all."

"Ah, I gotcha. You want to get up a game of Madden later?"

"I don't know. Eric is in the doghouse. No telling what mood he'll be in later."

"It's why I'm single. Don't need all the drama in my life."

"You're single because no one on this campus wants to date you," Dayton joked.

Curtis clutched his chest. "Ouch. I'll let you have that one." He looked at his watch. "I'll check in on you later. I gotta get over to the library. I'll see y'all later. Say hi to Carmen for me."

Dayton smirked at the request. While he knew Carmen and Curtis had dated two semesters ago, she had no feelings for Curtis other than them being friends. He wasn't sure Curtis didn't still pine for her. But he had no intention of playing the jealous boyfriend. He would give her the message, but he would also keep an eye on Curtis' behavior.

CHAPTER THIRTEEN

Zeborah knelt alongside the crate with a caulk gun, sealing any cracks and holes he found before Todd arrived.

He'd spent the night setting up a miniature lab in Todd's dorm room after Zeborah got back from helping Kevin. Zeborah didn't mention his visit to LaChard, but he did tell him about the terrible accident and death on the road leading to campus.

"So, how's it coming?" Todd stepped around to the opposite side of the crate.

"Jusa few more things and I'll be done with my end. Tha leeches inside are alive. All that's left is tha soil solution. It's over there on tha desk. You havta mix it."

He watched Todd approach his desk to find a set-up of test tubes, beakers, a Bunsen burner, and a microscope. A small experiment tray with a large leech and scalpel on it sat in the center. A faded sheet of papyrus bound to leather was beside the tray. On it, an ancient text made up of a mix of symbols, letters, and numbers scrolled in four lines.

To the right, on the table, were three jars. One contained a thick red liquid; the second contained dirt, and the third had granulated white powder.

"Bring me some soil from the crate."

Zeborah stood, scooped out a handful of black soil in one hand, and walked over to the desk. He knew the procedure well enough Todd didn't have to tell him where to put it. He poured it in a circle around the leech.

"I'm getting better at summoning the weather," Todd said. "I created the rainstorm last night. You know what that means?"

"Your new abilities are stable."

"After this next infusion piece here, I should be fine until the spring moon. Not to mention my powers of influence will heighten. The next woman I choose, I'll be able to manipulate her better."

"As long as you can maintain the cloud coverage over all of Bruckner, it's all I care about. If I'm gonna be busy durin' tha day, the last thing I need is to get burned by the sun because you're weak."

"You have nothing to worry about."

Todd picked up the jar of liquid, opened it and picked up the leech by its tail. As he dipped it into the liquid, he read from the papyrus. He spoke in a whisper, his lips moving fast and making smacking sounds. He finished the first line, then placed the leech back on the tray. Next, he took the jar of powder and removed a pinch of it. He read from the second line as he sprinkled the powder on the leech. He took the last jar, covered the leech with soil while reading the third line. He placed his hands along the edge of the outer ring of soil and pushed it all in, completely covering the leech. In his final act, he picked up the scalpel, sliced his left palm and made a fist over the mound of dirt. As his blood dripped onto it, he spoke the final line aloud.

"For with this hand and this blood, I commit my immortal body to you to house the power you grant me until such time I

make my transference and offer unto you a mortal soul as a sacri-
fice for my ascension."

Todd picked up the tray, carried it to the crate, and placed it
on the top of the soil. He dug a deep hole with his bloody hand.
Satisfied with the depth, he took the tray and poured the contents
into it. Then, after a moment, he covered the hole.

"The soil is ready, Zeborah."

Zeborah placed four copper wires deep into the soil. He
followed the wires to a small transformer where the other ends
connected. He double-checked the connection, tugging on them
to be certain they were secure before he plugged the unit into the
wall socket.

"Ready." Zeborah stepped behind the unit and turned it on.
Taking hold of the lever, he gently pushed it back, applying a light
charge to the soil. He leaned forward to see the topsoil tremble.
The leeches squirmed and writhed near the surface.

He charged the crate for a full minute before Todd waved for
him to stop. As Zeborah turned it off, Todd placed his hand on the
side of the box.

"I feel them settling. The one carrying mine and the ancient
blood should expel the combination soon. The soil will do the rest
by allowing the mix to seep into it."

"How fresh is tha food already in there tha rest are feeding off
of?" Zeborah said.

"What I have in there should be enough to sustain them for
now. We will need to find more food for them. Do three more elec-
trocutions in fifteen-minute increments. I need time to heal this
hand."

"Your healing is taking longer now."

"All part of the ascension." Todd walked to his bed and lay
down. "I'll walk the campus again later."

Zeborah performed the electrocution as instructed. Afterward,
he settled into a dark corner of the room to rest.

An hour later, Zeborah awoke to find Todd still resting. He quietly left the room. He climbed the stairs to the first floor, stepped out into the lobby, and spotted David in the office doing paperwork. He turned and saw double doors propped open, leading to a lounge. He heard a TV on inside. Curious, he went to investigate. He sensed a presence nearby. It was followed by a faint voice calling out *Eh!* from behind him. He turned to the front door. A horrible pain erupted in his stomach. He lurched forward as something tried to claw away at his insides before yanking him toward the door. He screamed and half ran/half stumbled out of it, knocking into a student entering the dorm.

He tripped down the stairs, tripped over the curb, and fell face down on the ground. Within seconds, the pain had subsided. Zeborah got to his feet, looked around curiously as he rubbed his belly.

"What tha hell was that now?"

CHAPTER FOURTEEN

Carmen's eyes snapped open. She laid still; too afraid to move. She couldn't tell if she had been asleep or had just been jolted back into consciousness after having an intense daydream. Either way, the vividness of the visions danced behind her eyes.

She could see the tall white guy, laying on the cold ground looking bewildered. Just moments before, she was walking on campus and spotted him in the lobby. Determined to find out why he caused her to have headaches, she made a beeline to the dorm, pointed at him and yelled out *Eh!* to get his attention. As she drew her hand back, he stumbled out of the dorm in her direction. Carmen backed away swiftly, fearing he could grab her.

The world around her started to liquefy into a myriad of colors, causing her head to spin. The colors swirled around her. She searched for something to grab onto. She became dizzy. Her legs gave out, and she fell backward. She closed her eyes, anticipating the impact her body would make on the ground. But she abruptly stopped falling.

She opened her eyes and found herself in her bed.

She gradually sat up on her elbows and looked around her room to get her bearings. She slid her legs over the side of the bed. But as she stood, what she had experienced was more than a dream. The hand she had pointed with had gone to sleep. She shook it to revive the feeling in it and then walked to the window. She experienced weightlessness with each step.

At the window, she looked to Chambers Hall. She saw a small gathering in front. She recognized David as he came down the steps and spoke to someone who had his back to her. They walked him to a bench and as he turned around to sit, her head twinged.

Carmen called Maria but hung up before she answered. Within seconds, it began to ring. Carmen stared at it, tempted to answer, but she couldn't bring herself to do so. After ten rings, the phone went silent. Suddenly, Carmen's cell phone rang. She ignored it and left the room.

She staggered down the hall to the bathroom. Gripping the sides of one of the sinks, she leaned over and took deep breaths. A feeling of nausea came over her and she dashed into the stall. She heaved, but nothing came up. Tears streamed down her face, as she couldn't shake the feeling that she was vulnerable to . . . something. She got up the courage to go back to her room and called Maria on her cell phone.

"Hola, Carmen. I saw jou called. Everything okay?"

"I don't know, Abuela." Carmen swallowed hard. "I'm not feeling very well right now."

"What's wrong, my love?"

"I'm feeling weak and dizzy. I've been having these headaches since yesterday and, Aye Dio Mio, I'm feeling scared."

"Scared? About what?"

"I don't know. It's like I can feel something terrible around me and I don't know why."

Carmen paused. "Abuela, are bad headaches a part of becoming a medium?"

"Headaches?"

"Si. Like migraines?"

"Migraines? Well, it's been known to 'appen to some people, the headaches, but bad ones like that? It's not common."

"What does it feel like coming in contact with a spirit?"

"Depends on the spirit. Why are jou asking?"

"I was just wondering. Forget I said anything. I got to go."

"Carmencita, don't hang up on me." There was a hint of worry in Maria's tone. "Jou asked for a reason. Tell me what has 'append?"

Carmen got into her bed and moved to the corner. She looked out the window at the gray sky as she took a deep breath.

"Yesterday, I passed this guy on campus, and like a couple of seconds later, I got this intense headache. Then I ran into this girl who was asking about the school, but she disappeared. I saw her later out my window. I went to talk to her, and she disappeared again. I stepped into the spot she was in, and I got another headache. And then I had a dream about that guy who I passed and in it, I somehow dragged him out of a building he was in, and I woke up feeling dizzy and funny and . . ."

"Parade," Maria interrupted, "This man jou passed, did he disappear?"

"Like right away?"

"Period."

Carmen took a minute to recall what happened. "No, I don't remember him disappearing. But I did see him twice."

"This headache? It 'appened twice?"

"This first time it wasn't intense. Not like the second."

For a moment, Maria grew quiet. "Jou said jou had a dream about him? Jou removed him from a building? How?"

"I don't know. I pointed at him and somehow did it." Carmen wiped a tear running down her cheek. "Abuela, do you know what this means? Am I a medium?"

"If jou physically passed this man, he's no ghost. And ghosts do not occupy dreams. They normally seek jou out to talk or tell jou something. He did neither. Did he?"

"No."

"Hm. Okay. Let me talk to jour aunt and see what she can tell me, and I'll call jou back. There's a reason he's making jou feel this way."

"So, he is a cause of this?"

"Possibly. Just wait until I can call jou back."

"What about the girl?"

"Let's take one thing at a time. The man is more a problem for jou than the girl," Maria said. "Are jou in jour room now?"

"Si."

"Stay there and I'll call jou back in a few. But I don't want jou to be worried? If something is going on, we'll figure it out, okay?"

"Thank you, Abuela."

"Call jou back." Maria didn't hang up right away. "Carmencita?"

"Yes?"

"Nothing." Maria hung up.

Knowing Maria was going to investigate the matter made Carmen feel better. She put her phone down, brought her knees up to her chest, and continued to stare out at the sky. Her phone buzzed. A text message from Dayton read, "Comfort food for dinner?" She smiled and typed back, "Perfect timing. Sounds like a plan."

A streak of lightning lit up the sky briefly, catching her attention. Thunder boomed before the rain came.

CHAPTER FIFTEEN

Eric and Kim drove to the end of the walkway that led to Wakeford Hall. They sat in silence. Kim saw his reflection in the passenger window while he glanced at her.

"What're you going to do now, apologize?" She turned to him. "I mean, what the hell, Eric? First, I told you we needed to be at the sale before one. We missed all the prime stuff. Then you disappear for an hour at the game store."

"I told you to call me as soon as you were done. I texted you twice, and you didn't respond."

"I said be in front of Macy's at four. Typical of you to forget what I say."

"That's not true."

"If I were Curtis or Dayton or one of those idiot friends of yours, you would have met me where I said. You're unreliable. I can't count on you for anything."

"You gotta be kidding me. I can't seem to win with you. What do you want me to do?"

Kim waved him off and turned to the window. "Whatever."

The rain picked up. Eric turned the windshield wipers on and as the glass became clear, he saw a Mustang coming toward them, headed toward the main gate. It slowed down as it approached. Eric couldn't see the driver as it stopped alongside them. As it did, the rain stopped. The driver appeared to be watching them.

"The hell is this about?" Eric rolled down the window as he stared at the driver's window. "Can I help you?"

The Mustang's window lowered an inch, not enough to see inside but enough for the driver could see out.

"Who is that?" Kim said as she leaned forward to see.

The car's engine revved, then it crept on its way.

"That was weird," she said.

Eric turned to Kim and sighed. "Look, I didn't make you miss the sale on purpose."

"What's the holdup?" Dayton said, sticking his head in the window.

"Jesus Christ!" Eric jumped while clutching his chest. "Scared the hell outta me."

"Sorry. Just making sure you two are okay." He saw Kim turn away from him. "You got to be kidding me."

"What do you want?" Eric grumbled.

"What I want is the car. I'm supposed to take Carmen out soon." Dayton held his hand out for the keys.

"Perfect timing!" Kim opened her door.

Eric slapped Dayton's hand back and scrambled to get out as Dayton stepped back.

"I'll walk with you," Eric said.

"I don't need you to walk with me." She opened the back door and removed her bags. "Good night, Dayton."

"Hey, I have an umbrella in the back if you wanna borrow it," Dayton called out, but Kim ignored him. She jogged to the dorm. "You never cease to amaze me. Now *that* is a perfect woman there and you keep messing up with her."

Eric watched her as embarrassment overtook him. "It wasn't my fault."

"It never is."

"What's that supposed to mean?"

"Excuse me." Dayton slid into the driver's seat, slammed the door, and put the car in drive. He kicked up water on Eric as he sped away.

"Hey! You're gonna make me walk back to the dorm?" Eric screamed after him. Dayton honked and waved goodbye.

A crackle of lightning sent Eric running for the dorm. He dashed across the road without looking. White light from a pair of headlights engulfed him. He heard the car brakes lock, followed by the tires' screech as it slid on the wet surface. Eric froze as the fender struck him and knocked him off his feet. He skidded across the wet blacktop, stopping on his side facing the car. His eyes widened as he stared at the silver Mustang horse logo.

The passenger door opened, and someone ran to him. "I think you hit him."

The driver's side door creaked opened followed by the sound of shoes clapping against the ground as the driver approached. Eric did a double take as Todd stood over him.

"Todd, git his arm. Help him up," Zeborah said. "You ain't hurt, are you?"

"No, no, I don't think so." Eric raised himself and allowed Todd and Zeborah to lift him.

Todd let go the second he recognized him. "Not you again." He made an exasperated sigh. "Figures, of all people, *you* bolt out in front of my car."

Eric stood straight. "Aw, Jesus! Seriously? You coulda slowed down, you know."

"I was doing the speed limit."

"You skidded into me. You don't skid if you're going the speed limit."

"You must have flunked physical science to make such a stupid statement. Your dumb ass comes running out into the road without—"

"My *what?* What did you say to me?" Eric stepped closer to Todd. "Who you think you're talkin' to? You must be itchin' for me to slap the hell out of you."

"You better put some space between us, boy."

"Boy? I'll show you a boy!"

"Make your move."

"Okay, okay." Zeborah slid his arms between them and pushed them apart. "No one got hurt here. Les'all calm down."

"Tell your partna here to calm down. First you do your little drive-by. Revving the engine. I know what that means." Eric pointed at the Mustang. "You nearly run me over then gonna talk shit? You lucky after the stunt in the dorm I don't—"

"You don't want none of this, trust me. Keep it moving," Todd said.

Eric rushed Todd. Zeborah put him in a bear hug. Eric struggled in his grip.

"Todd, git back in tha car, now!" Zeborah said.

Todd smirked before walking back to the Mustang and got in.

"Get off me!" Eric yelled.

"Not 'til ya calm down." Zeborah held on until Eric stopped resisting. "Listen, do yourself a fava. Don't git into any kinda confrontation with him." He let him go.

Eric gave Zeborah a perplexed look. It wasn't what he said, but the way he said it. It sounded like a warning.

"As long as he doesn't cross my path again, we'll be fine."

Zeborah walked back to the car. He turned and motioned with a wave for Eric to step back before getting in.

Eric did as Todd and Zeborah drove off toward the back gate.

———

"What in tha hell, Todd? We don' need ta draw any unnecessary attention and you try an kill a student?"

"I wasn't trying to kill him. I wanted to see how he responds to being goaded into a fight. I got my answer."

"Why him?"

"Why not?"

Zeborah stared at him. "You're targetin' him. You don' target anyone unless there's somethin' you . . . *shit*! Tell me it doesn't have ta do with tha girl in tha car with him. That's who you was lookin' at, wasn't it?"

"I'm just testing the testosterone levels of certain people right now. You have nothing to worry about with me and any females on this campus."

"Don't be too sure," Zeborah said under his breath as he looked out the window at the place he collapsed earlier.

"What's that supposed to mean?"

"Let's just git off this campus and see if we can't git Kevin a hidin' spot back in the south end woods. I've had enough of this place for now."

"Afterwards, we'll run a more important errand."

They drove in silence through campus and out along the road through the woods.

CHAPTER SIXTEEN

The road before him consisted of several twists before it came to a fork with a signpost for two signs hanging on a signpost that pointed to I-95 North and South.

They went left, heading south. As they neared a turn, Zeborah spotted the remnants of a dirt road trailing off into the wood.

"See where dat goes," he said.

Todd turned onto it, and they drove until they came to a clearing surrounded by a ring of trees. At the opposite end was a rundown cabin.

"Probably housed someone who worked at the school," Todd said as they came to a stop. "This will work. You can bring the van here. I don't think anyone will see it from the road."

They exited the Mustang. While Zeborah looked back toward the road, Todd approached the cabin for a better look.

The front door had been scorched. A square window to the right of it with a busted pane allowed him to peer inside before going in.

"See anything?"

"Deserted."

Todd turned to open the door, but Zeborah walked past him and went inside first.

"Coupla chairs and a table. All broken, it looks like. Somethin' that looks like a couch over by tha wall. I see two doors in tha back." He looked at Todd. "Bedrooms?"

"Doesn't matter. What's the ceiling look like?"

Zeborah walked around, looking up and surveying the ceiling. "I don 't see any holes. Seems solid."

"Kevin and Rakim can stay here. With any luck, this place has a cellar; you can put Rakim down there. We'll get one more crate to store here as a backup." Todd wandered into the cabin and looked around. His eyes shimmered in the darkness. "Yes, this will do nicely. We lucked up with this. Walk back to the campus and get the van. Let's get it out of sight. I'll meet you back at the dorm." He turned and exited the cabin. "I have something I need to take care of."

"I'll go pick up Kevin and bring 'em here in the van. Safer to transport Rakim that way."

"Makes sense. Good thinking. I'll meet you at the dorm in an hour." Todd got into the Mustang and drove it away.

———

Sy Taylor placed a closed fist up to his mouth and yawned into it. His eyelids grew heavy. He turned the heat off and cracked the window of the semi-cab, allowing the chilly night air in.

He had been on the road for seven hours, minus the hour he took to stop, eat, and let his food digest, hauling bathroom fixtures. He thought he could make it through the night to Virginia, but fatigue had crept up on him. After a decade of doing long hauls, he knew to listen to his body.

Slightly invigorated by the air, he glanced over at his cup

holder and noticed he still had some soda left in a plastic bottle. He retrieved it, unscrewed the cap with his teeth. He spat it onto the floor. He drank down the last of the dark, warm liquid, belched, then tossed the bottle into the back of the cab. He saw the exit for Bruckner coming up and thought *I could just pull into one of the gas stations and rest. The owner wouldn't mind.* But by the time he finished talking to himself, he'd driven past the exit ramp. *Oh well. Let's see how much more I have in the tank.*

He drove another mile and a half and didn't realize he had fallen asleep until the truck drifted to the shoulder and shook as it kicked up gravel. He straightened up, shook his head, and said, "Nope. Not gonna make it."

He glanced out the right side of the cab and saw the shoulder was flat, not a ditch, with enough room for him to pull off the road and park. By law, he could park ten feet from the blacktop and rest, but only for a limited amount of time.

Sy drove the semi off the road and onto the dead grass. He put the truck in park, turned the ignition off, then retrieved a reflective caution triangle from behind his seat. He exited the cab and walked to the rear of the truck. There were few cars passing, but he wanted to be sure should someone come off the road, they would see the caution triangle. The second he placed it on the ground, the lights of a car fell upon him. The throaty sound of a Mustang filled the air. Sy stood erect as the driver got out. A young black man stepped into the light between them.

"You okay?" Todd asked. "I saw you pull over."

"I'm fine, just had to take a break."

Todd looked over the truck. "What you hauling?"

"Fixtures."

"Long haul?"

"Pretty much. Hey, thanks for your concern. I'm good though."

"Okay." Todd started back to his car. He stopped abruptly and turned to Sy. "You travel this road a lot?"

Sy folded his arms. "What business is it of yours?"

Todd put up his hands. "Hey, I was just going to say watch out for troopers or police. Don't want you to get harassed."

"I'll be fine."

Todd continued back to his car. He revved the engine and peeled off onto the blacktop.

Sy glanced at his watch and thought, *I can do a 30-minute nap.* He looked at the highway and saw a few cars go by. They didn't notice him. *I'll make it an hour.* He walked back to the cab, climbed back in, and locked the door.

In the rear of the cab, Sy had a makeshift bedroom. A cot to sleep on, a small solid nightstand, and on the floor next to it he kept a tire iron in case he got into a situation requiring the use of a weapon.

Atop the nightstand sat an old-fashioned wind-up alarm clock, the kind with the bells on top. Being a deep sleeper, its loud ring was sufficient for waking him up.

He set the alarm to go off in one hour before he lay down on the cot and drifted off to sleep.

Twenty minutes into his nap, someone banging hard on his door awoke him. Groggy and aggravated, he slid off the cot, made his way to the door, and glanced out the window. No one was there, so decided to unlock the door, opened it, and peer out.

A passing car's headlights illuminated the area. Sy expected to see the police or state trooper cruiser, but there was no one.

The same loud banging happened again. This time from the passenger side. Sy looked over his shoulder at the door. The banging stopped, but started up once more.

"Oh, someone wants to play games." He slipped back into the cab, retrieved the tire iron, and exited on the driver's side. He crept around the front of the truck and paused at the corner of the grill. He counted to three before rushing around the corner, the tire iron raised up to his shoulder.

There was no one there.

Sy knelt to peer under the trailer. He moved back to the driver's side and knelt. Seeing no one, he climbed back into the cab. After closing the door behind him, he turned toward the back to put the tire iron back. He froze.

In the darkness, he could make out the silhouette of someone crouched down near his cot. The sounds of bone cracking and snapping filled the interior as the person's head jerked from side to side.

"Hey!"

The intruder stopped moving. They let out a series of guttural grunts before bleating like a goat. Two glowing red eyes appeared in the dark.

Sy opened the door and rushed out. He ran to the front of the truck, turning as he raised the tire iron again.

The intruder was already out of the cab and running toward him. Its contorted face, a cross between human and goat, let out a demonic bleat. It crouched seconds before it leapt at him.

Sy swung. The intruder caught his arm as it brought him to the cold ground. Its icy fingertips clutched his throat, and it squeezed his extended arm with the tire iron. It pried open Sy's hand. The intruder punched him in the face before standing, taking hold of his collar, and dragging him to the passenger side of the truck.

"Get off me! Let me go!"

The intruder tightened their grip as they continued to haul him to the back of the trailer. Sy tried to plant his heels into the ground to stop himself, but it did no good. As they passed the rear tire, he saw the front end of the Mustang that had stopped earlier.

"Help! Someone, help me!" he screamed.

The intruder stopped, let go of his collar, and straddled him. Their face contorted and morphed back to a human face. His red glowing eyes shimmered as he smiled at him, exposing fanged canines. He struck like a snake and bit Sy in the neck.

His nerves burned as his body seized up. Within seconds, he was paralyzed. Sy heard the car trunk open. He was lifted off the ground and placed into the trunk.

The smell of decomposition hung heavy in the air around him. Sy heard his kidnapper moving around down by his feet, creeping his way up to his head. His face came into view. The man held up something in front of Sy's eyes resembling a large worm. He placed it on his head. He showed him another one, took hold of Sy's jaw and cheeks, squeezed, and shoved it inside his mouth. Sy could feel it squirm as it lodged in his throat. An open bag of soil being poured over his face would be the last thing he saw before he blacked out.

CHAPTER SEVENTEEN

The room phone woke Carmen. She listened to the ringing. Her eyes darted to the opposite side of the room to Kim's bed. Confident she had her bearings, she got up to answer her phone, but Kim hurried in and picked up the receiver.

"Hello?" she listened. "Hi, Dayton. She's sleeping right now." Kim turned and their eyes met. "Oh wait, she's awake."

"Tell him I'll call him right back," Carmen whispered.

"She's gonna call you back." Kim nodded. "Okay." Kim hung up. "He's in his room. Whoa, you okay?"

Carmen sat on the edge of the bed, wiped her forehead with the palm of her hand and looked at the sweat she had cleared off.

"I'm just a little weak. Can you pass me my cell?" she extended her hand to Kim. "When did you get back?"

"About fifteen minutes ago. I've been in the hall talking to Michelle." Kim handed the phone to Carmen and watched as she checked it. "Expecting a call?"

"My abuela is supposed to call. Wait, what time is it? Hay Dios Mio, she was supposed to call like two hours ago."

"Everything okay?"

"Yeah, just something I needed to talk to her about." Carmen tried to get up, but dizziness forced her back down. She covered herself in a thick blanket Maria had made for her. "I'm gonna have to tell Dayton I'm not up for going out." She used her cell to call him. "Hey sweetie, I think I'm sick."

"Sick? What happened?"

"I woke up from a nap and just feel weak."

"You want me to come up and spend the evenin' with you?"

"You don't want to be around me. I'm completely out of it."

"We'll cuddle. I can hold you and make you feel better."

"Cuddle? Yeah, okay. You with your active hands." Carmen smiled as she raised the blanket close.

"Okay, I don't need to hear any more of this," Kim said. "I'm out."

"Hold on, babe," Carmen covered the mouthpiece. "Where are you going?"

"Over to the Commons. You and Dayton can have the room."

Carmen went back to her call. "You sure you want to come up here? I'm telling you, nothing will be going on."

"I'm not sittin' with Eric while he's sulkin.' Let me make an overnight bag and I'll be over," he said.

"You're not spending the night, Dayton. Just until curfew ends."

"See you soon."

Carmen chuckled as she tossed her phone onto her bed.

Kim went into her desk drawer, retrieved a bottle of flu medicine, and placed it on the end of Carmen's bed. "You two have a fun time."

"How did the shopping go? I heard you two left late."

"You rest and we'll talk about it tomorrow." Kim got her umbrella and left.

Carmen sat with her back against the wall. With her eyes closed, she listened to people moving around the hallway and their muffled conversations outside her door. After a while, she climbed out of bed and went to the window to watch for Dayton.

A misty rain covered the campus, making it damp. She watched the Chambers Hall's entrance. Butterflies fluttered in her stomach in anticipation of seeing him.

The feeling was interrupted by the sound of a deep groan followed by two low resonating croaking noises from the right. It sounded muffled, like the voices of her neighbors through the wall. She heard it a second time and realized it came from outside. She lifted the window and put her head out.

The sounds traveled on a breeze, moving toward her like an approaching wave. Carmen tilted her head a little toward the south end of the school, where it was more pronounced.

She spotted the Mustang from the previous night driving down the road toward Chambers Hall. The groans and croaks grew louder. The car stopped before the driveway leading to the parking lot.

A tall, young man came ran down the driveway. The driver stepped out and the two of them walked to the back of the car. They met at the trunk and talked. The driver pointed from the trunk to the dorm. The other shook his head and pointed to the south gate. The driver responded with a shake of his head. The groan and croak sounded again.

Carmen went to her closet, retrieved a pair of binoculars, and returned to the window. She placed them over her eyes and adjusted the focus. She recognized the driver as the man she saw the night before. Panic surged through her body as she watched the driver unlock the trunk door. He lifted it and leaned farther into the darkness of it.

A blood-curdling scream from a man erupted into the night

sky. Carmen nearly dropped her binoculars from fright. The man lifted his head, looked around, then fell back into the trunk. The cry continued.

Help me! Help me!

Carmen heard laughter from below. She saw Michelle, Debra and two girls coming out of the dorm.

"You guys don't hear that?" Carmen called down to them.

"Excuse me?" Michelle called up to Carmen.

"Somebody's calling for help. You don't hear it?"

The girls grew quiet and listened. Carmen pointed in the direction of the Mustang, but the girls just shook their heads.

"Damn girl, classes haven't even started yet and you're losing it?" Debra said. Her friends laughed.

Carmen returned to observing the driver as he rose out of the trunk and slammed it shut. The cry became muffled again. The driver suddenly turned in Carmen's direction.

She put the binoculars down and stepped back from the window. The cries morphed back into groans and croaks. Then she heard a loud bang, like a stick of dynamite going off.

Silence followed.

Carmen cautiously approached the window and looked through the binoculars and scanned the area. The driver and car had gone.

As a breeze came through the open window, she smelled something rotten, a combination of vinegar, rotten eggs, and garbage. It stung her nostrils and churned her stomach. It took her a moment to recognize it, decomposition. She remembered the odor from the time Maria's neighbor died in their apartment and sat there for several days before being discovered.

Frightened and nauseated, Carmen snatched up her cell and raced from her room. She darted down the hall at top speed and stumbled to the abandoned phone booth. It no longer housed a phone, but it still provided a private place to talk away from roommates. She stepped inside, closed the door, opened her phone, but couldn't press a button because her hands wouldn't stop shaking.

"Stop shaking, Carmen. Calm down," she whispered.

She closed her eyes, took a deep breath, and exhaled. When she ascertained a semblance of calm, she hit redial on Maria's name. Maria picked up on the second ring.

"Abuela?" Carmen's breathing quickened from panic. "Abuela, tengo un problema."

"Carmen? ¿Qué pasa? What's the problema?"

Carmen cried. "Estoy muy asustada. Something terrible happened."

"Mira, calm down. I can't help jou if jou don't calm down."

Carmen shut her eyes tight and covered her mouth until she eased her breathing.

"I'm calm," she said.

"Okay, muy bien. Now, what 'appened?"

Carmen told her about the cries for help no one else heard. The man she saw in her dream. The decomposition smell. After she finished, Maria whispered a prayer.

"Okay, I want jou to listen to me. I spoke with jour aunt about all jou told me earlier. I never suffered from headaches like jou described, but she said it has been known to happen. Jou see, usually the ability develops naturally over time. Jou sense things as a child and the older jou get, the ability allows jou to see and speak to the dead.

"However, there are a rare few whose ability needs a boost to start working. Someting has to awaken it, and the headaches are a result."

"Abuela, you're saying I have the ability?" She bounced on her heels with excitement. "Yo tengo que llama mama."

"No. Don't call jour mother and tell her. It will only make matters worse," Maria warned. "Jour mother never had it or understood it and she will only get in the way of me helping jou. No. We'll work this out together."

"I should come home."

"What for?"

"So, you can help me."

"Jou want the easy way out again."

"What? No, that's not it."

"Carmensita, this ability is with jou for the rest of jour life. I can help you no matter where jou are, mi amour." Her tone was comforting. "Now, take a moment to get jourself together. Stay on the line because I have more to tell jou."

"Okay."

Carmen heard Maria put her receiver down. At that moment, someone pounded on the door, causing Carmen to jump and scream. She saw a yellow blur through the frosty glass. She opened the door and the girl from the lobby stood before her.

"You!"

"I didn't mean ta frighten you," she said. "Those girls down tha hall said you were in here."

Carmen looked out the booth at Michelle as she walked back into her room.

"You actually spoke to them?"

"I told'em I needed to speak to tha Spanish girl. I had ta describe you 'cause I don't even know your name."

"Oh. Thank goodness for that. It's good to know someone else has seen you."

"'Scuse meh?"

"Nothing. Forget I said anything. It's Carmen. My name is Carmen."

"Carmen. That'sa pertty name. I'm Savannah, after the beautiful city of Savannah, Georgia."

"Nice to meet you, Savannah."

"Why, thank you. Pleasure's all mine. I saw you last night, but

I didn't have time ta talk. But listen, I need to speak to you now. It's about—"

Carmen put her hand up. "I'd love to sit and talk, but I'm on hold with my abuela."

"Your what?"

"Abuela. Grandmother."

"Oh granny. I hope she's doin' aright. You tell her Savannah says hi."

A smile formed on Carmen's face. Savannah's good-natured disposition made her feel happy, and she wanted to giggle. Not out of disrespect, but because of how sweet Savannah behaved.

"I will. Excuse me."

"But I–" Savannah stepped forward as Carmen shut the door. "Okay, well I'll wait. But we do need ta talk. You're really the only one I can speak to."

"Give me a few," Carmen said.

"You still there?" Maria asked.

"I'm here." Carmen shuddered. A chill engulfed her body. It lasted only several seconds before it was replaced with soothing warmth.

"Now let's take this slow. Jou told me your headaches started when jou passed this man on campus. Jou have seen him several times now and tonight with another man. So, he is not a spirit. But if he is the cause, there are a couple of reasons for it.

"Sometimes if a spirit is attached to a person and haunting them because of a curse and it meets one of us, it may lash out. Either it will attack jou or the person it's haunting. If he reacted to jou in any way, that might be what happened. Understand, not all spirits jou encounter jou will see."

Carmen grew anxious. "Okay. So, this guy is cursed, maybe? Possibly?"

"Si. But that may not be the case. Jour aunt told me jour abuela suffered from severe headaches after encountering a dark spirit. She said I was too young to remember. She would come home after helping someone who had dealt with a malevolent being."

Carmen's heart pounded like it was about to come out of her chest. "Abuela, what kind of evil would make my head hurt like a bomb went off in my skull?"

"For it to affect jou the way it did, it's an old type of evil," Maria took a deep breath and said, "Te cruzaste con algo malo. Evil is walking on your campus."

"Hay Dios Mio, something's after me?" Carmen panicked again.

"Carmen, stop it. Calmate y escuchame."

Carmen covered her mouth as she did her best to regain her composure. She looked out the door and saw Savannah pacing back and forth.

"I'm sorry."

"No more sorry. Learn how to keep jour calm. Now, I have never encountered anything like that. My contacts have always been positive in nature. But listen to me. I'm not sure exactly what jou came across on campus, but I don't want jou to stay clear of this man and anyone he is near. I will find out for sure what it might be and let jou know." Maria grew quiet for a moment. Carmen heard her mumble something to herself. "There is one more thing."

"Seriously, Abuela. I don't think I can manage anything else."

"This isn't a terrible thing. With jour abilities awakened the way they were, there is a chance there will be a spirit coming to warn you of this evil. It may even reveal to jou what it is before I do."

"What do you mean?" Carmen said.

"Each medium in the familia first encounter is usually with one spirit who reaches out and tries to help. They pass on information. It helps them cope with their abilities or with a problem they are trying to solve."

"What do these spirits look like?"

"They'll appear as people. Jou won't know it's a spirit at first. One of the signs they are is they tend to be insistent about speaking to jou."

"I won't even know if I am talking to a dead person?"

"Sometimes they tell jou they are dead. They can also be silent and use body language to communicate. Jou may even feel them close by. They can give off the chills or warmth depending on their, como se dice, disposition."

Carmen looked at Savannah, who stood against the wall across from her. "Abuela, I don't know if I can handle this. I know I was curious about being able to do it, but now, this is too much."

"Jou're going to have to own this. Jou cannot treat this like it's some easy college course. Jou're one of us now. And Carmen, remember what I said. Eso es así. Te quiero, Carmen. All will be fine. Get some rest and I will call jou soon."

"Te amo, abuela." Carmen ended the call and sat on the stool affixed to the floor. It scared her to know not only could she communicate with the dead but at any time, they could reach out to her, and she wouldn't recognize they were not alive.

She opened the booth door and saw no sign of Savannah. She figured she got tired of waiting. She stepped into a chilly spot. She shivered a little as she headed solemnly back to her room.

"Hey, Carmen, you okay?" Michelle said as she stepped out of her room.

"Dealing with some family stuff. Oh, that girl Savannah you spoke to. You know where she went?"

"Savannah?"

"The one in the yellow dress who was looking for me. She said you told her I was in the booth."

"I didn't see any girl in a yellow dress."

Carmen's eyes widened. "Okay. Thanks."

"You sure you're okay?"

"I will be." Carmen opened the door to her room, stepped inside, and leaned against the door. She rubbed her arms as she recalled what Maria had said about feeling a spirit's presence. "Holy shit, Savannah's my contact."

CHAPTER EIGHTEEN

C*rack. Sizzle. Pop.*

"Cut the power!" Todd said.

Zeborah pushed the lever on the transformer to the left. The ceiling light went from dim to bright as the hum from the unit dissipated. A thin veil of smoke rose from inside the crate. Zeborah removed the wires as Todd placed his hand on the top of the soil and closed his eyes.

"They're moving to feed off the new body." Todd opened his eyes. "They're hungry. With two bodies in there now, this should sustain them until the ascension."

"This man isn't gonna be missed, is he?"

"I checked his cab. He had no pictures of family or a wedding ring on, which means he's single. No one will look for him."

"What about his haul?"

"I took care of it. This isn't my first rodeo, you know."

Zeborah picked up a gauge and examined it. "We have ta be careful with this thang. Tha amount of 'lectricity we used could cause an outage in the buildin.' We need ta make note of our power limits." He placed it down and said, "We should stick to usin' tha lab for tha major power needs."

"We're not moving these bodies, if that's what you're alluding to."

Todd dug deep into the soil until he found a large leech. He took hold of it with two fingers, removed it, and brought it close to his face.

"Nature's true vampire. Fascinating little creature, isn't it?" He licked it from tail to head. "I thank you for your support in this endeavor."

"Don't mistake muh help for support." Zeborah walked to the desk and picked up the parchment. "I never believed this thang would even work. I still don't."

"Despite your witnessing my increase in power. Once the ascension is complete, I'll be unstoppable. The coven will bow down to me. And you, Kevin, and Rakim will reap the rewards and have whatever you wish under my leadership." Todd put the leech in his mouth and ate it. Blood ran down his chin and he wiped it with his fingers, then licked them.

"What I want you can't give me," Zeborah said under his breath.

Todd approached Zeborah as he chewed. He cupped Zeborah under his chin and studied his face. He pushed him away, huffing in disgust.

"You're *still* pining over that slut?"

"She weren't no slut."

"Keep telling yourself that. Forget the fact she took off with some rich sonofabitch and left you standing in the rain like a fool." Todd sneered.

"You know, your story never set right with me. I never found proof Savannah ran off with anyone. You never liked her 'cause we were in love."

"I didn't like her because she got in the way. You were losing focus because of her." Todd put his finger in Zeborah's chest. "Get this straight, nothing else matters but this. Especially some little frilly blonde-haired bitch like Savannah. Get your head back in the game and commit yourself one hundred percent to this."

"Or what?"

Todd dropped his finger, grinned, and placed both his hands on Zeborah's shoulders. "Or I kill you."

"Git your hands off me."

Todd grinned, wiped Zeborah's shoulders, and backed away. They stared at one another.

"You can finish tha work yourself. I'm goin' out."

"Out where?"

Zeborah turned from him and left the room.

———

Zeborah left the dorm and headed to the south gate. His anger with Todd had hit a boiling point, and he needed to distance himself. He crossed the quad and made his way to the guard booth. He found it empty, and the gate had been locked. He glanced around to make sure the coast was clear before he launched himself into the air and over the fence. Landing quietly like a cat, he strode down the road.

At the second turn, he stopped, closed his eyes, and called out to Kevin telepathically.

I need some normalcy for a moment. I had ta walk out on Todd.

Why are you communicating with me this way?

Walkin' to you. Didn't wanna catch you off guard.

You're good. I'll listen out for you.

Moments later, Zeborah made his approach to the cabin. Kevin emerged from the inside, wiping his hands together. He turned up his collar, adjusted his pork-pie hat, which veiled his eyes in the darkness, causing them to glow a faint silver. They met midway.

"What'd he do now?"

"Killed a trucker and put him in tha crate for those leeches. Said he took care of everythang so as not to draw attention, but there's another issue you need ta know 'bout. He got his eye on another girl. Even picked a fight with tha boyfriend." Zeborah narrowed his eyes. "Least I believe he's tha boyfriend."

"So, it begins again."

"You speak to tha Coven?"

"I did. The elders voted."

"And?"

"And we've all been excommunicated."

"Why us? Todd's tha one who stole that spell from tha archives and set this sick plan in motion."

"They're holding us, especially me, responsible as the ones who didn't stop him, especially after what he did to Rakim." Kevin paused and took a deep breath. "We're on our own, for now."

From inside the cabin came an inhuman scream, followed by the banging of wood. Kevin motioned with a tilt of his head for Zeborah to follow him.

Upon entering the building, Zeborah threw his hand up over his nose. The smell of rancid flesh stung his nostrils. He followed Kevin to a door to the left of the kitchen. He opened it to a flight of stairs leading down to a basement.

They descended the stairs to an unfurnished space containing broken furniture and old boxes of clothes strewn around. A lit lantern hung from an overhead beam. It gave off an eerie glow. Toward the back of the basement, shackled by his foot to a stone pillar, sat Rakim. His mouth covered in blood, and half of a human body lay in the corner. Rakim punched a wood pillar, causing the ceiling tremble.

"Enough!" Kevin said as he handed his hat to Zeborah.

Rakim crawled toward them, hissing like a cat.

"He's gettin' worse," Zeborah said.

"I'm going to have to get him an animal, maybe a deer, to feed on. Have to start weaning him off human blood since we're so close to the campus."

"You can always feed him Todd's leeches."

Kevin didn't respond. He waited until Rakim couldn't go any further. "Listen to me, Rakim, I need you to fight this change happening to you... Back up!"

Kevin yanked Zeborah back as Rakim stretched out a clawed hand and swiped at them. Rakim stood, ran back to the desecrated body, and tore a kidney from it. He threw it at them. Kevin rushed him, putting Rakim into a sleeper hold and applied pressure. Rakim began to sink to the floor until he blacked out.

"He's losin' it," Zeborah said.

"Back upstairs." Kevin took his hat from him and put it back on.

They retreated to the upper floor. Kevin shut the door and secured a lock at the top.

"That gonna keep him from escapin'?"

"He's out for now. I'll get a better lock tomorrow."

"We may have ta kill him."

Kevin gave Zeborah a disapproving look. "Wish you had the same quick sentiment for Todd as you do for Rakim." He headed for the front door with Zeborah in tow.

"There's somethin' you should know." Zeborah stopped. "I don' know where she came from 'cause I never sensed her when I scouted tha campus."

"Spit it out."

"I think there's a medium on campus."

Kevin stopped. "A medium?"

"I'm not a hundred percent sure. She could be just gifted, but . . ."

"But what?"

"Tha last time that kinda sickness happened ta me, we was in London durin' tha blitzkrieg. 'Member my reaction to tha old woman in that curio shop? This? Ten times worse."

"Does Todd know?" Kevin asked. Zeborah shook his head. "Don't say a word to him about this, you understand? Get me a description of the girl and where she's staying. I'll take care of the rest. If you're right, this might be the advantage we need." Kevin looked away. "A young medium."

Kevin continued out the door and around to the side of the cabin. Hidden behind a large tree sat a restored 1940 Norton 16H motorcycle. He took hold of the handlebars, put up the kickstand, and pushed the bike to the road.

Zeborah followed.

"Where you goin'? What about Rakim?"

"You stay and keep an eye on him. He should be out for the next couple of hours, so he won't give you any trouble. I'm going to meet with LaChard."

"Who exactly is LaChard? Ya never quite explained him to me."

"Maurice LaChard is the head of the LaChard coven. He controls this territory, not including Bruckner University. However, his vampires are forbidden to go near the school. To avoid temptation. Vampires who break his rule are banished from the territory and their names sent to all the other covens, making it hard for an ousted vampire to find refuge elsewhere. In the one hundred and fifteen years the LaChard coven has regulated this area, they've had less than thirty incidents with mortals."

"He doesn't sound too ruthless."

"He used to be. Now he's older. He's become more diplomatic about matters. If any vampire has an issue while in his territory, he opens his doors for a sit-down or audience, as he likes to call it, for them to voice their concerns and get his help. Back in the day, if a vampire came to him under false pretenses, they were dealt with by extreme prejudice. If he discovered a banished vampire had broken a law or harmed another vampire, he'd have them tortured and killed. Eventually, the other covens heard about his tactics and threatened to kill him and his entire coven if he didn't stop. He knew he couldn't take on over a dozen other covens, so he stopped. He's an excellent mediator now."

They made it to the road. Kevin mounted the Norton 16H and turned it on.

"Going forward, be careful contacting me telepathically. Todd is strong enough now he could intercept our conversations. That's why we use cell phones," Kevin said.

"Good luck with this LaChard guy."

Zeborah watched as Kevin revved the engine of the motorcycle and rode off into the night.

CHAPTER NINETEEN

They stood in the center of the room for five minutes, locked in an embrace. Each time Dayton started to loosen his grip, Carmen squeezed him, letting him know he had to continue to hold her. Something was amiss.

"What's wrong?"

"I just need for you to hold me." Carmen buried her face in his chest and started to cry.

Dayton lifted her head and saw Carmen's watery eyes. Carefully, he used his thumb to wipe the tears from the corner of her eyes as she tried to stop crying.

"Never feel you can't talk to me, ya know? No matter what, I'm here."

"I know." She forced a smile on her face, but it dropped to a look of concern. "Mirda, I'm going through something I'm not ready to let you in on. It's a family thing and until I understand it better. . . I'm sorry."

He kissed her on the forehead. "Let's just lay down and cuddle. Or we can go down to the lounge and watch tv."

Carmen led him to her bed and lay down. Dayton took his

shoes off and joined her. She settled her head on his chest and stared at the wall.

"Do you believe in ghosts?"

"What?"

"Ghosts," Carmen said. "Spirits and such."

"You asking me if I believe they exist?" She nodded against him. "Well, I've never actually seen one, but yeah, I do."

"How would you react if you saw one or if one tried to communicate with you?"

"I guess it depends on how it came at me. If it did the kinda things they do in movies, like throwing plates or moving furniture, I'd probably run for my life. But if it looked like a person, I don't know, I guess I would try to talk to it." He looked down at her head. "Why you ask?"

"Just something I've been wondering about. I got hooked on one of those medium shows on cable over the break and it got me to thinking about how it would feel to be able to talk to a spirit."

"Don't know if I'd want that power."

"Really?"

"How can you live a normal life? At any given moment, the dead can just appear and start talking to you. I mean, what happens if some spirit decides to keep you up all night wantin' to talk? Or someone evil tries to communicate through you?"

Carmen lifted her head and looked at him. "Like what kind of evil?"

"You know, like a serial killer or criminal. They always talk about the nice folks in the family who reach out from beyond to say they're okay. It'd be interesting to know how they — Hey, what's wrong?" He sat up as he watched her turn pale.

"You think serial killers would want to communicate?"

"I think we need to stop talking about this. You look like you're about to have a panic attack."

Carmen put her head back down on his chest and closed her eyes. Dayton stroked her hair until she dozed off.

———

Kim let the door slam behind her, startling Carmen and Dayton. Their sudden movement made her jump.

"I didn't know you were still here. I'll stay at Kathy's tonight. Her roommate isn't coming back this semester, so she has an extra bed."

"We're not doing anything," Carmen said.

"I can't sleep in here with Dayton next to you."

"Isn't like you have anything I haven't seen before." Dayton grinned. Carmen elbowed him in the gut. "I'm kidding."

"I see why you and Eric are such great roommates. You're both jerks," Kim chided. "Eric didn't call, did he?"

"No," Carmen said. "Did something happen?"

"Nothing I feel like getting into." Kim went to her drawer and got a pair of pajamas. She put items in a book bag and headed for the door. Dayton scrambled out of the bed and stepped in front of Kim.

"Hey. You know you're his everything," Dayton said.

"I would get out of here by 4 AM. The R.A. goes on duty at five."

"What makes you think I'm spending the night?" Dayton watched the smirk grow on her face. "Thanks for the heads up."

Once Kim left, Carmen turned on her back and watched Dayton slide back in next to her.

"I'm worried about the two of them," Carmen said.

"I think the closer we get to graduating from this place, the more tension is gonna grow. We don't know what will happen after we graduate."

"True." She sat up. "Can we talk?"

"Of course. What's on your mind?"

"What if there was something strange about me?"

"Like what? Like you have a sixth toe?"

"No, *estas tonta*, I mean–"

"I love it when you speak Spanish to me." Dayton cracked a wicked smile.

"I'm being serious, Dayton." Carmen glanced at the floor to gather her thoughts. "Okay, what if I had this weird thing that got passed down in my family and it only affected the women? And let's say it wasn't something necessarily bad, but if it got out I had this thing, I would be treated differently. And us staying together would cause people to treat you differently. Could you handle being with me?"

"Uhh," Dayton scratched his chin. "I guess so. I mean, you're still you, right? It's not something that would endanger our lives, is it?"

"No."

"Okay, well then, yeah. I could stay with you. You're the same girl I fell in lo . . . I mean, the girl I fell hard for."

Carmen smiled. "Were you about to say in love?"

"No." Dayton shook his head.

"Yes, you were. *Que Lindö*."

"I wasn't going to say love," he said cheekily. "Like. I was gonna to say *like*."

Carmen leaned forward and kissed him. She lay back on the bed and, as he wrapped his arms around her waist, she broke the kiss.

"Thank you. That's really what I needed to know. Get the light. Let's get some sleep."

Dayton grumbled, got up, and shut the light out. He lingered by the switch for a moment to calm himself. Then he got back into bed, and they spooned. Carmen gripped his arm around her. After a while, they fell into a deep sleep.

CHAPTER TWENTY

Kevin parked in front of a large Victorian house on a dead-end street. He turned the engine off on his Norton 16H, stared at the home for a moment. A light illuminated the second-floor parlor. Through the large bay window on the first floor, LaChard's servant headed to the door to greet him.

He dismounted the bike and hurried the walkway. The house's exterior had been beautifully restored. The huge porch greeted him like an old friend with its wide staircase. Stained glass windows adorned the upper portion of the house as well as around the trim of the lower windows. The wood had been meticulously shellacked. The inviting smell of wood burning from a fireplace came out of the brick chimney in the rear of the house.

As Kevin's foot touched the edge of the porch, the door opened and a well-dressed black man holding an oil lamp greeted him.

"Evening, sir. Mister LaChard is expecting you in the second-floor parlor," the servant said.

"Thank you. I know the way." Kevin handed him his hat as he passed him and made a beeline up the long wooden staircase.

Shadows danced from gas lamps light in the second-floor

hallway. The warmth from a fireplace greeted Kevin as he stepped into the parlor. He unbuttoned his coat and removed it as he walked to the center of the room next to a large round table with flowers on it. To his left, LaChard, a man whose looks favored Clarke Gable, stood before a high-back chair, talking to an individual sitting in it.

The servant came up behind him and took his coat.

"Excuse me, sir, your guest has arrived," the servant announced.

LaChard looked up, smiled and crossed the room with an extended hand. Kevin met him halfway and gave him a firm handshake.

"Ah, Kevin, wonderful to see you."

"LaChard, thank you for taking an audience with me. I appreciate it."

"Oh, how I miss such manners. You are most welcome. How could I refuse an audience with a member of one of the oldest vampire covens in the Americas? Accomplished occultist, as well as one of the librarians of the largest collection of ancient spells, books, and scrolls. Which you owe me a peek at the Egyptian book of the dead you acquired."

"I haven't forgotten," Kevin said.

"I have to say, though, the way you went about seeking an audience with me wasn't a pleasant one."

"Unpleasant, but necessary. I will explain."

"Better than your coven leader's son, I hope."

"What does Richard have to do with this?"

"An incident such as this mandates I contact the head of the coven whose member caused the atrocity. You know my team works fast. They found traces of saliva in the wounds and discovered... Well, you know what they found, so I had to have Richard come to sit and hear what you have to say." LaChard gestured to the chair.

Kevin stepped back. "LaChard, pardon me, but this is to be a private council between us. I no longer recognize Richard as the head of the coven, nor will I participate in this audience in his presence."

"Yes, you will. Let's not make this any more difficult than it has to be. I don't want to waste time arguing the politics of the situation. So, let's be cordial and get down to the matter at hand. Shall we?" LaChard extended his hand toward an empty chair across from the high back.

Kevin nodded and crossed the room to the chair. As he sat and saw Richard, dressed like he was going to a nightclub, Kevin nodded to him in a gesture of respect. Richard didn't return the nod. LaChard took his seat between them.

"Now then—"

"Before we begin, I want to say this sonofabitch and his three cousins are no longer considered members of the Barnes Coven. The council met last evening to—"

"Excuse me, Richard?" LaChard interrupted. "With all due respect, shut your mouth and don't speak again until I have given you permission. Kevin called this meeting, not you. You are here to listen. Understood?"

Richard shifted in his seat and folded his arms like a child throwing a tantrum.

"It is," Richard said.

"And what?"

"And it won't happen again."

"Adopt some manners before you become the head of your coven," LaChard chided. "Now first, let me say I didn't like having a body brought to me with your message. But I have known you for years, Kevin, and you don't do things for the sake of doing them. Speak."

Kevin leaned forward. "My cousin, Todd Anderson, got his hands on an ascension spell that appears to be working. He is now in the final stage of the spell, and I fear if he completes it, it will lead to many of our kind being slaughtered. I, therefore, ask permission to kill him on your soil."

"What ascension spell is in his possession?" LaChard said.

"The *Daemon Assi Ascension* spell."

"No vampire has ever successfully performed it. It's considered a sick joke created by a witch in 1384 as an act of revenge. I heard it was lost in the Gains Coven fire a century ago. How did Todd find it?"

"Alexander Gains gave the spell to Sofia Callaway, a collector, and member of the Barnes Coven, as a courtship present. She attempted to use it against Alexander because he was unfaithful to her. It drove her mad. After her death, the contents of her collection were divided up and much of the literature ended up in the Barnes archives. I oversaw all the occult work in the archives, so I know all about this. Todd sought it out and took it from there."

"Why did he seek it out?" LaChard asked.

Kevin glanced at Richard. "Maybe it's better I show you. With your permission, I would like to conduct a Coven Fusion."

LaChard raised an eyebrow. "Very well, Richard, we will need your blood."

"With all due respect." Kevin raised his hand. "It's better if we use mine. Although Richard is the heir apparent, I don't trust him to show you things the way they happened."

"You may proceed."

Kevin moved to the center of the room. LaChard signaled to Richard to take position across from Kevin as he stood between them. Kevin made a fist, extended his pinky, exposing his sharp nail, and he carved the Barnes Coven Crest into his palm. Richard did the same to his hand. LaChard carved two circles into his hand, in the palm and the backhand side. He extended his bloody hand. Richard put his hand on top of LaChard's. Kevin put his hand under and closed his eyes.

Kevin's memories traveled through his blood, then connected with LaChard and Richard, and the three were transported to the Barnes Coven's Keep. They stood before a medieval hall, lit with torches and decorated with beautiful oak carved tables, chairs, and sideboards against the walls.

In the center of the room, a large circle of well-dressed coven members cheered at an event before them. Kevin positioned himself so LaChard and Richard could see Todd in a fistfight with Richard.

"This was a year ago," Kevin said.

———

Richard, in the center of the circle, had taken hold of Todd by his shirt collar and punched him, causing him to lose his footing. Todd scrambled to his feet, swung, and missed as Richard ducked. He jabbed Todd in the ribs and backed up.

"Disrespect me!" He stepped up, struck Todd with a hard right, sending him to the floor. "Bet you'll think twice about going over my head."

"You have no right denying me a position on the council," Todd said.

"I have every right. I govern it. And as long as I am overseeing the council, only natural-born vampires will sit there. I'm not taking your disgusting breed. Some vampires' leftovers he didn't want to finish killing."

Todd rushed Richard and punched him in the chest. Richard fell backward, stunned for a moment. Coven members tried to help him up, and he pushed them away.

"Well, you can hit after all." Richard smirked. "Okay, leftovers, how about we do it this way?"

"Don't call me that."

"But it's what you are. Aren't you the one always complaining no one in the coven recognizes you for being the vampire—?"

"You know damn well what I mean."

"You're a leftover, Todd. That's all you will ever be, you pathetic mutt. What are you going to do, leftover? Go cry and tell the surrogate you call a father I called you names? A true vampire fights their own battles."

————

"Kevin?" LaChard said. "What is leftover? I've never heard this term."

"It is a derogatory term created by the prodigal son on the other side of you. A leftover refers to a human who has become a vampire because the one who bit them never returned to drain them. They're usually humans whom we harvest for food and feed on. It's a rule if we do not intend to feed on them anymore, we must end their lives, so the thirst doesn't develop within them."

"And Todd is one of these harvest people turned vampire?"

"He became one by accident."

"You know the details?"

"I do."

"How?"

"Because I am the one responsible for turning him."

Kevin and LaChard returned their attention to the events in the circle.

————

Todd readied himself to attack Richard as the sounds of laughter filled the hall. Before he moved, Riad and Elster, Richard's best friends, tackled him to the floor. They beat Todd with a flurry of punches.

Todd struggled to fight back. He clawed at the legs of his assailants, hoping to drag one down.

The crowd chanted, "Leftover! Leftover!"

Todd cried out for help.

No one interfered.

"Enough of this!" a booming voice called out. "Cease your actions this instant."

The crowd stopped cheering as Todd's adopted father, Andre, followed by Kevin, Zeborah, and Rakim, in his human form, infiltrated the hall. Richard, Riad, and Elster backed away, revealing Todd on the floor in a bloody heap. On his hands and knee, Todd spat out blood and tried to stand. Kevin and Zeborah helped him as Rakim and Andre watched.

"Don't touch him," Andre demanded. "He can get up on his own."

Kevin and Zeborah moved away. They watched as Todd got to his feet. The bruises on his face healed before their eyes.

"He disrespected me," Richard said.

"I couldn't care less what he did to you." Andre pointed his nose in the air as he turned away from him. "And you," he pointed at Todd. "How could you allow yourself to be beaten upon?"

"Father. . ."

"I am not your father. I did not make you. I agreed to take you as one of my own and you embarrass my name by allowing these three to beat on you."

"I didn't allow—"

"Silence! You're a disgrace to my name and a disgrace to our kind. You'll never be a true vampire." He turned to Kevin. "Take your "cousin" out of my sight. From this moment on, he is your burden to bear, not mine. Maybe this will teach you why we don't accept mutts into our fold."

"I'm not a mutt or a leftover," Todd shouted.

"Why don't you take a walk in the sun and do us all a favor and burn," Richard said.

"Why don't you just leave," Riad said.

Andre turned and exited the hall with the crowd in tow. Richard and his friends continued to mock and laugh at Todd as they trailed behind.

Todd stood silently with his cousins. His eyes burned red.

"Don't let them get to you," Kevin said.

"I'm leaving. If they don't want me here, I'm not staying."

"You can't let 'em bully you out tha coven," Zeborah said. "We'll stand by you."

"You mean it?"

"Of course," Kevin said.

"Come with me. There's something I want to do to ensure this coven pays a price for mocking me." He turned to Kevin. "I'll need a parchment and three books from the archives to help me with the spell."

"What spell?" Kevin asked.

"The Daemon Ascension."

Kevin backed up. "No, Todd. You can't use that. No vampire has ever—"

"You're either with me or not."

"Todd?" Zeborah stepped up. "Let's go git it."

Todd led the way out the hall with Zeborah and Rakim behind him.

Kevin stood in silence, his head down.

The image melted away and the three men were back in LaChard's parlor.

**scene break?

LaChard snatched his hand away from Richard's and looked at

him in disgust. He smacked him hard with the back of his hand, causing his lip to bleed.

"Step away from me, you privileged piece of shit," LaChard spoke through clenched teeth. "Sit and don't you dare move."

Richard scowled at Kevin, then took his seat.

"The Daemon Ascension, what proof do you have it's working?" LaChard said.

"Rakim. Todd bit him because he abandoned helping with the spell. Because he did this during the third stage, his bite's now poisonous. If he bit a mortal, they would go into anaphylactic shock and die. But biting another vampire, it has caused Rakim to regress into an earlier form we once held. Half bat, half-vampire."

LaChard's eyebrow turned up into an arc. "Where is he now?"

"With Zeborah. We have him contained."

"How vicious is he?"

"You saw the condition of the body I sent you." Kevin looked at Richard. "There's no way to turn Rakim back. If we kill Todd, we might stop the regression process."

"That's speculation," LaChard said.

"Yes."

"This speculation stems from?"

"Todd's bite also gives him a special bond with Rakim. He can manipulate him into doing whatever he wants. The closer he gets to obtaining his goal, the stronger the influence gets," Kevin said.

LaChard turned to Richard. "Have you seen Rakim? Is what he says true?"

"It's true," Richard said.

"This happened at the coven house?"

"It did."

"You let them walk out of your coven with him in that condition?"

Richard straightened up in his seat. "They were banished because of Todd's actions. What else were we supposed to do?"

"You lock him up until you find a cure or, in an extreme case with no cure, you kill an infected vampire. You don't send him out into the streets to do whatever he wants to do. What's the matter with you and your father?" LaChard yelled.

"Listen, no one wanted to go near that abomination."

"Instead, you push the matter off on an adjacent territory?" LaChard said. "If you're the future of the Barnes Coven, I feel remorse for the family."

Richard stood. "I don't need to sit here and be insulted."

"Then stand and be insulted. You put *my* territory and *my* coven in danger by letting both Todd and Rakim walk out of yours."

"How is this my fault? I didn't send them in this direction. This is the way they chose to come."

"By neglecting to oversee matters internally, you set off this chain of events. If they hadn't come here, it would've been somewhere else."

"What would you like us to do? Send an army of vampires down here to try to stop Todd? He has been excommunicated from the Coven, which means all claims on him are null. We have no control over him, we have no declaration on him, and we don't want him. To hell with you and your laws and the creature this bastard calls a cousin," Richard said.

"Have a seat, Richard." LaChard's eyes turned crimson. Richard hesitated, then sat back down.

"LaChard," Kevin raised a finger, "the final step to the spell leaves a window of opportunity for us to attack. He'll soon be vulnerable enough for us to kill him and . . ."

LaChard waved his hand and got up from his seat. He walked to the fireplace and stared at the flames. "What happens if he finishes the spell?"

"He ascends into an immensely powerful demon. He'll possess someone, effectively using them as a weapon. Their bites will be like a disease. Regressing any vampire they bite," Kevin explained, "and from what I understand from the readings, if a mortal manages to survive a demon bite, their blood will be poisonous to us."

"You said he can read your thoughts. How do you know he doesn't know about our meeting? Or any plans you have been brewing?"

Kevin walked to the center of the room, staring at the floor as he gathered his thoughts. "We have been providing him places where he can move around unnoticed. Where we all can blend in and help him get odds and ends. Do enough work to convince him we are on his side, so he doesn't read our thoughts. Along the way, we have been able to recruit people who can throw a monkey wrench in his plans and, possibly, aid in killing him."

LaChard towered over Kevin. "Where is he now?"

"Bruckner University," Kevin said.

"You put a vampire like that on a campus full of students?"

"Todd doesn't drink from humans for nourishment anymore. It's one of the conditions of the spell," Kevin said.

"What's he doing for food?" Richard said.

"Trust me, you don't want to know."

"Kevin, he's a vampire in a populated area. There are instincts that cannot be contained. If history has taught us anything, it's a vampire like Todd is going to get overconfident and try to mess with a mortal and . . . wait, did you say he will possess someone? This wouldn't happen to be a mortal, would it?" LaChard glared at Kevin, who nodded. "Okay, okay, okay, stop." LaChard held the side of his head. "Don't talk anymore." He walked away and stood by a window at the far end of the parlor.

"There is no counter spell for this?" LaChard said.

"No. Believe me, I have searched. The host has to be killed for the spell to end. We don't have a lot of time."

LaChard stared out the window. After a long silence, he turned back to Kevin.

"You made Todd what he is, and I get the sense you're feeling responsible for him. But Todd is the one seeking vengeance, not you. Take such burden off your shoulders. You have my permission to kill him."

"Thank you, LaChard."

Richard stood. "Thank goodness."

"I also grant you a one-time favor, but only come to me should you need my help. Now go. I don't want to look at you anymore tonight."

Kevin turned and headed out the door into the hall. He glared back at Richard.

"We'll settle up soon," Kevin threatened. "I promise."

"I'm sure we will," Richard said.

Kevin headed down the stairs, retrieved his things from the servant and let himself out into the wintry night.

CHAPTER TWENTY-ONE

Dayton emerged from Chambers Hall and found Eric sitting on a bench along the walkway, writing in a notebook. He yawned and stretched as he approached him. Eric looked up just as he got close and smirked.

"What?"

"You must've had a good night. It's almost lunchtime. Carmen wore you out, huh?" Eric said.

"Funny. Nothing happened. We just cuddled." He rubbed his neck. "Man, I'm hurtin'."

"You know, these dorm beds weren't designed to hold two people."

"Yeah, I think it's the school's idea of a sick joke." Dayton pointed to the notebook. "What's that for?"

"Hmm?" Eric looked at the notebook page. "Here." He handed it to Dayton. "It's a list of my bad habits."

Dayton read the pages and laughed, but his face turned serious the closer he got to the bottom.

"Wow."

"I need your help, bro. You seem to have it together. I need to change for Kim, and I don't know how."

"With all this? We need to find one thing to focus on."

"Well, what about my being late all the time?"

"I have tried to help with that, but you turn around and go back to your usual self. You have to want to change."

"Yo, yo, yo? What's goin' on people?" Curtis stepped out the door. "What's good?"

"Chillin'," Eric said. "How's work-study going?"

"Only been a couple of days, but I like it so far."

"Best place to work, if you ask me. You got access to all the study materials," Dayton said.

"Ain't that the truth? Do you know how some people graduate college cum laude? I'll be lucky if I graduate *thank you laude*." They all laughed. "What's this?" he snatched the notebook from Dayton and read it. "E, man, what on earth did you do to Kim *this* time?" Before Eric could respond, Curtis cut him off, "We need to help you out, man. Because you keep this up, you're going to lose your investment."

"My investment?" Eric said.

"Your relationship. You have invested time and energy. Not to mention money. You need to protect that investment cause if you don't, you will lose her." He put his hand on Eric's shoulder. "Dayton, I ask, how do we help this man?"

No one said a word. Curtis looked back at the list, shaking his head as he scanned the page, then handed the book back to Eric.

"Okay, this is what we have to do. We're going to have to change the way *we* do things with Eric. We're all going to make sure whenever he has someplace to be, he gets there. I mean anyplace he needs to be from class to meals to time with Kim."

"No problem," Curtis said.

"In fact, it might be best if we don't even start doing anything with him if we know he has to meet Kim, including *Madden*," Dayton said.

"What?"

"You wanna help, Curtis, you have to make sacrifices," Dayton said.

"But all the fun stuff?"

"It's that stuff getting him in trouble."

"Yeah, you got a point," Curtis added. "You know, if it doesn't work, I'm sure I can find a book on it. I'm just saying."

Eric's cell phone vibrated. He removed it from his pocket and saw he had a voicemail. "Give me a second." He stepped away from them.

"How are things going with Carmen?" Curtis said.

"Don't start."

"What? I'm genuinely asking. You two look good together."

Dayton gave him a suspicious look. "There's a punch line in this somewhere."

"No, there are no jokes or anything. She's a really great girl. You're lucky to be with her."

"Don't you mean lucky to have nabbed her?"

"C'mon man, I didn't mean it like that."

"Look, I know you two went out a couple of times and I'm guessing there are some feelings in there still stirring."

"Dayton, what I feel for her has nothin' to do with what you two have. I'm not jealous. I'm not mad or all up in my feelings. All I am saying is I'm happy she wound up with someone like you, and I hope it all goes well."

"Thank you."

"You're welcome," Curtis smirked. "Of course, you know if you mess up . . ."

Dayton turned to kick him in the ass, and Curtis jumped out the way, laughing. Dayton shook his head in disbelief, then started to chuckle.

"Hey, that was Kim." Eric approached them. "She wants to get together later to talk. I told her we can meet at the fountain. She supposed to be back on campus around four."

"This is the perfect chance for you to begin again with Kim," Dayton said. "We're going to get you to the fountain thirty minutes early. She sees you already there. It will give her hope."

Eric nodded. "Good plan. Let's get inside."

They went inside Chambers Hall. As they crossed to the lounge, Zeborah and Todd stepped out of the stairwell. Todd, dressed in a suit, strolled with an air of arrogance and saw them checking him out. Instead of going around them, he made it a point to walk through them, again. As he did, they could smell the heavy cologne he wore.

"What'd he do, bathe in that stuff?" Curtis covered his nose. "Kinda early to be stylin' and profilin,' don't you think?"

Todd stopped, turned, and eyeballed them, trying to figure out who made the remark. Zeborah tugged on his arm, signaling him to keep walking. Todd yanked away from him.

"I like to dress like an adult and be clean," Todd said. "I mean, I guess I could roll out of bed and throw something on. I, at least, know how to make it look good."

They all noticed they were wearing wrinkled and disheveled clothes.

"Twice you've had something smart to say," Curtis accused.

"Is it? Do yourself a favor and don't make me say it a third time," Todd threatened.

"You workin' my last nerve, bro," Curtis warned. "I don't know who you think you are."

"Obviously, someone better than you," Todd said with a smirk.

Curtis moved like a runner off the starting block toward Todd. Dayton leapt and seized Curtis by the arm as Eric got in front of him and put his hands on his chest to keep him in place.

"Chill, Curtis, it's not worth it," Eric said. "Let's go. We have better things to do."

"Sounds like a marvelous idea," Todd said. "Come on, Zeborah, the ladies await."

Todd turned to the door, but Dayton approached him.

"Hey, wait a second." Todd and Zeborah stopped.

Dayton kept his distance. "Listen, you're new here. Let me give you a bit of friendly advice."

"Friendly advice, huh? I could always use *friendly* advice." He clasped his hands in front of himself and pursed his lips. His posture screamed arrogance. "Lay it on me, dude."

"Okay," Dayton exhaled to keep calm. "Here's the thing. We respect our women around here."

"*Your* women. I didn't realize there's a claim on them."

"No one stakes a claim on any of them. But we do treat them with respect," Dayton said.

"And you're telling me this because?"

"We're getting this vibe from you." Eric approached him. "This whole player slash attitude thing you got goin' on. If that's how you roll, then fine. But respect our women if you plan on doing whatever it is you plan on doing. 'Cause whatever this is you're playing at isn't going to end well for anyone."

Todd looked at Zeborah as he pointed a thumb at Eric and chuckled.

"Let's go, Todd," Zeborah said.

"One sec." He turned and looked at Dayton. "Okay, you I hear. You want me to respect *your* women, fine." Todd pointed a finger at Eric. "As for you, I don't get it."

"What? What don't you get?" Eric said.

"Each time our paths crossed you've stepped to me. What's the deal?"

"Like my man, Eric said, it's a vibe we got," Dayton said.

"You two must be close friends. Got each other's back, hmm?

A word of advice, and you can take this however you like. Worry about yourself. Don't concern yourself with me or my business or even my vibe, okay? After this moment, you stay out of my way; I'll stay out of yours. We cool?" Todd smirked. "Worry about your own woman problems, brotha."

Eric and Todd stared at one another for several seconds. Todd walked out the door. Zeborah stared at Eric, started to speak but changed his mind and followed Todd out.

"Eric, is he talking about you and Kim?" Curtis said.

"Sonofabitch," he mumbled.

Eric walked to the door and continued to watch Todd as he stood alone at the curb. A moment later, Zeborah drove up in the Mustang. Todd turned and looked at Eric. He wiggled his fingers goodbye before getting into the car. Eric punched the front door in frustration.

CHAPTER TWENTY-TWO

armen awoke with a start, looked at the time, and cursed out loud. It was 1pm. Dayton had forgotten to reset the alarm before he left. Ignoring a mild headache, she scrambled out of bed, gathered her toiletries, and hurried for the door. Throwing it open, she nearly collided with Savannah. Startled, Carmen screamed and clutched her heart.

"Aye, Dios Mio. ¿Lo que está mal con usted? Usted me asusto casi hasta la muerte." Carmen sounded shaken. "You can't do that to me."

"I been waitin' here quite a while for you, darlin.' Woulda knocked, but I didn't wanna wake you."

Carmen lowered her hand and stared at Savannah, who, smiling, brushed back a strand of hair from over her eye.

"So, how does this work? Do I have to invite you in or do you just, I don't know, come in?"

"I don't like ta jus walk into anyone's livin' space. An invitation would be nice. May I?"

Carmen stepped to the side and extended an arm. Savannah

nodded and walked in. Carmen watched her as she closed the door.

"Why didn't you come through the door like a normal ghost?" Carmen said without clearly thinking about the words she chose. "I can't believe what I just said."

"Um, excuse me? I'm not a ghost. I'm a spirit," Savannah said. "It's okay. I guess that's a common mistake. I didn't even think about doin' that. But like I said, invitation is always nicer." She touched Carmen. "You gonna be okay?"

Carmen detected the chill of her touch on her arm and shivered.

"I'm working on it," Carmen said.

Savannah walked around, smiling. "Well, isn't this nice? Which side is yours? No, no, lemme guess. This one ova here." She pointed to Carmen's bed. "I can feel your energy ova here." She sat down on the bed, folded her hands, and placed them in her lap.

Carmen couldn't get over how alive Savannah appeared.

"You're my contact, to speaking with the dead?"

"I'm the first spirit you ever talked to? Whew, well, what a relief. I thought you were ignorin' me on purpose last night."

"I didn't know you were dead. You don't look dead."

"Well, bless your heart. But I am quite dead."

"Are you in . . . pain?"

"No. I'm not hurtin'."

"How did you know to come to me?"

"I didn't exactly. You see, I could sense someone nearby had the ability, I jus couldn't pinpoint who. Out of tha four people who walked past me in the lobby, you were the only one who responded ta me. And of course, in tha hall last night."

Carmen approached her, rubbing the split on her arm where Savannah had touched her. "Um, are you, or I should say, were you a student here on campus?"

"No. I was brought here."

"Brought here?"

"Tha man who killed me has been carryin' round my body. Because he refuses to bury me, I can't be at rest. So, here I am."

A chill shot down her spine. "You were killed? Why? Does your family know? Do you need me to call anyone? How can you–?"

"Darlin,' calm down. It's okay. I don't need you ta contact anyone for me. I'm here to try an help you. And in return, you can help me. But we can't do that if we're all nervous, now can we?" Savannah smiled. Carmen shook her head. "No, we can't. Now c'mon ova here to tha bed, sit yourself down, and breathe." Savannah patted the spot next to her. "I'll tell you what I know."

Carmen calmed her breathing as she sat down on the bed. "I'm okay."

"Okay, now, there are these two men. Their names are Todd and Zeborah. Don't ask me who in their right mind would give a person that name. But anyway, I met these guys about a year ago. They were going to school in the town where I worked."

"You went to school with them?"

"No, I waitressed at this dinah the students would come to. I met them there. Zeborah was such a gentleman back then. Just as sweet an kind. You could tell he came from a proper family." Savannah gushed.

"You had a thing for him, didn't you?" Carmen grinned.

"It shows, don't it?" She tucked her hair back, then giggled. "Yes, I liked him. He started courtin' me, you know. He stole my heart," Savannah sighed. "But we ladies sometimes make mistakes in judgment about a man. And I made mine. But I don't wanna dwell on that. He and Todd are cousins who dabble in what my granny used to call dark arts. Only they called it their 'experiment,' but it's no experiment. Todd's the one proficient at it. Zeborah seems ta be along for the ride, but it doesn't mean he's any less dangerous."

"Dangerous in what way?"

"With Zeborah, if he takes a likin' to you, he'll get close to you and get inside you," Savannah pointed to her head. "Get inside here an take over. There were times I would spend the night with him, and he'd put me in a trance. Nothin' made me blackout, but he would do it and put these leeches on the back of my hand and let 'em bite me. He said they were to help with the experiment, and I was helpin' him toward greatness," Savannah said.

"Why would you stay with a man who would do that to you?"

"Oh, he eventually stopped." Savannah smiled again. "He apologized for what he forced me ta do and changed his ways. He asked me to run away with him."

"Run away? Why?"

"Todd. See, he was forcin' Zeborah to use me 'cause he didn't like how close we were becoming. He told Zeborah to leave me, but I guess he didn't realize how much we loved each other." Savannah stood, then crossed the room. She wore a troubled expression on her face. "We were s'posed to meet behind a diner we loved to go to and run off."

Carmen got up and went to console her. Savannah glided back with her hands up.

"You can't touch me," Savannah said gently. "Touching me would be bad. At least, I think it would be."

"But you touched *me*." Carmen withdrew her hand. "What happened after that?"

"While I waited for Zeborah to show, someone hit me from behind and I blacked out. I woke up in a box of dirt. I heard Zeborah talkin' to someone I didn't know 'bout how Todd put a girl out of her misery. I assumed he meant me."

"Zeborah betrayed you?" Carmen said.

The lock on the door clicked and swung open. Carmen spun around as Kim entered the room and smiled at her.

"You're up. How you feeling?" Kim said.

Carmen turned around. Savannah had gone. She hurried to

the window, looked down, and saw her standing below. She waved at Carmen, smiled, and disappeared as she sauntered away.

"I'm better," Carmen said, rubbing her hands. "I'm, um, you know what, I'm fine. How are you feeling?"

"Better." Kim joined Carmen at the window. "You're pale. You sure you're okay?"

"I'm fine."

"I didn't mean to barge in on you last night. You two are like how Eric and I were in the beginning," Kim smiled., "God, such an awesome feeling, being in love. Not being able to stand being apart. Getting warm tingling feelings at the sound of their voice. Why can't it always be like that?"

"You guys have been together since freshman year. You just need to find a way to adjust and move forward," Carmen said.

"What if we can't adjust? I've never even tried to date anyone else. How do I know if I have options?"

Carmen's mouth dropped in shock. "You're lucky you don't have a boyfriend like Savannah."

"Who's Savannah?"

"What? Savannah? She's a girl I . . . Never mind her. Let me ask you this. Do you want to date other people?"

"Well, no, but—"

"So why bring it up? Unless you aren't feeling Eric anymore . . . *Mira*, promise me you will talk this problem out with him. You guys can overcome this issue." Her voice quivered a bit. "Promise me."

"Okay. I'll work it out," Kim said.

Carmen hugged her and then took her toiletries and left.

Kim took out her cell and called Eric so they could meet up later to talk.

CHAPTER TWENTY-THREE

The guards didn't see Kevin as he walked through the gate. They were too busy talking to one another. He made no attempt to announce himself. He strolled across the campus until he came to a map of the university grounds on a message board. Kevin placed his finger on the spot where he stood and drew an invisible line to the row of female dorms.

"Okay," he mumbled to himself. "There's four of them. Just have to find the right one."

Kevin adjusted his coat, then started to walk down dormitory row. Each one he passed, he closed his eyes and searched for a ripple effect in the air. It would mean the medium was close. So far, he sensed nothing.

Near Wakeford Hall, he experienced a sensation as though someone had hit him with a sledgehammer. He realized he'd inadvertently started a link between him and the medium. He stopped, placed his hand on the back of his neck, and willed the pain away, breaking the link.

"Oh, you're a real strong one," Kevin whispered to himself. He faced the dormitory and scanned the windows, hoping to see the face of the medium looking out to see the source of her own discomfort. With the link broken, she had to be curious.

He walked backward, taking in the entire scope of the building. He could see heads moving past windows. One of them, on the third floor, opened and a young Hispanic girl put her head out and looked around. She looked distressed.

"There you are," Kevin muttered.

She touched the side of her head before retreating inside. Kevin walked to a bench close to the dorm's entrance and waited. Ten minutes later, she emerged and walked in his direction. He watched her as she approached. The closer she got, the more he could feel her aura fighting to connect.

Kevin had the ability to control his detection from mediums. It had taken years for him to learn the technique. He would create a dead space around himself so the medium's ability to summon a spirit or latch on to one couldn't find him, only empty space.

This allowed him to follow her at a safe distance.

Trailing six feet behind her, he observed her searching as though on guard for an attack. She led him to a row of empty benches behind the administration building. There she took a seat at the farthest one and took out her cell phone. Kevin looked around. They were alone. He sat at the one farthest from her and watched peripherally.

She stared at the phone in her hand, fumbling with it until she decided to use it. As she placed it to her ear, he lowered his fedora and pretended to be asleep as she listened to her call.

———

"Hola?"

"Abuela, soy yo," Carmen said. "I know you were supposed to call me, but something happened this afternoon. I met my spirit contact."

"Que? Are jou sure?"

"Positive. She came to my room to talk to me. She tried to talk to me last night after we spoke. I just thought she was an annoying new student. I feel those headaches around her. Not as intense, but still." A grin formed on her face. "But this is a good thing, right?"

"It is." She sounded pensive. "I have news for jou. I called your aunt and some friends and told them what happened. They said the intensity of jour headaches are linked to an evil on campus."

"Abuela, I know. The spirit told me," Carmen said. "That's the other reason I'm calling."

"What did she say?"

"Two guys who practiced dark arts. I guess it's black magic."

"No, Carmen, ella está mal. Your severe headache is from encountering los muertos en cuerporeal." Maria now sounded distressed.

"The corporeal undead? What does that mean?"

"It is the dead walking in physical form. They're not of the spirit world. They have risen from the dead and walk about. Son como los zombis."

Fear moved through her body like falling dominoes as Carmen's hair stood on end. She tried to ignore the sensation. "Abuela, zombies aren't real."

"Living in the Caribbean, I heard stories of the dead being brought back to life."

"Abuela, esto no es el Caribe. They don't raise the dead here," Carmen's tone rose.

"No me lebantes la voz. I have been at this far longer than jou. I know what I'm talking about. Los muertos están entre nosotros."

"Abuela, there are no zombies on campus. If there were zombies, wouldn't Savannah tell me there were?"

Maria grew quiet for a moment. Carmen could hear her heavy breathing despite the noise of passing students.

"This spirit? Is she recently dead?"

"Yes, she was killed," Carmen said.

"She told you that. She knows how she died and has accepted the fact she is dead?"

"Si, abuela. Ella sabe que está muerto."

"It's not entirely rare for a new spirit to know and accept their death," Maria said. "But she *is* a new spirit and for her to know there were other forms of los muertos vivientes around would be, ¿Cómo se dice? Unusual."

Carmen tucked her head down and brought the phone closer to her mouth.

"What other forms, Abuela?" Carmen said.

"¿Qué?"

"You said other forms. What other forms of the undead are there?"

"Ghouls, zombi, vampire, mummy–"

"¡Esperate! Ghouls? Hay abuela, por favor. None of those exist."

"No? Jou're over there talking to a ghost."

"That's different."

"Why? Because she told jou she's a ghost?"

"Abuela, I know she's a ghost because of what you told me and from what I have seen."

"Why is it hard for jou to believe me about these other things? ¿Por qué?" Maria said.

Carmen looked to her right and saw a man standing there. He adjusted his hat as he looked at her, nodded politely, and walked away in the opposite direction.

"I'm sorry, Abuela. This is all new to me and I–" In her mind, she could see the monsters Maria mentioned. She couldn't grasp the idea any of them, in the forms she had known from movies and books, walking around. Though Savannah didn't fit her idea of any ghost she had ever had in her mind.

"No need to apologize, Carmen. But don't dismiss what I have told jou."

"Maybe I should come home," Carmen said. "Maybe I'll be safe there."

"What the spirit's name?"

"Savannah."

"Savannah has come to jou for a reason. It's jour obligation as a medium to help her," Maria said.

"I have to go. Love you." Carmen ended the call without waiting for a response.

She sat and took in the entire conversation.

After a moment, she called Dayton.

———

Kevin walked to Chambers Hall, processing what he had just heard. Now that the medium had connected with a spirit, he would have to let things play out. The fact she's getting help from her grandmother, who is, no doubt, a sage in these matters, meant she's invested in understanding her abilities.

The real issue had to do with the spirit. She had some knowledge of the fact Todd dealt with the dark arts. The only way she would know that was she would have had to have had dealings with him while she was alive. He groaned in frustration.

He spotted Zeborah walking toward him, searching through his pockets before taking out his room key. Kevin blew a low whistle, getting his attention. Zeborah looked up at him, then motioned with a tilt of his head for Kevin to go to the back. He made a left onto the driveway. Kevin followed.

They didn't speak until they were in Todd's room.

"Where's Todd?" Kevin said as he approached one of the crates.

"He's circlin' tha campus. He dropped me off at tha gate. He should be here in a minute."

"I found your medium."

"And?"

"And nothing."

"You didn't do anythang to her?"

Kevin ran his hand over the top of the crate, then removed the lid. He peered down at the dirt before reaching in and removing one of the leaches. Holding it so the mouth wouldn't bite him, he caressed it with his thumb.

"From what I can tell, she's just coming into her powers. Not sure if she will be much of a threat yet. But we all need to stay clear of her. She's extremely sensitive to our presence in her current state and. . ."

The door opened and Todd walked in. His eyes fell on Kevin.

"What the hell are you doing here?"

Zeborah stepped forward. "Kevin just wanted ta see how tha setup looks."

"The truth is, Zeborah had a run-in with a medium," Kevin said. "I came to investigate."

Todd stepped into the room and slammed the door. He looked from Kevin to Zeborah. "Where the hell did a medium come from around here?"

"I don't know. I guess she's always been here," Zeborah replied.

"Always been here? Aren't you sensitive to mediums?" He turned to Kevin. "How is it he didn't pick up on her before now?"

"I don't know, but we know what she looks like, so it shouldn't be too hard to avoid her."

Kevin watched Todd's eyes roll over red as he clenched his fists. His breathing increased as he crossed the room. His face morphed into a goat for several seconds, then turned normal. Kevin stepped between them and prepared to stop him. Todd paused, cracked his knuckles as he steadied his breathing, and stared at the floor.

"I find it odd," Todd lifted his head and glared at them, "that a medium would show up out of the blue. You scouted out the campus before we made our move here, right? How come you didn't sense the presence of a medium then?"

"Don't blame him. There's no way to pick up on a medium unless they're close by," Kevin said. "She may have been off campus at that time."

"I want you to kill her."

"Oh no, no. I'm not killing a medium."

"I'm not asking."

"She's a student. I kill her, and the school will call in the authorities to find out what happened."

"You've done it before with no problems."

"She was old, and times were different."

"Remind me what you did to her?" Todd moved close to Zeborah.

"I got inside her head and drove her mad but Todd—"

"I don't think it would draw much attention if you did the same. Think about it. She's a student under a great deal of stress with classes. She may even have personal issues going on. You get where I'm coming from?" He took the leech from Kevin's hand, then consumed it.

Kevin looked into Todd's eyes and could see the hate and contempt in them. Todd smirked and Kevin shuddered as he realized Todd was serious about him killing the medium. He stepped closer to him, raised a finger, and bared his fangs.

"Get this through your demonic head. I only kill if I need to." He pressed his finger into Todd's chest. "You don't dictate where or why I need to kill, understand?"

"Then I expect you to manage the situation accordingly. I don't need this now. Mediums are beneath me anyway, more of a fly in the ointment than anything else."

Kevin started for the door. He paused as he touched the doorknob, allowing for his canines to return to normal. He flung the door open and left the room.

———

Todd leaned against the wall, staring at Zeborah as his face morphed from human form to demonic and back. He let out an inhuman chuckle before speaking.

"A medium. Well, this changes some things." He straightened his face. "I'm going to move forward with finding my host here on campus."

"What?"

"I'm not wasting my time running around the town looking for a girl. In fact, I already have one in mind and as soon as I find her, I'm going to begin working toward the final steps of my ascension."

"Todd, you heard what Kevin said."

"And you heard what I told him? I'm extending that same sentiment to you. Especially since this is your fault."

"My fault? I walked this here campus and never picked up on anythang," said Zeborah.

"Did you actually *search* for anything unusual around here?" He approached Zeborah. "First, the Rucker Brothers mysteriously figure out what I am. Then you come here to find me a place to lie low and finish my work only now, there just *happens* to be a medium here. Doesn't it seem odd to you?"

"What you tryin' to say?"

"You saw what I did to Rakim." He drew his free hand and slashed him across the face, leaving four marks. "That was me being merciful. You betray me now and I will do far worse to you."

Todd shoved him. Zeborah turned away, shut his eyes tight, and started to strain. Gradually, the wounds closed until there was no trace of them.

"You gettin' paranoid."

"You forced my hand, dear cousin," Todd said. "You know, it's been a little too active around here. I think I need to get acclimated to these surroundings on my own and weed out any other issues you may have missed. I think it would be best if you stay with Kevin for a while."

"What about tha experiment? You need me here." Zeborah pointed at Todd's face. "You don't seem ta have control over this stage. You can't even keep your face straight."

Todd removed the Mustang keys from his pocket and tossed them to Zeborah.

He crossed the room to a dark corner to sit in a chair. As his body became enveloped by the shadows, his eyes glowed auburn.

"I have more control than you think," Todd growled. "Now, leave me."

Zeborah left. He thought about saying something, but changed his mind.

Todd sat motionless until he heard the growl from the Mustang. Moments later, the motor faded into the distance. He rose from his chair, moved to the bed, and sat on the edge. He stared at the crate. He closed his eyes, relaxed, and listened to the leeches moving around inside. With his hearing becoming more acute, he had become aware of sounds no one, including his cousins, could hear. He only needed to stick to his regimen a little while longer until his body would be ready for the final stage.

In this relaxed state, he allowed his face to contort. His lower jaw elongated to a v shape as the skin of his cheeks rippled back to his ears. In his mind, he saw the face of a goat demon and concentrated on replicating the image. But his mind began to drift, and he couldn't hold the form for too long.

His thoughts about Kim. He liked her. Their connection on the train appeared natural. He just needed to make sure she was the right one to be a host. He needed to manipulate her into committing to the life Todd had planned for himself. He had to fracture her will. A host with a will too strong could be combative.

He lay down on the bed and allowed himself to rest. The morphing tired him.

CHAPTER TWENTY-FOUR

The tower clock chimed at fifteen to, Eric shifted to the other side of the fountain so Kim would see him better. He'd arrived a half hour before he needed to be. She would be surprised to see him there early.

The moment he moved, she appeared at the end of the walkway. She did a double take. Eric smiled and waved to her.

"You're early." Kim covered her mouth to hide her surprise.

"I'm on time." He embraced Kim and kissed her on the cheek. "Look what I found."

He removed a piece of paper he'd pocketed and handed it to her. He waited for her reaction. She put her hand up to her mouth to cover her surprising response.

"This is the math test I wrote my number on the day we first met," she said. "You kept this?"

"Yes."

She threw her arms around him and hugged him tight. Casually, she broke the embrace. Seeing tears on his face, she wiped them away with her thumbs and smiled.

"You know how to confuse me, you know that?" She struck him in the shoulder with her fist. "Damn it, Eric."

"I am going to change."

"You always say that. You do it for a few weeks and then you turn around and do the same thing all over again."

"Well, see, it proves I'm dependable." He laughed, but Kim didn't. His smile dropped. "C'mon Kim, give me a real chance to prove to you I can be there for you." He took her hand. "When you need me to be."

"Eric."

"Tell you what. How about we go out tonight to Sully's?" Eric said.

"Seriously?"

"Yeah. I'll pick you up around six and we'll head out to eat."

"You need to have a reservation for that place."

"I know. If you want to get seated at seven, you'd better be on time," Eric joked.

"You made reservations?"

Eric took the test paper from her, turned it around and showed her the front. "You gave me this because you wanted to be with me. I want to keep it that way."

"Actually, I gave you my number because I felt sorry for you."

"*What?*" Eric seemed taken aback.

Kim cracked a smile as Eric embraced her. She shook her head in defeat and leaned on his shoulder.

"I can't stay mad at you," she whispered. "Don't make me regret my decision this time."

"I promise I'll be on time," he said.

They stayed in their embrace until it drizzled, and they didn't even care.

CHAPTER TWENTY-FIVE

The drizzle turned into a mist, but Carmen and Dayton didn't mind. The tall trees provided shade on a sweltering day and delivered protection from the rain. Carmen welcomed it. She hadn't been right all day, and it helped to soothe her nerves.

They had walked along the river's edge behind Wakeford Hall until they came to a bench under a tree near the bank. Dayton put his arm around her and cradled her. She gave him a half-hearted smile, then winced as she touched the side of her head. She looked around for Savannah.

"Still feeling bad?" he said.

"Hm? Oh, I'm okay. Just a passing headache. I'll be fine," she said.

"How's your abuela doing? You said you spoke to her. She's okay?"

"She's good." Carmen looked around again. "She's fine."

"Hey?"

"Hmm?" Dayton leaned in, kissed her gently on the lips, then kissed her on her nose.

Carmen placed her hand on the side of his face. "Que Lindö," she smiled, and kissed him back.

"What's got you so preoccupied?" He held her hands. "Talk to me. Don't shut me out. I have strong feelings for you, Carmen. I want to be a part of your life, but to do that, I need you to be able to confide in me."

"I'm going to ask you to give me time, okay? What I'm going through, I'm trying to get the hang of."

"Anything I can do to help?"

"Not now, but I will let you know."

"You sure there's nothin' you wanna to tell me? After our conversation last night, I—"

"Yes, I'm sure." Carmen stood. "Let's walk. How's your day going?"

Dayton and Carmen locked fingers and walked back to Wakeford Hall.

"Okay, I guess. Trying to get Eric to get his act together for Kim. Oh, and "Supafly" moved into the building. This guy has a big ego. I tell you I have never seen a guy so full of himself. The only thing bigger than his ego is his roommate," Dayton said.

"Wow, one of those again?"

As Dayton talked, she spotted the Mustang come out of the driveway of Chambers Hall. It made a right, then stopped alongside the curb. The tall white guy got out of the car, walked to the front of it and looked toward the south gate. Carmen winced and touched the side of her head.

"Carmen?" Savannah called out from behind her.

Carmen looked back, saw Savannah approaching, and tried to ignore her. "Hey, why don't we go to the Commons and hang out there?"

"Carmen? Hey, that's him in the car, Zeborah."

"You want to hang in the Commons?" Dayton said, surprised. "You hate hanging in the Commons."

"Well, how about the library? Somewhere, where it's quiet."

"Hey darlin,' you hear meh? That's Zeborah." Savannah stepped up beside her. "Hey."

Carmen glanced at Savannah, shook her head, and mouthed the words, "Not right now."

"But you need ta know what he looks like."

Carmen locked her eyes on Zeborah and stared as he touched the side of his head. She slowed down to a stop. She took in his size and features. He turned in her direction and their eyes met. An empty and cold feeling poured through her, followed by another one, like a thousand tiny spiders crawling up her back. She shuddered.

But Zeborah turned his attention back toward the south gate. On impulse, Carmen put out her right hand and tried to grab Savannah's arm. She withdrew.

"Can't touch meh,"

"That's him? I've seen him before," she whispered.

"Seen who?" Dayton looked where she was staring. "Oh, that guy is Don Juan's runnin' buddy."

"You two crossed paths before?" Savannah stepped into her line of sight. "That's not good. You're gonna have ta avoid him now."

"Avoid him? How can I? This is a campus," Carmen said.

"I'm pretty sure it's a big enough campus you two won't have to cross paths," Dayton said. "Wait, why would you have to avoid him?"

"What?" Carmen turned to Dayton.

"You had a run in with him?" Dayton pointed to Zeborah.

Carmen slapped his hand down and pushed him back. "Don't point at him!"

"What's wrong with you?"

"Just stay out his way. Ima lie low for a bit, until it's safe to come back around ya," Savannah said.

Carmen spun around to her. "Why?"

"Why what?" Dayton stepped around in front of her, but she moved him out of the way to look at Savannah.

"I just gotta feelin' I need to stay clear of you to not put you in danger. Don't fret, I'll be back." Savannah looked in the direction of Zeborah just as Kevin walked up to him. She turned and fled in the opposite direction.

"Am I in danger?" Carmen yelled. "Aye Dios Mio!"

"What the hell is going on?" Dayton said.

Carmen spun around. Her eyes wide with anxiety. She moved into him, striking Dayton in the chest with two fists. "You need to stay away from him."

"Why are you mad at me? What did I do?"

"Dayton, promise me you'll stay away from him." Her eyes welled up with tears. "Stay clear of Zeborah."

"Who is Zeborah? Wait, that's his name? How did you find that out?"

"Never mind, you just need to stay away from him. We both do. In fact, I'm not coming near Chambers Hall again this semester until—"

"Okay, I'm staying clear of him," Dayton said. "I see him coming. I'll cross the street."

Carmen wrapped her arms around him tight, buried her head into his chest and cried. "Hold me. I feel safe in your arms."

Dayton held her. They both looked in Zeborah's direction.

The two men and the Mustang were gone.

CHAPTER TWENTY-SIX

"You're a fraud and I'm coming for you," the voice said before abruptly hanging up.

Patricia 'Sister Cora' Keller couldn't relax after the call. The man's voice haunted her for hours. For ten years, she had been claiming to be a medium while robbing people of both hope and cash. She had her fair share of threats and multiple confrontations. But the way this man called her a fraud, lingering on the 'aud' part of the word, scared her. She considered calling the police, but they weren't huge fans of hers after she lied about talking to the spirit of the victim of a murder and botched the investigation. She would have to face this one alone.

To help calm her nerves, she made a hot toddy and snuggled under a thick blanket in bed. As the alcohol kicked in, she started dozing off, but awoke to a series of loud bangs downstairs in her library. The first one made her sit up and listen. The second and third made her get out of bed and go to her bedroom door. It sounded like books were falling off the shelf. Sister Cora put on her robe, tied it and went into her top dresser drawer, removed a revolver, and made her way to the stairs.

As she descended, the banging became more erratic. She creeped into her office but saw nothing out of place.

She opened the door leading to the library and saw a light on. A shadow floated around by the shelves. She raised the revolver, extended her arm as she took aim and breached the library.

The light went out, the door shut, and darkness engulfed her.

She stood still for a moment. She raised her free hand out in the light switch's direction but paused. Air from someone's nostrils blew into her palm.

Somewhere further into the library, footsteps approached. She fired the revolver in their direction.

The footsteps halted.

"You missed me," a voice whispered.

A sharp pain shot through her outstretched hand. She screamed as she dropped the revolver and was dragged to the floor. Something gnawed on her hand as it growled.

"Stop! For God's sake, stop!"

"Make it stop, medium," the voice said.

"She is no medium," a second voice from behind her said.

"Get this dog off of me!"

The lights came on. Sister Cora saw what had her. A creature, half human and half bat, its fangs buried deep into her hand; her blood oozing down its lower jaw. It seemed to smile at her. Her body began to shudder from a mix of fear and adrenaline. She shrieked so loud and hard it caused her eyes to tear. The outburst didn't faze the intruders.

"A liar's blood is as delicious to him as an innocent. The tainted flavor can be especially nutritious if the person is under duress." Kevin knelt before her, cupped the side of her face, caressing her with his thumb. "You're trembling. You're afraid. Surely, with your *skills,* you have encountered our kind before."

Sister Cora shut her eyes and began to cry.

"Look at me or I kill you." He squeezed her face. She opened her eyes. "My name is Kevin. I'm here because a mutual acquaintance of ours suggested I pay you a visit because, although you are a charlatan—"

"I am no charlatan."

"Rakim."

Rakim bit down harder and Sister Cora screamed.

"Do not interrupt me again. Now, although you are a charlatan, you have managed to acquire quite a collection of rare arcane books." His eyes moved to Rakim. "Rakim, you can let her go." Kevin observed him open his mouth. Blood ran from her wounds. "I'm in need of three things. Once we have them, we will leave you."

Sister Cora put her bloody hand to her stomach, placed her other hand over it and pressed them to her body. She shook from fear.

"If this is about the séance, I am sorry."

"The Tao Shen Book of Demonology. Where is it?"

Sister Cora looked at him. "F-F-Fifth case from the right, third shelf."

"Zeborah, go get it."

Zeborah stepped out from behind her and went to the fifth bookcase. After a moment, he returned with a weathered, hard covered book whose paper edges had turned yellow.

"The original copy of *Le Livre des Mediums;* the one only a true medium can read. Where is it?"

"Third case, fourth shelf."

"Zeborah, go get it." Kevin continued to gaze at her. "So, we're clear. I can sense the presence of a medium and they most certainly can detect me. They're respectable beings with great power, and it makes me sick running into someone masquerading as one."

"Got it," Zeborah said.

"Take Rakim back to the car. I'll finish up here."

"We're gonna have to make a stop."

"I know. I'll be out in a minute."

Kevin rose as Zeborah took Rakim by the arm and led him out of the library.

"I *am* a medium," Sister Cora said.

"I don't know what you are, but what I do know is you are now out of business." Kevin leaned over. "I should drink you dry. Or drink enough for you to suffer a heart attack or fall into a coma. But I think I will spare you."

Kevin dragged her to the center of the library by her collar, then ransacked the shelves, creating a pile of books before crossing the room to a reading desk with an oil lamp on it. Opening the desk drawer, he found a box of blue tip matches. After retrieving them and the lamp, Kevin poured the oil in a zigzag across the floor and emptied the rest on the pile. Then took a match, stuck it with his thumbnail and dropped it onto the trail. The flame snaked toward the pile and within seconds, the books lit up into a bonfire.

"We have a few moments before your house burns down to the ground." He smiled. "No one will know what happened here if you cooperate."

"Why are you doing this to me?" The tears that streamed down her face caught the reflection of the fire and shimmered orange. "Listen, I won't practice as a medium again. I promise," she said.

"Typical of one who is afraid for their life." The fire began to catch the shelves behind him, but Kevin didn't seem to care. "I don't believe if I leave you to your own devices, you will give up your ways. There is one reassurance I can make to ensure you won't go back to your old life."

Kevin bore his fangs. Sister Cora found the strength to move and tried to crawl away from him.

"No!" she screamed.

Kevin watched her try to scamper away. Like a cat playing with a mouse before it kills it, he allowed her to crawl out of the library and to the stairs. She attempted to climb them as Kevin approached her.

"The longer you resist this, the worse the outcome is going to be," Kevin chided.

Sister Cora ignored him and hoisted herself up the stairs. Kevin grasped her ankle, snatched her back down to the floor and straddled her again. He caressed her hair, leaned in, his eyes shimmering.

"Now look at me."

Sister Cora shut her eyes. "No! No! I won't!" She shook her head.

Kevin seized her by her chin, held her head straight, and whispered, "Open your eyes."

Sister Cora did as commanded. Kevin cracked a smile and leaned in closer.

"A man came in here wearing a mask, angry you helped his wife. He burned your house down. You barely made it out alive and you plan to leave and start your life over elsewhere. Understood?"

His words traveled through her head. Finding their way into her mind, they set in and became one with her thoughts. After a moment, she couldn't think of anything but what Kevin had told her.

She nodded.

"Wonderful." Kevin stood, picked her up and carried her from the house, laid her on the walkway before strolling to the awaiting Mustang parked across the street.

"What're those books for?" Zeborah asked.

"They're a gift for someone. I've got a plan brewing." Kevin pointed to his head.

"How did you know about her?"

"I cashed in my help card with LaChard. I got in touch with him about the medium on campus and he told me about this fraud. He asked I get rid of her and in return I could take her books for payment."

"How did LaChard know this fake had 'em?"

"Doesn't matter. I'm only glad he knew."

"You jus' gonna leave her there?" Zeborah asked.

"Let's get to LaChard and let him know the deed's been done," Kevin said.

Kevin watched as the side of the house went up in flames. It wouldn't be long before the entire house would be consumed.

CHAPTER TWENTY-SEVEN

The first week of classes had been quiet. Todd had been able to move about without any worry. The medium had not shown herself or been near the science building where he spent much of his time. Because of this, he welcomed Zeborah back but confined him to the lab to keep watch over the leeches. He provided him with his own set of keys so he could come and go as he pleased.

Todd would arrive in the morning after the building opened and he and Zeborah would spend the day cultivating the soil, assessing the effectiveness of electricity on the leeches to help them grow faster. He let them feed off him so his blood would mix with the bodies they fed from deep in the soil.

Todd nurtured this batch specifically for the final stage of his ascension. Genetically altered, these would be the ones to be used on the host to incapacitate her. The bigger they became, two glands, one containing Todd's blood and the other acting as a filter, formed their mouths. After biting the host, the gland with Todd's blood would burst and their teeth would function as an injection needle, pushing his blood and their saliva into the host's veins. The host's blood, while being ingested, would filter through the other gland to prevent it from mixing with his. The more of his tainted blood in her veins, the easier it will be for him to control her body once inside her as the demon. She would be filled with evil fluid and spirit. Her soul would be repressed until he destroyed it.

"You want, I can put soma those on ya back," Zeborah said as he watched Todd place the last of three large leeches strategically on his upper right arm. "Run a lesser risk of them being seen."

"This is where the good veins are. They would only annoy me being on my back." Todd pulled down his sleeve. "I'm going to go get some air."

"You don't mind, I wanna check in with Kevin. Rakim has been actin' edgy."

"Fine with me. It's 10 am. Be back here within the hour."

They left the lab. Zeborah took the back stairway while Todd left through the main entrance. He walked through a group of students headed to the lecture halls on the third floor. Once clear of them, he hurried to the second floor. He spotted Kim rushing through a set of double doors. His heart jumped with excitement.

He changed his original course and went after her. The hallway wasn't crowded, but he still had to go against oncoming students. He skimmed against the wall and attempted to close the gap between them.

Ahead, Kim made a quick left and disappeared into a classroom. Todd stopped and stared at the door. He debated whether to look in or come back in an hour.

Several students emerged from the room with loose papers in their hands and walked in the opposite direction. A second group came out. Kim took up the rear alongside Michelle.

"This is the second time since classes started Professor Webber has been absent. How are we supposed to learn anything if she's out all the time?" Kim said.

"Girl, this might be the easiest class we'll have going into graduation. Just roll with it," Michelle said.

"This better not mess up my GPA."

"Anyway, Ima head over to the Commons. You wanna come?"

"I have to run to the bookstore real quick. I haven't picked up the novel for English Lit yet and—"

"Hey Kim," Todd said, getting her attention.

Her jaw dropped from surprise. "Well, hey, I was wondering if I would bump into you."

"It's great to see you again." He gave her a big smile. "How have you been?"

"I'm fine. Can't complain. I guess you've been busy getting acclimated, huh?"

"Trying to get acclimated. This is a big campus. A newbie can get lost around here. Been moving stuff here from storage. You know how it is."

"Oh, Michelle, this is Todd. We rode in on the train together."

"We've met," Michelle said. "I'll see you over at the Commons."

"Okay, see you there." Kim waved goodbye as Michelle sized up Todd before walking away.

"Let me see. The last time I saw you, you were waiting for your ride. I guess he finally showed up," Todd said.

"He did, and I let him have it, of course." Kim chuckled.

You deserve better, he thought.

"Are you headed to class?"

"No, I'm on my way out for a quick walk. I've been up in my lab getting an early start. I have a lot of work to catch up on."

"You have your own lab here in the building? Must be nice to have personal lab space to work on an experiment." Her tone indicated a mixture of envy and admiration. "I should be so lucky."

"Well, if you meet the people who pull the proper strings, anything is possible."

"Yeah, it's all about who you know. Well, don't let me keep you. Nice seeing you again."

"Headed to class?"

"No, my class is canceled. I'm going to head over to the Commons for a while."

This is my chance to get her alone. "Hey, since you're free, how would you like to go see the children?"

"What children?"

"The leeches, I mean. I'm used to calling them my children."

"You already have them here?"

"I have them in the lab, yes. I mean, unless you want to meet up with—"

"No, no, I'd like to see them."

Perfect! "Okay, let's go."

They took the main staircase to the fourth floor, then walked down the hall to the second to last lab on the right. Black construction paper covered the vertical window embedded in the door. A plastic sign with the word LAB on the top and below it the word VACANT hung from the door. Todd changed the word to OCCUPIED. He removed a key from his pocket, unlocked the door, and stepped to the side.

The shades on all the windows were down. A large crate sat in the middle of the room. Fluorescent ceiling light gave the room an eerie feel. On a counter behind the crate sat beakers, burners, and multiple trays with soil samples on them. Wires from a small transformer were embedded in the soil.

Kim inched into the room, her eyes fixed on the crate. She walked to the side of it and peered inside. She didn't see anything but dirt and wires.

"Where are they?"

"They're down in the dirt." Todd locked the door and came to stand on the opposite side of the crate. "The electricity is what brings them to the surface."

"There aren't any on top here?"

"They usually retreat after a few minutes of being shocked." Todd caressed the surface. "Nope, they've gone back down." He stared at her, smiling at the curiosity on her face. It excited him to see she wanted to know more. "Maybe I can try to coax them." He stepped to the transformer and switched it on.

A snap followed by the crackle of electricity and the hum of the unit powering up sounded in the lab space. Kim stared at the dirt, a glimmer of anticipation in her eyes. Todd watched her with great interest.

The soil shook. Over the next several minutes, a black two-inch-long leech emerged, breaking the surface while squirming. Todd picked it up and turned the power off. He came over to Kim and held his hand open. He presented the fat leech. The tail hung over the side of Todd's hand. Its body glistened.

"Oh my God. Isn't that thing going to bite you?" Kim looked astonished.

"I fed them yesterday so they're not hungry right now." Todd held it up by the tail before her. Kim backed up. "Want to hold it?"

Kim shook her head. "Why is it wet after it's been in the dirt?"

"Wet soil allows the current to flow better. Plus, the electricity causes them to secrete an enzyme that makes them look wet." He turned it over for her to see the suction mouth. "Here's how they bite you."

"Revolting."

"Come." Todd walked over to the counter and placed it on a pan with soil. The leech wiggled. "This kind of leech, its body absorbs nutrients from the soil. I treat it with a special solution they thrive on and provide a tasty morsel for it to feed on. Helps their blood content increases."

"Tasty morsel?"

"I feed them mice or rats. Usually, I have two or three leeches attached to one of the animals. They can feed at the same time.

Now, I have discovered because of the overwhelming speed of their own blood production, *their* blood contains certain properties that could be used to combat anemia."

"How do you administer their blood to a host?"

"By extracting the hemoglobin out of the leech and injecting it directly into the bloodstream."

"You're telling me that thing can cure anemia?"

"Not cure but fight against it. My research is still a bit young, but I'm getting close. I don't want to say too much on the matter." Todd said, "Don't tell anyone what I'm doing. I don't want people snooping. At my last university, a couple of guys tried to sabotage my work."

"My lips are sealed." She mimed zipping her lips. "This is amazing, Todd. I have never heard of anyone trying this."

The lock to the door clicked, getting their attention. Kim turned to face the door as Zeborah walked in and their eyes locked. He froze with a stunned look on his face.

"It's okay, Zeborah, I invited her to come to see them," Todd said.

"Why?"

"Why do you think? She wanted to see the leeches." Todd turned back to Kim. "You'll have to excuse my cousin. He gets nervous if people get too close to them. They're delicate."

"I'm sure."

"Here." Todd took her hand and turned it palm up. "Don't be afraid." He picked up the leech and placed it gently in her hand."

"Ew!" Kim started to draw back, but as it started to move in her hand, she became intrigued. With her free hand, she placed her pointer finger on top of it and gently pet it from head to tail. "It feels. . . cold."

"Yeah, this guy, he's not homeothermic. Most of them aren't." He watched her with interest as she raised her hand closer to her face to get a better look at it. Kim appeared more fascinated than scared.

"How does it see? I don't see where the eyes might be." She turned it over before he could answer and stared at the rows of needle-like teeth in its mouth. Her eyes widened as her mouth contorted from a mix of disgust and amazement. "Look at all the teeth."

"Ah!" Zeborah grabbed the side of his head, screaming. He leaned up against the wall with a painful and pinched face.

"You okay?" Kim turned her attention away from the leech.

"Got a killer headache, is all."

"Is this attributed to that issue you told me about a week ago?" Todd asked him.

Zeborah shrugged. "I think so."

Todd turned to Kim. "He gets migraines. My apologies about this."

"No, no, it's no problem. I know that feeling. Do what you need to do." She put the leech in the crate. "I need to go, anyway. I'll see you around."

"Wait." Todd snatched a pad and pen off the table, wrote his phone number down and handed it to her. "Let me know if you want to come back. Call me and next time I can show you how the blood works on samples I have."

Kim glanced at the number and started to make a comment but decided against it. She took it and put it in her bag.

"I'll let you know," she said. "Impressive work." Kim turned to Zeborah. "Feel better."

Kim left.

"What tha hella you doin'?" Zeborah seethed. "I told you not ta mess with these students."

"Did you see how she responded to the leech? No one has ever responded to them like that." Todd crossed the room. "This is good. I won't have much coaxing to do."

"I recognize her. I know what you're thinkin.' You need ta forget it."

"What I need to do is move as fast as possible. We already lost a week fumbling around with. . . wait, what happened to your headache?" Todd sneered.

Zeborah touched the side of his temple and slid his hand down his face to his side. He took a step back and folded his arms.

"I had ta get her away from you. No usin' students. We agreed. You shouldn't be letting anyone in here, either." Zeborah crossed the room to the crate, repositioned the wires in the soil, then patted them in before adjusting the transformer. He took the leech Kim had handled and buried it.

"Zeborah, why did you come back here? You told me you were going to see Kevin."

"I forgot somethin'."

"No, you didn't. You suspected I was up to something." He strode across the room. "You were trying to catch me?"

"I'm bein' cautious."

Todd stepped around the crate, seized Zeborah by the throat, and stared into his eyes. "You tell Kevin if he wants to keep tabs on me to come and do it himself. Go tell him, right now." Todd released his grip, placed his hand on the side of Zeborah's face, and caressed his cheek with his thumb. "What happened to you? You used to not care so much about mortals. Why do you now?"

Zeborah gripped Todd's wrist and pushed his hand away. He sneered at Todd before turning and storming out of the room.

Todd finished straightening up. He thought about Kim and how it wouldn't take much work to get her on his side. But he remembered one detail he had to get out of the way: the boyfriend.

CHAPTER TWENTY-EIGHT

Kevin heard Zeborah approaching before he saw him. He rose from the floor of the main room of the cabin, yawning as he waited for him to come into view. He could tell from his body language he was upset.

"What happened?"

Zeborah didn't answer him until he came inside. "He's eyeballin' the coed's again."

"I have to move my timetable up. You haven't sensed the medium around, have you?"

"No. She might be avoidin' me."

"Okay, I'm going to have to find her. You stay here until I get back. Todd knows where you are?"

"He does. He sent me to see you. He thinks you have me keepin' tabs on him. Told me to tell you to come do it yourself."

Kevin contemplated his next move. He knew where Carmen lived, but if he got too close and she picked up on him, she may not come out. If she weren't in the dorm, him sitting around waiting for her could draw unwanted attention. He looked at his watch. Classes were already underway. She could be anywhere on the campus.

"Tell you what. Go back to him in a half-hour. Tell him you spoke to me, and I'll be over to see him later. There are a couple of places I can check to see where the medium might be."

"What you plan to do to her if you do find her?"

"I'm not sure yet. It's been a while since either of us have crossed paths with her and there's no telling what she knows how to do now." Kevin went to the back of the cabin. "Thirty minutes."

"What about Rakim?"

"He's asleep. You don't have to worry about him."

Kevin put on his coat and hat, went out a backdoor, and walked through the thick wood around to the east end of the campus. A seven-foot chain-link fence separated the campus from the woods and ran the length of the university. Kevin followed it until he saw the administration building and just beyond, the back of the university library. There were no people nearby. He launched himself over the fence, landed a foot away from it, then approached the library.

CHAPTER TWENTY-NINE

Carmen ended her mid-morning jog behind Wakeford Hall. She took a seat on a bench and stared at the lake for a few minutes before calling Maria. She thought of Savannah. She had not seen or heard from her since the day they saw Zeborah. And come to think of it, she hadn't seen him either, but it didn't mean he wasn't out there.

"It's a good chance he is avoiding jou to, Carmensita. Take this to be a good sign," Maria told her. "If Savannah feels it necessary to come to jou, she will. Don't stress jourself trying to contact her."

"I don't like this, Abuela. Everything just started and stopped. I don't know if I'll ever be in control of this power, and that scares me." She caught herself getting choked up. "Why was I cursed with this?"

"Jour not cursed. What jou have is a blessing. To be able to help the dead find the peace they did not find on this side. Jou don't fear it, jou embrace it. Only spirits looking to speak to jou will reach out and they don't come if jour stressed. Jou must breathe." Maria grew silent for a moment, then said, "Let me teach jou something I learned to help my body and mind. It's a breathing exercise to help keep jou calm. Do this twice a day, in the morning and evening. It can help with jour stress."

Maria practiced the series of deep breaths with Carmen, instructing her to inhale, hold her breath, then purse her lips to exhale. She performed this for one minute. She closed her eyes and breathed steadily for another minute.

A sense of calm washed over her. Her mind cleared and almost immediately, a thought came into her head.

"Abuela, are there any books that can tell me what I need to know about my abilities?"

"Si, there are books, but they can't *teach* jou how to use jour abilities, only explain. I know jour anxious to understand but jou need to be patient and let me help you."

"You're not here to help me directly. At least if I have something to help guide me, I can begin to get some direction. Ask the right questions. It could make it easier for you to help me."

Maria grew quiet for a moment. "There is one jou could try to look for. Ask for Mediana de historia by Isabella Garcia. It has been reprinted a few times since the 50s, but it is the most accurate book about mediums jou will find. But it is only a blueprint."

"I'll check the library here and see if they have a copy. We have a bookstore in town. I can check there too." Carmen sighed. "Thank you."

"Jou don't have to thank me." Maria paused and said, "I'm proud jou are taking this seriously."

"There's no other way to take it. I'll call you later." Carmen ended the call.

———

After a quick shower, Carmen packed an empty composition notebook into her book bag with a couple of pens and started for the door. The phone rang, but she ignored it. Halfway down the stairs, her cell phone buzzed. She looked at the number, saw it was Dayton, but didn't answer.

She trekked the long way to Günther Gabel Library. A six-story brick building home to an extensive array of books, archives, and resource materials. It also housed the mass communications center. It was a study hall, a meeting place, hang out and a place to grab a quick nap. Second only to the Commons, many students spent a great deal of their free time in between and after classes there.

Carmen headed for the information desk to inquire about the book. Lying that she needed it for an assignment, the clerk redirected her to the second-floor kiosk. She saw Curtis behind a computer inputting data and froze.

"Damn it," she whispered. "Oh, well." She approached him. "Hey, Curtis."

He looked up from the computer and beamed. "Hola, Carmen. How are you?"

"I'm fine. I didn't know you were working here."

"Yeah, this is my station. You're looking well."

"Thank you."

"I'm surprised to see you here without Dayton."

"I do have schoolwork to do, you know. Some things I have to do without him." There was a hint of sarcasm in her voice. The smile fell slightly from his face, and she knew Curtis had picked up on it. "I do need some assistance."

"Sure, sorry. What do you need?"

"I'm looking for a book called Mediana de historia written by Isabella Garcia."

Curtis typed on the computer, then pressed enter. He stared at the screen as it flickered and green letters scrolled across.

"It's not coming up. Let me search by the author." He typed again and waited. "Hmm nope. Nothing. What's the book about? Maybe we have another on the subject you're looking for."

"Mediums. You know, like people who can talk to the dead? I need it for English Lit."

Curtis returned to the computer and input the new information. "Okay, I have several books here. Let me print this out for you. Go down to the 200 section. Anything else?"

"Yeah, would you happen to know where I can get some books on the undead?"

Curtis looked up at her. "The undead? You mean like zombies and shit?"

"Really?"

"Excuse my language. But that kind of stuff?"

"Not just zombies. Anything pertaining to the undead. And I need it in non-fiction."

Curtis typed in more information and printed what came up on the screen. He tore them from the dot-matrix printer and handed them to her.

"There you go. If you need anything else, anything at all, don't hesitate to ask. I'm here for you." Curtis gave her a warm smile.

Carmen glared at him before looking around to make sure no one could hear what she was about to say.

"Look, I know things didn't work out between us and we agreed to stay friends, but it makes me uncomfortable doing that."

"Doing what? All I did was smile."

"I can see it in your eyes."

"I don't know what you mean."

"You look at me like you're still in love with me. You make comments about me not being with Dayton and . . ."

"Whoa." Curtis put his hands up. "Hey, I didn't mean anything by it. I'm sorry if it came off like—"

"I don't want there to be any problems, you know."

Curtis nodded. "I understand." His face turned serious, and he said, "Excuse me, I have some books I need to file. If you require any other services, you can ask for Susan or me. Hope you find what you need for your class."

"C'mon Curtis, don't do that."

"I don't want to cause any problems." He walked away from the kiosk, took hold of a cart of books, and pushed them down the hall.

Carmen looked at the papers, read the titles, and then headed to the nonfiction section. Halfway there, she sensed a twinge in her head, but it subsided.

———

The fourth floor was the best place to go if one wanted to work in silence. Unlike the other floors, with their crowded study areas where talking was tolerated, this floor was like a tomb.

It housed the largest collection of reference books, from law to theology. A virtual maze of long rows, six-foot-high shelves, and fluorescent lighting. The redolent smell of old books filled the air, and, for many students, it soothed and relaxed them. During midterms and finals weeks, those who were cramming for exams often occupied the rows. The prime areas were the last rows that had no outlet at their end. Because they had a wider spacing, a student could tuck themselves into a corner, spread out their materials, and work on the floor in peace.

Carmen walked to the end of the last row at the south end where it was private. Only the hum from the florescent light over-head broke the silence. Setting the books down, then sitting cross-legged on the floor, she removed a pen and notebook from her bag and began crafting a list. Starting with the corporeal undead Maria told her could affect her medium powers. Mummy, zombie, ghoul, and vampire. Lastly, removing the book on the top of the stack marked *Undead Creatures of Legend,* Carmen began her research.

She needed to know what Zeborah was. Based on the descriptions in the books, he wasn't a mummy or a zombie. Both of those creatures were mindless and lacked humanity in any form other than their appearance. He might have been a modern-day ghoul; a killer who ate the flesh of his victims. The remaining information she read unsettled her and, in the silence, she let her imagination grow. In her mind, he was devouring someone's arm to satisfy his hunger and ingesting their flesh to steal their soul.

"There you are," Savannah called from the entrance of the row.

Carmen screamed, tossing the book out of her lap. "El Amor de Dios!" She put her hand over her heart while trying to ease her breathing. "Savannah?" She sighed with relief. "There you are." Her tone went from relief to anger in seconds. "Damn it, Savannah. How many times do I have to tell you not to sneak up on me?"

"Sorry, darlin'." Savannah glided as she walked down the row, smiling. "I been lookin' all around the campus for you. I finally picked up your trail here. This is a beautiful library."

"Yeah, it's great. Hey, thanks for abandoning me. You disappear on me and don't bother to send a message or anything. I'm beginning to have some serious trust issues."

Savannah sat down across from her. "I'm here now." She looked at the books. "Why are you readin' books on mediums? Isn't your grandmamma one? I thought she was helping you."

"She's helped me as best as she could. She suggested a book to help, but they didn't have it here, so I got what I could to get the information I need." Carmen exhaled to calm herself. "I can't do this if I don't understand my abilities. Even if I have to spend time doing old fashion research."

"You have me too, you know."

"You? You happened to find me at a time I'm coming into my abilities. I've got a thousand things happening at once and I—"

"Whateva I can do to help, I will. Some help is better than none." Savannah gave her a reassuring smile.

"You're right. For now, we work piecemeal. Okay. But you can't run out on me again."

"I won't. I'm back to stay. It's safe for me to be with you now."

Carmen shut the book. "I'll focus on my abilities. You help me with this business with Zeborah. Now, my abuela said based on my symptoms, he's one of the undead. You had a relationship with him. Tell me what I need to know about him."

Savannah's demeanor changed. The smile fell from her face like a flower wilting. From instinct, Carmen extended her hand to comfort her, but her fingers passed through her. Savannah's form turned transparent until Carmen touched the floor.

"I'm dead, remember?" She drew her hand back. "I don't know how to explain this. What he is. . . If I told you, then you gotta destroy him."

"Savannah, listen to me. I know you had something special with Zeborah, but he'll hurt me physically. He may even pose a threat to others on this campus. Midar, I'm not going to go to the police or anything. If this is a supernatural issue, I can try to address it. If we can't trust one another... Do you trust me?"

"I trust you, darlin'," Savannah fixed her face to a grin. She looked at the spines of the stack of books and pointed to the third one.

Carmen removed the top two and glanced at the cover titled *The Undead*. Savannah motioned for her to put it on the floor between them. She put her fingers under the lip of the cover. Her finger passed through it. Savannah sighed in frustration. She tried again; her eyes focused on the cover.

"You need help?"

"I got it." Savannah opened it to the table of contents. She scanned the list before she turned the page to the next listing. "I didn't find out what he was until after I died. Weren't no way of me knowin' 'cause, well, how can you tell he's a monster? He looks so human." She ran her finger down the page. "I can sense when he is near. His kind can also see me. That's why I abandoned you. I didn't want them to see us together, otherwise they would know what you are."

"*Them?*"

"He's not alone. One of them is extremely smart and I know if he saw me there will be problems, so Ima have to be real careful." Savannah stopped scrolling. "Here."

Carmen saw Savannah's finger, nearly translucent against the paper, hovering between two words, vampire and wraith.

"What's a wraith?" Carmen asked.

"Not that one." Savannah looked back down the row with a frozen stare. "No. . . no."

"What?"

"I can't stay. I have to go." Savannah started to dematerialize. "I'm so sorry. I told you everything I can for now."

Carmen hopped to her feet. "You can't leave now. I thought we're supposed to trust each other!" Carmen looked down at the book. "What were you trying to show me?" She knelt and picked it up.

As Savannah disappeared, a long shadow appeared on the floor at the mouth of the row. It began to shrink, indicating someone approached. Carmen began to feel cold. The shadow stopped. Carmen fixed her gaze on it as it stayed still. Four brown fingers appeared, gripping the edge of the shelf. Gradually, an impeccably dressed in a grey suit and matching fedora, stepped into view and blocked her exit. He said nothing as he looked her up and down. Thoughtfully, he removed his hat, grinned, and nodded.

"Forgive me if I startled you. I'm looking for the periodicals. Do you know where I can find them?"

"The periodicals are on the first floor toward the back of the building." Carmen gripped the book, preparing to use it as a weapon if she had to.

She watched his eyes as they fell on her hands. He looked as though he were studying the way she held the book, then he looked back at her face.

"It's quiet up here. You can practically hear a pin drop. That's how I knew you were here. I heard you talking to someone a moment ago."

"I was talking to myself. Studying out loud." She held up the book. "Just... you know."

"Mind if I ask what you're studying?"

Carmen looked down at the pile of books. "Nothing too—" She lifted her head. He now stood closer to her. His eyes were wide. He stroked the rim of his hat.

"How?"

Like the arm of a marionette being manipulated by a puppeteer, His hand waved before her face. He joined the tips of his pointer and thumb, then closed his eyes.

Do you hear me? His voice resonated in her head.

Carmen dropped the book, shut her eyes tight, and massaged the sides of her head. She started to back up to the wall. Her head pounded in excruciating pain from Kevin's vocal intrusion.

"I hear you."

You are breathtakingly beautiful. He began his charm. *Spanish?*

"Puerto Rican," Carmen said.

No hay rosa es tan bella como la flor antes que yo.

Carmen blushed. She tried to turn from him but couldn't. "What are you?"

"Call me, Kevin." An arm wrapped around her waist, followed by a hand cupping the back of her head. She opened her eyes to him, holding her like a lover. The pupils of his eyes shimmered silver. "Aye Dios Mio." Kevin smiled and parted his lips as though he were about to kiss her.

Her voice trembled. "I have a boyfriend."

Kevin nodded as his arm slipped away and he placed his hand alongside her face. He moved so fast it took a moment to process what he had done.

"Zeborah told me about you, medium. You don't know how long I have waited for someone like you." Kevin rubbed his hands down her arms, took her hands in his, and leaned toward her face, gradually opening his mouth and exposing his fangs to her. Carmen tensed up. Taking a step closer, he tilted into her neck, gently kissed her jugular, then looked back into her eyes. "Let me assure you, I am not here to kill you."

His eyes reminded her of Dayton's, honest and sincere. She sensed she could trust him. She wanted to stay connected to him. "Is Zeborah like you? How come I'm not having migraines from you?"

"I have my ways of controlling that effect." He glanced down at the books. "And why are you reading books about mediums?"

"I'm still learning about my abilities with my contact."

"How new are you to your abilities?"

"A week or so."

"Interesting. And who is your contact?"

Carmen fought the urge to answer him. A warm energy moved through her. Some of it moved across the top of her skin, like electricity dancing over water. Her whole body tingled inside and out.

"What're you doing to me?"

"Will the person who has been in contact with this medium show yourself," he said above a whisper.

"Let go of me!"

"Don't resist me. You'll only harm yourself." He tightened his grip on her hands. "Show yourself. I demand you do."

Carmen tugged her hands from his, and as they separated, Savannah appeared between them. She looked from Carmen to Kevin, who stared back at her, shocked. Then she disappeared through the shelves.

"Savannah, come back," Carmen said.

"Now this complicates things." Kevin looked at her. "You're not ready. I can't use you yet."

"What are you talking about? Use me?"

"I was never here. You will not remember this meeting." Kevin passed his hand before her eyes, then caressed her face.

The connection broke between them. Carmen collapsed onto the floor. Her brain couldn't focus back on what she was doing before she blacked out.

CHAPTER THIRTY

It took Carmen a moment to recall where she was. Her mind had trouble focusing. She heard echoes of a voice deep within the recesses of her brain before it faded. She looked around on the floor, saw the books, knelt and began to stuff her belongings in her book bag -. Her hands shook as she tried to zip the bag closed. Grunting in frustration, she stopped and made a fist, willing her hand to stop trembling.

"Are you okay?" Savannah appeared through the shelf.

Carmen screamed and fell backward into the adjacent shelf. "Stop doing that!"

"I didn't mean to scare you."

"You didn't mean. You don't *mean* to do a lot of things. I have to get out of here."

"What happened to you jus' now?"

"What do you mean?"

"What did he tell you?"

"He who?" Carmen looked at her, confused. "What do you mean?"

"The man who was jus' here," Savannah said.

Carmen shook her head.

"Oh no, what did he do to you?"

"Look, Savannah, I don't have time to play guessing games." Carmen held her head in her hand. "This is so stressful."

"Why don't you ask your handsome boyfriend to help you?"

Carmen hoisted the book bag on her shoulder. She made her way to the end of the stacks. Savannah followed.

"What? Why don't you ask him?"

"I can't. He doesn't know about my ability."

"You haven't told him?"

"Trust me, he's not ready to hear this. I don't think Dayton could even handle it." Carmen exited the row and walked into him. "Jesus!"

"It's only me," he said. "Handle what?"

"Are you following me?"

"I was downstairs talkin' to Curtis, and he said you were in the building. I know you like comin' up here and..." He looked behind her. "Who you talkin' to?"

"No one." She adjusted her book bag. "I'm thinking out loud."

"You should tell him," Savannah said.

"I told you no!" Carmen said over her shoulder.

"Told me no about what?" Dayton said.

"Huh?"

"Told me no about what?"

"He can help you. You have to trust him. If he loves you, he'll understand."

"Carmen, what's goin' on?"

"Everybody be quiet!" Carmen screamed. She pushed her way past Dayton, putting distance between him and Savannah. "I can't think. I need to process all this."

"Hey, calm down. Why are you flippin' out like this?" Dayton stepped toward her. "Carmen, talk to me."

"Leave me alone!" Carmen began to cry. "You wouldn't understand." Her eyes shifted toward Savannah, who had taken position behind Dayton's right shoulder. "I have to figure this out on my own. Once I understand what's happening, then I can tell him."

"Carmen?" a voice called from behind her. She turned and saw Curtis approaching. "Hey, was that you who screamed? You okay?"

"I had a —"

"She's fine," Dayton said.

Curtis looked into her tear-filled eyes. "She's not fine. What happened? You need me to call security?"

"Security for what? Nothing's wrong," Dayton said.

"She's screaming and crying; her face is flushed and you're standing over there."

"What're you implyin'?"

"I'm not implying anything. I'm simply responding to what I see."

Dayton made a beeline for Curtis. Savannah grasped to stop him, forgetting for a moment she was a ghost. Curtis stood in front of Carmen to block Dayton from getting to her.

"Don't." Dayton waved his finger at him.

"Get your hand out my face, Dayton."

Curtis smacked Dayton's hand away. Before Carmen could react, Dayton decked Curtis across the face. Curtis, in turn, smacked him. They grappled with one another, tussled, fell to the floor, and started fighting.

Disgusted, Carmen took off running. She bypassed the stairs leading to the lobby and went for the fire exit. She burst through the door, continuing to run down the stairs to the first floor. She paused at the door, her hand firmly gripping the handle.

Closing her eyes, she took several deep breaths. The tears subsided. Her racing heartbeat slowed as she calmed down. Carmen tried to clear her mind, but didn't know the proper way to do it other than to think back to the last few minutes and blank out what happened. Before her, Dayton and Curtis were arguing while Savannah watched.

Then all went black.

There was no sound, no images, only a vast and soothing darkness. Carmen searched for something, but was not sure what. The stairwell fell away. Weightless, she floated between two worlds. Exhaling, all the stress and tension within her faded. It was then she sensed a presence somewhere in the dark.

Hello? Is someone there?

"Hello?" a distorted feminine voice answered.

Hi, can you hear me?

"I can hear you. Keep talkin', I think I can find you."

This is unbelievable. Who are you? Are you a spirit?

"I am. Where did you come from all of a sudden? I didn't know there was another like you here." The voice sounded closer.

What do you mean?

"Another who can hear me. I already met one who can see and talk to me. Maybe you can help us. She can't call me like you can. She doesn't know how."

I can see and talk to spirits, if that's what you mean. Carmen became excited. *Come closer.*

A feeling of warmth passed through her like a gentle wave. Invisible fingers brushed against her face before passing over her shoulder.

"Can you feel me?"

I can. I can't see you.

"I'm right next to you. . . Wait, Carmen?"

Carmen opened her eyes, looked to her right, and came face to face with Savannah.

"Savannah? That. . . That was you just now?"

"Yes. I was upstairs watchin' the boys fight and the next thing I knew, I detected this presence in the air." Savannah became excited. "And then I hear this voice. This person and I was drawn to it, you know, but I couldn't see, and I hear you talkin' but it doesn't sound like you and—"

"Savannah, calm down." Carmen held her hands up as a smile started to grow. "Calm. That's how I did it, Savannah. I have to find peace, and I can reach out to the dead." Tears of joy streamed down her face. "I can call you now. I can call for help."

"Great." A somber look came over her face. "Carmen, you don't remember what happened upstairs? The man who visited you?"

Carmen stared at her. "I don't."

"He made you forget. They do that sometimes."

"They who?"

Savannah dematerialized. "It's in that book, the word right before wraith. Tell your grandmamma, he made you forget. I can't speak it."

"Wait, why?"

"I'm only here to help, darlin'. You have to be the one to find the truth."

CHAPTER THIRTY-ONE

Kim left the Commons and sprinted to the fountain. Her heart nearly leapt out of her chest seeing Eric on time. She embraced him and gave him a deep kiss. For the last three weeks, Operation Kim, as Curtis called it, kept Eric punctual. His friends stuck to their promise and made sure Eric cut back on any activities that would make him late.

"Missed you at breakfast," Eric said.

"I was running late this morning."

"You were running *late*. I see." Eric cracked a smile. "Well, I don't know how you expect this relationship to work if you can't be on time."

Kim playfully slapped his shoulder. "Shut up. It wasn't my fault. Carmen had me up most of the night. I didn't get my full eight hours."

"What's going on with her, anyway?" Eric took Kim's hand, and they started walking. "She's been acting funny since we got back."

"I wish I knew. She keeps saying nothing's wrong, but I know her too well. She's kept me up to talk. Leaving the room to talk to her grandmother in private. She's got the jitters, too."

"The jitters?"

"Yeah. Any little noise she hears or a knock at the door has her jumpy. I caught her several times coming into the room and looking cautiously around. Like she was expecting someone else to be in there with us. I heard her call out the name of a girl, Savannah, in her sleep. I asked her about it, but she told me she didn't know anyone with that name."

"You think she might do something to herself? You talked to the R.A. about it?"

"It hasn't reached that point. She's not showing signs or mentioned she's depressed. I don't want to jump the gun without giving her a chance to tell me what's up."

"What a way to start the semester with your roommate," Eric said.

Despite the overcast day being chilly, they walked and took in the early afternoon. Kim put her head on Eric's shoulder.

"You know I have to say I'm extremely impressed with your concerted effort to change," Kim said.

"Dayton and Curtis had a small hand in all of this. Ninety-eight percent of this is me. I am going to stick to this, I promise."

Kim stopped. She turned to him, cupped his face in her hands, then kissed him. He slid his arms around her waist and held her close. She put her arms around his neck.

"I am tryin' to do better," Eric said

"I know."

"And you know there isn't anything I wouldn't do for you."

"I do."

"I don't want to lose you."

"Okay, where is this coming from?"

"I just," he dropped his hands.

She dropped hers. "I'm scared."

"Scared of what?"

"This is it. Months from now we're graduating and. . . I don't know. Something Curtis said to me got me thinking if we don't make it, what happens beyond this?" He shook his head. "Know what? Forget I said anything. Let's just live in the moment."

"I didn't realize you were thinking so far ahead." She wrapped her arms around him and buried her head in his chest. "I love you, Eric. If you're unsure about anything else, be sure of that."

They stood holding one another for a moment. Kim raised her head. Something caught her attention.

"What?"

"What's going on over there?" She pointed. Eric followed her gesture.

Curtis, Dayton, and Carmen were coming from the library; all three were in a heated argument. Carmen kept trying to pull Dayton back while telling Curtis to walk away.

"What now?"

———

"You ever put your hands on me again. You better have your affairs in order," Curtis said.

"Stop it, the two of you!" Carmen screamed.

"Is that right? I'd like to see ya try to do somethin' to me." Dayton balled his fists. "I'll make you go night, night."

Curtis moved in. As he drew his arm back, Eric caught him from behind and dragged him backward.

"Chill, chill."

"Get off me, Eric."

"Not 'til you calm down, bro."

"I'm sick of this!" Carmen said. "I'm sick of the both of you." She walked off.

"Carmen! Carmen, wait." Dayton hurried to catch her.

"Hey, girl." Kim stepped in front of her. "Whoa."

"I'm not in the mood, Kim. Let me go."

"Not like this. You come with me."

"Kim, let me," Dayton said.

Kim held up a warning finger. "You stay back. I'm sure whatever this is, you had a hand in it."

"Wow, really Kim?" Dayton said.

"Carmen, look at me." Kim took her hands as their eyes met. "Take a walk with me. Let's talk. Doesn't matter what about."

Carmen started to cry, and she nodded. Kim put her arms around her and let Carmen sob on her shoulder. She looked over at Dayton, frowned, and led her away.

"Kim? Let me know if you need anything," Eric said.

"I got this, Eric. I'll talk to you later."

As Kim led Carmen away, Eric shoved Curtis. "What the hell's going on?"

"Your boy here punched me."

Dayton turned around. "You need to stop putting your nose in business where it doesn't belong."

"I just wanted to help."

"Carmen doesn't need your help. She's my girlfriend, not yours. She wants help. She can come to me."

"Well, she didn't want *your* help. Did she?"

Dayton rushed toward Curtis. "I know what you were doing. Ever since I hooked up with Carmen, you've resented me for it. You see us in the middle of a serious discussion and swoop down, thinking you're coming to her rescue."

Eric stepped between them. "Okay, enough now."

"Bro, you're reading way too much into this." Curtis took a step back, gesturing he didn't want a confrontation. "I heard screaming; I came upstairs. I thought something physical had happened."

"And you thought I had hit her?" Dayton said.

Eric turned to Curtis. "You didn't think that? C'mon, you've known Dayton since freshman year. You know he wouldn't hit a woman, especially Carmen."

"You know, this is fucked up." Curtis shook his head. "A girl got assaulted up there a couple of semesters back. How am I supposed to know... I hear *leave me alone,* that's not what was happening? You should be happy I even care."

Eric held up a hand. "Curtis, man, you have to understand. . ."

"Tell you both what, handle your girlfriends' problems on your own from now on. I won't step in or say another word. But just so your Midwestern, corn-fed ass is clear, I don't want Carmen. I'm not interested in her, and I couldn't care less what happens to her or you from now on."

Curtis headed back to the library. Neither of them attempted to stop him.

"You know he doesn't mean any of that. He'll be back to playing *Madden* with us in a couple of days. What happened up there?"

"I lost my cool."

"You know Carmen would never backslide."

"I know. I'm honestly not mad at him. Whatever is going on with her is what's buggin' me. She won't talk to me about it."

"Well, Kim's got her now. If there's anything to be found out, she'll get it out of her." Eric glanced at his watch. "There goes my romantic afternoon. Let's go get some food."

CHAPTER THIRTY-TWO

Carmen didn't speak the entire walk back to Wakeford Hall. As they approached the walkway under their window, she saw Savannah. Her hands pressed against the glass as she looked down at them. Carmen froze.

"What's wrong?" Kim followed her gaze up to the window. "What're you looking at?"

Carmen continued to stare as Savannah mouthed *sorry* to her. She shook her head and spotted a smooth stone in the grass. She picked it up, gripped it like a baseball, and drew her arm back, aiming at their window.

"What are you doing?" Kim wrestled the stone from her hand. "What's the matter with you?"

"Thanks a lot!" Carmen screamed at Savannah. She turned to Kim. "Not you." She shook her head as she dropped her chin to her chest. "I'm sorry."

"You want to see the nurse? Or maybe a guidance counselor?"

She lifted her head. "We need to go someplace to talk."

"We can talk in the lounge."

"No, not in the building. It might be better if we talk off-campus somewhere. I can't be here right now."

"Well, we can go to town to the coffee shop I like to hang out at. Or we can go to the diner and get a booth."

"I can do with some ice cream. The diner it is." She looked up at the window. Savannah had disappeared. She looked around and spotted her in the doorway of Wakeford Hall. "Let's grab the shuttle." Taking Kim by the arm, she half walked/half dragged her to the front gate to an idling shuttle van.

"Jesus, Carmen." Kim struggled to keep up.

"Where are you goin'?" Savannah yelled at her.

Carmen ignored Savannah as she opened the van's side door, pushed Kim inside, and said, "The diner."

———

Carmen requested the waitress seat them in the back once they arrived. She ordered a milkshake and an ice cream sundae for herself and told Kim to get whatever she wanted. The waitress returned a short time later with Carmen's order and a diet soda for Kim. Carmen dug into the sweets and didn't speak for several minutes.

Then she told her about the incident in the library between Dayton and Curtis. Kim listened as Carmen intermittently drank her milkshake until she slurped tiny drops into the straw.

"Remember, I told you about my abuela and the mediums in my family?"

"You said it's skipped you."

"Well, apparently it didn't."

"Hold on, you have been talking to *the dead?*"

"It's more than that. I can see them too. Well, one at least."

Kim chuckled a little. "You see dead people?"

"You think this is funny? You find humor in this?" Carmen's

lips quivered. "I've been walking around campus being followed by a spirit and you think this is a joke?"

"Carmen, I didn't mean it."

"You know what? Forget it." Carmen looked away from her. "Waiter, can we get the check over here?" She turned back to Kim. "I'll deal with this on my own."

Carmen jumped up, tossed her money on the table, and started to leave.

Kim reached for her arm. "Stop. Take it easy and sit down and explain this to me. How was I supposed to react, huh? C'mon, sit back down. I'm here for you, like always."

Carmen saw the sincerity in Kim's eyes. She let out a gentle sigh before sitting back down. Kim placed her hand gently on top of Carmen's.

"Now, what exactly has happened?" Kim said.

Carmen told Kim what had happened, leaving out the parts about the evil she had been warned about. She didn't feel ready to tell Kim.

"So, this Savannah girl, has she told you why she needs your help?"

"She's not being clear with me. I asked my abuela what it could be, and she gave me a laundry list of things. Then I went today to the library to find some books on. . ." Carmen stopped, and a blank expression came over her face.

"What did you find in the library?"

Carmen's brain couldn't piece it all together. Her thoughts were fragmented. She could remember up to the moment Savannah pointed to one of the books.

"I can't remember what happened." Carmen shut her eyes and said, "*Maldito sea.* Savannah tried showing me something in a book," then opened them.

"It's okay. Don't stress yourself."

"That's just it! I'm trying not to stress any of this. If I'm from a line of mediums, all of this should be easy. I shouldn't have to run around reading books and trying to figure things out. I mean, I should be able to tell a spirit from a real person, right?" She wiped tears from her eyes. "Why would my abuela and my family put this on me?"

Kim leaned in. "I don't think you can blame your family for this."

"They gave me this ability."

"Yeah, I mean, I get what you're saying, but you've always had it in you. It's just coming out now and maybe the reason is because you couldn't handle it until you were older."

"Does it look like I'm dealing with this, Kim?"

"Well, you're not shying away from it. That's one thing you don't give yourself enough credit for. Put a challenge in front of you and you always step up and figure it out."

"This is different."

"It's unique." Kim grinned. "Chica, you need to trust yourself. And you gotta stop stressing so much."

"It's hard not to. You never know when you'll get contacted by the dead."

"Does Savannah just show up out of the blue?"

"Pretty much. She just pops up and she scares the hell outta me."

"And you haven't told Dayton? Carmen, you have to tell him. Dayton is an understanding guy. I'll even go with you to talk to him."

"I don't want you to tell him or Eric, either. Once I know what is going on and what we're dealing with, then I can talk to him."

"Okay, fair enough." Kim played with the straw in her drink. "Do I have to worry about you. . . well. . . doing anything to yourself over this?"

Carmen shook her head. "No, I'm not gonna hurt myself. I

wouldn't keep that to myself." She exhaled. "I think I just needed to talk this out."

"Well, now I don't know what I'm supposed to do with this information. I mean, how can I help? Anything I should be looking out for?"

"Honestly, being able to tell you is enough. If you see or hear me acting funny, you know why." She grinned. "There is one thing, though. I feel like I need to tell you this. There's this guy who moved into Chambers Hall, supposedly some Don Juan, and he has a friend. Stay away from them." For some reason, Carmen couldn't remember either Zeborah or Todd's name. "Dayton mentioned them. They've been causing some issues with the ladies," Carmen lied.

Kim patted the top of Carmen's hand. "Okay, I'll do that. And listen, I'm going to act as normal as I can, girl. As far as I'm concerned, this discussion doesn't leave this table unless you bring it up. Just give me a heads up if you and Savannah decide to have a late-night chat."

Carmen smiled before looking out the window.

CHAPTER THIRTY-THREE

"You have no idea where he is?" he asked Zeborah.

"He's not even respondin' to me telepathically."

Todd couldn't shake the feeling Kevin was somewhere doing something behind his back. Though he had pledged to help Todd after they were banished, his behavior of late made him wary. He and Zeborah had waited for two hours for Kevin in the lab, but he never showed.

"You used your phone?"

"I did."

"And still nothing?"

"Nope."

"Okay, I'm not sitting around here anymore. I'm going back to the room. You want to wait here, you can."

"I'll let him know."

Todd left the lab and took the back way out of the building. Once on campus, he walked fast, his thoughts on Kim. He had found his host. He required a little more time to draw her closer to him, and he needed to facilitate a breakup between her and her boyfriend. They had to discover *his* weakness, his fear, and exploit it.

By the time he arrived at Chambers Hall, his mind raced with ideas of how he could mess with the couple. A hand touched his shoulder. He spun around to see Zeborah.

"I heard from Kevin. I know where he is," he said.

"Where?"

"He's waiting for us in your room."

———

Todd and Zeborah found Kevin standing behind the crate, his hands buried deep inside the dirt. His eyes shut. His lips moved rapidly, as though he were praying.

"What are you doing?" Todd said.

Kevin opened his eyes. He glared at Todd, then looked to Zeborah. He removed his hands. They were covered with leeches.

"I must have lost track of time," he said.

"Were you feeding the leeches?" Todd rushed across the room. "You taint these with your blood and they're useless to me."

"I wasn't tainting them, just checking something." Kevin brushed them off. The more stubborn ones wouldn't let go. He snatched them off. "By the way, I found the medium in the library. It appears she is taking her newfound abilities seriously. Had a nice stack of books with her. She's in full study mode." He pointed to Zeborah. "She mentioned you, by the way; by name."

"What?" Zeborah looked confused. "How does she know my name?"

"I'll get to that in a minute. First, I wanted to tell you I'm removing you from campus. You will take over my duties overseeing Rakim."

"You're jokin'. I don't wanna do that job," Zeborah said.

"You won't have any trouble with him," Kevin said. "I need to be here to keep an eye on things."

"Ah, so my suspicions were correct. You *do* want to keep tabs on me," Todd said. "This is a rather slick way because of a stupid medium you're refusing to take care of."

Kevin wiped the dirt from his hands and took position between Zeborah and Todd. "Okay." He nodded. "Okay." He took a deep breath, exhaled it then looked at Zeborah. "I see we're going to play this game. Tell us, Todd, what happened to Savannah?" Kevin waited for Zeborah's expression of surprise to form.

"Savannah?"

"Yes, Savannah, Zeborah's girlfriend," Kevin said.

"The mortal he had delusions of love for. She ran off," Todd said.

"To where?"

"How the hell should I know where she is? She's probably a thousand miles away."

"Oh, I doubt that." Kevin walked back to the crate. "Did you know some spirits tend to occupy a space close to where they died? And sometimes, if their physical body is moved, they will follow it." He clasped his hands together. "They attach themselves to it and linger. And then they will do something interesting, and this is the important part, oftentimes they reach out for help to those who can hear them. Like a medium."

"This is all fascinating, Kevin. What does this have to do with Savannah?" Todd chided.

"For starters, she's dead."

"What?" Zeborah yelled. "What'd ya mean she's dead? How do you know?"

"Once after I found the medium, I saw Savannah trying to hide from me. Then again, while crossing the campus in the medium's room window at Wakeford Hall. That's the girl's dormitory across the way. This means they've linked up."

"Listen to yourself. That's moronic," Todd said.

"Well, you can ignore it if you want to, but as long as *she's* walking around with the *medium,* Zeborah can't be on this campus."

Todd didn't say a word. Zeborah walked to the bed and sat down. He covered his mouth, trying to hide the shock.

"D-Did you speak to Savannah?" Zeborah said.

"No," Kevin said.

"You don't know how she died?"

"I have a theory. I believe I might even know where her body is." Kevin kept his eyes on Todd.

Zeborah stood. "You have to take me to her."

"No," Kevin said.

"Watch your step, cousin," Todd warned.

"I don't have to because you're already near the body," Kevin said.

"What do you mean?"

"Tell him," Kevin said to Todd.

"Tell me what?"

"I have no idea what you're talking about." Todd feigned ignorance.

"You killed her and put her in there with your leeches." Kevin pointed to the crate. "Along with another body. That's what they have been feeding on and whose blood you have been consuming."

"You're crazy," Todd said.

"Am I?" Kevin started to fume. "Savannah was about to reveal to the medium that Zeborah is a vampire. The only way she would have known, since Zeborah, Rakim, nor I never told her, is someone revealed it to her before she died." Kevin leaned in, pointing to his chest. "You were the last to see her alive."

Zeborah stepped toward Todd. "Is this true?"

Todd slid his tongue against his inner bottom lip. "I knew one day I would regret the fact you have the power to communicate with the dead." He glared at Zeborah. "She was a distraction. You spent all your time chasing a pathetic mortal woman instead of handling the matters at hand. So, if anyone is responsible for her death, it's you, Zeborah. You left me with no choice."

Zeborah attacked Todd. Seizing him by the throat, they glided across the room, slamming into a wall. Zeborah lifted him off the floor.

"You sonofabitch. I should rip your throat out." Zeborah exposed his fangs.

"Let go of me." Todd bared his fangs.

Zeborah threw him across the room into the closet door. Todd struck it hard but stood his ground.

"You were jealous of us."

"No, Zeborah, he wasn't jealous of you two," Kevin said.

"You don't think so, huh?"

"I'm beginning to understand the other function of the leeches. They're not entirely an alternative food source. Blood doesn't just carry nutrients. Some believe the soul of a person travels through their veins. Savannah was a wholesome girl with a beautiful soul. Consuming her soul made him stronger. She's now connected to all this."

"Call it collateral damage, Zeborah. Savannah's body serves the greater purpose," Todd teased.

"Zeborah, go outside and cool off. I'll be out in a minute to join you."

Zeborah strode over to the desk and slammed his fists down on the desk. The legs buckled and splintered as it smashed to the floor before he stormed out.

"I'll get him settled with Rakim, then come back. I'll take my residence in the lab so you can do whatever it is you need to do in peace here." Kevin tilted his hat and headed toward the door. "I'll be back within the hour."

"You happy now?" Todd said.

Kevin left without responding. Todd stood engulfed in silence. He walked to the crate, removed a leech, and ate it fast.

————

Finding Zeborah fuming and pacing in the parking lot, Kevin approached him with reservation. He respectfully took his hat off and cleared his throat. Zeborah looked at him.

"You're worse than the coven. You refused to handle him properly and now look where we are!" Zeborah said.

"The coven figured, as did I, the spell would kill him, as it has done to other overzealous members."

"Admit he's better at decipherin' spells than you gave him credit for. We underestimated Todd's smarts in all this." Zeborah stopped pacing and stared at Kevin. "Where is the medium now?"

"Why?" Kevin saw hope in Zeborah's eyes. "You're not tracking down the medium for answers to Savannah's death."

"You know I loved her. It wasn't a ploy to make her a vampire."

"I know. But you sealed Savannah's fate the moment you allowed yourself to be in love. You exposed her to Todd. We need to stop him before he completes the ascension, and the problem is we need to wait until he's close to the end because there's a small window of time that he will be at his weakest."

"We tried before, and what happened? We screw up again and this whole campus and our Coven will die."

"I know, Zeborah. But at least for now, he hasn't set his sights on any of the coeds."

"Besides the mortal female I met?"

Kevin's eyes turned crimson. "What female?"

"A girl he met here on campus. He showed her the leeches earlier."

"You let him bring a girl into the lab and you didn't tell me immediately? What the hell, Zeborah?"

"He brought her in while I wasn't there."

Kevin shook his head. He turned away from him, looked across the yard, and spotted Carmen and Kim coming from the shuttle bus. He crossed the road to the grassy knoll, stood behind a bush, and watched them. Carmen touched the side of her head as she got to the door of Wakeford Hall. Kim approached her with a concerned look, but Carmen waved her off and went inside. Kim lingered in the walkway.

"That's her," Zeborah said as he approached Kevin. "The girl from tha lab with Todd. Tha one standin' there." He pointed to Kim.

They watched as Kim marched down the walkway, stopped halfway, opened her arms, and smiled as Eric came and embraced her. They kissed.

"Oh, shit." Zeborah turned away.

"She has a boyfriend. Does Todd know that?" Kevin asked.

"I don't know. But this is bad."

"I know."

"No, you don't understand. The guy she's kissin'. Todd's gotten into an altercation several times already with him," Zeborah said.

"How bad of an altercation?"

"Wouldn't take much for the two of 'em to go to blows."

Kevin continued to watch as Carmen reemerged and hugged Kim before turning to Eric and started talking.

"Well, it just got more complicated. They all know each other." Kevin tugged on Zeborah, forcing him to look. "What're the odds of this?"

"That changes things, doesn't it?"

"Let's go." Kevin headed in the direction of the library. Zeborah followed. "You have to stay off this campus. Too many eyes know who you are." He took hold of his arm, and they stopped. "Do you trust me?"

"Yes, I trust you."

"Then this is what's going to happen. We'll let Todd have his space for now and let things play out with this girl. If he does what he normally does, he will anger the boyfriend, and all will go south for everyone involved. It gives us enough of a distraction for me to work on the medium. She'll be the weapon I need. By the time comes for the ascension, I'll use all three of them to put an end to this whole mess," Kevin said.

"What about what he can do now? The morphing?"

"Don't worry about it. He hasn't merged with the demon yet and he won't for a while."

Kevin led Zeborah to the fence behind the library. Once certain no one was looking, they leapt over it and headed back into the woods.

CHAPTER THIRTY-FOUR

Four parchments instructed how to complete the ascension. They provided the practitioner with the specific incantations to allow one's body to open to demonic influence. Meaning the demon could pass on certain abilities to the practitioner and in return prepare their physical form to be overtaken. The final stage would allow the demon and practitioner to become one. But for it to happen, one ritual had to take place before the possession so fusion between vampire and demon could happen. That ritual was missing.

Todd discovered this while researching why the last two vampires who tried the ascension spell died from madness. The last page, he learned, had been replaced with part of an exorcism ritual taken from an old biblical text. It was rewritten in the Coptic language to blend in with everything else. Even the parchment had been changed; treated papyrus, not flesh, like the others.

It took Todd several months to locate the real page. He discovered it hidden deep in the catacombs on the Coven's home grounds in the crypt of the only vampire who had completed the ascension.

After retrieving it, he hid it. Even Kevin had no clue Todd had the page. He had secretly begun the final ritual before things had gone south at the previous school. But he had done enough for it to take effect on his ability to change his appearance. And now with Kevin and Zeborah gone, he settled in; it was time to prepare for the final stage.

Todd locked the door. Next, he covered the small window with a sheet, immersing the room in darkness. He knelt beside the crate and slid his hand alongside it. His fingertips traced over the grooves until he found a loose plank. Carefully, he plucked it back. It creaked. He opened it more, slid two fingers into the gap, and pinched down on a rolled parchment made of dried human flesh tied with twine. It resembled leather with its worn look. He placed it on the floor and replaced the plank.

He took two handfuls of dirt from inside and walked to an open space. Using his fists like a sieve, he proceeded to make the shape of a scarab beetle on the floor. He finished, went back into the crate and dug deep until he found the larger leeches attached to the body of one of his victims. One by one, he removed six and placed them at the ends of the scarab's legs and antennae.

Next, Todd picked up the skin, untied it, unrolled it, and placed it under the scarab. Satisfied with the setup, he went to his knapsack, removed two black candles along with a stick of incense and matches. Placing the candles on either side of the skin, Todd lit them and the incense and finally, placed it above the skin.

He genuflected, bowed before the skin with outstretched arms, and read the words etched in vampire blood written in the dead Coptic language:

"This body is your vessel. This flesh for you to command."

He picked up one of the leeches.

"As I consume this living thing to make one with my body, so shall we become one upon the ascension."

He placed it in his mouth and ate it.

"Accept me as your willing companion, one of the living dead. And grant me my desire for vengeance."

Todd repeated the incantation five more times; he consumed a leech each time. He leaned forward and touched the ground with his head.

Thunder clapped. His body seized. Something took hold of the back of his head and yanked so hard his head bent back. Fleshless fingers pushed his eyelids open like forceps, forcing him to look up at the ceiling. He saw nothing, but he perceived the presence of something evil in the room. The oppressive atmosphere enveloped his body, tearing his mouth open. An invisible one covered his. A vile, rotting breath seeped into him. He tried to cough, but the invading breath forced itself deep into Todd's body. Like congestion, his lungs filled, making his breathing tight. The invisible mouth removed itself.

He doubled over and breathed in deep. The breath the evil entity had passed into him spread through him. Its rage made his face shift and contort. The flesh of his face stretched, causing small slits to open and drip blood. Then it elongated to resemble a Kuria death mask, exposing his gums and lips while causing bags under his eyes to droop. A voice spoke to him. Its foreboding tone forced him to submit to feelings of fear.

"The essence of what you will need to complete the ascension is inside you."

Tears of blood streamed from Todd's eyes. "Thank you. I am grateful for this gift."

"You have found another to be the host?"

"Yes." Todd lowered his head as if he were about to pray. "I believe I will have her before the rise of the new moon."

"Continue to nourish what I have put in you."

"How long do I have to do this?"

"Until you are ready for the new host."

Todd lifted his head. "How do I nourish it?"

"Kiss a mortal in the grip of fear. The essence inside you will know what to do." The demonic entity placed a hand on his head. "Summon me no more."

The candlelight went out, and the presence dissipated from the room. Todd's face returned to normal.

Todd wiped the bloody tears from his face and sat in silence. The demon's essence traveled through him, settling in the pit of his stomach.

CHAPTER THIRTY-FIVE

Eric walked into his room to find Dayton in his bed with one arm behind his head, staring up at the ceiling with his headphones on. He sat up on his elbows.

"Sup?" Eric said.

Dayton took off the headphones. "Nothin' much. Where you been all this time?"

"Had a lab, then I caught up with Kim. We're supposed to get together later at the Commons." Eric dropped his book bag and sat on the edge of his bed. "You okay?"

"I don't know." He sat up and put his back against the wall. "Things aren't making sense lately."

"What do you mean?"

"That thing with Curtis today and what's going on with Carmen." Dayton paused for a moment. "Lemme ask you. Do you think Carmen's sneaking around on me?"

"Sneaking around on you? Carmen? She loves you to death. Why would you think that?"

"All this weird behavior all of a sudden. She's acting jumpy. I try to talk to her and she's in a hurry to go somewhere else."

"Could be stress."

"Kim hasn't said anything to you?"

"Not really, no."

"I must have done something."

"She would have told you if you did. I wouldn't get worked up about this. Whatever is going on, she'll open up to you when she's ready."

"Look at you giving relationship advice," Dayton quipped.

A loud rap at the door cut Eric off before he could respond. "It's open!"

They watched as Curtis stuck his head in. For several seconds, no one spoke.

"Hey, mind if I step in?"

"I'm good." Eric looked at Dayton. "You okay with him in here?"

"Whatever."

Eric waved him in. Curtis closed the door behind him but kept his distance and his hands behind his back.

"Dayton, man, listen. I'm sorry."

"Save it. I'm the one who's sorry. Things have been kinda crazy lately with Carmen and I didn't mean to take it out on you. I get it. You two have a history. I guess I was. . ."

"Jealous." Eric and Curtis said in unison.

"I'm not jealous."

"Yeah, you are, and you deserve to be. She's a wonderful girl." He dropped his hands to his side, and they saw he had a book with him. "While putting some books back at work, something told me to go back upstairs to where you guys were and look around. In the last row, I found this sticking out from under the bottom shelf. She must have dropped it. I took a moment to look through it and, well, I dog-eared a page you should see." He offered Dayton the book.

"Toss it," he said, and Curtis complied. Dayton looked at the cover. "The Corporeal & Incorporeal Dead?"

"I remembered she asked me about books on mediums, then I find this. There's stuff in there about zombies, vampires, and demons."

"Okay." Dayton opened to a dogeared page. "Spirits, Ghosts and Haints." He read the page. "What do you think this is about?"

"I don't know anything really about mediums, only what I've seen in the movies. They talk to ghosts and stuff. Maybe, well. . ."

Dayton looked up from the book and over to Eric.

"C'mon, Curtis. You think Carmen is trying to talk to ghosts?" Eric said.

"I'm just saying that's not the kind of thing you come into the library to read for leisure. I'm thinking, Dayton, you should show it to her and ask her about it. Maybe it will spark a convo about whatever is going on with her."

Dayton looked back at the book, shook his head, and closed it before putting it on the foot of the bed.

"Honestly," Eric began, "I'd say give her some space. Let her come to you with her issues. I wouldn't—"

The power winked out in the entire building, bathing them in darkness.

"What the hell is this now?" Eric said.

———

"Aw, damn."

Todd yanked the transformer's plug as sparks flew from the socket. The smell of smoke and electricity filled the air. Immediately checking the ceiling lights and realizing nothing was working, he rushed to the window and opened it to air out the room. Shifting next to the door, Todd intended to go out and see if the blackout only affected Chambers Hall or the entire campus.

Upon opening the door, he heard David screaming as he accessed the stairwell at the end of the hall.

Todd closed his door and covered the crate with the lid, and threw a large comforter over it. He gathered up the transformer, shoved it into the closet, and listened.

"Someone in here got a fridge or a microwave." He heard David unlock the door across the hall from his room. "There's gonna be hell to pay if this. . . Yep, I knew it."

Todd heard a switch being turned. The lights came on in his room. David slammed the door, then knocked on Todd's.

"Just a second." Todd checked to make sure nothing looked out of place before opening the door. "What's up?"

David peered over Todd's shoulder into the room. "We okay in here?"

"Yeah, busy with homework. What happened to the power?"

"Someone using an appliance tripped the circuit breaker." David finished his scan of the room. "What's that burning smell?"

"A desk clock sparked and burned out."

"Well, don't plug it back in," he warned. "I bet it's them idiots on three." David turned and left.

Todd went back and checked the transformer. It was fried. He would have to wait until the next day to buy a new one in town. He decided to get some air and check out the scene on campus. Maybe if he were lucky, he would see Kim again. He took his keys and headed out the back door.

Moments later, he strayed into the Commons and surveyed the small crowd. Students mingled, played various board and video games, or waited to get food from an area called The Grill. He spotted one student with a chocolate milkshake and found himself craving one. While he didn't need or eat regular food, there were some things he did like the taste of. Chocolate was one of them. He ambled over to the line and waited his turn to order.

He spotted Kim sitting by herself at a corner table, reading a book. He became anxious. While sipping on her drink, she glanced in his direction. Their eyes met, and she waved. Todd smiled and waved back. He ordered and paid for his milkshake, then walked to her table.

"That's three times in one day," Kim remarked.

"Yeah, I needed to get a cold drink." He shook his cup. "Chocolate."

"Black and white." Kim shook her cup at him.

"Satisfying choice. You're waiting for someone?"

"My boyfriend."

"Back to his carefree ways again?"

"I'm early. But he'll be here soon, I'm sure."

"Care for some company while you wait. Someone to vent to?" Todd smiled, "Your own *Personal Jesus?*"

"Pull up a chair." Kim pointed to an empty chair from an adjacent table. Todd slid it over and sat down. "Depeche Mode."

"Excuse me?"

"'*Personal Jesus*'. Depeche Mode sings that."

"Whoa now." Todd put up his hands while sliding back from the table. "I'm scared of you. I'm impressed. I kind of like the Marilyn Manson version myself."

"How are the leeches doing?"

"All tucked away and resting." He looked around. "Is this all there is to do around here at night?"

"On campus, this is it. You haven't been in here until now?"

"I've passed by the place. I haven't been out much on campus in the evening because of my work."

He watched as Kim observed a group of guys enter the Commons. She looked relieved at first, then disappointed. As she turned her attention back to him, he saw her eyes glance over to a foosball table as two students walked away from it.

"You play foosball?" Todd asked.

"It's been a while."

"You up for a quick game?"

"Well, I don't know." She looked at the door. "Eric should be here soon."

"One game, while you wait."

They looked at one another. He gave her a reassuring smile as he held up a single finger. She relented.

"Why not?" Kim took up her milkshake and followed Todd to the table.

CHAPTER THIRTY-SIX

Carmen found herself back in the reference section of the library, but something was off about her surroundings. The aura was different.

The closer she got to the aisle she had been sitting in, the stronger the odor of rancid flesh mixed with wet earth after a rainstorm grew. She looked down and saw she was walking in black soil. Her bare feet sank into it. The coldness seeped between her toes.

She walked faster. Beneath the soil, several slimy things squirmed. She looked down again. *Earthworms*! But she noticed many of them clung to the top of her feet. She stopped to pull them off, but they wouldn't come loose. She squeezed one. It exploded between her fingers, covering them in blood. Carmen cringed. She tried to scream, but it came out as a muffled cry. These weren't worms, but something else. She glanced down again. One of them had grown fat as it fed off her blood.

She ran in the opposite direction, but black soil covered the entire floor. She searched for an escape but couldn't find a clear path. A hand rose out of the soil a few feet away. A second hand adjacent to the first appeared. They planted themselves palm down on the topsoil and pushed.

A mound formed. Bits of it trickled down the sides as a freed itself. It sat up in a sitting position, facing her. It lifted its right hand, which contorted into the shape of a claw. Soil poured from its mouth as it started to moan. With its left hand, it wiped away the dirt from its face to reveal a rotting corpse. It took its clawed hand and peeled away the rot. The face beneath started to become clear, but not recognizable at first. It shook its head, causing the dead skin to fall away, then looked back at her and smiled, showing off sharp canines.

Once freed, it limped toward her and with each step; the face became clearer until the thing which stood before her was Kevin. He caressed her face. The moment he touched her, he spoke one word, "Todd".

"Who is Todd? Wait, I know you." She touched the side of her head and started to concentrate. Forcing herself to remember him and, in her mind, seeing a blank face with cracks like a roadmap running through it. It started to flake as the image melted into Kevin's features. "I remember you did something to me. Tried to make me forget."

Kevin lunged and brought her down. They began to struggle with one another. He managed to get on top of her and pushed her down to the soil.

"Get out. Get out of my head!"

"Get off me!"

The earth closed in around her. She tried to call out for Maria but couldn't. Kevin's icy hands seized her throat. In her panic, she called to Savannah in her mind. The world around her went black.

Within the darkness, a pair of hands seized her waist and started to pull her deeper into the earth. Kevin let go of her throat.

A second set of hands took hold of her ankles and tugged hard. *I got you, darlin'! I got you.*

Carmen slid down through the soil and, within seconds, was bathed in light. Her body landed on something soft.

"They almost had you," Savannah said from down by her feet.

Carmen sat up, looking around, and found herself in her dorm room bed. "What the hell happened to me?" Irritations on her wrists caused her to look down to see fingernail markings on her skin. Her eyes then met Savannah's who stood at the end of the bed.

"Kevin. He almost had you."

"Kevin? Why do I feel like I know that name?"

"He's Zeborah's cousin."

Carmen braced herself as it all started to come together in her mind. She slipped out of bed, went into her book bag, and removed a book Savannah and she had been looking at in the library and began to thumb through it.

"Where is it?"

"What are you lookin' for?"

Carmen stopped on a page titled *Vampire*. She saw Kevin's face in her head. She remembered the fangs. "I'm going to need a whole lot more help than you, Savannah."

———

Blood spewed from his mouth as Kevin convulsed on the cabin floor. Zeborah tried to stabilize him. His arms flailed, striking him across his jaw. Zeborah fell backward. Kevin let out a throaty growl as his body bent into an arch and his eyes rolled back into his head.

"Kevin?" Zeborah shouted.

Kevin stayed locked in the arch position for several seconds. A gurgling sound replaced the growl. Streams of blood ran from the corners of his eyes. He fell flat onto his back and lay motionless until his eyes returned.

He sat straight up in a trance state. This lasted for a minute, then he leapt to his feet. Without saying a word, he broke into a run through the woods back to the campus.

He launched himself over the fence, walked across the quadrangle, and took the walkway behind Wakeford Hall. He strode into the building's shadows and scaled the wall to the roof. The trance wore off.

It took him a moment to realize he was no longer in the woods, but on the roof of Wakeford Hall. Kevin walked to the edge of the roof, peered over the side, and saw several girls exiting the building. Pressing his hands on the sides of his head while closing his eyes, Kevin tried to remember what prompted him to come here. Hearing Savannah's voice coming from inside the building speaking to someone caused him to open them swiftly.

Discovering a lip running the length of the building under the windows and carefully climbing down onto it, her voice sounded louder, but from below. While climbing down once more, his headache returned. *Savannah is with the medium*, he thought. Kevin suppressed the headache so no link could be made and approached the window but was mindful to stay in the shadow while peering inside.

Carmen sat on her bed. Her phone was a few inches in front of her. Savannah stood in the corner on the opposite side of the room, watching her.

"No, Carmensita, that's not a good idea," Maria said through the speaker.

"I need to tell him. I can't do this alone."

"Jou're not alone. I am here for jou."

"You're thousands of miles away. I know you mean well, but

what can you do besides give me advice?" Carmen's voice cracked. "And after what happened with my dream, I'm scared."

"What dream?"

"After I talked with Kim, I came back here to lay down. I fell asleep and started to dream. It was so vivid. I could smell the books, and the ground was covered with black dirt. He rose from the ground, faceless at first, then his face appeared, and he said something, a name, Todd." Carmen took a second to catch her breath. "He had fangs. Do you know what that means?" She paused, then said, "He's a vampire. If you can't help, I can at least summon Savannah if I need help."

"Wait, Carmen, jou summoned the ghost of Savannah?" Maria interrupted. "Jou figured out how to summon her? Aye Dios Mio. It took me several jears to learn and jou did it on jour own. It means jou're getting stronger."

"Did we just forget what I said about the vampire?"

"I heard jou."

"And?"

"And jou had a vision, not a dream. Because it was of one who is considered undead, and a strong one from how jou describe what happened, it's the reason for its intensity. Jou see, there are different kinds of vampires, Carmen. Jes, they drink blood, but they do not all behave the same. Their actions are often as myste- rious as they are. Vampires don't like us, and they will do their best to avoid contact. I heard of mediums who have had contact with them and what I can tell jou is this one you had the vision of picked up on you and is deciding how to handle the situation."

"You know for sure?"

"I don't know anything for sure. I have never come across a vampire before. But if this other one jou had in jour vision didn't try to kill jou when he first met jou, then I suggest jou lay low. Stay clear of him if jou feel him coming near. Summon Savannah and have her tell you what she knows about this vampire. She's the connection. If she wants jou to intervene with this vampire and her, jou call me back and we will work this out together."

Carmen glanced over at Savannah. "What if Savannah doesn't tell me what I want to know?"

"Jou threaten to stop talking to her. She's alone and jou're the closest thing she has to a friend. She will tell you. Confia en mi." Maria sighed. "I'm going to do more digging and see if mi Madre wrote anything down in her diary about vampires." Maria grew quiet for a moment, then said, "I still don't like the idea of jou telling this boy about what you are. Se debe tener en la familia."

"He's my boyfriend," Carmen said.

"If he were jour husband, that would be one thing. But what if jou tell him and he rejects jou, huh? What if he breaks up with you, then decides to spread it around the school that jou're a medium? What then?"

"He's a good man. He won't turn on me. He cares a lot about me," Carmen countered.

"That's right, he does. He put up a fight today for her honor. He loves Carmen," Savannah said. Carmen shot her a disapproving look. Savannah dematerialized.

"Be extremely careful how jou approach this. Men are not as understanding and strong as they like to appear. Jour Abuelo had a hard time dealing with my abilities, even though he never showed it."

"But Abuelo kept your secret. He never told any of us about what you could do. That counts for something."

"If jou still have the candle, I gave jou freshman year, light it tonight and say a prayer."

"There's more to the vision I haven't told you about."

"No more tonight. Go and rest. Clear jour mind."

"Thank you, Abuela," Carmen said. "Buenas noches."

"Buenas noches."

Carmen ended the call and sat still on the bed. After a moment, she stood and shuffled towards the window.

Kevin climbed back up to the roof. He looked down to see if she would stick her head out and caught Savannah walking across campus with a man who looked like a truck driver. They were talking, but he couldn't hear what they were saying.

"Who the hell is this now?" He whispered as he watched them disappear into the night. He communicated with Zeborah. "Zeborah, we have a situation. It looks like I'm going to have to work a lot faster than I thought."

"Are you okay? You was seizin' up, then ran out of here."

"It was the medium. I'm fine. Seems her powers are growing. And my ability to make this one forget things is temporary. She remembers who I am and what I told her. She now knows Todd's name. The only saving grace is she doesn't know why. I can't let her find out yet. And there's more."

"Is it bad?"

"I spotted Savannah with some trucker. I've never seen him before, but I have the suspicion Todd's killed him. Also, the medium has a grandmother, who is too a medium, now helping her."

"Which means we can't touch this girl now," Zeborah said.

"But I can stop her from getting any more help, that's for sure."

"How?"

"First, I'll take out Savannah, then find out where her grandmother is, get her out of the way and get those books in her hands."

"When do you plan to do all this?"

"We start tomorrow." He closed his eyes. "Shit, she has a boyfriend, but he's not involved. Not yet, anyway."

"How do you wanna handle him?"

"Leave the boyfriend alone for now. She's going to need comfort after what I do."

"You care about her comfort?"

"Don't go there."

Kevin broke the link as he jumped down from the roof into the darkness behind the dormitory. He decided he needed some time alone to think and headed to the science building.

CHAPTER THIRTY-SEVEN

"Now that's rare, even for Chambers Hall," Curtis said. "Two blackouts minutes after one another. I've never seen David so pissed."

"Remember last semester what's his name had a fridge and microwave in his room and caused a brownout in the middle of the night? I thought David would hit the roof then," Eric countered. "They need to do an upgrade on these buildings, anyway. All this money we pay and the buildin' runnin' off 1930s wiring. Lucky we didn't have a fire." He glanced at his watch. "Kim's gonna kill me."

"I got you. She'll believe me if I tell her."

"That's cold, man. You sayin' Ima liar?"

"I'm saying your truths need a side order of extra truth from time to time."

Eric strode as he shook his head. "I don't know why I keep hanging out with you."

"You gonna miss me once we're out of this place," Curtis said. "I hope they have some of those sweet onions for the burgers at the Commons. "

"I meant to ask you, what exactly happened between you and Carmen. I don't think I ever got the full scoop."

Curtis hung his head a little while he let out an exhausted sigh. "We started as friends, and we were good. Always hanging out, studying together, and all that. Then we went to the movies one night, got a little too cozy, and started making out. Apparently, I took it to mean something more than she did. I kept trying to label us."

"You sleep with her?"

"No. I wanted to, but not for the sake of doing it. That's what's messed up." Curtis stopped walking this time. Sadness filled his face. "I still have strong feelings for her, but I know how to keep them where they belong. At the same time, it's hard to see her with Dayton and not wish it were me. I tried to date her, and it just fell apart fast. After a little time, she said she wanted to stay friends and I…damn."

"You took it literally."

"Yeah, but it's one of those things you can't go back to once you cross a certain line. Anytime I do or say anything now, I'm always worried she thinks it's because I'm still in love with her. Not because I genuinely care about her needs."

"Isn't that what love is?"

"In dictionary terms, yeah. When it comes to someone's feelings, not so much." Curtis looked at Eric and wiped his eyes to keep the tears from falling. "I'm worried about her. I know Dayton is a good man and all, but still, I can't help it."

Eric nodded. "I get it. Sorry I brought it up."

"It's all good. Let's get you to where you gotta be."

They made it to the Commons in silence. Eric opened the door to go in first. Curtis grasped his arm and dragged him back out.

"What?"

"Is that Kim over there?" Curtis pointed in the direction of a couple walking away from them.

Eric followed his finger. "I think you're right."

"Who is that she's with?"

———

Kim and Todd walked across campus to Wakeford Hall. After giving Eric an extra five minutes, Kim decided to leave. Todd, deciding he would go back to the dorm to rest, accompanied her.

"You sure you don't want to go back and wait for him?" Todd asked.

"He knows the deal," Kim said. "This will keep him on his toes."

"I learned an interesting fact about these leeches a while back," Tod said, changing the subject. "They don't like rough skin." He cracked a smile as he watched Kim become fascinated and repulsed at the same time.

"What do you mean, they don't like rough skin?" Kim asked.

"People and animals have a texture to their skin. Men, in general, have rough skin. Women don't. Leeches like to feed until they're fat enough to fall off, much like ticks. But my study has shown they don't particularly like to work for their food. They like to clamp down and feed. It's all quite natural. But if they have to fight or struggle to bite through the flesh, they're not too happy about it."

Kim scrunched her face up and shook her head. "You like them?"

"It took a while to get used to them. Now I enjoy working with them."

"I don't understand why God would make such a revolting thing. What purpose does it serve?"

"All living things serve a purpose to nature. Take your

boyfriend, for example. Now, why would a seemingly intelligent man keep a woman like you waiting?"

Kim laughed. "Oh, that's smooth."

"Was it?"

"No. Nice try though."

"I'm not trying to imply anything. I'm saying every time I run into you, you're waiting around for him. I wouldn't keep my girl waiting."

"The way you talk, it sounds like you don't keep ladies waiting much."

"What're you saying? I'm a player?"

"Hey, I'm callin' it as I see it."

"I never thought of myself as a player. I admit I have a certain suaveness, but I'm not a ladies' man at all."

A couple of girls walking past stared at Todd. One whispered to the other, and they laughed. Kim grinned as they swooned over him.

"Uh-huh." Kim turned to him. "I'm sure."

Todd stopped and placed his hand on her shoulder.

"I live a lonely life, Kim. Much of my time has always been toward my work and my cousins. They are the only constant in my life. I don't put much trust in anyone. My former family constantly berated and bullied me. And as for women, well, women have always been a distraction, and not in a pleasing way. After being hurt a long time ago, I keep my relationship with women strictly platonic, and even that's difficult." His voice trembled as he defended himself. "It's hard living the way I do."

"Todd, I wasn't trying to insult you. It's called an observation."

"You call me a player, yet your relationship wouldn't be one I call charmed."

"Okay, *that* was rude," Kim said. "First off, you don't know me well enough to make such accusations. Second, you come off as an easy-going guy. I did not think you would take what I said person-ally. Forget I said anything."

"Kim, wait."

"Whatever. See you around." Kim walked away.

"You touched a nerve. I didn't mean to bark at you," Todd said as he caught up to her. "Forgive me."

Kim saw the sincerity in his eyes behind the apology.

"Listen, you seem like a nice person, and I had fun playing foosball, but you need to check the anger issue you have."

"My cousins say the same thing to me. Can we be friends?" Todd put out his hand.

Kim hesitated, then shook it. "Friends." She looked into his eyes and became mesmerized by them. For a second, she thought they had changed color, slightly glowing crimson before turning back to a dark brown. A powerful migraine hit her. Todd's face flashed behind her eyes. She shook her head while blinking and stumbled a little, but regained her footing.

"You okay?"

She put her hands up as she took a deep breath and started to feel better. "I'm fine." Her gaze landed over his shoulder. "You finally showed up."

"Sorry, we had a blackout in the dorm and—" Eric stopped as Todd turned and looked at him. "What the hell is this?"

"Eric this is—"

"I know who this is," Eric interrupted as he moved forward on Kim, his gaze fixed on Todd. "What's the deal?"

"I don't think I understand what you mean," Todd replied.

"Then allow *me* to clarify," Curtis said, catching Todd off guard. "Why you with my man's girl?"

"I'm simply walking her back to her dorm." He looked back at Eric. "Wait, you're her boyfriend?"

"Yeah, that's exactly who I am!"

"Todd and I met on the train on the way back. I ran into him at the Commons while waiting for you," Kim chimed in. "Nothing's going on."

"Oh, so you knew she had a boyfriend and decided you were gonna walk her back to her dorm, huh?" Curtis said.

Todd turned to him. "Where do I know you from? Oh yes, the parking lot. So, you're what, his right-hand man or something?"

"Who I am is none of your concern."

"Curtis, c'mon. Let's walk Kim back to Wakeford."

"No doubt." Curtis stepped past Eric and took Kim gently by the arm. "C'mon."

"What's wrong with the two of you?" Kim nearly tripped. "Curtis, I can walk on my own!"

"I'm sorry." He let go and put up his hands. "You lead the way."

"I'll see you around, Kim," Todd said.

Eric stopped and turned to Todd in one fluid motion. "What did you say?"

"Eric, what's wrong with you?" Kim tugged on his arm to get his attention.

"I said I would see her around. And I was addressing her, not you." Todd looked at Curtis. "And I'm not talking to you either, so you don't need to comment."

Curtis stood speechless. He glanced at Eric who looked as though he were trying to figure out what to do. After a second, he started to walk back toward Todd. Kim tugged on his hand. Eric withdrew from her.

"Curtis, get Kim back to the dorm." Eric's eyes were fixed on Todd. "Ima keep the black knight here at bay."

Curtis encouraged Kim to walk with him. She complained as she started down the path.

"And you standing here is supposed to do what?" Todd said.

"Listen to me carefully, playa. I don't want to see you around my girl, you hear me? Stay away from her. Do yourself a favor, find another girl to get friendly with. Because if I catch you near her again, I won't be as nice as I am now," Eric said in an eerily calm tone.

"You know, maybe you should turn your attention to your girl and her needs and stop worrying about me." Todd folded his arms. "I mean, if you were where you were supposed to be tonight—"

Eric balled his fists and prepared to punch him. "I swear, you say one more thing—"

"What? What are you going to do?" Todd stepped forward. "You're not going to do a thing!" He smirked. "You think you can take me? Wanna try it?" He stepped closer. "Go ahead and put your hands on me and see what happens." He leaned in and whispered, "Please."

Eric relaxed his fists. He studied Todd's expression and wisely decided to back down. He took several steps back as he raised a single finger at him. Todd looked confused at the gesture. Then Eric turned and followed the path to Wakeford Hall.

———

"You have a lot of nerve. How dare you embarrass me like that?" Kim said. "Embarrass you? I'm rushing to get to you, and I see you walking off with some other guy." Eric pointed back down the path. "That guy, no less."

"Hey, um, I'm just gonna go back to the dorm," Curtis said. "Y'all have stuff to discuss."

"Good looking out, Curtis. I appreciate it."

"No problem. I'll catch up with you," Curtis said. He started to say something to Kim but changed his mind and walked away.

"A guy like that has a track record, Kim. I see him with you, and I know you're not talking classwork."

"You see me around another guy you think I'm cheating?"

Eric leaned back in surprise. "I never said you were cheating."

"You know, first you stand me up at the Commons, now you're acting jealous. I don't get it?"

"Where is this going? I was late because we had a brownout in the building. Why are you attacking me?"

"Because you're attacking my character. And Todd didn't mention a brownout."

"You want me to call Curtis back and confirm it? Or maybe ask Carmen to ask Dayton what happened."

"Eric, I'm not going to rest on the words of your roommate to confirm whether you're having electrical issues. The bottom line is you're starting to slide back to your old ways again."

"I'm late one time and now I'm reverting to my old ways. Why would you—?" Eric looked back and saw Todd still standing where they'd left him. "You were talking to him about us. Weren't you?" He turned back to her. "Why are you talking about our relationship with some guy you just met?"

"Eric, I'm talking about what I see happening."

"I don't want you seeing him again."

"What?"

"I forbid you to see him."

"Oh, you *forbid me* to speak to people. You don't tell me what to do." Her hands shook with anger. "You got some nerve."

"Wait a minute."

"No, Eric, I got it. You've made yourself loud and clear. I'll start by not being around you and your bitterness."

"What the hell is your problem all of a sudden?" Eric watched her walk away into the dorm.

He stood, stunned and confused. Then he glanced back down the path. Todd was gone.

CHAPTER THIRTY-EIGHT

Kim entered her room, rubbing her temple. Anger coursed through her body, up to her head. She hurried to her desk for some aspirin as the argument with Eric played over in her mind. Carmen came in and immediately, like a bomb going off, the headache intensified. For a split second, she thought she saw Todd's face flash before her eyes. Kim steadied herself against the desk.

"You okay?" Carmen said.

"Yeah, just a headache. I had an argument with Eric."

"Seriously? I thought things were going good between you two."

"They were. They are. Eric started throwing a fit over some guy he saw me with. We were just talking, and Eric flipped out."

"Well, I'm not even gonna comment." Carmen started to pass her, but froze. She turned and gazed at Kim. "What is that?"

"What is what?"

Carmen sniffed. "You don't smell that? It's like rotten garbage or something."

Kim tugged on her own shirt, sniffed, and shook her head. "I don't smell anything"

Carmen sniffed and then looked down at Kim's hand. She took her wrist, smelled it, and withdrew. "What did you touch? It's on your hand."

"I didn't touch anything." Kim sniffed her hand. "You know what it could be. I shook hands with that guy I told you about. He's been doing some experiments with leeches. Probably had some residue or something on his hand. Funny I don't smell it."

"He should wash his hands." Carmen started to go past her, but stopped. She started to sway and touched the side of her head. She stumbled sideways and collapsed onto her bed. Kim rushed to her. "Aye Dios Mio, I'm so dizzy."

"You need some water?" Kim tried to help her sit up, but Carmen fell back over. "I'm gonna get you something to drink."

"I need to lie here for a minute." She glanced at Kim. "Guess we're both having a night. I'm feeling drained. I had a conversation with my abuela I'm still coming off of."

"Leave it to the people we love," Kim quipped. "I'll be back. I'm gonna grab us some sodas from the vending machine." Kim hurried out of the room.

Carmen's dizziness washed away like a receding tide. Sluggishly, she sat up on her elbows. After taking a couple of deep breaths, she apprehensively swung her legs over the side of the bed. Stabilizing herself, she slid forward and her feet touched the floor. Immediately, she was drawn to Kim's desk.

An intense heat suspended in mid-air, approximately where Kim's head would be if she were standing there. Carmen extended her fist. The high temperature began to irritate her skin, but she didn't pull away. Her fist trembled as the hotness closed around it, almost crushing her. Fighting the desire to cry out in pain as the indents of fingers appeared above her wrist. Something had her in its grip.

"Let go of her!" Savannah screamed as she materialized next to her and reached out into the hot spot. "Git your hands offa her, I said." She brought up her other hand and seized something invisible.

Carmen could feel the grip begin to loosen as Savannah fought against the invisible force. She wrenched her fist away.

Savannah screamed like she were in pain as both her hands were lifted above her head. Then she was thrown across the room like a ragdoll.

Something struck Carmen in her chest, knocking the wind out of her as she fell to the floor.

A pane of glass in the window shattered. The heat dissipated.

Carmen stared up at the ceiling in shock. Savannah appeared alongside her and tried to help her up, but couldn't get a grip.

"You okay darlin'? I can't seem to help you," Savannah moaned.

"What the hell was that? A spirit?" Carmen whispered.

"It didn't feel like one of me. Its hands weren't normal. Felt like a lizard, one of them little reptile thangs." Savannah clasped her hands together. "So wrong."

Carmen caught her breath as she massaged her wrist, and she glared at the broken pane.

"Whatever it was, I think it followed Kim back here and was waiting for me. Waiting for the right moment." She turned to Savannah. "We can't do this alone. I don't care what my abuela said, I'm telling Dayton."

"What about Kim? What are you gonna tell her?"

"It's not after her. So, nothing."

"But—"

"I know what I'm doing. Kim knows enough, so if I need her, I'll ask her. I need Dayton for this."

"I can try to find whatever that thang was."

"You do that."

Carmen retrieved her cell, and typed Dayton a text message to meet her as she headed out the door.

CHAPTER THIRTY-NINE

Carmen arrived at the library steps where she had texted Dayton to meet her. She spotted Savannah walking toward the other side of the campus, presumably following the bad spirit that had invaded her room. A sense of relief washed over her, now that Savannah had something to occupy her time.

She went over in her head how she would break the news to him. The best way would be to come out and say it. Make it quick, like pulling off a Band-Aid and give him a moment to process it. Dayton was an open-minded guy. He wouldn't be quick to judge her. She believed it in her heart.

As she sat down to wait, a terrible thought occurred to her. If this evil on campus did follow Kim back to the room to get to her, what would it do if it came across Dayton? If it sensed they were boyfriend and girlfriend, would it attack him? Was she about to put him in danger?

"Stop thinking that." She buried her head in her hands. "I can handle this?"

"Can you tell me what *this* is?" Dayton said.

Carmen looked up and saw Dayton standing a few feet away. She stood and approached him. "You got here quick."

"I was already out walkin' when you texted me. I came right over." She hurried to him, wrapped her arms tight around his body, and hugged him. He returned the gesture. "You wanna finally talk about what's going on?"

"Hold me. It'll help me get my thoughts straight."

Dayton continued to embrace her. He didn't speak the entire time as she nuzzled her head into his chest. She sniffled before wiping the corner of her eye. He let go to look at her.

"What's wrong?"

Confusion and fear traveled through her. Carmen folded her arms against her body, then bit her bottom lip. She fought the urge to bawl as the soft, caring sound of Dayton asking, "What's wrong" echoed in her head. The sincerity of the question made her feel at ease about telling him. Her eyes widened as she took a deep breath and exhaled it slowly.

"Estoy muy asustada."

"What?" Dayton looked perplexed.

"Do you love me?" Carmen said.

"Do. . . do I love you?" Dayton shook his head. "I don't under-stand. . . why you would ask me that?"

"Just answer me," Carmen pleaded.

"Yes, I do love you," Dayton assured her.

Carmen closed her eyes and smiled. She dropped her arms in front of her as she relaxed. She lowered her head, opened her eyes, and stared at the ground for a moment before looking up at him.

"I've been going through something hard to explain. It affects the women in my family. I found out about it recently and with everything else I need to worry about this semester. . ." She took hold of his hands. "I don't know the right way to say this to you. So, I'm gonna come out and say it."

"Mami, what's wrong? What happened?" Dayton asked, concerned.

"I'm. . . I'm. . ." Carmen struggled to get the words out.

"You're what?"

"I'm a medium."

"You're a medium, what?"

Carmen saw the confusion in his eyes. She let go of his hands and stepped back. "A medium."

Dayton looked her up and down. "Okay, so you're a medium. So what? I don't care what size you are; I still love everything about you."

Carmen's mouth dropped open in shock, but turned into a smile as she burst into laughter. "Oh, baby. Que Lindo." She stepped back toward him. "Not a *size* medium. A medium as in, I talk to the dead. That kind."

Dayton smiled, but as Carmen laughed, he turned serious.

"Holy shit, Curtis was right!"

"What?"

"Curtis brought me a book he found. Said you were looking through it and it had all this stuff about mediums and ghosts, and he said you might be one!" He backed up. "I can't believe this. Oh my God, I mean Aye Mi Dios. That's what you say, right?"

"It's Aye Dios Mio. Dayton don't freak out. Please. The last thing I need–"

"I'm not freaking out!" He heard himself scream. "I mean, I'm sorry."

"Dayton–"

"Shh." He placed a finger to his lips, then put up his hand. "I need a minute." He backed away as Carmen watched him, trying to gauge a change in his response. "Curtis found a book about mediums. He said you may have left it in the aisle."

"You said that. Yes, I was reading it, but I need you to—"

"Hold on." He put his hands behind his head and turned his

back to her. He stared across the campus for a moment, then turned back. "I want to make sure I understand this. You speak to the dead?"

"Yes."

"Have you always spoken to the dead?"

"No."

"You said this recently started happening?"

"Yes. Shortly after we came back to school."

"Does anyone else know this?"

"Kim and my abuela, you're the last person I intend to tell."

Dayton stared at her, studying her face. "How did you learn you were a medium?"

Carmen rubbed her hands together. "My abuela told me about it running in my family. Also, a dead girl named Savannah started visiting me in the dorm. She's been trying to warn me about an evil presence on this campus."

"Is she here with us now?"

"No, she's out looking for something that attacked me in my room."

"You were attacked?"

"Well, not so much attacked as, well, grabbed."

"And you didn't think to call me right away?"

"And tell you what? A dark spirit was in my room and me, and a ghost were trying to figure it out?"

"Yes! I'm your boyfriend. You should feel comfortable tellin' me these things." He palmed his head with both hands. "What the hell did I just say?" His hands slid off his head and down to his sides. "This is for real."

"Yes. I wanted to tell you, but I wasn't sure if I could. Or if I should." Carmen took his hand. "I need you, Dayton. I need your stability. I need your help to try to figure out the basics of what I can do while I figure out how to stop whatever this is after me now. My abuela can only do so much. Savannah is still tryin' to figure herself out. Please, Dayton."

He walked to the steps and sat down. With his hands folded, he lowered his head and closed his eyes. He looked as though he were praying. Several seconds went by before he opened his eyes again, but he didn't look at her.

"It all makes sense now." He lifted his head. "The thing is, I can't help you."

Carmen folded her arms tightly again. "You can't or you won't?"

"I can't." He stood. "Because I don't know a damn thing about mediums. So, what Ima have to do is skip class tomorrow, go to the library and find every single thing I can to read so I can help you get through this." He shook his head. "I'm not letting you do this alone."

"I'll come with you."

"No. I need to go alone. I have a pretty good idea where to look and if Curtis sees you looking for those books again, he's going to start thinking what he told me was true. I'll get what I need and meet you at your dorm around lunch."

"There's more you need to know."

"One thing at a time. Let me deal with this first before we worry about me getting involved in everything else." He wrapped his arms around her and said, "Te Amo, Carmen."

Carmen covered her mouth. Tears of joy trickled down her face as she leaned in and kissed him. A great weight had been lifted off her shoulders. She turned her head to face the campus as she leaned into him again and saw Savannah watching them in the distance. She waved for Carmen to come to her.

"I need to handle something." She looked up at him. "Meet me at the fountain." She looked at Savannah.

Dayton looked too. "Medium stuff?"

"Okay, we're not gonna call it medium stuff." She chuckled. "But yeah. I see Savannah."

"That's a good start, telling me you see her now. I can start to get used to it."

"I'll meet you in ten."

Dayton kissed her and then started in the direction of the fountain. Carmen turned in Savannah's direction. She had disappeared.

"You told him?" Savannah appeared alongside her.

"Savannah, I swear, you're gonna stop doing that. It scares me." Carmen covered her heart.

"I'm not doin' it on purpose. Forgive me."

"Did you find the thing?"

"I lost it somewhere ova by that big black buildin'." She pointed to the science building. "I walked round tha sides but nothin'."

"Great. And yes, I told Dayton. He took it . . . He's gonna help."

They stood together in silence. Carmen could see Savannah wanted to comment, but instead, she turned her back to her.

"What is it?" Carmen asked.

"This thing that came at you t'night. It's got me feelin' some kinda way." She turned back to Carmen. "I feel scared."

"You can feel fear?"

"I can feel certain thangs. And right now, I feel scared for you because I haven't been honest with you." She started to reach out to touch Carmen, but retracted her hand. "Please forgive me."

"For what?"

"Say you forgive me. Just say it."

"Okay, I forgive you. What am I forgiving you for?"

Savannah hesitated, then said, "Zeborah is a vampire."

Carmen froze. Even though Maria had told her the possibility of Zeborah being a vampire, hearing it from Savannah sent chills down her spine.

"Say that again," Carmen said.

"Zeborah is a vampire. He is one of tha undead."

Goosebumps blanketed her arms as her heart raced. "How do you know he's a vampire?"

"After I died, I followed him. I saw him kill this girl and her friend near a motel not far from where I worked. He and Todd bit them and drank their blood. Kevin helped get rid of tha bodies."

"You're tellin' me three vampires are roaming around? Why are they here?"

"That there's the thang, I don't know. But I think it has to do with these crates they been haulin' around."

"What crates?"

"These big ole wooden crates filled with dirt. I can go find out what's in them for you."

Carmen shook her head. "You knew all this time and you had me tryin' to guess things and figure out what we're dealing with here? How could you, Savannah?"

"I told you what I thought you needed to know, darlin'. I'm still new to this."

Carmen stepped away from her. "I can't be around you right now. I think you should go. Leave me alone for a while. You've done enough for now."

"Please don't walk away from me. I can still help."

"Not tonight. I want to be with Dayton. If I need you, I'll call you." Carmen walked away. "Vampiros, fantasmas, los muertos vivientes. Dios me da fuerza. Esto es demasiado." Savannah tried to follow her but froze as an invisible force tugged at her stomach.

She touched her belly. The world around her spun out of control, then went black. A flash of light behind her eyes made her dizzy. After the darkness fell, she found herself standing in Todd's lab.

"Hello, Savannah," a voice said from behind.

She spun around. Kevin stood behind an open crate with a

gaping hole inside. She noticed dirt surrounding his feet. Savannah covered her mouth in shock.

"Where did you come from?"

"Even in death, you're a problem," Kevin seethed. "I need you gone, Savannah. You're a hindrance to my plans."

"I don't understand what you mean."

"The medium you have been in contact with. She has to come into her powers gradually. She doesn't need you confusing her and sending her on a wild goose chase."

"I am bound to her. She needs muh help."

"I have a use for her and you're getting in the way."

"What use?"

"Don't make me have to force you from this campus. We can do this the easy way or the hard way. The choice is yours."

Kevin leaned into the crate. Savannah watched as he lifted a decomposed corpse out and sat it up. It had long, faded hair and a dirty yellow dress.

"That's me," she breathed. "What happened to me?"

Savannah felt a pain in the pit of her stomach. She screamed and fell to her side as Kevin palmed the head of the corpse. He closed his eyes and whispered in Latin.

"What are you doin' ta me?"

———

Carmen met Dayton at the fountain. A calm rushed over her with relief. But as she picked up the pace, her name echoed from a distance.

"Carmen! Carmen! Help." Savannah shrieked.

Carmen stopped and looked around. "Savannah, what's wrong?"

"Help me! He's got me!"

"Who's got you?"

"Caaarmen!"

Carmen shut her eyes and concentrated on Savannah. In the darkness, she saw her in the distance, struggling to get free of something with grey eyes. Carmen started to run toward her, her hands outstretched. "I'm coming."

Savannah broke free and started running toward her as the entity pursued. She stretched out her hand, stumbled, but regained her footing and made a beeline to Carmen. The more she screamed, the more muffled her voice became. They were only a foot from one another when the entity lunged. It took hold of Savannah, bringing her down into the blackness.

Carmen skidded to a stop. The entity looked up at her. Its gaze penetrated her head, causing a massive migraine. She clenched her teeth, groaned in pain, and fell.

The entity stood; its body looked human in form but off-white, swirling like a tempest. It lifted Savannah from the floor by the back of her neck. Below the eyes, a mouth appeared, opening like a maelstrom. The center was a black pit. It leaned toward Savannah's neck while its gaze fixed on Carmen.

"No, don't." Carmen pleaded, as the pain in her head intensified.

"I'm sorry, darlin'," Savannah said.

The entity's mouth clamped down on Savannah's neck. There was a crack of thunder around them, and the mouth expanded as it began sucking Savannah into its body. She cried out in agony as it ingested her. Her body turned to ash. As the maelstrom closed, the entity nodded its head.

Carmen was shoved backward. Within seconds, she struck the ground hard. She opened her eyes and saw the night sky over her.

"Carmen, are you okay?" Dayton's face appeared above her.

"What?" She sat up. "Savannah." She scrambled to her feet and looked around in panic. "Savannah, can you hear me? It's

Carmen. Answer me." She shut her eyes. "No, no, no, no. Answer me. Where are you? I can't see you."

"What happened?" Dayton pleaded with her. He placed his hands on her shoulders. "Look at me. Tell me what happened."

Carmen opened her eyes and stared into his. "S-S-She won't answer me. Something's got her. This thing got Savannah."

"What thing?"

"I didn't get to her in time." Tears welled in her eyes. "I can't hear her anymore. She's gone."

———

Kevin's eyes rolled back white, and his fangs grew as he opened his mouth. He raised the palm of his hand, put it on the face of the corpse, and continued with the strange incantation.

Savannah's dematerialized form spewed out of him like breath leaving the body on a cold day.

Kevin's eyes returned to normal as he sighed with relief. He dropped the corpse back into the crate and covered it with dirt.

"Now to deal with Abuela."

CHAPTER FORTY

By 8 AM, the sun was fighting to punch through a radiation fog that had formed in during the early morning hours, blanketing the campus. A dense haze made it nearly impossible to see. Students went to breakfast, doing their best to stick to the concrete paths and avoid running into something.

Curtis spotted Carmen and Dayton sitting on the library stairs, waiting for him to arrive. Covering a yawn with his fist, he waved to them, his keys jingling in the loop around his finger.

"I want you to know you two gonna owe me for this," he said. "I'm not supposed to let anyone in who isn't part of the staff."

"We appreciate this," Carmen said.

"Whatever you need, I got you," Dayton said.

Curtis' eyes fell on Carmen's sullen face. She looked like she hadn't slept. "You don't look too good."

"Rough night."

Curtis turned to Dayton. "I'm gonna have to stay with you."

"No need to."

"I have to. You get caught and you're both gonna have problems and not just with the two security guards in there." He tilted his head to the side. "This way."

Carmen secured her backpack. Curtis led them down the stairs and around to a staff side door. They entered quietly.

They passed by a series of offices and elevators, took a left, and proceeded up the stairs to the first-floor level. The silence was deafening. The building had an eerie feel to it with no one around.

They followed him to a narrow hallway with eight doors, four on each side. He led them to the last one on the right and opened it. They found themselves in a study room, complete with a table and several chairs. Curtis closed the door.

"Okay, give me your list and I'll get the books for you."

"We don't have a list. We thought you could just leave us in the section, and we find what we need," Dayton said.

"I can't do that."

"You can take me then. I know where I have to go," Carmen said.

"Tell me what you need, and I'll bring it."

Dayton and Carmen exchanged looks. Carmen nodded.

"Okay, remember that book you showed me last night? We'll need a couple more of those on the subject," Dayton said.

"This really couldn't wait until the library opened?"

"She has a project coming up and needs to do an outline due today at 11. And after everything that happened. . ."

"Okay, I got you. I know what to look for. Stay here and don't make a sound. I'll be right back." Curtis left the room.

Dayton sat down. "Have a seat." He waited for her to sit. "How you feeling?"

"Not good. I spent half the night trying to find Savannah and the thing that took her."

"You gonna to try to call your grandma? Maybe she can help."

"I don't even know what to tell her or how to explain all this." Carmen rubbed her temple. "I'm so exhausted."

"Did you talk to Kim?"

"I thought about it, but she and Eric got into something, and you know her and her issues." Carmen took his hand. "Thank you for being here."

"You don't have to thank me."

"I got so mad at Savannah last night for holding out on me. I stormed off. I should have stayed with her." She chuckled. "I'm talking about her like she's real."

"She is real." Dayton took a seat across from her. "Doesn't matter if she's a spirit or not. She has a bond with you, right? That makes her real. What was she holding out on?"

Carmen hesitated. "Let's wait until we have the books. It's easier if I show you."

Dayton nodded. "Okay."

Curtis returned with a stack of seven books. He placed them on the table. Carmen removed the backpack, opened it, and took out two notebooks and several pens. She passed a notebook to Dayton. She took two books off the pile, looked at the covers, and placed one in front of her.

"I'll start with this one about the corporeal dead. You look through this on medium abilities. It should give you an idea on... well, you know what I need to know."

"How else can I help?" Curtis said.

"I think we're good. Can you give us the room? We won't leave."

Curtis glanced at the book in her hand and then at the stack. The book on the top, *Corporeal Myths, and Legends,* made him make a "hmm" sound. "Okay, I'll be back."

He left.

Carmen and Dayton worked through their books in silence. After an hour, Dayton realized Curtis had not come back to check on them.

"It's ten. Where do you think he went?"

"Who?"

"Curtis?"

Carmen put her pen down and stretched. "I don't know. You learn anything?"

"Quite a bit. Some of this stuff is scary. This says mediums not only can connect with the dead but with other forces as well. They can experience anything from intense headaches, chills, even blackouts, especially if the being is malevolent."

"They say what kind of malevolent beings?"

Dayton looked back at the book. "Restless spirits of those who did wrong when they were alive. Evil entities. And here is something about what you're reading about; the Corporeal dead. I have no idea what that is."

"It's the undead." She pushed her book over to him. "The second paragraph is what Savannah revealed to me. It's also what my abuela believes is passing through this campus. And I'm pretty certain, I came in contact with one yesterday in the library. I think he tried to make me forget."

Dayton read the page without any reaction. Then went back to his book, flipped to the glossary, found what he needed, returned to the page and compared the two.

Carmen sat back and watched Dayton's face as his lips moved, but nothing came out. He turned the page and read the rest. He ingested the information, then pushed the book out of the way. He retrieved one of the books he had already glanced through and set it between them.

"I," he paused to take a deep breath then looked up at her. "You believe there are vampires on this campus? That's what made you, I mean, tried to make you forget."

"It's a lot to take in, I know."

"Well wait, I'm not sayin' I don't believe you, but can I pose a theory? I found this." Dayton slid the book closer to her and pointed to the middle of the page. "An older and more experienced medium can hurt an inexperienced medium, especially if they are in tune with dark elements."

Carmen took the book from him to read the paragraph. "You think he's like a dark medium?"

"It's possible."

"Possible, but not likely. Savannah was sure of what she told me, and my abuela pretty much confirmed it. I have no reason to doubt either of them, Dayton."

"Okay." He looked around the table at the books. "Maybe if we keep looking we can find a, you know, reasonable explanation."

"You don't believe me. Do you?"

"Well." He turned to look at her. "I can believe in the spiritual. I mean, who hasn't had a run-in with a ghost or spirit or somethin', you know? But a vampire is a different kind of . . . It's hard to wrap my head around. All these books we been readin' is grounded in some kinda fact or reasoning. Vampires are, well, Hollywood."

Carmen stared at him in silence. She heard Maria's warning in her head about this moment.

"Dayton, what's on this table, no matter how far-fetched you think it is, is affecting me in some way. It also killed Savannah. And it's out there on our campus right now, probably looking to hurt me or some other poor student. Whether you believe in it or not, the point is it has to be stopped. So, either you're in on the whole deal, or you let me do this alone. But you can't half-ass this. You can't choose to believe one thing and not the other."

Dayton glanced at the books again. "Did Savannah happen to tell you who this vampire might be?"

"His name is Zeborah."

"The guy that hangs out with Todd?"

"Who's Todd?"

"Don Juan. The one who moved into our dorm." Dayton turned to her. "Eric's been having beef with him since he arrived."

"They're living in the dorm? Dayton, we have to tell someone."

"Tell who?"

"Campus security. The police. You have a killer living in your dorm." Carmen jumped up. "We have to go."

"Hold on." Dayton stood. "This is all speculation. We don't know for sure what they did or who they are."

"We know enough."

"All the information we know is from you being a medium and these books. You go callin' police or campus security accusin' them of murder, you'll have to tell them how you came up with it all. Think about what you're going to say," Dayton pleaded.

"You can back me up."

"I'm your boyfriend. No one will believe me because they'll think I'm protecting you. And your abuela can't help because she's not even here. The last thing I want is for you to get hurt in any way."

Carmen sank back in her chair. "We don't do anything?"

"We keep reading and learning what you can do. We figure out your weaknesses and how to guard against them from harmin' you. If they really and truly are vampires, they have been around long enough to know how to attack you." Dayton took her hands in his. "We get all that down, then we can make a move."

"We need to be cautious from this point on. Maybe we should see about taking over this room and working from here. It would keep me off campus and won't raise suspicions."

Dayton nodded. "Maybe Curtis can help us." He looked at his watch. "Let's go for a walk after this. I need to clear my head."

CHAPTER FORTY-ONE

Kim decided to play hooky from class. Her argument with Eric still lingered in the forefront of her mind and the best place to clear it was to hang out at her favorite hideaway in town, *Roland's Coffee House*. She packed a novel in her pocketbook, put on her coat, and left the room with thoughts of a Chamomile tea and a blueberry muffin.

She breathed in a lung full of fresh air. In the midst of her exhaling, her eyes fell on Eric seated at a bench. They locked eyes. He didn't move. Neither did she.

"We need to talk," he said.

"Talk about what, Eric?"

"What happened last night? You blowin' up at me like that."

"It's too early to do this right now."

"I'm not here to fight or argue. I want to clarify something I said about not wanting you to see Todd."

"You said forbid."

Eric folded his hands in his lap and glanced at the ground. He shook his head as he mumbled, "Yes, that's what I said." He leaned forward. "Kim, there is something wrong with this dude. If you had seen how he stepped to me, you would have thought you two had something going on."

"You think something going on with us?"

"What? No, I have no reason to think that, and I never have. I'm not jealous of none of these cats on campus. But he's a different story."

"You're jealous of him."

Eric approached her. "I don't trust him around you is what it is. He doesn't care you have a boyfriend, and it shows. Now I'll figure out a way to deal with him, but you? The way you went off on me . . . you gotta explain that."

Kim stared into his eyes, caught like a deer in headlights. She tried to search for the answer from within, but nothing came to her. She couldn't explain the split-second desire to defend Todd.

"I don't know. Saying you *forbid* me to do something. After all we've been through, you might as well have said you don't trust me."

"It wasn't about you."

"Fine, if you say so. Thanks for clearing that up. I gotta go."

"Kim."

Kim walked away, stopped, and looked back at him. "For the record, I'm not *interested* in him. He happens to be working on a fascinating science experiment that we got into a conversation about. I don't have any control over his behavior or how he is towards you. But I'm also not going to let anyone disrespect me."

"Wait a minute."

"I'll talk to you later if I feel like it." Kim disappeared into the haze on her way to the shuttle.

———

Roland's Coffee House had been designed to mimic a living room, with various sofas and high-back chairs, coffee and pedestal tables, and intimate lighting. Smooth jazz played over the speaker system, making for a relaxed atmosphere. Newspapers and magazines were available for customers to read, as well as ample sockets for laptop use.

Kim had been going to Roland's for solace since her sophomore year. The staff knew her so well that as she walked through the door, they immediately prepared her order.

She took the seat in a corner by the window. From the outside, one would have to get up close to the window to even see her. After settling into a large high-back chair, she held the mug of tea with both hands, sipped it, and began to relax.

Someone knocked on the window. She looked and saw Todd waving to her.

"Oh shit." She sat up and waved back. "How did he see me?" She followed him with her eyes as he went around to the door and waltzed in.

"Hey there." He took a seat in the chair across from her.

"Hey."

"How are you holding up?"

"Fine, I guess. What's up with you?"

"I had to pick up a few wires for the experiment," Todd explained. "I'm waiting for the store to open, then I can get what I need and head back."

"Oh."

"Hey, if I'm disturbing you, I'm sorry. I can go."

"No, no. You're fine. I didn't expect to run into anyone I knew from campus here."

An uncomfortable silence fell between them for close to a minute

"Listen," Todd broke the silence. "I didn't mean to cause any drama between you and your boyfriend last night. I have a way about me, that's. . . well, you have to know me to understand."

"What's done is done. You don't owe me anything." She sipped her tea. "Life moves on." Kim peered out the window.

A young African American man, maybe a year older than Eric, holding a cup of what she assumed to be coffee, stared through the window. His attention fixed on Todd before it shifted to her.

"I felt I owed you that much." Todd tried sounding sincere.

"Uh-huh." Kim stared at the young man, who inched closer. He mouthed the word "*mutherfucka*" before taking off, running across the small parking lot.

"Well, I'm gonna go. The store should be open by now. Um, how are you getting back to campus?"

"What?" Kim looked at Todd.

"How are you getting back?"

"Same way I got here. The shuttle."

"You want a ride back?"

"After what happened last night, Todd?"

"What? I'm offering you a ride back to the campus if you want it. I'll even drop you at the gate and keep going. I'm not going to drop you off in front of your dorm or anything."

"I don't need the gossip."

"Hey." Their eyes locked. "Why do you care what others think or say? You don't want the ride because you'd rather ride on the shuttle, fine. But if you're worried about what people might say because I'm dropping you off. . . I'm just being nice."

Kim leaned back. She could feel something strange happening between them. As though he were trying to force her to decide in her head so her mouth would speak it. She resisted.

"Why are you pushing the issue?"

Todd's eyes widened. "I guess you're not as honest as I pegged you for."

"Wait, what does that mean?"

"You said what's done is done. From the way you're behaving, I guess it's not true."

The weight of his words forced their way into her mind. Instead of resisting, she agreed with his sentiment. But in the recesses of her mind, she heard herself say, *don't let him guilt you into anything. You go by your own accord*!

"Todd, wait."

"Yes."

"Don't guilt me into riding back to campus with you."

Todd blinked and took a step back. "You're right, my apologies."

Kim sat back in her chair and sipped her tea. "If you pass back by and I'm here, I'll take the ride."

"See you later, then." Todd walked out. As he passed the window, he waved to her.

Kim started to eat her muffin, closed her eyes, and tried to relax.

CHAPTER FORTY-TWO

Todd walked to his car and kicked the back tire out of frustration. "I suspected her to be strong-willed, but didn't figure she could fight off my advances like that. She was weakened the night before but somehow, overnight, my effect on her wore off. Okay, it's a minor setback. A different approach is now necessary to get into her head."

He opened the trunk and removed a shoebox filled with dirt. Digging until he found a leech, he used his free hand to roll up his sleeve then he placed it on his arm to feed.

While lowering the sleeve, thoughts of how to get one to bite Kim so his blood could transfer to her consumed him. A blood link would help his case. The thoughts were interrupted by the sound of a cobalt black Dodge Charger going by. The windows were tinted, making it impossible to see inside. It stopped, idled for a moment before driving away.

Todd watched the Charger drive away, then put the box on the front seat before heading toward the electronics store.

A half-hour later, as he returned to the car, Kim emerged from *Roland's*. He rushed to get in and rolled up his sleeve. Squeezing the leech near the head, he removed it from his arm and put it back in the box.

"Hey," Todd called out. "Still want that ride?"

Kim hesitated for a moment and opened the door. Todd picked the box up and held it as she got in.

"What's that?" she asked as she put the seat belt on.

"It's one of the large leeches. I'm transplanting it into some new soil. You take a look if you want." They started to drive as she opened the box and saw it lying on top of the dirt. "Pick it up."

"You must be crazy," she chuckled.

"I already fed it. It's not going to bite you. Slide your hand under it and hold it from the bottom."

Kim slipped her hand under the leech and held it in her palm. The creature didn't move.

"Sorry for all the drama last night," Todd said.

"What?"

"I haven't been having a lot of good experiences with the men on this campus. I have a particular way about me. Rubs other guys the wrong way. I speak my mind and well. . . I'm sorry."

"Yeah, well, I get that you're you, but you were really out of line. And things got real. . . never mind, it's not any of your business." She glanced at him. "It might be better if we didn't spend any more time together like last night."

"You think so, huh?"

"If it's gonna cause these kinds of issues, yeah, I do."

"That why you decided to ride back with me, to tell me this?"

"Out of respect."

"How is this out of respect?"

"Would you rather I walk around campus ignoring you? Acting as though you don't exist? Wouldn't be right. And it's not fair to Eric for me to be seen running around with you, with it being known you two don't like one another."

Todd cracked a smile, nodded, and said, "I understand both

sides of this deal. He doesn't know me and got jealous of seeing us together. You were being practical. Trying to convince him nothing is going on, but he's being protective of you. At the same time, you two aren't married. And even if you were, you're still your own woman. You have the right to make friends, go places, and experience life. You live it how *you* want, not like how others want you to."

Kim glanced at him. "It's not always easy."

"Yes, it is. If more people took control of their lives and didn't let other people dictate their actions, living would be much better." He stopped at a traffic light and turned her. His eyes darted to the leech in her hand, then back to her face. "Look, you're a cool person to be around. I like you. I'm not trying to take you from your man, but at the same time, I'm not going to let someone else's jealousy dictate my life."

A car behind them beeped its horn. Todd raised a middle finger and proceeded under the traffic light. From the corner of his eye, he could see her looking at him with a wary expression. He realized he had let his emotions get the best of him.

"You okay?" she asked.

"Sorry, I just get fired up sometimes," he said calmly. "I get it. I'm not the easiest person to get along with, and I don't try to fit in. But—"

"Ow!" Kim jerked in the seat as she extended her hand, making a claw. "I think this thing is biting me."

Todd drifted to the shoulder of the road and parked.

"Let me see." He took her hand in his. With his free hand, he held the leech. "Stay still." The head stuck to her hand briefly before it let go. It left a bloody circle where its mouth had been. "He did. I'm so sorry. It doesn't look like it was feeding. Probably bit you out of instinct."

"Great. Let's get back to campus so I can clean this. I'm not going to get sick. Am I?"

Todd removed a napkin from the glove compartment and handed it to her. "No, you'll be alright." Todd placed the leech back in the box and put it on the back seat. "I guess meeting me later for a game of foosball is out of the question, huh?"

"Seriously?"

Todd laughed. Kim couldn't hold it in and laughed with him. He drove away from the shoulder and continued to the university.

At the gate, he waited for the automated arm to go up. A Charger sat behind him.

Todd parked by the shuttle vans. He got out and went to open the door for her and Kim scanned the area.

Was she checking to make sure no one saw us?

"Thanks for the ride."

"No problem." He shut the door. "Hope to see you later for that game."

"We'll see."

Todd got in and back in drove to Chambers Hall.

CHAPTER FORTY-THREE

Kevin used the fog as cover to travel to the roof of Wakeford Hall, the medium book tucked in his coat. He had no concern about not being invited inside. Dormitories were some of the rare places where vampires didn't need an invitation to breach in since no one person claimed occupancy.

Finding the side exit door locked, it didn't take too much strength to pry it open. Then stealthily make his way down the stairwell to their floor. Cracking the next door wide enough to see down the hall.

Carmen was leaving her room. Kevin counted to ten then, moving faster than the eye could see, he was at her door. Gripping the knob and with applied pressure, he leaned into the door and pushed up. The door opened easily, allowing him to slip in, shut it, and glance around the room, trying to figure out which side was hers.

Starting with the dresser drawers and neatly lifting clothing in hopes of finding personal letters tucked away with names on them. Then, moving to search both desks. Rearranging papers at first but making sure that he returned them to their rightful place.

In the bottom drawer of the desk, he found a shoebox. Upon opening it, an envelope addressed to Carmen from Maria sat atop a pile of pictures. "*New York City,*" he said to himself. He lifted the envelope, and his eyes fell upon a picture of Carmen and Maria together at Christmas. "*You must be grandma. I'll have to make it a quick trip to pay you a visit. No telling what Todd would do with me gone too long.*"

Once Maria's face was committed to memory, the items were placed back in the box and shut it. He removed the book from his coat, placed it on top of the box, and put everything back under the drawer.

Footsteps outside the door caught his attention, and he rushed to the closet. Before he could get the door open, the footsteps passed by. He heard voices murmuring in the hall. The residents were up. Kevin waited by the room door, listening until the coast was clear.

Kevin left out the same way he came in. Once on the roof, he noticed the fog had lifted. With the campus coming to life, he couldn't risk climbing down without someone spotting him. As he contemplated his next action, a loud screeching noise erupted by the front gate. His speed ability got him to the edge of the roof in time to see smoke coming from the back tires of a Dodge Charger as its engine revved.

CHAPTER FORTY-FOUR

The security guard jumped back into the booth as a car smashed through the automated arm, sending splinter projectiles in multiple directions. It sped toward Chambers Hall.

"This is the north gate. A driver has blown through here in a black–"

The Charger's brakes locked, sending the car into a loud skid cutting off Todd's Mustang. Michelle scurried to get out of the way as she crossed the road. Others watched with curiosity as the car came to a smoky stop a foot away from them and sat idling.

"Hey, jackass!" Michelle yelled. "People are walking here!"

Todd got out of his car as the Charger's driver's side door opened. Robert stepped out. Neither man said anything to the other.

Robert ducked back into the car and emerged with a nine-millimeter handgun and magazine. He slapped the magazine into the gun, racked the slide back, and took aim at Todd.

"Oh shit, gun!" Michelle shouted.

Todd winked out of the way seconds before Robert squeezed off six shots, striking the Mustang.

The security guard ran to the action. Robert turned, and without saying a word, took aim.

Michelle darted across the road and tackled him as Robert fired right above the guard's head, missing him by inches. The two stayed down until Robert turned his attention back to Todd.

As they scrambled to their feet, Todd circled to the back of his car and peered around the front bumper. Robert still had the gun raised as he approached him.

Robert spotted Todd. He fired twice, and the bullets struck the taillight, shattering it. Todd leaned back and stayed out of sight. Robert fired six more shots at the side of the car. Once he was empty, he slipped the magazine out and let it hit the ground. He purposely waited to reload a fresh magazine.

He wanted Todd to make a run for it.

———

Kevin seized the moment and leapt down from the roof. He ran toward Chambers Hall and watched in horror as Robert removed another magazine from his back pocket and slapped it in. Todd started to make a run for it. Robert opened fire again. Students scattered and screamed as the air filled with the odor of gun smoke. Robert kept missing. Kevin could tell he wasn't taking time to aim despite the fact he had the gun pointed at Todd.

"What the hell is he doing?" Kevin wondered.

Todd stumbled onto the steps as Robert headed toward him.

"I'm going to kill you all!" Robert yelled. "You're dead men. You hear me?"

He opened fire at him again. A bullet hit Todd in his calf, but he never went down. He cried out and limped, but he regained his footing and bolted.

Kevin smelled garlic in the smoke. Robert had laced the

bullets with it. Kevin's eyes turned red as he launched himself into a tree across from Chambers Hall.

———

"Jesus Christ. . . Run!" a student yelled from inside the Chambers Hall vestibule as Todd rushed in and tried to bar the doors.

Robert climbed the stairs to Chambers Hall, the gun now down by his side. He smiled like a man possessed as he saw Todd through the glass. He raised the gun and aimed.

"Stop!" a security guard shouted. "Lower your weapon."

Robert turned, took aim, and fired a single shot grazing the guard's shoulder. The guard fell backward, then scurried behind a nearby tree.

"Shit," Robert mumbled. He turned back to the front door and kicked it.

The door didn't budge.

Todd backed away and raced to the stairs. Robert fired at him through the window and grazed him in the arm. Todd changed direction and went into the office.

Sirens blared in the distance.

Robert ignored them. He punched the glass, cutting his knuckles, and reached inside. Finding a trashcan blocking the door, he knocked it over, pushed open the door, and burst into the dorm.

Robert turned to the office and saw Todd in the corner. David stood on the other side, too scared to move. Robert turned the gun on him.

"Run."

David bolted from the office and went out the front door. Robert aimed at Todd. Someone grabbed him from behind. A pair of sharp teeth clamped down on his shoulder. He cried out in pain and began shooting.

"Run. Get to the room." Kevin screamed. "I got him."

Todd crossed the hall and disappeared down the stairs while Kevin held on to Robert. He heard the police cars pulling up to the dorm outside.

"Why attempt this?" Kevin said.

"Dwain is dead. I have no vested interest in this."

"They're going to lock you up. Once they do, you're no longer any use to me."

"Then kill me. Let me be with my brother."

"Inside. The gunman is inside!" David said to the police.

"If I do this, you have to promise to help me one last time. After you're dead. Then I'll release you from our agreement."

"You have my promise. One last time."

"You cannot die by my hand for this to work." Kevin turned him around and touched his forehead to Robert's. "I bind your spirit to me. Rest shall only come once your oath is fulfilled."

Kevin shoved him. Robert raised the gun and aimed. Kevin backed up as Robert stepped out into the vestibule.

"You bit me. I'll come back as one of you!"

"I bit muscle, not vein. You will die. See you soon." Kevin disappeared into the stairwell behind him.

Robert fired five shots at the door as he crossed the vestibule. He paused halfway as he caught movement out of the corner of his eye. He turned and observed a deputy with his gun drawn.

"Put the weapon down on the floor right now," he commanded.

Robert spotted two more officers and realized he couldn't escape. The effects of Kevin's bite coursed through his body. Numbness crept down his left arm, followed by a powerful pain in his gut. He doubled over and vomited blood. Fear started to set in as he became aware he was dying. Fighting against the pain, he stood erect, aimed the gun at the deputy, and opened fire.

Robert didn't stop until he had emptied the entire magazine. And he didn't reload. He dropped his gun as bullets struck his body from multiple officers returning fire. Within seconds, he was dead.

CHAPTER FORTY-FIVE

Maria exited the small elevator in her prewar apartment building with her shopping cart in tow. Once she cleared the lift, the door closed. The sound of metal hitting against metal echoed through the hallway. Leaning on the cart, she began to push it toward her apartment at the end of the hall, past a flight of stairs. It seemed a mile away. Her day had been eventful, first Mass, followed by lunch with a friend and finally food shopping. *I still have to call Carmen back about the shooting.* Carmen had been so shaken up about it, she neglected to bring up the issue with her abilities.

Stopping short of the stairs to get her keys from her purse, the effects of her exhaustion that started to overtake her was interrupted by a chill that went through her and crept into her head. It lingered only for a moment.

"Are jou trying to contact me?" she said, suspecting it was a spirit and waiting for it to pass through her. "Jou want to talk?"

Nothing happened. Maria continued to push the cart toward her apartment and glanced up the stairs as she passed them. A nagging feeling someone would be standing there caused her stare. Her cart struck something, forcing her to turn to look.

Kevin stood before her, his eyes glowing crimson. "Buenos Noches, Maria."

Maria froze as he reached out with a single finger and placed it over her lips.

"Don't speak," He drew back his hand. He bore his fangs, "You know what I am? Nod if you do?"

Maria nodded. She tightened her grip on the handle of the cart.

"I need for you to listen to me very carefully." He took a step back. Maria crossed herself. "Carmen. I need her. The abilities she possesses are an asset to my mission."

"What mission? What have jou done to her?" Maria spoke above a whisper.

"I don't have time to get into that. Rest assured she is fine. But your so-called help is no more than a hindrance and I have come to insist you cease providing her guidance."

"No."

Kevin sighed. "I wish I had the time to press upon you the importance of why I need you out of the way, but I don't." He stepped forward, leaned over, and took hold of the sides of the cart. "I will implore to your age and wisdom and state again, cease any assistance to Carmen."

Maria pushed on the cart hard. "I will help my Carmensita in any way possible. Jour evil is not as strong as jou believe it to be."

Kevin closed his eyes. Maria started to feel a headache coming on fast. Within seconds, it was as if her skull were on fire. She let go of the cart, held the sides of her head, and stumbled back a few steps. Kevin opened his eyes. After several seconds, her pain went away. Her eyes widened with surprise.

"You've never encountered someone like me, have you? I can control your ability to feel my presence. I was the spirit you thought passed through you. I have a lot of knowledge about mediums because I am also one." He nodded. "Yes, Abuela, I have the ability as well. And I am the best chance for your Carmen to defeat the evil on campus. With you in my way, she will certainly die."

"I cannot abandon her. And how do I know jou won't corrupt her?"

"You don't."

"Then I can't."

"Then you leave me with only one choice."

"Jou kill me and—"

"Kill you? No, killing you would only upset Carmen, and that wouldn't be advantageous to me." He pushed the cart out of the way. "Forgive me, Abuela, this is going to hurt."

Kevin brought her down to the floor and covered her mouth. Maria tried to shut her eyes. He pressed his fingers into her cheeks and her eyelids opened. Locking his eyes with hers, he forced her to stare directly into his pupils without blinking. As he made his own dilate, hers expanded. He spoke without moving his lips. His words invaded her consciousness.

You're going to call Carmen and tell her she's on her own. You will tell her there is no more you can do to help her.

A loud pop went off in Maria's head. She could feel his words buzzing in her head, followed by the sensation of a thousand tiny needles scratching over her brain. She tried to drive him out, but he pushed back. "No," she said into his hand. She fought back in her mind. *Get out of my head.*

Stop fighting me. Let. It. Happen. Kevin kept repeating his demand.

Maria stopped struggling. His words melted into her brain. She shouted. "Get off me. I have to call my Carmen!" She repeated it several times before she started to physically fight back.

He stood and backed away. "You have to make an important call, don't you?"

Maria got to her feet. She staggered a bit as she faced him. Her eyes widened, and she yelled, "Intruder in the building! Intruder in the building!"

Locks began to turn up and down the hall. Kevin glared at her. Just as he started to speak, a door creaked open behind him. He bolted down the stairs.

A young African American woman stepped out into the hall and, seeing Maria in distress, rushed to her aid.

"What happened? Are you okay?"

Maria glanced at the stairs, turned to the young woman, and said in a daze, "I have to call my Carmen."

CHAPTER FORTY-SIX

In the hundred years Bruckner had stood, there had never been an attack on the grounds. Robert's assault changed the way people were allowed on campus. Security went on high alert. Two guards were put on post at the main gate, and they allowed no one on campus without current valid identification. A retention block had been positioned to prevent cars from speeding onto the campus, and an officer from the sheriff's office stood on duty, along with security.

For the time being, the south gate stayed on locked down. No students were allowed in or out of the south end of the campus until further notice.

———

The headlights of Michelle's car fell on the sign on the closed gate, and she let out a frustrated scream. Michelle had forgotten the back gate closed early and now was forced to make a U-turn and headed back down the road. The grey clouds made dusk feel much later.

Without warning, a deer bolted out in front of her car, causing her to mash down on the brakes. The car stopped inches from hitting it in the rear. The animal stared at her briefly, looked to its right, let out a loud snort before darting off into the woods. While leaning back in her seat, clutching her chest, something tapped on her passenger window, compelling her to look.

A strange animal with hellish red eyes stood at the window. A hybrid; half-man, half-bat with talons for fingers, a small flat nose, and ears. It opened its mouth, exposing two long sharp canines, and let out a cry like a wounded seal.

Michele let out a bloodcurdling scream. She slammed on the gas. The creature smashed the glass with its head and crawled into the car. It straddled her, pinned her to the seat, and bit down into her neck.

The car lurched forward and sped up. As the creature jostled on top of her, its back pressed against the steering wheel, causing the car to weave across the road. It opened its mouth long enough to allow a blood-soaked Michelle the opportunity to uppercut it. The blow only succeeded in making it angry. It bit down again.

The car left the road, sped through the woods, and crashed into a large tree.

She and the creature were pinned against one another. With its jaw locked on her neck, it continued to feed until she didn't move anymore. It let go and stared at her as the life left her twitching body. She spat up a glob of blood before her head slumped to the side.

The creature placed its talons on the shoulders of the seat and pushed. A loud crack resounded as the seat fell back, laying out like a bed with Michelle looking as though she were napping. It let out an inhuman screech before it crawled out of the window and scurried off into the woods as the rain came.

Kevin stood before Michelle's car, staring at her corpse through the windshield. As Zeborah approached, dragging

Rakim's sleeping body behind him, Kevin pointed a single finger at Michelle.

"After I promised LaChard this would not happen again." He lowered his hand. "You had one job. Just one. Do you realize the danger you put us all in?" He looked at Rakim. "Where'd you find him?

"Hafa mile that way." Zeborah pointed in the direction he had come from. "Passed out under a tree."

"Effects of gorging himself on youthful blood. Get him back to the cabin and I don't care what you have to do. Bolt him to the floor if you have to. He cannot get out again." He turned back to Michelle's body. "It's going to take me some time to clean this up."

"She's gonna be missed, isn't she?"

"I'll figure out how to cover this up. Go take care of him."

Zeborah hoisted Rakim onto his shoulder and made his way back to the cabin. Kevin turned to the vehicle, removed Michelle's body, and carried her deeper into the woods to bury her.

CHAPTER FORTY-SEVEN

Thanks to the botched attempt on Todd's life, the police discovered he and the Rucker brothers were behind the fires that nearly destroyed two buildings at Huntington. The police questioned Todd for three hours trying to get answers as to why Robert tried to kill him, but his ability to artistically dodge questions proved frustrating.

Three days after the shooting, they brought Kim in for questioning, since one student reported they had seen her with Todd moments before. Eric found out after Debra, who witnessed her getting into a police cruiser, told him in front of Dayton and Carmen. But Kim provided no help for the police, and upon her return to campus, Eric was waiting. Dayton and Carmen stood by and observed a surprisingly calm Eric listen to her explain what she told the police.

"So now what?" he said.

"That's it. They don't need to speak to me anymore," she said.

"Okay, why?" He stopped talking, shook his head. "I." He folded his arms. "At this point, whatever I say now is gonna start something."

"What do you mean?"

"I can't understand why you were in his car to begin with. There's a shuttle bus you could've taken back."

"It was an innocent ride. Don't make it into something it's not."

"This fool has people tryin' to kill him." Eric grew testy. "God only knows what he's into and you're pretty much telling me to let it go? I can't."

"Eric, I'm tired. I don't feel like talking about this anymore. Why can't you just be happy I'm safe and leave it at that?"

"Because I got the feeling even after this, he's not gonna leave you alone. Especially after word gets out you didn't roll on him to the police." Eric stepped closer to her and lowered his voice. "I don't know why he's got his eye on you, Kim, but you need to stay clear of him."

"I'm not going down this road with you again." Kim walked away.

"Why you?"

"What?"

"Why does he keep tryin' to get next to you? He knows you have a boyfriend, but he keeps tryin'. Why?"

Kim walked back to him. "What are you trying to say?"

"I'm not tryin' to *say* anything. I just find it odd after I confronted him and had a conversation with you. You two manage to find one another off campus and he talks you into getting a ride from him."

"You think I'm cheating on you?"

"I didn't say—"

"You're implying it."

"Kim?" Carmen stepped between them. "Is it possible you said something to him that made him think he could pursue you?"

Kim's glare shifted to Carmen. "Seriously?"

"Yes."

"I thought we were girls."

"Chica, you know I would go to the ends of the earth for you. I'm not standing here pointing fingers or blaming anyone. But the truth of the matter is Todd is up to something no good, and you've caught his eye. I've seen this happen back home. Some guy gets it in his head, a particular girl is his and he'll do anything to possess her, especially if she's not interested in him. All she has to do is acknowledge his presence, and he thinks she wants him." Carmen took Kim by the hand, led her away from Eric, and gestured for him to stay back. She spoke softly. "You have to stay away from Todd."

"Nothing's going on between us except what's going on in Eric's mind."

"This isn't about Eric. There's something not right about Todd. I can feel it. You need to cut ties with him and do it sooner than later. Evil walks with him."

"Is this some of your medium talk?"

"If I say yes, will you listen to me?" Carmen didn't wait for a response. "I have never steered you wrong, chica. In all the time we have known each other. Don't listen to me because of my ability. Listen to me as your friend."

Kim stared into Carmen's eyes. She saw the worry and sincerity in them. She took a deep breath, sighed, and turned to walk away.

"I'll see you later," she said.

Carmen watched Kim until she went into Wakeford before she turned to Eric and Dayton.

"Eric, I'll stay on her about this."

"Whatever, Carmen. I think I need to handle this another way." Eric glanced at Dayton. "I'm going to deal with this fool myself."

"What?" Dayton and Carmen said in unison.

"It's obvious the only way to solve this problem is to have a one-on-one with him for the last time."

"N-N-N-N-No bro, you don't want to do that." Dayton's voice filled with panic. "I know you're pissed off, but trust me, this is not the way to go."

"Dayton, man, I don't see no way around this."

"After he just got shot at you, wanna go and do something stupid like confronting him over Kim?"

"Who are you calling stupid?" Eric replied. "Kim is my girl and I'm not—"

"Okay, I didn't mean you were stupid. I'm sayin' the situation is. Todd's a . . . well, he's. . ." Dayton looked at Carmen.

"Eric, let me talk to Kim. I can convince her to stay away from him," Carmen pleaded.

"You can do whatever you want. I'm not letting this go on." Eric turned as Dayton attempted to grab his arm but missed. Eric stormed off to Chambers Hall.

"Let me go try to talk some sense into him. Call me if you need me, babe." Dayton kissed Carmen, then hurried after Eric.

"Watch what you tell him," she called after him.

Her cell phone vibrated in her pocket. She saw Maria's number and pressed a button on the side of the phone to send the call to voicemail. A second passed, and the phone vibrated again. She answered it.

"Abuela, I can't talk right—"

"Carmen, it's mom."

"Mom? Why are you calling from Abuela's phone?"

Isabel paused and then said, "Don't get excited. Abuela is in the hospital. She's been there for two days."

Carmen stopped walking. "What?"

"She's fine. It's nothing too serious. She had some kind of episode in her hallway. One of her neighbors found her screaming your name in hysterics. No one knows what triggered the outburst and she wouldn't say why she wanted you, but she wouldn't stop. They had to call an ambulance to take her to the emergency room. Doctors think she might be showing early signs of dementia."

"I'm coming home."

"There's nothing you can do by coming home. She's fine right now. They have her under observation." Isabel paused before continuing, "She wanted me to tell you something. I don't know what it means. . . she said she can't help you anymore and something about being careful of who talks to you. Do you know what she means?"

Carmen stood silent, taking in the words Maria left for her. She knew she and Isabel would get into a fight if she tried to fill her in on what happened up to this point.

"She's helping with an assignment about Old San Juan," Carmen lied. "You know how Abuela feels about watered-down history. I meant to call her back about it and, well, I kinda flaked on it."

Isabel sighed. Carmen knew she bought the lie. "Even in a moment like this, she's still thinking of you. You have to do better by her."

"I know, mom," Carmen said, putting on the best guilty voice she could. "I'm sorry. What room is she in? I'll call her and apologize."

"She needs her rest right now. I'll let her know I spoke with you." Isabel mumbled something in Spanish. "I'll check with the doctors to find out the best time for you to speak to her."

"Please do."

"Te amo, Carmen. I'll call you soon." Isabel ended the call.

CHAPTER FORTY-EIGHT

Carmen changed direction and headed for the rear of the dorm. Her mind raced as she thought about Maria in the hospital. Deep down, she knew it wasn't dementia. Nervousness set it, followed by a feeling of abandonment.

Both Savannah and Maria were now out of her life. If she didn't know better, she would swear some force out there was taking out those who could aid her. And while Dayton was ready to step up and help, he wasn't ready to be a major player yet. Especially now, with Eric deciding he wanted to challenge Todd.

With her arms folded and head tucked down, she picked up her pace, rushing to get to a lone bench near the water. She collapsed on it and had one good cry. All her anxiety came out in those couple of minutes she allowed herself to be vulnerable. Finally, she wiped her eyes with the back of her sleeve and exhaled hard.

"That's better," she said, fanning her eyes with her hands. "I gotta figure out the next step."

"I know the feeling all too well," a soothing male voice said from behind.

A hand landed on her shoulder as she started to turn. A sudden jolt, like she hit her funny bone, passed through her. It traveled into her head, causing a twinge followed by a cold sensation.

Don't turn around. Can you hear me? She heard a voice in her head. She nodded. *Very good. Close your eyes and concentrate on my voice, and use your internal voice to speak. The one you use to think up answers to questions.*

Carmen closed her eyes and began to concentrate. *Do you hear me?*

I hear you. That's good, you learn fast.

Who are you?

Who I am is not important right now. What is important is what happens next. First, understand I did not want to come to you like this. I had other plans, but the shootout has forced me to take other measures. By now you know Savannah and your abuela can no longer help you.

Are you the reason they're gone?

Yes. I will take their place to prepare for what is coming. They're not proficient in dealing with this kind of evil. The voice paused then said, *First thing you need to know is the dead coming to you are linked, exclusively, to a specific individual. In this case, all who have been in contact with Todd. Not all his victims will seek you out, only those who desire to see an end to his evil.*

Whatever help you decided to give Savannah when you two met brought you into this fold. You are bound now to see this through, even with her gone. Until the threat is vanquished, you have no choice. The voice paused again. *A plan was already set in motion to stop Todd, but got unexpectedly interrupted. It needs to be set right again, and I require your assistance.*

No.

I beg your pardon.

I don't know who or what you are. I am not helping you. How do I even know what you told me is the truth?

The voice stopped speaking. Two cold hands took hold of her head from behind. Carmen flinched from the touch. Gradually, the hands warmed up. The heat sensation traveled through her. The fingers of the right hand caressed her hair slightly, soothing her.

"I have left a gift for you. In your room, under your bed. Only you will be able to read it. The words will make no sense to anyone else. Consider it a gesture of goodwill on my part, which is something I rarely give. Do not take it for granted like the two others I tried to help, and they misused it."

"You were in my room? How do you even know where I stay?" Carmen said.

"Oh, I know a great deal about you. Remember this as well." The fingers pressed into her head and the warmth became an agonizing headache. She wanted to scream but couldn't find her voice. "I can break your mind. I can go in here and cause memory loss, stroke, and even death. Make no mistake, medium, my use for you is a means to an end." Her body was pushed forward as pain radiated into her gums and teeth. "You will only feel this pain from me *if* I want you to. I am watching you and I can appear at any time. You won't know I'm there." The fingers released their grip from her head. Carmen fell onto the cold ground. "See you soon, medium."

The pain in her head dissipated. Within seconds, she scrambled to her feet and spun around, looking for her assailant. There was no one in sight.

CHAPTER FORTY-NINE

Carmen nearly took the door off the hinge as she burst into her room. Kim had gone. She rushed to her desk, opened the bottom drawer, removed her keepsake shoe box and found the book sitting on top. She sat on the floor, opened a random page, and started to read a part on mediums being in the presence of demons. Particularly how not to communicate with them. She flipped the pages back to the beginning and looked within the tablse of contents for anything on vampires.

Her eye caught the section entitled undead. She turned to the page and on the back, she read the information.

Vampires: *These creatures walk the thin line between the living and the spiritual plain. This makes them susceptible to a medium's presence. The spiritual half wants to connect, but the living portion wants to avoid it. For this reason, mediums suffer painful reactions such as headaches, muscle torsion, and, in some instances, blackouts.*

While they are considered immortal, they can be killed by way of fire, sunlight, and heart trauma.

Mediums, however, pose another threat to vampires through telepathy. A well-trained and experienced medium can get into the mind of a vampire and confuse their thoughts by appealing to their spiritual side. It's worth noting this process works better on older vampires whose age has worn them down. Younger vampires will mentally fight back. The advantage to this is due to their youth and arrogance, they can leave a window of opportunity for the medium to breach their minds. The disadvantage is they will viciously fight back physically and mentally to expel a medium.

An inexperienced medium is well-advised not to challenge a vampire of any age.

Refer to the section on telepathy and the undead for guidance on how to tap into telepathic abilities.

There was more, but none of it gave a clear path to battling vampires. She searched the book for telepathy, found the small section on vampires, and started to read.

On Vampires – *Getting inside the head of a vampire is difficult, but not impossible. It requires solid concentration. Your mind cannot drift even for a second or the vampire will attack. Like calling a spirit while in a calm and semi meditative state. . . .* I know how to do that. *. . . must be out of reach of the vampire. Too close of proximity and it can get hold of you. Their touch, combined with their ability to get inside your head, will make it impossible to fight back as your body will be under attack physically and mentally.*

At your distance, the goal is to penetrate the mind. Concentrate, first on making a mental link with the vampire. You want to throw it off by speaking to it telepathically. It will be confused by your voice and will try to then form a connection. Because their abilities are predatory and they're used to attaching weaker minds to make their prey more susceptible, connecting with yours will be difficult. Your mind will be on the defense. As they will try to acclimate themselves to your telepathy pattern, this will be the window you need to get inside their mind. You will know you have achieved this when their voice resounds like an echo and your mind feels like it's on ice . . . . Nice, a brain freeze . . . . *now you can—*

"Hey!" someone shouted from behind her as they knocked on her door. Carmen looked back to see Michelle, cleanly dressed and wearing a smile. "What's going on?"

"Nothing, just looking over something real quick."

"Have you seen Debra? I can't get into the room. I knocked, but there's no answer."

"Nope." Carmen turned back to the book as waved her hand near her face. "Did it get warm in here?"

"I guess she's out. And I feel fine. It's not hot at all." Michelle stepped into the room. "Mind if I come in?"

"No." She turned back to Michelle. "Where have you been? Haven't seen you in a minute."

"Running around campus." Michelle started goose necking around the room. "Your roommate, Kim, she's still with Eric, your boyfriend's roommate."

"Yeah. Why?"

"I saw her in one of the labs in the science building alone with Todd. Not a good look after what happened."

Carmen hurried to her feet. "How long ago was this?"

"About twenty minutes ago."

"Twenty?" Carmen looked at her watch, then the clock on her desk. "I couldn't have been by the lake that long."

"What happened?"

Carmen took her cellphone from her pocket and called Dayton. He didn't answer. She texted him. "I'm sending Dayton a text. I'm going to the science building. Hopefully, he talked some sense into Eric. Can you show me where you saw them?"

"Sure."

"You sure you don't feel warm? It's giving me a bit woozy."

"I'm fine."

Carmen lifted her bookbag, shoved the medium book inside, and left the room with Michelle in tow.

CHAPTER FIFTY

Kim held the leech in the center of her hand and began to caress it. She didn't feel as repulsed by it as she had been before. She brought it closer to her face, examining its texture and shape.

"You're sure I'm not gonna catch something from this?"

"No, they don't transmit disease." Todd stepped up alongside her and touched the top of it. "At least I don't think so." He grinned.

Kim smirked. "Funny." She took hold of its sides and started to lift it. It gave a slight resistance. "I think it's latched on to my hand."

"Okay, wait a sec, don't pull." Todd hurried to a counter and retrieved a pair of tongs and a lighter. He returned, clasped the tongs around the leech. "Yeah, he got you. I'll get him off. Hold still." He lit the lighter, brought it close enough for the heat to disturb it, and the leech let go. "There."

Kim looked down at her hand and saw a speckle of blood. She walked to a sink in the corner, ran water under it until it was clean, then put a paper towel over it. "Funny, I didn't even feel it this time."

Todd placed the leech back into the crate. "I wanted to thank you for looking out for me with the cops. I appreciate it."

Kim approached him. "I didn't say anything that wasn't true."

"Still, you know how it can be with the cops. I'm glad it happened after you got out of the car." He gave her a weak smile. "I'm glad you didn't get hurt."

"Here's the thing. It might be in both our best interests if we don't hang around one another for a while."

"Huh." Todd took a seat on a stool. "Because of what happened? I get it if that's the reason."

"It's pretty much the main reason."

"Forgive me but I have the strangest feeling that's not the rock-solid reason you don't want to come around me." Todd folded his hands and placed them in his lap as he leaned forward as though he were about to tell her a secret. "Your friends got on you about this. Probably told you I was some evil guy."

"Of course, they said something to me. They're concerned. But I had to weigh everything too, Todd. People got seriously hurt and one died. What if this happens again to you?"

"It won't. Trust me. But I am curious. You said not be around one another for a while. What do you mean? If you don't want to see me—"

"What I'm saying is let things cool off around here. Being seen with you feels like it's going to cause issues I don't need to have to deal with right now."

"And yet you came here to tell me this, alone, in the lab."

Kim fixed her mouth to respond but decided not to. She knew what he was insinuating. She chuckled at the irony.

"Didn't need to do this in front of a campus audience," she said.

"Wouldn't want Eric to find out and he gets jealous," Todd replied.

"No, I guess I wouldn't." She saw the surprised look on his face. Her response caught him off guard. "But this isn't about Eric, this is about you and me. I don't have a problem having a casual convo with you or getting up a game at the Commons, but I don't like having to defend myself for being around you. If we let some time pass from this incident, then things won't feel... you know."

Todd nodded. "I understand. So long you're clear about this move you want to make."

"What does —?"

"Why don't you come out and say this is about Eric finding out we were together and he's ordering you to stay away from me?"

"Ordering me? What is it with you men thinking I can be told what to do?"

"C'mon Kim, it's obvious what this little meeting here is really about. And the simple fact we're still discussing this means you're conflicted about what you want and deep inside you don't want to have to make a choice." Todd held up a hand. "It's all good. You do you." He slid off the stool and walked back to the crate.

"Why are you getting defensive? You and I are not dating. We don't have some side thing going on between us. You're making it sound like I got caught sneaking around with you and want to end a relationship that doesn't exist."

Todd stood with his back to her, his hands in the crate as he spoke. "I don't like people trying to dictate other people's lives." He lowered his head. "Treating people like property." He subtly brought his right hand up to his mouth. He held it there for a moment before dropping his hand onto the side of the crate.

Kim looked down at her hand, lifted the paper towel, and glanced at the bite. It had stopped bleeding. She considered his words. "He's not dictating my life. You haven't been in many long-term relationships, have you?"

"I've never met a woman worthy of a long-term relationship with me," he said.

Kim chuckled. "Did you say worthy?"

"Yes. Worthy as in worth my time. A woman worth building a relationship with." Todd turned to her. "I stopped trying a long time ago. I don't date. I don't like dealing with the pettiness of women. I say this is what I want. If you want that too, then let's cut the crap and let's do this." Todd approached her. "This is who I am; upfront, honest, and to the point. If I'm digging you, I'll admit it. And yes, I move fast. I get what I can or what I want from them, use them up, and wash my hands of it all."

"That's why people think you're a player," Kim said.

"Most guys wish they could do what I do. Which is why they hate me. The kind of women I attract. No guy in his right mind wants those women. They want to hook up with them and have fun, but they don't want them for girlfriends," Todd said.

"Some do," she said.

"Those men don't want to be challenged by a woman. By that I mean smart, has their head on their shoulders and makes them think." He paused. "Like you."

"Todd."

"I'm saying you're the kind of girl–"

"I know what you meant. You don't think you'd ever find someone someday?"

"I don't know. What I want is a woman with whom I can share my life and the essence of my being. A woman I can join with and become intertwined with on every level possible. Share the depths of her soul," he said.

"Wow, that's, um, intense," Kim said.

"It's what I want. Probably never find it."

"Well, you never know. There's always someone out there for everyone. You have to make a connection."

Kim and Todd stared at one another. She noticed he were chewing. His gaze went through her, a warm sensation flowing through her body. The wound on her hand tingled. She scratched it. A sharp, shocking pain radiated down her nerves, but before she could cry out, it subsided. Then she heard Todd's voice in her head.

Connections are important. And new possibilities.

"How?" She touched the side of her head. "How did you?"

"What?" he said and touched her hand.

She enjoyed the feeling, but she couldn't get herself to draw her hand away. She watched as Todd closed his eyes. Her hand with the bite felt as though it were melting into his. He pushed his body into hers as though he were trying to invade her.

"Let go of me," Kim said.

"I simply want to connect with you. Isn't that something you want as well?"

Kim shut her eyes and strained with all her might from him. The sound of a gunshot went off in her head as she stumbled backward away from him.

"If there is anything I'd want for you and me, is to be friends. I do like talking to you." Her statement poured out of her unconscious mind. She winced as she touched the side of her head.

"You okay?" Todd motioned toward her, but she retreated.

"I'm fine. Just. . ." she held up her hand. "I need a moment."

Kim felt like a part of her were missing. She clutched her stomach, took several quick breaths. The feeling subsided.

"Need me to get you some water?"

"I'm okay now." She gave him a wary look. "I should go. I think I've stayed long enough. See you around."

"Hey." Todd approached her. "At least let me walk you out. I don't like the way you look, and I don't want anything to happen to you like you falling down the stairs."

"Fine."

Todd stepped in front of her and led the way. He opened the lab room door, stood to the side for Kim to pass, but she stopped short and stared. Todd turned to see what she was looking at.

Carmen and Michelle stood before them.

CHAPTER FIFTY-ONE

Carmen extended her arm, blocking Michelle. They stared at one another in awkward silence. Carmen's eyes shifted back and forth from Todd to Kim. A cold, empty void unfolded between her and Todd, and it made her uneasy. Their eyes locked. Hope seemed to leave her body. She couldn't let her fear show.

"Kim?" Carmen swallowed hard. "You okay?"

"I'm fine. Why wouldn't I be okay? Why are you sticking your arm out like that?"

Carmen ignored her and glanced at Todd as she took her hand. Calmly, she guided Kim out the room and to her left. She gazed at the wound on her hand.

"What happened?"

"Nothing. It was an accident. I'm fine." Kim jerked her hand away. "Don't make a big deal out of it."

"Why are you snapping at me?"

"I'm not *snapping* at you." Kim touched the side of her head. "I need to go lie down. My head hurts."

Carmen saw her start to wobble. Michelle rushed to their side and started to place her hands on Kim's back, but Carmen interjected.

"I got her," Carmen said.

"Allow me." Todd stepped forward with an extended hand.

"She said she's got her!" Michelle said.

Todd put his hands up and retreated. "We were just leaving,"

"*She* was just leaving. You," Carmen pointed, "are going to stay right there."

"Am I?"

Todd smirked. Carmen scowled, but the slight tremor in her hand gave away her fear. Kim watched both of them in confusion.

"You didn't have to come down here. I can handle myself. Wait, how did you know where I was?"

"I told her," Michelle said.

Todd noticed Kim didn't respond to Michelle. His eyes widened, and he took two steps back.

"You know what? It doesn't matter. I wish everyone would stay out of my business!" Kim lashed out.

"I'm concerned, chica," Carmen said.

"I'm outta here." She winced as she touched the side of her head. "S-S-So long, Todd." Kim spat her words like venom. She turned on her heel and headed down the hall.

"I'll keep an eye on her." Michelle followed her.

Once they were gone, Carmen looked back at Todd. His eyes were fixed on her. A twinge in her head pulsated and then withdrew.

"You're the one my cousin talked about." Todd stepped out of the room. He towered over her. "Hello, medium."

Carmen shuffled back, putting distance between them.

"You stay away from us, you hear me? Stay back."

"I have to give you credit. Waltzing in here with no weapons and a ton of inexperience." He advanced on her. "What exactly was your plan, you and your friend there?"

Carmen stopped. Todd did the same. Certain he could not reach her, Carmen closed her eyes and started to concentrate on trying to enter his mind. She tried calling his name, waiting for him to respond. After several seconds, she opened her eyes.

Todd stood inches in front of her. "You can't be serious. You *actually* tried to connect with me?" He palmed the side of her head. His hand was like an ice pack. "Let me show you how it's done," he shut his eyes. "*Medium!*" His voice resonated like a megaphone in her head.

Carmen screamed so hard her throat went raw. Todd placed his hand on her shoulder and pushed her hard enough to cause her to fall. Carmen held her head in her hands as she writhed on the floor. She clenched her teeth in a vain effort to curb the pain. He knelt next to her.

"Somebody needs more practice." He tapped the tip of her nose with a finger. "I have no quarrel with you, nor do I wish to. But if you try this little stunt again, I'll do some permanent damage to that pretty little head of yours." His eyes shifted, and he looked past her. "The cavalry is coming. I'll take my leave."

Todd rose and headed back the way they had come.

"Carmen! Oh my God, what happened? Are you okay?" Michelle knelt next to her as she struggled to sit up. "Did he do something to you?"

Carmen watched Todd close the door to the lab and nonchalantly head out the back stairway. The pain melted away.

"That was stupid, Carmen," she said aloud. Tears began to stream down her face. "What was I thinking?"

"I got your back, girl." Michelle sat next to her. "Whatever you need. We got to stick together dealing with guys like him."

"Where's Kim?"

"On her way back to the dorm. Something's up with her. She kept acting woozy."

"He did something to her. Todd. . ." Her voice trailed off until she passed out.

———

Todd went to the roof of the science building. He walked to the edge and scanned the campus. With Kim succumbing to him after the bite from the leech and the medium scared of him, he was elated. He called out to Kevin.

If you're on the campus, come to the roof of the science building. I have news for you. Todd proceeded to sit, crossing his legs, his eyes shut. His thoughts moved to Kim as he tried to pick up on her presence. He could feel her walking with purpose. A hand landed on his shoulder. His eyes snapped open. "You're here fast."

"I was already on my way to the campus," Kevin said as he stepped around to face him. "What is it?"

"I took care of the medium. She knows now not to cross my path." Todd rose to his feet, smirking the entire time.

"What did you do?" Kevin said through clenched teeth.

"What needed to be done?"

"Where is she? Is she alive?"

"I didn't kill her, but I did teach her a lesson about trying to get inside my head. A brazen move on her part. But I wanted you to know, so you don't have to worry about her anymore. She won't be a problem, and we can begin the final steps of the ascension." Todd patted him on the shoulder.

"Why do you insist on causing this type of chaos? I told you I would handle it." Kevin stood by Todd's side. "After the Rucker incident and Rakim killing a student, I would think—"

"What? He killed someone?"

"It's not important. The body has been dealt with along with the vehicle they were in. But it's only a matter of time before a search is made for them. All the more reason for you to curb this behavior. If you give these people around here any cause to come after you again and they decide to search your room or the lab." Kevin stopped as Todd raised a hand.

"I think it's time we alter things a bit because, honestly, this is getting tiresome with you bitching at me about my behavior and what I've been trying to do." Todd placed his hands behind his back as he turned to Kevin. "I'm thinking I need to advance the timetable on making my next move."

"It's too early. According to the spell, we have to wait until the next new moon."

"We haven't exactly followed every single step by the book. I have had to improvise a few times, and it worked out fine. I can't see any harm in picking up the pace."

He studied Kevin's reaction, waiting to see if he would complain or comply.

"Okay. Let's say we do that. Have you given any thought to exactly how we're going to get off this campus? The south gate is locked down and there is no way we're getting by security with these crates without them being inspected."

"I've given it some thought for sure. I have a plan; one I believe will work." Todd scratched his chin. "You know, there is something else I have been meaning to address with you. Actually, it's more of a question I have."

"Okay."

"How did Robert know where I was?"

"How the hell should I know?

"I only ask because I also find it interesting Kim happens to be friends with the medium. And both her and the Rucker's were on your watch," Todd said.

Kevin took a step back. "What are you insinuating?"

"I'm not insinuating anything. I simply find it coincidental, that's all."

Kevin folded his arms as he gave him a wary look. "Exactly how did you know it was the medium you came across?"

"Don't change the subject."

"My question is relevant. Did you sense it, or did she sense you? Did you have some kind of connection?"

"Actually, she showed up with a spirit in tow."

"What do you mean, she showed up with a spirit?"

"We were leaving the room. I opened the door, and she was there with some ghost girl with a lot of mouth on her," Todd smirked as he watched Kevin's expression turn to confusion. "Why don't you look into *that* while I move things along, and I'll let you know should I need you again."

Todd turned and headed back to the stairwell.

CHAPTER FIFTY-TWO

A professor discovered Carmen. He helped her to her feet and took her to the dean's office. She called campus security to take her to the infirmary. By the time Dayton arrived at the science building, she was being escorted out. She convinced the guard to let Dayton take her, and he didn't object. Michelle followed.

They headed to the nurse's office. However, once out of sight of the guard, they went to Wakeford Hall. Carmen told Dayton everything from the mysterious stranger and the book to what had happened with Todd.

"Well, someone out there wants to help you in this fight. You want me to comb through this book with you and see if I can help?"

"This book reads like a manual to help with my abilities. Not much you help with. What you can do is get me more information about vampires. This book doesn't tell me much." She stopped to embrace and kiss him. "Thanks."

"Hey, um, I'm gonna go check on Kim for you," Michelle said.

"You do that," Carmen replied.

"Of course, I'll do that," Dayton said.

"I need time to rest and get myself right. I've never been so exhausted." Carmen watched Michelle enter Wakeford. "Thank you for not getting on me about confronting Todd."

"You were looking out for Kim. I would've done the same for Eric. I'm sorry I got there too late." Dayton hugged her. "I'm gonna go to the library to do research. If anything, I'll check on you this evening. Go get some sleep."

Carmen watched him head back across campus before making her way to Wakeford Hall. As fatigue set in, her mind filled with thoughts of how she could have handled Todd differently. She kept beating herself up for not being better prepared. She could hear Maria chewing her out for rushing into a fight she had no chance of winning. She should have read the section fully.

As she made her way up the stairs to her room, Michelle met her halfway.

"She just had another fight with Eric," she said.

"Eric's here?"

"No, on the phone. She's really pissed off."

"I don't need this right now," Carmen moaned. "Did you hear what it's about?"

"I'll give you one guess." Michelle folded her arms. "I'll hang back out here; let you have your space."

"Thanks for the heads up." Carmen removed her keys and hurried to her room. She rushed in to find Kim standing in the center of the room, a large Principal of Accounting textbook at her feet. She looked up and wiped the tears from her eyes.

Carmen closed the door then picked up the book and tossed it onto Kim's bed before embracing her. Kim welcomed the hug and sobbed into her shoulder. Carmen closed her eyes. She could sense a tremor between them. As though something tried to push them apart, but Carmen held on tighter, refusing to be separated.

The tremor became cold until Carmen whispered, "It's okay. I'm here now."

It dissipated, and the resistance ceased.

"We had another fight." Kim watched as Carmen broke the embrace, went to retrieve a tissue from her desk, and handed it to her. "I call him to tell him I told Todd we're not to see each other, and he lost it."

"What exactly did you say to him?"

"I told him Todd, and I agreed we wouldn't hang around one another anymore." Kim paused. "And I didn't appreciate the fact he's pretty much dictating who I can be friends with, but I understand where he's coming from."

"Chica, you didn't. Not to Eric."

"Well, I had to let him know how I don't like being pressured." Kim sat on her bed. "Then he started screaming, and I hung up on him."

"You hung up on. . . How could you? All over some guy you hardly even know? What's with you and Todd?"

"Nothing. There's nothing more than friendship between us."

"Why do I get the feeling that doesn't matter to him?" Carmen shook her head. "I saw it in his eyes. He wants something from you."

"Well, it doesn't matter what he wants now, does it?" Kim said with teary eyes. "I'm not going to see him anymore. Uh, I hate this." Kim dropped her head in her hand and shook.

Carmen took the chair from her desk and sat in front of her. She touched her shoulder and sensed the tremor and chill more prominent.

"What's going on, Kim?"

"I don't know. I don't feel like myself. I feel stressed, angry for no reason, tired and fed up."

"Last semester blues," Carmen said. "You need to get some

rest. Maybe stay in from class tomorrow and get yourself sorted out. Take a mental daycation."

Kim gave her a weak smile. "That's a clever idea."

Carmen gripped her shoulder, and the cold sensation subsided. "How about we have a girl's afternoon out? We'll go to a movie or something later."

Kim hugged her tightly. She appeared to have calmed down. Whatever sensation Carmen sensed around Kim disappeared the moment they embraced.

———

Kevin watched Carmen emerge. He avoided the temptation to go inside and see if she was okay. He was relieved when he saw Dayton arrive and walk her back across campus to her dorm. Todd hadn't done any considerable damage to her. But their confrontation meant she had raised the stakes.

Half an hour later, he got a nagging feeling he should look in on Todd in the lab. He exited the stairwell and spotted Todd returning, limping toward the lab. He paused at the door, turned in Kevin's direction, lifted his shirt, and removed a leech which he ate.

From his distance, Kevin noticed several things. First the bruises where the leech had been. He looked like he had been repeatedly punched. Then the smell of fresh, damp earth. Not the kind in the crates. The dirt on the knee of his pants meant he had been somewhere digging.

Kevin continued to observe him as he swallowed the leech. He stared down at the bruise as it started to heal itself. His face contorted.

"Why are you consuming that foul blood?" the demon said within.

"Easy. It's only a little more of Rakim's blood. I needed to heal a bit." His face contorted back. "We saw what we needed to see. I won't take anymore from him."

"Sonofabitch!" Kevin whispered.

He hurried down the stairs and out the back of the building. He jogged to the fence and leapt over it. He raced to the cabin. Zeborah stood in the doorway; his face bruised from being in a fight.

"What the hell happened? He didn't get loose again?" Kevin pointed to his face.

"Naw, he ain't loose. I got too close feedin' him. Oh, Todd stopped by."

Kevin inspected Zeborah's face. "He struck you where he could incapacitate you." He stepped back. "What was Todd doing here?"

"Said he wanted to look in on Rakim. We went down ta see him and he got violent. Got Todd in his ribs. Think he bruised them."

"How'd you get him to calm down?"

"I didn't. Todd did. Not sure what he did 'cause he sent me out tha basement. But whatever he did worked. Then he left. Said he had somethin' to look into."

"I bet."

Kevin led Zeborah inside. They descended into the cellar, where they found Rakim in the corner sitting in a comatose state. Kevin knelt before him, passed his hand before his eyes, looking for a response. He got none. He cupped Rakim's chin in his hand, turned it to the right, and looked at his neck.

There were two puncture wounds where Todd had bitten him. Below one of them, a large leech fed on Rakim's jugular. Kevin wrenched it off, leaving a small, round bruise. He examined it.

"Which way did Todd go?"

"He headed back ta the road. Why?"

"Come on."

Kevin exited the cellar. They walked across the woods, over

the road and in the direction Michelle had crashed. Once they reached the site, Kevin made a sharp right and walked for another five minutes. Covered in the thick brush sat her car, but it had been turned on its side.

"That's not how I left that," Kevin said. He approached the vehicle and saw the earth beneath it had been disturbed. "He found the body."

"You said you buried her."

"I did. Under the car." Kevin moved closer. "Doesn't look like he removed her."

"What's this all 'bout? And why would Todd put a leech on Rakim?" Zeborah inquired.

"Todd said he saw a spirit with the medium. More than likely it's this girl Rakim killed," Kevin said, avoiding Zeborah's question. "Todd's final stage is taking its toll on this Kim girl. I picked up on his aura around her. The more time she spends around Todd, the more he's rubbing off on her. Literally. I read about this part, but no one has ever seen it before. It's only a matter of time before the medium feels it too. If this keeps up, he'll be able to control her without having to turn or glamor her."

"He'll be able ta possess her."

"Our dear cousin has become suspicious of me too, and he's moving up his timetable on the girl. Which means now I have to move mine up."

"How long you figure we got?"

"Weeks, maybe only days. Either way, we now need to move fast if we want to stay ahead of him. The medium is nowhere ready. She jumped the gun today, trying to go up against Todd. I think it's time to get her acquainted with the Ruckers. I'm going to need that demon book to pull all of this off."

"You seem to care more about them than you do our kind," Zeborah said.

"My dear cousin, it's my slight compassion for the mortals

that makes me care about *our* kind. Keep better watch over Rakim. If Todd comes back and puts anything on his body, wait until he leaves and then take it off," Kevin said.

"You never said why he put leeches on him in tha first place."

Kevin didn't answer. He headed back to the cabin to retrieve the book on demons.

CHAPTER FIFTY-THREE

Dayton sat in the library's study room, poring over multiple books on vampires. He learned a great deal about the disparages between folklore and supposed fact. At times, he had to stop reading because he scared himself.

He thumbed through a book about the psychology of vampirism just as Curtis arrived with another book and placed it on the table.

"I think that's about it on vampires. Man, you really going all out on this assignment for English lit, huh?" Curtis said.

"What?" Dayton replied without looking up.

"You said you were doing this for an English lit class you were taking." Curtis closed the door and started to look at the spines of the books. "You got enough here to write your own dissertation."

"Gotta maintain my GPA, ya know." Dayton finished writing a sentence. He placed his pencil down and said, "I appreciate the help."

"It's all good. So, is it true they're afraid of crosses?"

"Well, there's some debate about the religious aspect of all this. That's more grounded in folklore. But they do have issues being on hallowed ground. Makes 'em weak for some reason. And the sunlight thing is real. 'Parently, their blood is so thin sunlight heats it to a boilin' point."

Curtis flipped through the book he held, cringing at a gory picture of a vampire feeding off a young maiden. He turned the page again and stopped to read something.

"Huh. This says while they are considered the undead, they can walk the plain between the living and the dead. Their movements are so fast they cannot be seen by the naked eye." He looked at Dayton. "That's crazy." He went back to the book and turned the page. "They got enemies. This is interesting."

"Which book you reading?"

Curtis looked at the spine. "What Walks Between Plains: Vampires, Ghosts and Haints."

"What's it say?"

"Well, they list man as the primary enemy, mostly because of his resourcefulness. Ghosts are another because they're not solid and can actually pass through their body and cause harm to their internal makeup. They leave behind some kind of residue supposed to be toxic to them, the vampire, not the ghost. Witches, real ones, not the movie kind, have a unique connection with nature and can disrupt—"

"Wait, aren't witches human?"

"So are mediums, but they have them listed here."

Dayton scrambled to his feet. "Let me see!" He snatched the book from Curtis and read. "Because of their ability to draw the dead to them, a medium can lure a vampire to their death through a form of hypnosis. By appealing to their consciousness since they are devoid of a soul. . . what? This can't be real." Dayton flipped the pages to the back of the book. "Is this a non-fiction book?"

"What's it matter? It will make for an interesting paper." Curtis looked at his watch. "Hey man, it's almost time for dinner. You coming?"

"It's that late?" Dayton looked at his watch.

A knock at the door caught their attention. Dayton and Curtis exchanged looks.

"Someone's in here," Curtis said.

"It's Carmen."

Curtis opened the door. Carmen looked tired, but she forced a smile. Dayton opened his arms. She came in, placed a book on the table, and embraced him.

"I couldn't sleep. I tried to go to the Commons after Kim left, but after everything that happened today."

"What happened?" Curtis asked.

Carmen turned to him and broke the embrace. "Kim and Eric got into a nasty fight again about Todd. I consoled her for half the afternoon," Carmen said. "Anyway, how's the research going?"

"Found some interesting things. There's something in this book about mediums. Might be useful for your paper. But I didn't find any standout information." Dayton handed her the book. "Is that the book you told me about?"

"Yes."

"I didn't know you read French," Curtis said as he picked it up. "You want me to get you a French to English dictionary to get through this?"

"It's okay. I know enough to get through it."

"Okay, well, I'm out. I'm going to grab some food and figure out what to do with my evening," Curtis said.

"Don't you have homework or something?" Dayton called him.

"Eh, not really part of my evening plans, but I guess I should knock out some math homework. Catch ya'll later."

Carmen waited until Curtis closed the door.

"What did the medium stuff say?"

Dayton passed her the book. "It didn't really make much sense. Might be more fiction than fact, but see for yourself. Everything else I found is standard how to kill vampire stuff. Older vampires are supposed to be easier to kill than young ones. Do we even know how old Todd is?" Dayton glanced at the medium book. "Can you really read French?"

"I read it. It's in English." Carmen read the section on appealing to the consciousness. She picked up the medium book and looked for a match. "This is true. There's a piece here, talks about it, but there are some serious steps I have to take in order to do it."

"How can I help?"

"You can't, not according to this. They tell me what I can do and how to do it, but not exactly *how* to do it, you know. I can follow the steps but. . ."

"It's the execution you need to figure out," Dayton said. "I get it."

Carmen sat down and compared the books. Dayton returned to his notes but paid more attention to her reading. He saw the distressed look on her face. After a moment, he took the book from her and pushed it to the middle of the table.

"What?"

"I'm thinking of doing an internship with Indigo after graduation. You know, the marketing firm my dad started out with?"

"What are you talking about?"

"Interning for the summer while I try to get a full-time gig."

"What does that have to do with this?"

Dayton shook his head. "Nothing at all. That's why I brought it up. So, what's your plan after we get out of here? Back to New York?"

Carmen took his hand and exhaled.

"I have no idea what I'm going to do. Maybe go into the family business?"

CHAPTER FIFTY-FOUR

Eric spotted Kim leaving the cafeteria with her dinner wrapped up. He stopped in the walkway and waited until she saw him.

"I'm sorry," he said.

Kim stopped short, looking more surprised than anything. She frowned.

"What do you want me to say?"

"I don't want you to say a thing." He stepped closer. "Can we talk over here, out of the way of people?"

He pointed to a large tree whose shade supplied the right amount of darkness for privacy. Eric gave her space, and they went under the tree.

"Okay, go ahead and talk."

"I had time to think about what happened, and I just wanted to tell you why I acted the way I did, and I'm sorry."

"How many apologies do you think you have left for me to have to listen to, Eric? I feel like no matter what I say, what I do, it's never—"

"I'm afraid."

"What?"

"I'm afraid. That's why I lost it earlier."

"Afraid of what?"

"Of losing you. I'm afraid I've messed up so many times with you that you're ready to leave me." Eric trembled. "I'm trying to get my act together and then this clown shows up, trying to take you from me. And I feel like he's got your attention."

Kim sighed as she shook her head. "You know what's messed up? It takes some other guy to show me some attention for you to realize how important I am to you."

"Wait, what?" Eric looked confused.

"So, you're scared of losing me now because Todd appears to like me. Now you give a damn?"

"I'm not saying he's the direct reason—"

"Direct reason or not, it's not fair I get the brunt end of your anger because you're afraid. If you honestly think I'm interested in someone like him, then what have we been doing this whole time with our relationship? In fact, why do you even want to be in a relationship with me? If everything that happens is all about you and your feelings and your fears, what am I? Does anything become about *us*?"

Eric stared, dumbfounded. "What's going on with you? You know that's not what I am trying to tell you. In all this time we've been together, have you ever known me to—"

"There you go again; You!" She stepped closer. "Well, since we're so concerned about your well-being, here, take this." She shoved her food into his hands. "Now you can't say I don't care about you. Now you can eat."

Kim stormed off. Eric stood in stunned silence. The fear melted into anger. He threw the food into the tree's trunk. As he stepped out from the shade, he saw Curtis.

"Take it easy, Kim," he hollered. He turned to Eric. "Say, hey! What happened?"

"Man, I don't know how to feel right now. I'm pissed, I'm scared, I-I-I . . . I gotta do something about this Todd situation. Kim and I . . . I don't know what to do."

"I know what we need to do. Let's go eat and you can get this off your chest."

"I'm not hungry."

"Then let's walk. You're letting this guy get under your skin too much. You and Kim should give each other space for a couple of days. Let all this blow over. Too much is happening in one day. C'mon, we'll go to the Commons later."

Eric looked in the direction Kim went, before being led in the opposite way. He didn't see Kevin until it was too late. They bumped shoulders. Both of them stopped and stared at one another.

"My apologies," Kevin said. "My fault."

"It's all good. My bad," Eric replied. As he turned to continue walking, he said, "Where's Dayton? We should all go hang."

"He and Carmen are in the library working on some paper about vampires."

"Vampires?" Eric said.

———

Kevin's eyes widened, and he turned in the direction of the library.

As soon as he passed through the front door, he searched for her. He masked his presence so she wouldn't feel him there. He spotted Dayton removing a couple of books from a shelf. He followed him.

He kept a good distance. Dayton eventually led him right to the study room. Kevin stood feet from the door, thinking of the best way to proceed. Looking around, he spotted a sign with an arrow pointing to the archives. He followed it to a glass door that separated the archives section from the rest of the library. Beyond it, he could see dimmer lighting, no doubt to protect the works inside. The door was locked. He tightened his grip around the handle, lifted it while putting his weight into it. The lock snapped. Kevin went in.

There were seven long aisles of old books. He found the light switch and turned it off. He moved to the back of the second aisle, shrouded himself in darkness, and closed his eyes.

Hear me medium. I have returned as I have discovered you did not wisely use the book I gave you. You need to come to me now. He waited for her response. After a moment, he called out to her again. *I am in the library. Come to me in the archives. Come alone. Leave your boyfriend behind.* He opened his eyes and waited.

Within minutes, Carmen appeared at the door with an enthusiastic look on her face. She opened the door and seemed taken aback to find it unlocked. She looked around while keeping her back against the door as she came inside.

"I'm here," she said.

Do not use your voice, speak to me like a proper medium.

Carmen thought her words. *I hear you.*

Good. Embrace your ability like your abuela. Now, come to the second row and step in.

Carmen did as instructed. She saw Kevin's shining eyes glowing in the dark.

Why do you stand in the darkness? Step forward where I can see you.

I will reveal myself in time. Until then, know this. Time is not on your side. Focus on learning that book. Trivial books cannot help you. You need to learn how to use your abilities to protect yourself against this evil. You try facing off against him again unprepared, and he will kill you.

There isn't anything in any books about how to really fight vampires.

The book I gave you, you need to read it from cover to cover to get your answers.

I'm supposed to read all of that?

"It's all you should be doing," Kevin hissed as he spoke aloud.

"I need more than books. Give me advice. Tell me what to do so I can get a jump on things."

"You want someone to hold your hand and walk you through this, but that's not how this works." Kevin tossed the book he had brought. "Take that. If you need help from your boyfriend, so be it. He can read it with you."

"At least give me something else to start with. Something I can use in the meantime until I learn all of this."

"I will tell you this. Your unique ability to summon the dead makes your touch deadly for Todd. In order to use it, you have to be in the right frame of mind. The book will tell you exactly where on his body to touch him for it to work."

"What about the how?"

"I believe you already know the how. Read section two, first three pages. And I will send you one last piece of help. After tonight, I expect the next time we meet, you will be ready."

Carmen knelt, picked up the book, and glanced at the cover. "Ready for what?"

Kevin charged her. As she looked up in his direction, he tapped her on her forehead, and she collapsed. Taking her by the collar, he dragged her out of the room and left her laying at the entrance of the hall leading to the study rooms.

He went to a shelf, removed a random book, went back to the entrance, and threw it at the door he saw Dayton enter through. He levitated an inch from the floor and glided away, touching down at a safe distance.

Dayton came out of the room, saw Carmen lying on the floor, and rushed to her aid.

CHAPTER FIFTY-FIVE

Two hours later, Kim was surprised to see Todd waiting under a nearby tree. He held a small bunch of Gerbera daisies.

"You've got to be kidding me," she mumbled as she walked down the steps. He waved. Kim shook her head.

"Kim!" Todd followed her. "Kim, wait!"

"No."

He caught up to her and blocked her path.

"Here. The flowers are to say forgive me. It's nothing more than that."

Kim shook her head. "I can't accept these."

"Why not?"

"Are you kidding? After the incident in the hall? This will only cause more problems, and I don't need the drama."

"Okay, give them to your roommate then, as an apology, or put them in the lobby in a vase. Just take them. It would at least make me feel a little bit better."

Kim hesitated before she took them. "I have to go. Got some homework I need to do."

"You headed back to your dorm? I'll walk with you. I'm headed that way back to Chambers."

"Fine," Kim groaned. She had the feeling if she said no, he would follow her anyway.

She walked with enough space between them so no one seeing them would think they were a couple. For a few seconds, they didn't speak. He broke the silence.

"I have a question. While with the leeches today, I got to thinking if you had the choice, would you live in a world with more night than day or no day at all?" Todd said.

"What kind of question is that?" Kim replied.

"Hypothetical. Well, they live in dirt all the time. No light or anything, but they don't seem to want to be in sunlight. I wondered if they thought it was better."

"No sun at all? I don't know. I could never live without it completely." Kim stopped. "Although the darkness does have its advantages. You don't have to face many problems in the dark. Not being seen. The solace darkness can provide. It can be beautiful in its own way." She looked at him. "That's an odd question to ask me."

"Just making convo."

Kim spotted a group of girls coming out of the dorm head in their direction.

"I'll walk alone the rest of the way."

"Did I do something wrong?"

"No, I think it's better if I continue on alone," she said.

"I understand. I'll see you tomorrow then?"

"You'll see me *around*. We need to keep our boundaries," Kim said.

"Gotcha," Todd said.

As Kim headed to Wakeford Hall, she glanced back. She saw him still looking at her. She waved, then picked up her pace.

———

Todd waited until she went into the dorm. Smiling, he headed across the quad toward Chambers Hall. The warmth of satisfaction Kim was becoming his made him pleased. So preoccupied with his thoughts, he didn't hear the footsteps approaching behind him.

"Hey, Todd?"

He turned and four rounded ends of knucklebone struck him across his jaw. The pain surged through his teeth and up the side of his face as he spun around and fell to the ground onto his back. As he stared up at the sky, he heard a voice say, "Kick him!"

Eric's face came into view. He shook his right hand he had hit him with, and said through clenched teeth, "Get'chor ass up."

CHAPTER FIFTY-SIX

With her composure fully regained, Carmen sat with her face buried in the book about demons. Dayton sat across from her, staring intensely. She had read over the section Kevin had told her multiple times.

The book was a guide to understanding how they operate, their weaknesses, and the various kinds that manifested themselves in and around humans. With no glossary or table of contents, the reader had to read the book from cover to cover. Fortunately, the four sections were labeled.

The second section, entitled The Power and Impacts of Sensory Abilities, covered clairvoyance, spiritual and medium capabilities, and their effects as they are applied to battling a dark force.

"Okay, this talks about how I can draw out and/or put down a dark entity." Carmen ran her finger over the words. "By placing their hands on the sides of the head of someone possessed, then summoning the evil, one could rip out the entity attached to the host's body. Now in the case of the half-dead or walking dead, such as vampires, the summoning counteracts with their ability to glamor thus causing them to collapse from excruciating pain. While a medium can have this effect simply by being in their presence, using the ability to summon causes greater pain because of the direct physical contact."

Carmen began to cross-reference the information.

"I think we should call it for now," Dayton said. "You need to rest."

"I'm fine. I wonder if it's the same thing I did with Savannah."

"What?"

"I'm talking to myself. Wait." She flipped pages, stopped, and ran her finger down the middle of it. "Okay, there it is."

"Carmen? Look at me," he said. She did. "You had an episode out in the hall. It took you 45 minutes to get back to being yourself and you've been poring over those books for nearly an hour. Let's go get some food, then rest."

"I need to finish cross-referencing some things, and I don't wanna do it in the room around Kim. You can go. I'll call you later."

"I'll wait."

"Don't." She gave him a reassuring smile. "Go get your rest. I'll call you as soon as I get out of here, I promise."

Dayton kissed her.

"That's two books now. I hope whomever this is donating this information is really helping," he said. Carmen started to respond, but he held a hand up. "Call me."

Dayton left.

Carmen had to agree. The end of both encounters left her worse for wear, but she hadn't detected any sinister intentions. The books' information did help.

Thirty minutes later, she proceeded to gather up all the extra books, putting them into two neat piles. There was a knock at the door. She opened it and a work-study student, a short, pudgy girl with long hair and glasses, with a book cart behind her.

"Sorry to disturb you, but we're going to close up the rooms soon. You can still use other areas of the library if you want," she said.

"I'm finishing up now," Carmen said.

"Okay. Do you have any books you want me to take?"

"Yeah." She turned, took up each pile, and handed them to her. "Thanks."

"No problem. Have a good night."

Carmen shut the door and returned to her books. Another knock at the door caught her attention.

"I'm packing up n—"

She peered out into the hall in both directions and found it empty. Yawning, she shut the door; a hard knock resounded. She reopened it to see no one there. Huffing, she stepped out into the center of the hall.

"Hello, this isn't funny," Carmen said.

She tried the doorknob and found it locked. She checked the room to the left, also locked.

Carmen returned to her room and slammed the door. She gripped the knob, but it wouldn't budge.

"Aw, come on," she moaned. "Damn it, my books."

Carmen tugged on the knob. Gradually, the temperature in the air around her dropped. She saw her breath in front of her face. A migraine started to form.

From the far end of the hall, a fire extinguisher fell off the wall with a loud crash, startling her. One by one, like footsteps coming toward her, the lights in the ceiling winked out. Her adrenaline rushed through her body and her skin warmed.

A voice called out to her. "Carmen, I need you."

At that moment, she couldn't determine if who was coming for her was friend or foe. The combination of the voice and icy air frightened her. Deep inside, she found the strength to scream. Hot tears burned her cheeks as she sobbed. She pressed her back against the door.

"Caaarrrmennn."

Another light went dark.

"Go away! Leave me alone!" she shouted.

"*Carmen.*"

More lights flickered out.

"Stop it!"

The darkness skipped over her and continued down the hall, leaving her bathed in the only light left.

She saw the pale face of a young African American man materialized out of the blackness. As his body appeared, he stopped at the edge of the light. Trails of blood had trickled from the gunshot wounds and stained his shirt.

It took Carmen a moment to recognize him as the campus shooter. She remembered his face from the newspaper.

"Carmen, I need you."

Hot tears streamed down her face. Shaking her head, Carmen cupped her hands over her ears and squeezed her eyes shut to block out the voice.

"Please go away." Her legs weakened. She slid down the door onto the floor.

"I will not be able to rest until you have listened to me." His voice echoed around her head.

She pressed her palms onto her ears. He repeated her name. Wisps of his breath caressed her cheeks and neck over and over again.

Everything went quiet.

She uncovered her ears. The hum of the light filled hall. She turned to the right; the man kneeled inches away. He gripped her arm, sending hot searing pain through her body.

"Let me go!"

A pair of arms wrapped around her in a tight embrace.

Carmen peered over her shoulder and saw Michelle staring at Robert.

"Leave her alone," Michelle said.

"I have your attention?" he said. Carmen nodded. "There is a locker at the train station, 1763. Combination 4152. In it, there's a book bag filled with information about Todd. It belonged to me and my brother. Now it's yours. Go and get it. Bring it back to the campus and use the information to plan your attack against him. You need to know what you're up against."

"I know he's a vampire."

"I wouldn't be here if that's what you were up against. You're only going to get one shot at this. You miss the window to stop him. This whole campus will die. I agreed to come to you in death and damn myself for a moment to warn you. Go to the locker, get the information, and don't fail."

"What's the information? Be specific."

"Everything you need to know about what he is."

"How do I stop him?"

She retreated into the darkness.

One by one, the lights came back on. Carmen sat in Michelle's arms, shivering.

"It's okay. I got you. You're okay," Michelle said.

Carmen broke free of her, fell onto her side, and crawled away from her door, screaming. The work-study student turned the corner and ran to Carmen's aid.

"What's wrong? What happened?" she asked.

Carmen backed into the wall and brought her knees to her chest. Her face was pale from fright. She saw Michelle standing over her.

"You saw him. You saw what I saw!"

Michelle nodded. "I saw it."

"Thank God. We have to tell Dayton," Carmen said.

The work-study girl looked around. "Who is Dayton?"

Carmen pointed to Michelle; the girl followed her finger but saw no one.

"If I give you Dayton's number, will you call him for me?"

"I'll call him," she said. "I need a pen and paper."

"Not you. I'm talking to Michelle," Carmen said.

"Michelle who? I don't see anyone else down here."

Carmen's head hurt as she covered her mouth.

Michelle nodded.

"Oh my god," Carmen whispered, realizing Michelle's horrible fate. "Aye. . .Dios. . .Mio."

CHAPTER FIFTY-SEVEN

Todd rubbed his jaw as he stood up. It hurt, only because he didn't see the punch in time to roll with it. He caught a glimpse of Curtis moving into position out of the corner of his eye. He faced him.

"Not so tough now. Are you?" Curtis said.

"You're kidding me, right? Two against one?" Todd said.

"He's making sure you don't try to run," Eric said.

Eric swung and struck Todd again. This time Todd absorbed the punch and didn't lose his balance. The warm, coppery flavor of his blood seeped into his mouth. He spat out his blood.

"You feel better now?" Todd let out a lazy sigh. "If you're done, I'd like to go to my room."

"I told you to stay away from Kim. I guess this is the only way to get you to stop."

Eric got closer until they were toe to toe.

Todd eyed him up and down. Why don't you go back to your little hole in the wall, okay? Be satisfied I let you get a few hits off." Todd clenched his teeth. "Carry your miserable ass back to your room and play with your friends because you're out here dealing with something you can't handle."

"You best get outta my face," Eric said.

"Or what? What do you think you're going to do?" Todd taunted. He could see both fear and anger in Eric's eyes. "That's what I thought. Move." Todd purposely bumped him.

"Don't you bump me, bitch!" Eric grasped Todd's shoulder, spun him around and swung.

Todd caught his fist before it could connect and wrenched Eric's arm back. The tendons in his wrist bent. He crushed Eric's pinky into the rest of his hand and the bone broke. Eric collapsed and cried out in pain.

"You don't know who or what you're dealing with," Todd threatened.

Curtis circled around behind Todd \, put him in a chokehold, and attempted to toss him off Eric. Todd grounded himself as he applied more pressure to Eric's hand.

"Let him go," Curtis said. "Let him go or so help me. . ."

With lightning speed, Todd let go of Eric and spun around. Curtis' eyes bulged as Todd's fingertips dug into the flesh of his throat.

"Not so talkative now, huh?" Todd said.

"No, no, no, no!" someone screamed. Todd saw Dayton running toward him. He lunged at Todd and caught him around the waist. "Eric, go!"

Todd let go of Curtis, dropping him to the ground, and punched Dayton in the side, causing him to fall. Smiling, he turned his attention back to Eric. He strode to him, lifted him by his collar, and glared at him.

"You're lucky all you get is a broken pinky. You're not going to win this. Give it up," Todd chided.

He turned in time to see Dayton and Curtis approaching. They flanked him on both sides. He watched them. They took their positions. He fell back two steps, still holding on to Eric. He crouched slightly and parted his lips, revealing large canines on the top and bottom of his mouth. The whites of his eyes turned crimson.

"Bring it," Todd said in a demonic tone.

"What the fuck?" Curtis said.

"Okay. Okay, this is it!" Dayton yelled as he crouched to Todd's level. "Let's do this."

Todd released Eric and made a beeline to Curtis. Still in awe of his appearance, he didn't move in time. Todd gut-punched him so hard, he dropped like a sack of potatoes. He collided with Dayton, who tried to rush him. Todd held Dayton by the throat, bore his fangs, and leaned in to bite him.

Dayton let out a guttural scream of panic and tried to wiggle out from the grip. Todd got inches from his jugular. He laughed before shoving Dayton to the ground.

Curtis groaned. He saw him struggling to get up. Todd kicked him in the gut. Curtis went down again.

"How does that feel?" He leaned down and said, "Kick him!" He kicked Curtis one more time, turned to Eric, and prepared to attack. Eric, clutching his wounded hand, sat up as Todd pounced on him, got down on one knee, and snatched him by his shirt. Lightning flashed, brightening Todd's face as it contorted briefly.

"Oh my God," Eric whispered. "Please help me."

Todd turned his eyes up, tilted his head left so his right ear pointed toward the sky. He shook his head. "I don't think he heard you." His eyes circled back to look at him. "Look at what you've done. You've made me expose myself." He leaned closer. "I should kill you and send Kim into a world of grief. But then, I wouldn't get to see the look on your face once I give her a shoulder to cry on and lying in my arms for comfort." He smirked. "Perhaps I still will."

Eric struggled against Todd's grip. "Muthafu—"

"Whoa, whoa, whoa, slow your roll, homeboy." Todd held him still. "Don't try to get brave now after sucker-punching me." Todd slapped him hard across the face. "Better get a handle on your behavior, Eric."

Eric stared hard into his eyes, breathing heavily but staying calm.

Todd patted him on the shoulder. "That's better. So now, this is how this is going to go."

Before he could say another word, someone stuck Todd hard on the back his head. He crashed to the side in a sitting position. Carmen stood inches away with two hardcover books.

CHAPTER FIFTY-EIGHT

"Carmen, get outta here!" Dayton said.

She ignored him and struck Todd across the face with the books. He got to his feet.

They stood a foot apart, staring one another down. Carmen gripped the books and brought her arms back.

"You again. You didn't learn the first time, did you?" Todd rushed her.

Carmen backed up, taking tiny, quick steps while holding the books tightly until he was steps away from her. She then dropped the books and extended her arms. Unable to stop, he collided with her. She took hold of the sides of his head.

They cried out in unison. He grasped her wrists and fought to snatch her hands away, but she pressed her fingertips into his skull. Unable to let go, she convulsed.

Todd released her wrists and touched the sides of her head. Their eyes locked.

Carmen forgot what to do next.

You have made the gravest mistake of your life. He closed his eyes. *Now taste death.*

Carmen's screams intensified. She shut her eyes and fought through the pain, and struggled to force him out of her head.

"You're not that strong," Todd said.

Eric, Dayton, and Curtis came behind Todd and took hold of his arms and around the waist. As they held on to him, Carmen pressed harder against his temples. Todd's voice left her mind. She snatched her hands away and, with all her strength, she cold cocked him across the face.

Everyone fell backward. Todd toppled over on top of them. Carmen's legs collapsed under her. Wobbling, she tried to distance herself but tripped over her feet and hit the ground.

"Carmen!" Dayton rushed to her side and tried to sit her up. "Talk to me."

"I don't feel so good," she whispered.

Eric came too and tried to get her to her feet.

"Easy," Dayton said.

"The books," she said. "Get my books."

"Curtis, can you grab. . . ." Eric looked over in his direction. "Awe shit."

"What?" Dayton said.

Curtis lay passed out on the ground, face down. A campus security guard stepped into view, knelt next to him, and gently shook him on the shoulder. Todd had disappeared. The guard looked in their direction. He saw Carmen's condition and stood.

"You two set her down on the ground and back away!"

"We're helping her," Dayton said.

The guard took out his radio. "Dispatch, I need assistance on the quad. I have a student down, possible sexual assault victim." He touched the can of pepper spray on his belt. "I said set her down and back up!"

"What?" Eric screamed. "No one sexually assaulted anyone."

Carmen leaned into Dayton. "Listen to him. I'll sort this out." She caressed the side of his face and gave him a weak smile.

They placed her on the ground and did as instructed. Carmen glanced over at Eric, cradling his hand.

"Hands at your sides," the guard said.

"My pinky is broken," Eric said. "I gotta hold it. You think I can get some medical attention or something?"

"Once we sort this out."

"An ambulance or somethin'," he said.

"Quiet down." The guard radioed again. "We're going to need EMT as well."

"Copy that," a voice replied through the radio. "Miss, you okay? Did one of these men hurt you?"

"No," she shook her head. "They actually came to my defense." She looked at Dayton. "That's my boyfriend and his roommate. I was waiting for them when I got attacked."

"Did you see your assailant? Can you give a description?"

"No. He grabbed me from behind. Never saw his face." Carmen glanced at Dayton. She shook her head slightly, signaling him to keep the lie going.

The guard turned to Dayton and Eric. "Either of you see the assailant?"

"All I can tell you is he was a big guy. Pretty strong," Dayton said. "It took three of us to get him off her. He ran off before we could see his face." He pointed to Curtis. "He's our neighbor."

Curtis groaned as he tried to get up. Dayton asked the guard if he could assist him. He agreed.

"Eric?" Carmen shouted at him.

He glanced back at her. "Let's step out of earshot. We need to talk."

CHAPTER FIFTY-NINE

Todd's sudden appearance startled Kevin and Zeborah at the cabin. He looked disheveled as he staggered toward them.

"What the hell happened to you?" Kevin said.

"I got jumped."

"Jumped?" Zeborah looked perplexed. "Jumped by who?"

"Kim's boyfriend and his friends, and then the medium. And she's not as weak as I thought." Todd locked an angry gaze on Kevin. "They're lucky she showed up because one of them wasn't going to survive the ass-kicking I gave them."

"You got into a physical fight with those guys?" Kevin said.

"What was I supposed to do? Stand there and let them put hands on me? Oh no, they learned a lesson tonight." Todd's eyes shimmered. "I'm going to kill Eric if he comes near me again. I can't wait to take his girl."

"Todd, you didn't expose what you are in front of them, did you?"

"So, what if I did? It doesn't matter. They're not going to tell anyone. Especially now that the medium did her little stunt."

"What stunt?"

"Palmed me right here." He pointed to his temples. "It felt like she was trying to rip my insides out. I don't even feel like myself right now."

Kevin walked in a different direction.

"We need to lie low for a while," he said. "Need to get you off campus and have you come and go during the day like a regular student."

"Why?"

"Are you serious right now?" Kevin went to him. "Bad enough you were involved with that shooting, but then you go and beat up a group of students. You exposed your true nature, which, the last time you did, had us running for our lives. It doesn't matter if they don't tell anyone. The point is, they know, and I suspect, after the initial shock wears off, they're going to figure out how to kill you."

Todd's eyes returned to normal. He laughed.

"I don' see what's so funny," Zeborah said.

"They're not going to kill me. They wouldn't know how to kill me," he said.

"You're getting off campus. You can stay here, or I can arrange to set you up somewhere. You want to finish with the leeches? Fine. But you need to abandon this whole host thing with this girl."

Todd's smile fell as he folded his arms.

"That's the second time you've hinted at me abandoning this venture. And I'm getting the feeling this isn't about my wellbeing," Todd said. "I come to you and tell you I've been assaulted, and you don't even mention retaliation, not in the slightest."

"You want to go back to the campus and beat up on some mortals? Get revenge for your pride? Why not? Let's abandon all the work we have done for you to show off."

Todd stared at Kevin. With lightning speed, he grabbed Kevin by the shoulders.

"Todd, let 'em go!" Zeborah yelled.

Todd's face morphed into half-goat, half-man. A combination of inhuman screams and animal bleat erupted from his mouth. He leaned in as if he were about to bite. Kevin screamed in horror as he paled. Todd laughed. He shook Kevin like a doll before throwing him to the ground.

Falling on all fours, gnawing at the air, his face contorted more. Todd held the sides of his head and cried out in pain before falling face-first into the dirt for several seconds. Then, rising sluggishly, his face returned to normal.

"What in tha hell, Todd?" Zeborah helped Kevin sit up.

"Feel better now?" Kevin rubbed his neck.

"You now see how close I am to the ascension. You see what happens once I am provoked?" Todd stood and wiped himself off. He had a calm demeanor as he glanced back to the campus and mumbled something inaudible. "Of course. I went about this all wrong. I know how to get that sonofabitch. I know how to destroy him." He looked at Kevin. "At this moment, you have made me realize what I must do. Thank you, Kevin, for making me see the errors of my ways. I will return here in two hours and let you know what my next step will be."

Todd didn't wait for a response. He headed back through the woods toward campus.

CHAPTER SIXTY

Eric refused the offer to go to the hospital after the paramedic wrapped his hand. He assured them he would go the following day to have it looked at. As he stepped out of the ambulance, he spotted Carmen and Dayton giving a statement to an officer. He waited until they were done then the three of them stood off to the side and watched Curtis, still sitting on the ground, drinking water while being attended to by another paramedic.

"Your hand okay?" Carmen said.

"Todd dislocated it. They popped it back in and put on this splint." Eric examined his hand then looked at Carmen. "So, are we gonna talk about the fact there is a vampire on campus? That *was* a vampire, right?"

"Lower your voice," Dayton said. "We should wait until Curtis is done."

"We're going to discuss it, just not here." Carmen turned to Dayton. "Can you go get your car? There's someplace we have to go. I can explain on the way. We'll meet you at the main gate."

Dayton nodded and headed to Chambers Hall. Eric Curtis

spoke with an officer before he joined them. She told Curtis to come along but said nothing more.

They walked in silence to the main gate, where Dayton waited in his car. Carmen got in the passenger side, Eric and Curtis in the back. She told Dayton to take them to the train station, then she turned to face Eric.

"I'm glad to see you're not freaking out about this," Carmen said.

"I'm past the point of freaking out, Carmen. A brush with death will sober you up quick." Eric glanced at Curtis, who appeared to have zoned out. "Curtis said you and Dayton were studying vampires. If you knew what he was, why you didn't say something?"

"A heads up woulda been nice," Curtis said.

"Let me bring you up to speed. Then I'll tell you what the next step is."

Carmen proceeded to tell them everything. She ended with the bizarre visit she had outside the study room. She left out the part about Michelle helping her. She didn't want them telling Debra of her death.

No one spoke as Dayton made the turn on Main Street and headed toward the train station.

"You actually speak to ghosts? Like, have full-blown conversations with them?" he said, and she nodded. "That's crazy. I mean, not that *you're* crazy." He turned to Eric. "Can you believe she can do that? I'm rambling, huh?"

"All I care about is finding out how to stop this guy. I don't care about ghosts, the walking dead or anything else. Whatever's in that locker better be worth it," Eric said.

"Something that holds the key to stopping Todd."

"Stopping him from doing what?" Dayton said.

"I guess we'll know for sure in a few minutes," Curtis said.

CHAPTER SIXTY-ONE

The train station was empty, aside from the woman at the ticket counter. Their footsteps echoed as they walked to the far end of the building where the lockers were. Carmen paused before the wall of metal locker cubes.

"What's the locker number?" Eric said.

"Locker 1763. Combination 4152," Michelle said as she materialized alongside Carmen. "It's near the end to the right."

"Thanks," Carmen said. "Can you go back and look in on Kim?"

"Sure. See you soon," Michelle dematerialized.

"What?"

"Not you, Eric." Carmen made her way down to the far right of the wall and found the locker. There were four small dials with numbers on them going vertically near the edge of the door. She turned each one to the corresponding number, then turned the latch. It clicked, and the door opened.

A black bookbag had been stuffed inside. She took it out and handed it to Dayton. Eric snatched it from him, walked to a bench, and started to unzip it.

"Eric, wait, don't open it here. Let's go back to the campus and look through it," Carmen said.

"For what?" Eric tore the bag open and withdrew a handful of papers and a notebook. He rifled through them, glancing at a mixture of drawings, pages with symbols and bizarre languages. "What is this? None of this makes sense." He showed it to her.

Carmen took the papers while Eric looked through the notebook. She took her time, going over each page while trying to make sense of it. She passed each page to Dayton, who passed it to Curtis. They all reviewed everything in silence. One of the papers caught her full attention.

A copy of a hand-drawn image of a vampire touching the shoulder of a woman. Next to it, another drawing of the woman, but the vampire was gone. Her face appeared distorted. A phrase written at the bottom of the page read Final Demonic Ascension. She flipped it over to find nothing on the back.

"W-What's this mean?" Curtis pointed to the phrase.

"I don't know. Hold on to this for me." She handed it to Curtis and went to the next paper.

"Uh, you need to take a look at this." Eric turned the book around so everyone could see. Symbols with letters under them filled the page. They were in no particular order. "This looks like some kinda alphabet."

"It is the alphabet," Dayton said as he pointed to the letters. "See."

"The letters go with the symbols. But what are these symbols from?" Curtis said.

Carmen's eyes widened. She took back some of the pages Curtis held. She started to look through them again and found one with the symbols on them.

"We need to go back to the car. I need a pen," she said.

Eric snatched up the bookbag. They hurried back to the car, where she and Eric got into the back seat. He tore out a blank page from the notebook and gave it to her. Dayton got her a pen from the glove compartment.

"Curtis, look and see if there are more pages with these symbols and give them to me. Dayton, the book about demons is on the floor. Look and see if there is anything about demonic ascension."

"There's another page here. Different symbols. You got these in your pile?" Eric showed Curtis the page. Curtis shuffled through the papers, paused, and held one up with the matching symbols. "Put those to the side. We'll go through those next."

"Gimmie the alphabet page," Carmen said. Eric ripped it out and handed it to her. "Okay, let's do this."

The four of them got to work trying to make sense of it all. Twenty minutes later, Carmen stopped writing. She re-read what she had deciphered, and the blood drained from her face. Her hands became clammy as fear gripped her. She glanced over at Eric going back and forth with Curtis, who appeared to be going with the flow as they worked on the symbols.

"Okay, we got something here," Eric began. "Looks like Todd is searching for a female partner. Someone he can take back to his coven. There is mention of an experiment, but it's not clear what it is." Eric looked up. "This thing is all over the place."

"I'm trying to get these pages in order," Curtis said.

"It's not an experiment," Carmen said. "He's transforming." She offered Eric her paper. "Todd is turning into a demon."

Everyone's eyes fell on her.

"What the fuck do you mean, he's turning into a demon?"

"That's what it says. He's using some kind of curse or spell to change into one."

"So, he's not a vampire? So, the whole thing with the fangs and morphing face, that's demonic?" Eric started to panic. "What in God's name is going on around here? How did we go from some guy making moves on my girl to demons walking the earth?"

"Eric, stop yelling. It's not makin' the situation better," Dayton said.

"My man, she *just* said he's turning into a demon. The same cat trying to take Kim away from me." He began to tremble. "And this paper said he's looking for a partner, but not why. There's a connection here."

"C'mon, we don't know that," Dayton said.

"Does the book say anything about vampires turning into demons?"

"I haven't read anything yet."

"Then, until it tells me otherwise, I'm going off the belief that Todd is going after Kim because of this spell he's doing." Eric handed everything to Carmen. "We need to head back now."

"Eric's right," Carmen said. "We need to get back and properly go through all this, then plan our next course of action."

CHAPTER SIXTY-TWO

Carmen and Eric continued to review the papers and the information they had deciphered. Eric put his papers in order, so it began to make sense. Then he started to look through the book Dayton gave him.

"I wonder what kind of demon he's supposed to be," he said as he flipped through the pages. "This book names different types."

"I wish we could figure out what this spell is supposed to do. It would at least give us a clue as to why he wants Kim," Carmen said.

"You believe now?" Dayton called from the front seat.

"It makes sense," she said. "He doesn't seem fixated on any other girl except Kim. So there has to be a connection."

Eric closed the book and turned his attention to the bookbag. He dug around in the main section, but it was empty. He opened a smaller one in the front and removed a weathered brown leather-bound journal with a strap tied around it. A silk book marker stuck out the bottom in the center of the book.

"Found this." He offered it to Carmen.

Carmen took it and undid the strap. She took hold of the marker and used it to open the book. Neat handwriting in black ink filled the page. She read it quietly.

"This whole thing is messed up. It's like we're living in some kind of dream. These things aren't supposed to exist," Eric said. "It's not like we can call someone for help, either. This is bad."

"Eric? It's worse than you think," Carmen said. "Dayton, pull over."

"What's wrong?"

"You need to stop driving for me to read this."

Dayton pulled over onto the shoulder of the road leading to the university and put the car in park.

"What's happened?"

Carmen shifted as she brought the journal closer to her face. "Hopefully, the subsequent pages in this diary are clear to you, and you understand Dwain and me were not crazy. I am going to attempt to kill Todd Anderson with what little I know about what kills vampires. It probably won't work, but it's worth a try to stop him from finishing his plan to ascend into a demon. I'm praying he hasn't found a new girl to try to possess."

"What?" Eric said.

"He almost got Crystal. Probably would have succeeded if Dwain hadn't accidentally. . . I can't even write out what he did. But she is dead now and at peace, like my brother. This is my last entry because I don't want to think about this anymore. He needs to die, by my hand. I pray I'm not too late." Carmen paused. "It's signed, Robert." She looked up at the shocked faces. "He wants Kim so he can possess her. You were right, Eric."

"Lemme see that," Dayton said. Carmen handed it to him, and he looked over the page. He thumbed back to the first page, scanned it, then flipped several pages ahead. "This goes back eight months. He's talking about acing some math exams. This is a personal diary." He skipped ahead to the center of the book. "It starts right about here about Todd. Lemme see if I find something that'll tell us more."

"We need to get back to the campus, regroup and find him and kill him tonight," Eric said.

"Kill?" Curtis looked taken aback. "What do you mean, kill?"

"Okay, hold up Eric, before even considering that we need to prep. We don't need to go recklessly into this," Dayton said.

"What do you mean?"

"You know how to kill vampires and demons?"

"Get the drop on him and cut his head off," Eric said.

"Oh yeah, get a machete and slice him open," Dayton said sarcastically. "You're afraid of stepping on a cockroach. How you gonna kill a man?"

Eric and Dayton screamed at one another. Carmen tried to talk over them. Curtis covered his ears and, without any warning, let out a guttural scream that made everyone jump.

"Stop it!" Curtis opened the door, got out of the car, and ran to the rear. Everyone followed him. "Do ya'll hear yourselves? Vampires. Demons. Decapitations. I-I-I'm still processing what happened back on campus and you're over here talking about committing murder."

"Curtis, calm down," Carmen said.

"Don't tell me to calm down. I nearly got myself killed tonight by some. . . I can't even wrap my head around all this right now."

"All the more reason why we need to regroup and figure out the best way to handle this," Dayton said.

"Na, I'm sorry. You're on your own. I can't be a part of this." Curtis stepped back. "You can't ask me to do this. I can't kill someone."

"Curtis, he's not human," Eric said.

"That's not a reason to get my hands bloody. I'm sorry. You're on your own on this." Curtis walked away before running into town.

"This is great." Eric threw his hands up. "Now we have to worry about Curtis and his feelings."

Carmen took his hand. "Eric, look at me." He turned to her. "This is a lot to take in right now and if we don't do this right, we can be killed. It would be one thing if Todd feared us, but the simple fact he went toe to toe with all of us says a lot."

"He's gonna kill Kim. I can't just sit by and do nothing."

"You can't do anything if you're dead." Carmen's eyes teared up. "Kim's my girl. I wouldn't abandon her, but if we're going to stop Todd, we have to be smart."

"We need rest, and we need a plan," Dayton said. "I'm with you on this. Let's head back and check on Kim and make sure she's safe. Then we take things to the next level."

"What about Curtis?" Carmen said.

Eric looked from Dayton to Carmen. "We can't worry about him right now. He needs time to get his head together." He shook his head in disgust. "Let's get back."

"I have someone watching over Kim," Carmen said. "She hasn't contacted me, so I guess no news is good news."

CHAPTER SIXTY-THREE

I*'m on my way back to the campus. How is Kim?* Carmen waited for a response from Michelle but got none. *Michelle, do you hear me?*

Carmen opened her eyes as they drove through the university gate. She tried again and got no response. A sense of worry washed over her.

"You okay?" Dayton glanced at her.

"I will be."

"I'm coming with you to check on Kim," Eric said as he got out first.

Carmen didn't protest. She got out of the car and found herself standing face to face with Michelle, who wore a terrified look.

"I couldn't stop him. He pushed through me and somehow, he's kept me away from Kim," she said.

"What're you talking about?"

"Todd. He's in the dorm. He showed up here about 15 minutes ago and had Kim meet him in the lounge. They've been in there ever since. I can't get through the door to see what's going on."

"Dayton! Hurry!!" Carmen took off running, with Michelle following close behind.

————

E ric and Dayton broke into a run, trying to catch up with Carmen. They watched her nearly knock two girls over as they came out of the dorm.

Dayton stumbled, dropping the diary. Eric slowed to help him. Dayton urged him to keep going, but he went back for him and helped him to his feet.

They hurried to the dorm, entered the lobby, and were met by Carmen, who stopped them in their tracks.

"Go back outside," she said.

"Why? What happened?"

"Todd is in the lounge with Kim." Carmen gave Eric a gentle shove toward the door. "Go back outside and wait for me to try to deal with this."

"Oh, hell no! I'm goin' in there. Kim could be in trouble," Eric said.

Eric pushed Carmen to the side and rushed to the lounge door. He saw Kim through the window staring down at the sofa at Todd, who sat with his back to the door. Eric started to open the door, but Carmen snatched his hand away and pushed him back into the vestibule.

"She's not in danger, but you go in there all fired up. There's no telling what he might do." She turned to Dayton. "Take him outside, please."

Dayton took hold of Eric, but he struggled and tried to fight his way out of his arms. Fed up with his behavior, Carmen slapped him.

"Why'd you slap me?"

"Callate." Carmen yelled. "Listen to me. You need to—"

The door to the lounge opened fast, striking the wall. Kim stormed out, fuming, made a beeline for Eric and punched him hard in his pectoral muscle.

"What the hell is wrong with you?" Eric winced. An expression of disbelief on his face.

"What's wrong with *me*? I'll tell you what's wrong with me. I... no, better I show you." Kim took him by the arm and led him into the lounge.

Carmen and Dayton followed close behind. They circled around to the front of the couch, faced Todd and, one by one, they each had a different reaction. Carmen gasped. Dayton's jaw dropped in shock. Eric's eyes widened in surprise.

Todd sat before them with a swollen eye, bruises on his hands and face, and scratch marks on his neck. He saw Eric and cowered.

"Kim?" Todd called to her.

"I'm here." Kim stepped toward him, but Eric tugged her back.

"Stay away from him. He's dangerous!"

"Get'chor hands off me. You're the one that's dangerous. How could you do this to him?" Kim said.

"What the hell happened to him?" Dayton pointed at Todd's face.

"Todd said you, Dayton and Curtis jumped him." Kim folded her arms and stared Eric down.

"We got into a fight, but no one did *that* to him. He did it to himself." Eric turned to Dayton. "He got the best of us. Look what he did to my hand." Eric held up his hand, showing her his broken finger.

"I was defending myself."

"Kim, I don't know what kinda game he's playin', but we didn't beat him up. If anything, he beat us up," Eric said.

"Todd beat up three of you. I find that hard to believe."

"They surrounded me, kicked me while I lay on the ground, and scratched me," Todd said.

Dayton stared at him.. "What are you trying to do, huh? What is all this?"

"I'm telling my side of the story."

Eric forgot he was dealing with a monster. His mind switched gears, and he went into interrogation mode. "Why didn't you report us to security? Or go to the R.A.? Why'd you come here to Kim?"

"This is the closest building he could come to for help," Kim said.

"Kim, this fight happened about an hour or so ago."

"What do you mean, an hour? He said this happened twenty minutes ago."

"You didn't hear the commotion outside with the police and EMS? We've been. . ." Eric paused. "We were at Chambers this whole time filing a report because. . ." Eric held up a single finger. "How come he didn't he tell the R.A. at the front to call campus police? He crawls in here, calls you, has you harboring him in the lounge, feeding you some BS. You don't find it odd, Kim?"

Carmen smiled. "Nice, Eric."

"Well, if it were you, you would have come to me," Kim said.

"No."

"No?"

"No. You know why? Because I would have been too embarrassed to let you see me beat up. I would have gone to Dayton or Curtis for help. I would have gone to the people I knew would help me get payback. Or if it were this bad, I would have gone to campus police and reported them. I would come to you for sympathy." Eric glared at Todd. "The comforting arms of my girl."

Kim followed Eric's gaze to Todd, who resembled a deer caught in headlights. He stared hard at Eric, then at Kim.

"I could have stayed to talk to the police or gone to the R.A., but that would have pissed him off more. I came here because I figured if I told you, and you know him, you could talk sense into him." Todd's eyes were fixed on Kim. "He's had a thing against me since day one."

"Wow, Eric." Kim shook her head. "You really can't let this go. I don't know why you're so jealous of Todd, but you really need to find a way to deal with all this."

Eric looked confused. He glanced at Carmen and Dayton, his mouth moving, but nothing came out.

"Kim?" Carmen approached. "What in the hell are you talking about?"

"Don't tell me you don't see it. He's had an issue with Todd and our friendship."

Carmen turned to Todd. "What are you doing to her?"

"What do you mean? I'm telling—"

"No, you're doing something to her to make her say these things. Leave her alone!"

"Not you too, Carmen. He's not doing anything to me," Kim said. "Why are all of you against him all of a sudden?"

"He's trying to take you from me."

"Oh, for God's sake! Stop it!" Kim shook from anger. "Grow up, Eric. He's not trying to take me from you. And not for nothing. I'm not your property to take. I have every right to allow anyone I want in my life."

"Even if he's a vampire?" Eric caught himself. He covered his mouth, closed his eyes, and mumbled something into his hand.

Kim leaned in. "Did you say he's a vampire? Like, do you mean in the literal sense or figuratively? Like Dracula?" She sounded.

"Don't say it like I'm nuts. I'm not saying he turns into bats or wolves, but he has the fangs and the eyes," Eric said.

"He's telling the truth." Dayton stepped up alongside Eric. "Todd is a vampire."

"Kim, if you don't believe me, check his mouth."

Kim chuckled. "You're serious." She looked at all their straight faces. "This is ridiculous." She strode over to Todd and stared him in the face. "Open your mouth."

Todd laughed. "C'mon, Kim, you're not buying this, are you?"

"Why are you stalling?" Eric winced and placed his sprained finger into the palm of his other hand for support.

"This is the most ridiculous thing I ever heard," Todd said.

"Then open your mouth," Dayton said.

Todd struggled to his feet with a frown. He opened his mouth for Kim. She peeked inside and her mouth dropped open in surprise.

"I don't believe it," she said. Eric and Dayton moved closer. Carmen prepared to pull her back. "Your teeth are perfect."

"What?" Dayton said.

"He has the best set of teeth I have ever seen. No fillings or anything."

"What about his canines?" Eric said.

"Look normal to me," she said. They gathered around to see there were no signs of the vampire canines. "What are you going to tell me next?"

"It's a trick. I'm telling you, he had fangs."

"If he were a vampire, would he walk around in daylight? I thought vampires hated the sun," Kim said.

"Um, vampires can walk around in the daytime. They can't walk in direct sunlight," Dayton pointed out.

"You know what? Come to think of it, there hasn't been any sun out since he came here. Every day has been overcast or raining," Eric said.

"Okay, this is getting too weird. I don't want to hear any more of this," Kim said.

"You mean you don't want to hear the truth."

"Don't raise your voice at her," Todd bellowed.

"Keep it up and I'll put a stake in your chest," Eric threatened.

"Eric, stop it. Stop talking like you're in high school," Kim said.

"Stop acting like his bitch, catering to him!"

"ERIC!" Carmen screamed.

Eric didn't have time to react. Kim's hand came down hard across his face, causing him to stumble sideways and almost fall. The pain radiated in his skull. Eric clasped the side of his face, screaming after he let his broken finger go and stared in shock at her.

She slapped him again on the other side. Eric backed up. Neither one said a word. Todd placed a comforting hand on her shoulder. She allowed it.

There was no coming back from what he said. Eric knew it, Kim knew it and, worst of all, Todd knew it.

"I..." Kim closed her eyes and swallowed. "I don't think I want to be around you anymore. In fact, as far as I'm concerned, we never met."

"Kim, that's a bit harsh," Eric said.

"Well, at least I know where I stand with him. Todd is right about you. I-I can't even look at you now."

Kim rushed out the lounge, nearly knocking Carmen over as she stormed down the hall.

"Kim. Kim, wait." Carmen gave chase.

Dayton stepped to Eric's side and put a comforting hand on his shoulder. Eric turned to Todd.

"I don't care what you are at this point. So, help me God I'm gonna–"

"You're not going to do a damn thing." Todd got in Eric's face. "You see, I got you dead to rights. I kicked your ass earlier and now I've taken your woman. She'll be in my arms soon enough. You and your punk ass friends can't touch me."

"I'm not afraid of you." Eric shook with fear and anger.

"The last man in your position wasn't afraid of me, either. Believe me, your courage doesn't faze me."

They stared each other down. Dayton touched Eric's shoulder.

"Easy. Back away."

Eric stepped back.

Todd nodded. "Go on, back down. Pretty soon you'll be bowing down to me." He cracked his knuckles and headed for the door. "We're done here."

"You don't have to worry about anyone else finding out what you are. I have no intentions of saying another word," Eric said.

Todd stopped. "I'm not worried others will find out about me."

"I wanted to give you a little peace of mind because I don't want anyone in my way."

"In your way of what?"

"In my way of killing you," Eric said. "Believe me, I am going to kill you."

"Are you? Many have tried. As you can see, I'm still here." He smiled at Eric again. "He's a vampire." He broke into a heavy laugh as he exited the lounge.

Eric turned to Dayton and all the color left his face. Dayton ushered him to the sofa and sat him down.

"Head between your legs and breathe. Easy man," Dayton said.

Eric tried his best to breathe. Images passed through his mind of him and Kim during happier times, but they were muddied with images of Todd.

CHAPTER SIXTY-FOUR

Carmen came out of the 1stfloor bathroom with Kim who couldn't stop crying. She handed her a paper towel and put a comforting arm around her. They spoke quietly, with Kim nodding several times. Carmen gave her a hug, looked out toward the lounge, and saw Todd leaving for the exit.

"Go up to our room. I'll be up soon," Carmen said. "I need to take care of something."

"I don't want to speak to him. Tell him not to even call me."

Carmen hugged her again, ushered her down the hall, and chased after Todd. She spotted him shy of the front door. Michelle blocked his way.

"He's tryin' to leave," she said to Carmen.

Todd saw Carmen approaching. His face was now devoid of bruises. He cracked a sinister grin, said something in a language she didn't understand before walking through Michelle and out the door.

Michelle moaned in misery. Carmen rushed to help her, but she waved her away and pointed to the door. Carmen ran after him.

"Hey, Todd! You think you're slick, but your time is up. We're coming for you."

Todd stopped and glared. "Really. Well, let me quell the fire brewing inside you and tell you, I don't care. You and your little ghost friend and buddies are not going to stop me."

"I noticed you didn't mention I bested you."

"No need to include you in that conversation. And besides, I have something else in mind for you. No need to have Kim at odds with you, too. She'll need you for comfort due to the break-up. So, I tell you what. We're done here tonight. You go on back in there, help your friend, ease some tensions, and get some rest. You're going to need it."

Michelle appeared alongside Carmen. "I'm okay now."

Carmen nodded. "We'll be ready for you."

"Hopefully more than you were in the science building." He looked at Michelle. "And you, ghost, I'll be seeing you soon."

With that, he walked away.

"What do you think he meant?" Michelle said.

Carmen turned to her. She looked at the campus information bulletin board. "Oh."

"What?" Michelle turned around. A posted flier with her picture on it, along with a telephone number to call Debra, her roommate. "Leave it to Deb. She's a good friend."

"We have to let someone know you're dead, Michelle."

"You can tell them."

"I don't know if I should. They're gonna wanna know how I know you're dead and I don't think me telling them I speak to ghosts is going to go over well." Carmen looked down at the ground briefly, took a deep breath. "Michelle, do you remember how you died?"

"I remember being attacked." She pointed to the south gate. "Out there in the woods. Some kind of creature attacked me. I don't really remember a lot afterwards. I walked back from out there the day I came to you."

"What kind of creature? If we went back out there, would you know where I could find you?"

Michelle shook her head. "I don't know what it was. I guess I could show you. You want to go now?"

"No, we got too much else going on tonight."

The front door swung open. Dayton followed a distraught Eric. They all converged further down the walkway.

"How's Kim?" Dayton asked.

"Devastated. I'm gonna hunker down tonight and keep an eye on her."

"She never wants to talk to me again. Does she?" Eric said.

"Well, it's safe to say you're not going to make boyfriend of the year. I can't believe you. With what we're up against, you go and say that."

"I didn't mean it." Eric tightened his face to hold the tears at bay. "He pissed me off."

"I'm making a command decision. We're putting a pause on everything. We're all tired and frustrated. We need to sleep. We'll take the papers and the diary for safekeeping. If you need us. You know where we will be."

"Give me the diary. I'll be up late so I can try to get some reading done."

Dayton took it from his pocket and handed it to her. "Hope it tells you something."

Carmen nodded. Dayton put his arm around Eric, and the two of them walked back to Chambers Hall. She saw Kim watching her from their dorm window. Carmen took a deep breath and headed back inside.

Lightning danced across the sky.

———

K evin watched the lightning storm close in. It flashed and rumbled, shaking the earth beneath his feet.

"This is bad." Zeborah pointed to the sky. "That there's a sign he done did somethin' makin' him one step closer to this ascension. What we gonna do?"

Kevin shook his head. "I don't know."

"Nothing to do now but wait." Todd stepped out of the woods and into the clearing. His eyes were milky white, and he bared his teeth. His face had contorted again. "Tomorrow night, I make my final move."

Kevin frowned at Todd's appearance, but didn't back away. "What's happened?"

"The girl is but all mine now. The wedge between her and Eric is in place. Tomorrow, I seal the deal, and I will leave Bruckner with my host. I'll perform the final rites ritual during the next crescent moon." Todd said.

"Crescent moon? That's in three days." Kevin shook his head. "I'm not going to be able to find a new place for the ritual in time."

"You won't have to. I want you to prepare this area for Kim. Relocate one of the crates from the lab and bring it here. We will keep her buried until the time is right. Then, once we're done, I want you to prepare for our departure back to the coven."

"How do you expect us to get the crates off the campus? We have to go through the checkpoint to get them out of there," Kevin said.

"That's for you to figure out. Oh, and there is one more thing I need you to prepare."

"What am I preparing?"

"Not what, who. Rakim."

"Rakim? What do you. . .?" Kevin's mouth dropped open. "No, Todd." Helet out a bloodcurdling scream, clutching his stomach and holding his head, writhed in pain as Todd approached him.

"This isn't up for discussion. You're going to prepare Rakim to be released on the campus on the night we leave. The chaos will buy us the cover we need to escape. And so we're clear, you *will* aid me in possessing Kim, destroy this shell I am in, and finally kill Eric and his cronies." He knelt next to Kevin. "And the medium dies as well. Painfully. Understood?"

Kevin screamed. "Release me. Get out of my head."

Zeborah hurried to Kevin's aid, but Todd waved a warning finger.

"Don't make me hurt you, too," Todd said. "You're coming back to campus with me right now and helping me begin consolidating things. And to keep watch over my room. Eric may try something, and I gave the medium my word I wouldn't retaliate. I never said anything about you."

"I'm not killin' anyone on campus."

"I didn't say you had to. If he tries anything, I want you to subdue him with a bite and bring him out here. He can witness my ascension before he dies." Todd stood up. "Let's go, Zeborah."

Zeborah looked concerningly at Kevin, who nodded for him to go. Kevin's head returned to normal as soon as Todd and Zeborah left. He got to his feet and watched with fury as they disappeared into the darkness.

CHAPTER SIXTY-FIVE

A succession of gentle knocks awoke Eric in the early morning hours. Peering over at Dayton, sleeping with the demon book open like a tent on his chest, he considered waking him but thought better of it.

Opening the door without thinking, a hand reached out for him. Eric let out a scream that woke Dayton, who jumped out of his bed and rushed to his side. Both readied their fists to fight. They paused upon seeing Curtis with his hands raised.

"It's me," he said.

"Man, what the hell you grab me like that for?" Eric said.

"Sorry."

"Curtis, it's five o'clock," Dayton groaned.

"I know. I couldn't sleep. C-Can I come in?"

Eric waved him in. "What's up?"

"I wanna apologize for walking off. You know I'd never leave you guys hangin'. I been up all night pissed off with myself for leaving. However, I can help, you know I'm here for you guys. All of you."

Eric gave him a hug. "It's all good, bro. No one's mad at you."

He broke the embrace. "I couldn't really sleep either. A lot happened after you left." Eric filled him in on the details of what happened between him and Kim. "Not sure what direction we're gonna go in, but we're getting together this morning to try to figure things out."

"Let's meet at the library. It's safer to talk there," Curtis said.

"What do you mean, safer?" Dayton said.

"You forget Todd lives downstairs? If he's a vampire or demon or whatever, there's a chance he can hear us, isn't it? We can't go on making plans around here."

"I didn't even think about that," Eric said.

"We can meet in a couple of hours. I'll get us a study room."

"No." Dayton stepped in. "Let's find somewhere else to work. After what happened to Carmen in that area, it might be better to stay away from it. Can you arrange another place?"

"No problem. Call Carmen and let her know." Curtis started for the door. "I'll meet you over there."

"Curtis, it's five in the morning," Eric said.

"Text her then. Give her a time to come over, then let me know. I'll let you know where to go. I'm going to go over there now and start pulling information on vampires and demons." Curtis headed for the door in a hurry. "I'll be waiting for your call."

"Curtis, wait." Dayton handed him the demon book. "See if you can find matches for this book. You know, others like it. And look for anything on how to kill these kinds of monsters. I don't care what it is. Anything at this point."

Curtis looked at the book as he took it. "Best I go now. This will take a while."

Eric turned to Dayton. "Maybe I should go with him. Get a head start on things. You and Carmen can come later. I'm not gonna get any sleep at this point."

"I'll reach out then."

Getting his coat, then his phone off his desk, they bumped fists before Eric left with Curtis.

———

They worked for two hours, gathering books and marking off pages with pertinent information. They had amassed a total of fifteen books relevant to vampires and seven about demons. The archives didn't prove to be as great an asset as Eric had hoped with the information steeped in folklore. They did find two books explaining exorcisms, but to perform one, they needed someone who knew the ritual and the religion associated with the demon. The wrong holy man chosen to perform the exorcism could piss the demon off and do more damage.

"Well, that wasn't in the movie," Curtis chided after reading it.

At 7:30 am, they received a text from Dayton. He and Carmen were going to come to the library after breakfast. Curtis suggested to Eric that they join them and get some nourishment before they got back to work.

They all met in the cafeteria, choosing a table in the corner so they could speak privately. Curtis told them what he and Eric had found so far in the books. Dayton suggested they take shifts since they still had afternoon classes later in the day.

Carmen filled Curtis in on the details of what happened with Kim. Eric pushed his food away and began to stew.

"There is one more thing. I have been getting some help from a ghost." She looked to her left and nodded at an empty space by the wall. "I'm not going to get into the logistics of who it is, but she did tell me she was killed out in the woods by a creature of some kind." She looked at Eric. "I did find something in the diary. Robert mentioned there are three other vampires, Kevin, Zeborah, and one called Rakim. I know about Zeborah. Rakim, all he says is he doesn't look human. Kevin's the one who fed him information to stop Todd."

"Okay, how does that help us?" Eric said.

"For starters, I bet it's Kevin who has been helping me. We need to find him."

"Where would we even begin to look?" Eric said.

"I want to go out into the woods and look for the dead girl's body. I think if I find her, I'll find them." She turned to Dayton. "Maybe Rakim killed her. If so, that means they're close by."

"You not goin' out into the woods alone looking for vampires?" Dayton covered his mouth. "Why did that sound stupid?"

"How do you know they won't kill you?" Curtis said.

"I doubt it." She turned to look in the corner. "What? Where?" Carmen turned around. "Oh, oh."

Everyone looked toward the entrance and saw Kim crossing the cafeteria, looking disheveled but on a mission. She had her arms tucked in tight as she approached Eric.

"I need to speak with Eric alone," she said.

"Dayton, Curtis, c'mon. We'll be outside," Carmen said.

Kim waited until they were gone. Tears ran down her face. She didn't sit down.

"I hate to see you cry." Eric stood and put his hand out.

"Don't touch me!" She took a small step backward.

"I'm not," he said. "What I said slipped out. But still, there is no reason for me to say what I said."

"I can't believe you can't trust my judgment. Todd tried to make his move on me, but I told him I wasn't interested."

"All the girls on this campus. Why'd he choose you?" Eric shook his head. "Why are we talking about him like he's a regular guy?"

"Eric, I don't know where you got that fantasy in your head about him being a vampire, but you need to stop."

"I'm not going to try to convince you of what I, Dayton, and Curtis know." Eric stopped and closed his eyes. "Kim, if you don't ever want to speak to me again, that's fine." He looked at her. "But I won't let this man hurt you. You don't want to believe that, then I don't know what to tell you."

Kim stared at him for a long moment.

"Well, it's nice to know it doesn't bother you that I don't ever speak to you again."

"That's not what I meant."

"I have to go. I can't do this with you." Kim shook her head. "After four years. . ." Kim fled the cafeteria.

Eric sat for a moment. A fire burned in the pit of his stomach. He slammed his fists on the table, let out a scream, and shoved all the dishes onto the floor.

———

Ten minutes later, Eric walked out of the cafeteria to a waiting Dayton and Curtis. Without saying a word, Dayton took him by the elbow and beckoned him to the side.

"We're changing plans, completely," he said.

"What? Why?"

"Just come on."

They headed back across campus. None of them spoke. At the basketball courts, Dayton stopped and leaned against the fence. Curtis looked around, angst-ridden, before speaking.

"We should make a list," he said.

"Wait for Carmen," Dayton replied.

"We don't have to wait for her to make a list."

"Based on what? Folklore? Let's see what she has to say, then we can take it from there."

"Why do I feel I'm out of the loop on something?" Eric said.

"Here she comes."

Eric spotted Carmen walking toward them with her backpack on. She pointed to a bench across from the court and they followed her. She sat, and they gathered around her.

"Curtis, can you ditch work-study today?"

"I can ditch everything if you need me."

"We're gonna need weapons. Anything we can use against a vampire."

"Gotcha. Buildings and grounds have all kinds of tools. I can also make a run to the hardware store and pick up several items. We can make some stuff as well," he said.

"I want you to take Dayton with you. Eric is coming with me."

"Where are we going?"

"We're going to find the other vampires ourselves."

"The hell we are! We go as a group and do this," Eric said.

"No, we don't have time to do that. If we have to face off with Todd, we need to be two steps ahead. We have to be ready to strike back and if we don't have weapons ready, this will be a short fight!"

"You want me to go with you into the woods, unarmed and unprotected, to find a vampire? It hasn't occurred to you we'll get attacked?" Eric threw up his hands. "That's what you want to do?"

"It's not what I want, it's what has to be done. And you're not going in there unprotected. You have me and my abilities. We have a ghost ready to fight by our side." She stood. "I don't believe we're in danger from this one."

"You sure you wanna do this, Carmen?" Dayton said. "Maybe it will be easier to have me and Eric go. You and Curtis get weaponized."

"Dayton, at some point, I have to trust instincts and myself. This is an ability I have to live with. I don't have a choice in the matter. My abuela reminded me," Carmen paused and took a deep breath and said, "I can't always take the easy road and none of this is going to get easier. If this vampire's the one feeding me information, I need to secure our ally."

"But why Eric?" Dayton said.

"Because Kim is the one in danger, not you or Curtis." She looked at Eric. "I don't know what happened after we left you two, but she said that she's officially done with you. I walked back to the room with her and tried to calm her down, but I couldn't do anything for her."

"She's just mad."

"No, she's done, Eric. I know her. And if Todd thought he had a one-up on us last night, it's official. And Kim has classes today in the science building, so the chances of her running into him are pretty good," Carmen said.

Eric shook his head in defiance. "It doesn't matter at this point. Todd's not getting his hands on her."

"And we're going to make sure of that. Dayton, can we get your car?"

"No problem." He took the keys from his pocket and handed them to her.

Carmen handed them to Eric. "Pick me up here. I'm not going near Chambers Hall. I don't want Todd to pick up on my presence." She looked at Dayton and Curtis. "Let's meet back here in two hours. We can regroup and advance to the next phase."

"Which is what?" Curtis said.

"I have no idea. Guess we'll have to wait and see," she said.

CHAPTER SIXTY-SIX

Eric returned with the car and within minutes. They drove through the back entrance and onto the road.

Carmen stared out the passenger side window as Eric drove. Michelle leaned forward between the seats, looking left and right.

"Any of this look familiar?" Carmen said above a whisper as she glanced over at Michelle.

"No. I mean yes. I mean, no it doesn't look like where I had the accident. I think it's further down, close to where the fork in the road is."

"Eric, stop at the fork in the road up ahead. That's where the accident may have happened."

"What's she look like?"

"Who?"

"The ghost. Is she like transparent or vapor?"

"She looks like a regular person. Why would she look like vapor?"

"I don't know. I didn't mean anything by it. I was just asking. Until yesterday, I had never seen an actual vampire." Eric sighed. "I feel like I'm in the Twilight Zone or something. I keep replaying everything over in my head. It feels like every effort I've made was for nothing. God, I'm exhausted."

"He's a good boyfriend," Michelle said. Carmen nodded. "He really loves Kim."

"Yes, he does," Carmen said.

"What?"

"Not you. I'm talking to the ghost."

"Truthfully, though, the way you've stepped up and been leading the charge is impressive."

"I'm just goin' with it."

"No, don't sell yourself short. We're all following your lead at this point. I got your back."

"Aww," Michelle said.

"Stop it," Carmen blushed. "Not you, the ghost."

"There's the fork." Michelle pointed out the front window.

"Pull over here. On the side," Carmen urged.

Eric pulled the car over, stopped, and all of them exited the vehicle. They stood on the shoulder, looking around.

"Wow, it is quiet out here," Eric said.

"Michelle, do you remember where it happened?" Carmen said.

"I was coming up that way and this thing came from over there." She pointed to the woods across the road and pointed to the woods behind her. "I ended up over in this direction somewhere."

Carmen looked back at the woods across from them. "You up for a walk in the woods?"

"I don't like the idea of being caught in there, Carmen. I've seen enough slasher flicks to know that's not a good choice."

"I got your back if you want to go through the woods," Michelle said.

"Eric, we're going to have to go in there, anyway."

He turned to the woods. "There… what the hell is that?"

Carmen turned to see a half bat, half-human creature standing among a group of trees. It stared at them.

"That's it," Michelle said. "That's the creature!"

Rakim screamed and shot toward Eric. Carmen froze. Eric ran, but he tripped over his feet and tumbled to the ground.

Rakim was on him in seconds. He put all his weight on him so he couldn't get up. With his clawed hands planted on the blacktop, he leaned into Eric's face and growled.

Eric's screams came from deep inside. His throat cracked as he punched Rakim's face in hopes he would get off. Instead, it seemed to anger the creature. It swiped Eric's hands away and began to choke him.

———

"Carmen! Carmen, we have to help him!"

"Right!" She ran up behind Rakim and palmed both sides of his head. *Rakim let go of Eric.*

Rakim roared and tried to dislodge her wrists. Michelle appeared behind her and placed her hands over Carmen's. Their hands melded together as Michelle combined with Carmen. A surge of energy passed through Carmen, and she dug her fingertips further into Rakim's head while she concentrated hard to telepathically coerce him to let Eric go.

He howled as his body convulsed.

The most excruciating pain exploded in her head. It knocked Michelle out of her and sent her screaming in agony. The palms of a man's hands pressed against Carmen's ears; the fingertips pressed her temples. All of her energy drained. Her body went limp and was guided to the ground. Kevin's face appeared above her.

"Well, I am impressed, medium. I see you've been doing your reading and discovered how to get possessed by a ghost and use it to your advantage." He stroked her hair. "Sorry about having to hurt you. I couldn't let you harm Rakim. He doesn't know better." He stood. "Now stay still while I tend to your friend over here. Once I'm done, we can talk."

Carmen struggled to talk but couldn't.

Eric shouted. "Please, don't kill me!"

CHAPTER SIXTY-SEVEN

Kim crossed campus with her book bag filled with textbooks on her way to the science lab. She intended to spend the entire day away from her room and immersed in schoolwork. She didn't want to be around anything that could bring thoughts of Eric. Twice since the incident at breakfast, she had burst into an uncontrollable crying fit, forcing her to leave both math and english classes and hide out in the bathroom.

The lab assignment didn't require a partner. Kim settled into a corner station with a microscope, took out her notebook, and began to prepare her slates.

Hi, Kim. She looked up upon hearing Todd's voice. He was nowhere in the room. Chalking it up to her imagination, she turned her attention back to the microscope to look at the amoeba on the slate.

Kim?

"What do you want?" Kim looked up.

Other students watched her. The area where the leech had bitten her started to itch. She scratched it while searching around the lab.

"Everything okay, Ms. Morris?" Professor Skillman said.

"I'm sorry. I thought I heard someone calling my name." She glanced one last time, then went back to her assignment.

Look to your left. She saw him standing by the open door. He waved and mouthed the words, "I need to speak to you."

"No." She shook her head.

"I just want to talk."

Kim had an uncontrollable urge to lash out at him. A deeply pitted rage she didn't understand. She scratched the leech bite again and pounded the desk. She saw him smile and nod at her reaction.

You feel it, don't you? Come on out and I can explain.

"Leave me alone!"

"Ms. Morris?" Professor Skillman came to her. "Are you okay?" She looked at Todd. The smile fell from his face. "Where are you supposed to be?" She headed to him. He stepped back. "Can I help you?"

"I was saying hi to my friend Kim."

"You're disturbing my lab and from the looks of it, you're disturbing her. Walk away from my room, please," she said.

Todd glanced back at Kim, smirked and walked away. "Come see me, Kim. I'll be waiting."

Kim sat motionless as curiosity and fear clashed within her. She held the edge of the table for support as she started to feel dizzy. She shut her eyes until she was steady again.

"I'm sorry, I have to go." Kim opened her eyes and began shoving her materials into her book bag. She stumbled, getting out of her chair as she made a dash out the door.

She didn't see him in the hall, but she knew where he was. She took the stairs to the upper labs to his door. She opened it without knocking and found him inside tending to the crate of leeches. She slammed the door, then tossed her things on the nearest table.

"What's your end game?" she said.

"I don't know what you mean." He didn't look up from the soil

"Downstairs at the door? What are you trying to do to me?"

"I wanted to tell you I'm leaving Bruckner." He wiped his hands together, cleaning the dirt from them. "I decided it would be better for me if I transfer out of here. Besides, I need to do two more things then I will be through. I don't need to stay here to finish." Todd shrugged his shoulders. "It's for the best, anyway."

"Okay. You didn't need to track me down to say that."

"Well, you see, the reason why I needed to see you was to say I haven't been completely honest with you. I haven't only been interested in you because of your interest in my research. You possess a quality I find to be both attractive and necessary for my goals." Todd took her hand. "Which is why I want you to come with me. I need you to come with me."

Kim yanked her hand back. "You must be nuts! I can't leave school to go with a man I don't know. I don't even *know* you well to even consider leaving."

Todd placed a cupped hand on her cheek. "What I am about to do is going to make me famous. And the power. I want to continue to share it with you. You and I, together, we will be both revered and feared."

Kim swooned at the sound of his voice. His touch warmed her face, and it radiated down to the pit of her stomach. The leech bite stung. Rage bubbled inside her.

"Take your hand off me!" she demanded.

"You feel it again. Don't you? It's swelling inside you as it is in me. Don't you see? We were meant to be together." He placed his hands on her shoulders. "You're my proof my experiment has worked. The leeches have done their job. And now, I can begin the ascension phase."

Kim tore away and shoved him. "Get off me." She distanced

herself from him. "I don't know what the hell you're trying to do. But you won't do it with me."

Todd nodded. "I see, and I understand your apprehension. I want you to remember this moment, Kim. Remember, I asked first." Todd walked to the door and locked it. He turned to her, his eyes burned crimson. He bared his fangs. "Unfortunately, no isn't an option for you."

At the sight of seeing his fangs, she covered her open mouth and backed away from him, bumping into tables, then into the crate.

The leech that bit you injected you with enough of my blood that we are connected. You will be my host. My demonic persona will occupy your body, repress enough of your soul so you are conscious of what is happening but unable to stop anything from occurring. Todd zipped across the room and pinned her against the crate. He caressed her cheek. "Beautiful Kim. You will join me." He leaned into her ear and whispered, "in immortality."

Todd put his hand over her mouth and bit into her shoulder. The tips of his fangs broke her skin as he brought her to the floor.

Kim punched him as hard as she could across his face. He let go. She managed to get to her feet and stumbled toward the door. He rushed her and grasped the back of her shirt. She swung her elbowed and struck him in the cheekbone. Todd released her. She kicked him in his balls, and shoved him as hard as she could, sending him over the top of a desk.

A burning, searing sensation radiated in her shoulder. It crawled down through her skin to the leech bite, numbing her arm. The room spun as the effects of Todd's bite coursed through her. Her skin was on fire, her nerve endings tingled. She dropped to the floor and writhed in agony.

Todd stood over her.

The lock clicked. Todd looked in its direction. Kim could hear everything, but couldn't budge. The door opened, and she heard a gasp. She saw Todd smile. "The demon's venom is working. I've incapacitated her."

The next face Kim saw was Zeborah looking down at her as he walked over.

"I thought we were waitin'."

"Get her feet and let's put her in the crate," Todd said.

Zeborah and Todd lifted her body and set her down on the crate's moist earth.

"See you tonight, my dear," Todd said.

She watched as the lid to the crate passed over her head and set in place with a loud bang.

Kim lay in darkness.

———

Zeborah locked the lab door. He and Todd went up to the roof. Zeborah hung back while Todd walked to the edge and looked out at the campus.

"I'll need you to stay here and keep watch over Kim." Turning to face Zeborah he said, "In case the venom wears off and she wakes up and starts calling for help. Keep her quiet." He held up a warning finger. "Do not, under any circumstances, bite her. You taint her body with your vampiric fil-" he stopped short of saying filth. "Find a way."

Hate swelled inside Zeborah. He contemplated pushing Todd off the roof, but the fall wouldn't kill him. Break some bones, yes, but not give Zeborah the satisfaction he wanted.

"And what if someone comes lookin' for her?"

"They won't. She and Eric are through. The medium has her own issues to deal with. By the time anyone does notice she's missing, we'll be gone. But not before laying waste to the campus. We go amid the chaos."

Zeborah walked to the edge of the roof and surveyed the

campus. He looked back toward the woods where Kevin and Rakim were. He then glanced at Todd. A worried look showed on his face. He nodded and headed for the door.

"What's wrong with you?" Todd said, but he didn't answer. "Zeborah?"

Zeborah looked at him.

"Don't forget the bigger picture. The Coven forced my hand in all this."

"I know. I'll be in the lab."

"I'll be in my room getting prepared. I'll be to you by sundown."

Zeborah went back into the building and made his way back to the lab. His thoughts went to Savannah and how scared she must have been. being attacked by Todd and placed in the crate. Her body fed upon in the damp soil. Anger percolated inside. But his fury increased once he was back in the lab and his eyes fell upon the crate Kim lay in. His heart went out to her.

Zeborah started to call Kevin, but then, realizing Todd could sense and possibly intercept his telepathic communication, he opted not to try. Instead, he decided to wait for the opportune moment to sneak away and warn him.

CHAPTER SIXTY-EIGHT

Carmen sat in the back seat of Dayton's car and wrapped Eric's hand with an ace bandage from the first aid kit. Luckily, Eric had not done any more damage to his already injured finger after falling. He sat still as a statue, staring at the back of Rakim's head in the passenger seat as Kevin drove them up to the cabin. They parked and Kevin got out first, rushed around to the passenger side and took Rakim out. They walked back to the cabin as Rakim kept looking back at them.

"There," Carmen said as she finished. "You want to wait here while I go talk to him?"

"The hell I am. I'm not letting you go in there alone." They simultaneously got out of the car. "I thought that thing was gonna kill me."

"The fact we're both alive proves my point. They don't want to hurt us."

"No, just scare us to death!" Eric stared at the cabin. "Appropriate living conditions, I see."

Carmen started walking as Kevin emerged from inside and

approached them. They met halfway. Carmen folded her arms and gave him an angry stare.

"I chained Rakim back up." Kevin gestured to the cabin with his thumb. "You took the fight out of him, Carmen. Very good. You're understanding how to use your abilities in different ways."

"So, you are the one that's been helping me."

"I am."

"With books. Yeah, thanks," she said. "You've been a big help."

"Don't get smart. You're lucky I decided to feed you information, otherwise you'd be suffering from a nervous breakdown by now." He turned to Eric. "You're going to act that way against Todd?"

"What?"

"Screaming and stumbling all over the place. Crying out, "don't kill me"."

"My man, you sic that monster on us. What reaction did you think I would have?"

"Don't call him a monster. He's not a monster."

"Creature then!"

Kevin rushed him. Eric managed to get one punch in before Kevin brought him down and pinned his head to the ground. He bared his fangs.

"You're pissing me off. It's men like you who put your mortals in harm's way!"

"Stop it." Michelle appeared and tried to pull Kevin off Eric. "Get off him. Carmen, help me."

Carmen hurried over and joined with Michelle. Kevin let go of Eric at once and backed away.

"Don't touch me."

Carmen and Michelle separated. Carmen tended to Eric and helped him up off the ground. They turned to Kevin, who had now put distance between them.

"So, my touch can hurt you like it hurt Todd."

"If you're joined with a spirit, yes. Wait, you didn't know that? I thought you read about it in the book I gave you."

"I haven't had time. I flipped around in it and read some things here and there I thought I could use. This guy Robert wrote about you in his diary. So, we have no choice now but to come to you. Why are you hiding? Why are you attacking me, then disappearing?"

"I've never attacked you. I admit my tactics have been—"

"Hey, either you tell us how to kill Todd or—" Eric chimed.

"Or what?" Kevin took a deep breath to calm down. "Damn it! I really thought I had found the right ones for this." He buried his head in his hands. "Things with Todd are moving faster than I anticipated, and I hoped you'd be ready by now."

"What are you talking about?"

"We need to talk before we do anything else." He looked at Eric. "Where are your other friends?"

"Off getting weapons to kill Todd."

"Create an open text message for them for me, then give me your phone."

"What for?"

"Just do it," Carmen said.

Eric sighed, took out his phone, and created the open message. He tossed the phone to Kevin. He filled it in, then pressed send. He tossed it back to him. Eric read the message as Kevin went back to the cabin.

"You gave them directions to come here? Why?"

"We have a lot of ground to cover. Come inside when they arrive," Kevin said.

———

Dayton and Curtis arrived a half-hour later. Before either of them could ask any questions, Carmen ushered them all inside the cabin. Kevin stood in the center of the room. They could hear Rakim growling beneath them.

"What the hell is downstairs?" Curtis said.

"Trust me right now, you don't want to know," Eric said.

Kevin detailed everything, from the coven to the Rucker brothers, and why he and the others had come to Bruckner. He spoke uninterrupted for several minutes, after which he allowed them a moment to take everything in.

Carmen crossed her arms and held herself as if she were cold. Dayton placed his arms around her. She glanced at Michelle, who stood with a stunned look on her face. She looked over at Eric, who looked ill as he stared at the floor. Curtis looked pissed.

"So let me see if I got this right," Curtis began. "Todd's doing this because he was being bullied?"

"Do you think mortals are the only ones who are affected by bullying?" Kevin said.

"Honestly, I never even considered it. Of all the things I have ever heard of about vampires, getting revenge for being bullied isn't one of them."

"That's true," Dayton said.

"Who cares?" Eric crossed to Dayton. "We have to kill Todd now."

"You can't kill him now," Kevin said.

"The hell we can't. We know where he is in the dorm. We have weapons and a medium," Eric said. "What are we waiting for? Curtis, let's go."

Curtis started for the door. "Let's do this!"

Zeborah appeared before them, blocking their way. "You can't go" He looked over at Kevin. "He went back to his room to prepare for t'night. Say's we're leaving." He glanced at Carmen. "Ya found her."

"She found me."

Zeborah came into the cabin and stopped. He gripped the side of his head.

"Carmen? Do you know how to?" Kevin pointed from his head to Zeborah's.

"I think so." Carmen stood aligned with Zeborah. She closed her eyes. She suddenly drew a blank as to what to do. She furrowed her brow in frustration.

"Listen to my voice." Kevin walked up behind her, placed his hand on her shoulder and leaned into her ear. "This is going to happen in stages, okay?" He squeezed her shoulder. She nodded. "Now, clear your mind of everything. Create an empty space. Once you've done it, I want you to picture Zeborah in your mind. Make him as clear as you can."

Carmen concentrated. In her mind, Zeborah materialized within an empty space. "I see him."

"Good. Now I want you to create a barrier between the two of you. Create a slab of black glass. Make it so you can barely see him."

Carmen nodded and pictured the slab. It rose from the ground, separating them. She could barely make out his frame. "Okay, I did it."

"Let the image burn into your mind, then what you're going to do is tuck it away."

She started to turn her head. "What?"

"Focus, Carmen. Face forward." He tapped her head. She turned her head forward again. "A medium's mind works differently than others. It's a vast void that allows for large quantities of information to pass through from this world and the next. You can store this information in your subconscious now, and this allows you to go undetected by Zeborah. Push it out of your sight. Once you no longer can see it, open your eyes."

Carmen concentrated on moving Zeborah and the black glass further into the darkness of the void until they were both gone. She opened her eyes. He no longer held the side of his head.

"How did you know how to do that? What else can you show me?"

"It's a long story we don't have time for. It's why you should really read the book." Kevin returned to the center of the room. "He's ready to run again?"

"It's not only that. He done grabbed Kim and sealed her in one of the crates in the lab," Zeborah said.

"Whadya mean he grabbed Kim?" Eric shouted. He listened as Zeborah told them what had happened in the lab. His jaw slacked from panic. "We have to go get her!"

"Eric, wait." Dayton rushed to him and held his arm. "Listen to me."

"Get your fuckin' hands off me!" Eric tried to break free from Dayton's grip. It didn't work. He tried to punch him, but Dayton ducked, and he missed. They tumbled to the floor and Dayton hung on to him. "I gotta go get my girl."

"Calm down! We have to do this right." Dayton said.

Dayton and Eric wrestled. After a moment, Kevin yanked them apart with such strength both men slid across the floor to opposite sides of the room. Curtis helped Eric to his feet while Carmen helped Dayton.

"Enough of this. We all want to end this. Fighting one another, going off the deep in, and rushing into matters isn't going to help. We need to come up with a viable plan."

"Kevin, I can't stay here," Zeborah interrupted. "I'm supposed to be guardin' the girl. Todd goes back to the lab and I'm not there. We're gonna have some problems."

"Don't go yet. Did Todd say when he wanted to leave? Timewise?"

"Sometime t'night."

"He's going to wait until dark like the last time, which gives us a few hours to get things together. I need you to do something for me. Go back to the lab and summon Todd. I need him out of his room. There's something I need to get from inside there."

"What do you want me ta say I need him for?"

Kevin scratched his chin. "You'll tell him the Rucker's contacted Carmen and told her everything. You got this news from me because I spotted her with them. Then tell him her and her friends are regrouping by the library. That should buy us some time. Go and get back. Wait for me to summon you."

"I'll be waitin'." Zeborah took off out the door and through the woods.

"You have a plan?" Carmen said.

"The makings of one. First, I need you to take me back to campus and we're going to hang out in your room and wait for Todd to leave." He pointed to Eric. "I need Carmen with me as well."

"I can get her to hang in the lounge," Dayton said. "Visitation to the room is tricky."

"Just what are you thinking?" Eric said.

"I'm thinking we get Todd boxed in. Get him in the lab and take him out there. We'll get Kim out first to lure him to the lab, then close in on him."

"Won't he already be there with that other guy?" Curtis said.

"For now. Once I do what I need to in his room, I'll summon him back there and that should give you guys time to get Kim out, hide her, then we regroup in the lab and kill him. Trust me, with what I'm about to show Carmen, we can do this."

"Can I ask a question?" Curtis said as he raised his hand. "If he's able to beat us up on the quad, what makes you think we can get him in a confined space?"

"He's going to be weak in there. The demon keeps messing

with Todd's anatomy and in the heat of a fight, it's going to wear him down trying to protect him. It will show its true form and fight us. That's the best time to strike."

"That's the only way to catch him in a weakened state?" Dayton said.

"Or we wait until he tries to possess Kim, which also means you're going to have to catch him at the right moment. If you find him after he escapes the campus. He won't do it here."

"Or," Curtis said as he held up a finger. "There could be one other way, depending on if what we read is folklore or true."

"What?" Kevin asked.

"What if we lured Todd onto the hallowed ground? I mean, he's a half-demon, won't it work?"

All eyes fell on Kevin. He looked at the floor, thinking.

"Is there a reason it wouldn't work?" Eric said.

"It's a slippery slope." Kevin looked back at Curtis. "I mean, in theory, I guess it could work."

"Demons don't like anything holy. I read it in that demon book. They will react negatively to anything pertaining to God," Dayton said.

"What about vampires?" Eric turned to Kevin. "Can you go into a church and not be harmed?"

"You want to get Todd into a church?"

"I don't think we'll get him in the school chapel, Curtis," Dayton chided.

"Not the chapel." Before Curtis could finish, Carmen gasped. They looked at one another and she nodded. "Yes, we're both thinking the same thing. The university founder's gravesite. We can get him to that spot and kill him."

"You think he's gonna chase one of us into the area?" Eric said.

"Yes." Kevin nodded. "He's arrogant enough not to think the ground could be his undoing. How many graves are there?"

"Eight," Dayton answered.

"Depending on how old the graves are, they may be powerful enough to weaken him. Okay, so we have a where, we need to figure out the how. We can do that in the dorm. Let's get moving. Eric, I'm going to need to use the trunk of your car."

"It's my car," Dayton said. "What do you need to put in it?"

"Rakim."

CHAPTER SIXTY-NINE

"You gotta keep him quiet," Eric said over his shoulder to Kevin as they approached the gate.

"Don't worry about us. Just fix your face and act normal."

Eric gripped the steering wheel tight as he approached the security hut. He slowed to a crawl, showed his ID, as did Carmen, as she leaned over and presented it. The guard waved them through. He never looked in the back seat. Eric glanced in the rear-view mirror and watched Curtis and Dayton behind them in Curtis's car pass through the gate.

They drove in a single file and parked just shy of Chambers. Carmen started to get out and Kevin touched her on the shoulder.

"Remember what I told you about the black glass. Think of Todd this time. It will keep you off his radar."

Carmen nodded as she exited the car. She met up with Dayton and they walked hand in hand into the dorm.

Curtis went around Eric and Kevin and drove by without looking at them. He parked in the lot behind Chambers Hall.

Eric glanced in the rear-view mirror again to look at Kevin, but he had no reflection. "Of course," he whispered.

Kevin sat with his eyes closed. He looked as though he were meditating. After a moment, he opened them. Eric was staring at him.

"Talking to Zeborah."

"We waiting on him?"

"In a way." He looked past Eric out the windshield. "Watch for Todd." He sank down out of sight.

Eric stared straight ahead. After five minutes, Todd appeared from Chambers Hall and started to make his way across campus. He ambled like he had all the time in the world. He didn't notice Eric watching him.

"Okay, he's gone. I'm going to pull around back," Eric said. "What do you want to do with Rakim?"

"Leave him where he is for a moment. I'll get him a little later."

Eric parked the car next to Curtis'. Kevin went to the trunk and tapped on it three times. Rakim knocked back twice. Kevin followed Eric into the dorm.

On the main floor, Curtis was waiting for them. He explained how Dayton convinced the R.A. to let Carmen go upstairs with him for thirty minutes.

"I left the weapons with them in your room. I'm shocked David let Carmen go up, but he's keeping it to a hard thirty, so whatever we need to do, we have to in that time."

Eric and Dayton's room was located right off the stairwell exit on the third floor. Curtis knocked. Dayton let them in. Kevin stopped at the doorway.

"I need a formal invite. Either you or Eric."

"Come on in," Eric and Dayton said in unison.

Kevin stepped inside as Dayton closed the door. He stopped short as he glanced down at the array of weapons laid out before him. Two machetes, three hatchets, a crowbar, flares, axes, a sledgehammer, and a large pair of shears.

"I can tell you now the sheers won't work. You won't be able to cut his head off with those. Not sharp enough to cut through muscle," Kevin said.

"I told you," Dayton said.

"Who said anything about cutting? You can slice or stab with them if they're open," Curtis said.

"Okay, we're strapped for time. Carmen, I need you to come with me. We'll be back in a few minutes."

"I'm going with you," Dayton said.

"No, I only need her. I promise you no harm will come to her." He held out his hand. "Come, before Todd gets back. Then we can discuss the final plan to take him out."

Carmen crossed the room but didn't take his hand. Kevin nodded. Together, they left the room and headed down to the basement.

Kevin jostled the knob as he leaned against the door and forced it open. He and Carmen infiltrated Todd's room. Several of his belongings were packed in large duffle bags. In the center of the room lay a ritual circle with smoldering candles, melted down halfway. Carmen squirmed as she folded her arms.

"It feels cold in here. Not weather cold but something else."

"He's been communing with the demon. From the looks of it, he's been at it for a while. He must be satisfied with whatever that thing is telling him, or he wouldn't have felt to see Zeborah."

"Maybe he's done?"

"Maybe. But this isn't why I brought you here. Come." He led her across the room to an open crate full of dirt. "Summon Michelle."

Carmen closed her eyes. "Michelle? It's Carmen. I need you."

Michelle materialized alongside Carmen. She looked around the room, then tapped Carmen on the shoulder. They looked at one another.

"What is this place?"

"Todd's room," Carmen said.

"This is his room. What the hell kind of devil worship is he into?"

"Michelle?" Kevin called to her. "Time is of the essence. Please." He waited for Michelle to focus on him. "I'm about to ask you to do something I know you're not prepared for, but it's necessary. First, how well can the two of you fight?"

"I can take care of myself," Michelle said.

"I'm from the Bronx. We were born knowing how to fight," Carmen said. "And having two brothers also helped."

"One of you is going to have to be the dominant hand here. Usually, the supernatural being takes control and uses the host body to control the attack. Your combined force would be enough to do damage to any mortal. The main problem we have here is you're not fighting another mortal being, which means you need a double dose of power. I can help you get it, but I cannot help you control how you use that power, Carmen. You understand what I'm saying?"

"I think so. Me and Michelle combined aren't enough, so you're giving us a little extra something," Carmen said.

"Right. But by doing so, it's going to be up to the two of you to help instruct this aid as to what to do. You have to figure out how to work in tandem, as a trio in one body. This is not a request I'm giving you. You must do this."

"I'm ready."

"Then I think it's time to reacquaint you with an old friend."

Kevin put his hands deep in the crate and closed his eyes. He whispered words they couldn't make out.

He stepped back as a pale hand rose out of the crate and gripped the side. A head appeared next as Savannah sat up. She glared at Kevin as she climbed out of the crate.

"You sonofabich!" She said. "I could kill you!"

Carmen's mouth dropped open in shock. "Savannah?"

Savannah turned and looked at Carmen. Her eyes widened as she threw her hands up to her mouth. She began to bounce excitedly on the balls of her feet. They squealed like two teenagers and tried to embrace each other.

"Oh. My. God! Darlin, there you are. I thought I'd lost you," Savannah said. "Are you okay? Did they hurt you?"

Carmen wiped happy tears from her eyes. "I'm fine. I thought you abandoned me. I didn't know where you had gone."

"He sent me away." Savannah pointed to Kevin. "I couldn't reach out to you. But I'm here now." Savannah looked at Michelle. "Can she see me too?"

Carmen looked over at Michelle. "She can. This is Michelle."

"Nice to meet you," Michelle said.

"Ladies," Kevin said, getting their attention. "We have to go. Carmen, you can fill Savannah in with the details of what's happening." Kevin started for the door. "Maybe it's better you two disappear and wait until we get back upstairs to talk to Carmen. We can't run the risk of you being seen talking to yourself on the stairs."

"I can tell her what I know, Carmen," Michelle said. "Call us when you're ready."

"Okay."

Michelle motioned for Savannah to follow her. The two began to dematerialize at the door.

Kevin tilted his head toward the door. Carmen nodded and followed him. They stepped out into the hall.

"Now you're going to have to go off somewhere and practice with them before tonight," Kevin said. "Anywhere on campus you can go and not have issues?"

"I can probably go back to my room."

"Maybe you should do that now. I'll tell the others where you went, and we'll call you once we have everything in place."

"Okay, I can. . ." Carmen stopped talking and froze.

"What?" Kevin looked straight ahead.

Rakim was standing hunched over, looking at them as he blocked their path. His eyes were burning crimson.

"How did you get out of the car?"

"Funny you should ask." Todd stepped out from the hall leading to the side entrance. "I happened to hear him rolling around inside of the trunk of a car out back. Someone had locked him in there." He took a place behind Rakim and folded his arms. "And I know you don't own a car." He pointed to Carmen. "Where are you going with her? Or should I ask, where are you coming from with her?"

Kevin stepped in front of Carmen, shielding her. "She's mine. I am dealing with her in my own way."

Todd placed his hand on top of Rakim's head and petted him. "I knew something was up. Zeborah told me the brothers contacted the medium. Why would they specifically seek *her* out to give her information? They never operated on this campus. And why *today*? They've had more than enough time to appear before now?"

"I don't know what you're getting at."

"I've already dealt with Zeborah and his deceit. Now it's time to deal with yours. And then, I kill you, medium." Todd stepped back. "Rakim, kill him."

Kevin kicked Todd's room door open and threw Carmen inside. A split second later, Rakim tackled Kevin to the floor and bit him hard on the shoulder.

CHAPTER SEVENTY

Carmen watched through the open door as Kevin tried to fight back. Blood seeped through his clothes as he punched and kneed Rakim in a vain effort to get him to back down.

She crawled back further into the room; her fight-or-flight senses were high. She looked around frantically for a way out. She spotted the small window at the far end, but it was too small to fit through.

Kevin's screams hurt her ears. She could feel her emotions bubbling up inside. Fear, anger, frustration, and sadness all came colliding together. She managed to make it as far back to the bed as Rakim bit Kevin in the arm. Kevin screamed in pain as he tried to push Rakim's head off. Rakim let go then in a flash shoved him so hard into the room, Kevin went crashing into the crate, breaking it. Dirt and leeches were everywhere.

Carmen closed her eyes and frantically called Michelle and Savannah, but her panic made it impossible to concentrate. Still, she persisted. Until she heard a low growl close by. She opened her eyes. Rakim lumbered toward her. His monstrous mouth was wet with blood. He licked his upper lip, smearing it.

"Rakim," Kevin cried out weakly. "Cousin, this isn't you. Fight Todd's influence."

Rakim didn't listen. He continued to creep toward her, hissing and growling. Behind him, Todd appeared in the doorway.

"Too bad. You would have made an interesting host, I think."

Rakim lunged. Carmen put out her hands to stop him, but he froze. He shut his eyes and put his taloned hand up to the side of his head as he backed off his attack. He appeared to be in pain.

Carmen laughed nervously while getting to her feet. She called Michelle and Savannah again. This time, they appeared alongside her.

"We're here," Michelle said. "What happened?"

Carmen didn't answer. She watched as Rakim backed himself into the wall. Kevin regained enough strength to get to his aid.

"Look at me. Look into my eyes. I can stop the pain."

Carmen turned, and Todd pinned her against an adjacent wall. She tried to reach out and touch his face, but the choke hold kept her from raising her arms.

From the corner of her eye, she saw Michelle rush to her. Michelle's presence blended into her body and a powerful will to fight overcame her. She took his wrist and tore it back. She managed to work his grip loose enough to get a bit of air. Her other hand, not feeling like she had control over it, swung around and cold-cocked him across the jaw. He let go and backed up. He seemed more shocked than hurt.

Carmen took in heavy breaths before balling up her fists and getting into a fighting stance. Todd laughed and charged her. She swung hard and fast. A combination of one-two punch that forced him back. She inched forward, her guard up.

Todd cracked his neck, then put his fists up. His face contorted into the demonic goat for a split second before he punched her in the gut, sending her to the floor.

"Savannah? We could use some help here," Michelle called out through Carmen.

"Savannah, you might want to go across campus to the science building and look in on your boyfriend," Todd chided. "He may be joining you soon."

Carmen got her wind back. She rose and rushed Todd to take him down. Michelle left her body, and, in that brief moment, he took hold of her and tossed her into the bed. She bounced off it and onto the other side.

"You have to let her know what you're about to do," Kevin called out. "Work as one."

Carmen watched the bed get tossed to the side. Todd took hold of her. She spotted Savannah on the other side of the room. At first, she thought Savannah wasn't going to help because she hesitated. But then she ran toward Todd. She passed through him and fell into Carmen's body.

Todd, startled by the foreign feeling, let go.

"What're we doin'? You wanna hit him?" She asked.

"Yes!"

Savannah took over, and she swung repeatedly at Todd's face, striking him. Michelle joined and, in her head, she could hear the two of them cursing and crying out as punches and kicks landed against him. And they were having an effect. The harder she hit him, the more he seemed to lose his footing.

But another facial contortion seemed to give Todd an edge. He struck her across the face and sent her back to the floor. Michelle and Savannah separated from her and dematerialized. He stepped over her, raised his foot, but before he could bring it down, someone shoved from behind. Todd struck the far wall. Carmen looked up and saw Dayton standing in Todd's place. He helped her up.

Someone sped past him. Eric ran at him with a crowbar. He

brought it down in an arc, striking Todd in the back of the head and sending him to the floor. As he lay motionless, Eric kicked him several times and raised his weapon to strike him again.

"You can't kill him that way," Kevin said.

Eric glanced at Kevin, then lowered the crowbar. He turned to Carmen and stepped to her side.

"We got worried something happened. You didn't come back to the room," Eric said.

"Todd tried to kill us by siccing Rakim on us." Carmen pointed to Kevin and Rakim in the corner.

"What the hell is that?" Curtis screamed as, upon entering the room, he saw Rakim being tended to. He pointed to him with the hatchet he held. "What is that?"

"Take it easy." Eric crossed the room to explain to Curtis.

"You okay?" Dayton said as he embraced her.

"We need to get out of here." She broke the embrace. "We need to go get Kim and forget this plan. He's too strong." She rushed to Kevin. Rakim shied away from her. "Are you okay?"

"No. Rakim's bite." He winced from pain as he shifted his body. "He's poisoned my blood. I'm not going to be as big a help as I want." He touched her hand. "Zeborah is in trouble."

"I think I remember where the lab is. I'll go to him."

"Where's Eric?"

"I'm here." Eric walked to Carmen's side.

"Go get your girlfriend out of there and get her to hallowed ground. Don't try to leave the campus with her. You do and he will chase you. And he won't stop until he has her." He leaned in. "Go before he gets up." He sat back. "Go!"

Eric looked at Carmen. "We all need to go."

Carmen turned to Rakim. "I'm not going to hurt you. But we could use your help. Please, after everything Todd has done to you, you shouldn't live like this."

"Save your breath," Kevin said. "He won't listen to you."

"Todd is using you. He wants to set you loose on us. He wants you to poison us like you did Kevin. He doesn't care about you. He may have killed Zeborah. He may even kill you too in the end."

Rakim glared at Todd's motionless body. He glanced at Kevin before he turned away and stared into the corner.

Carmen rose to her feet, her eyes locked on Rakim. He looked over his shoulder, hissed at her, then cowered back. She looked at Kevin.

"We can't. . . after what you told us . . ."

"You let me worry about him."

"Carmen, let's go," Eric called to her.

Carmen hurried to join them at the door.

"Look out!" Curtis screamed.

Carmen turned in time to see Todd, back on his feet. He rushed toward them. Dayton stepped in front of her and raised the hatchet he had brought with him, ready to strike.

Rakim jumped on Todd and brought him to the floor. Todd struggled against him.

"Let's go!" Curtis yanked Eric by the collar. Carmen followed, then Dayton. They ran to the end of the hall, made a sharp right, and went out the door to the parking lot.

R akim and Todd wrestled on the floor, punching and clawing at one another. Rakim overpowered Todd, straddled and pinned him with his knees on his arms and grasped him by his throat.

"We madeth you whath you are," Rakim sneered in a raspy voice. "You will noth useth me to kihll anyone."

"I perfected you."

"You madeth me ah monsther!" He glanced over at Kevin. "Go. Help the mortalsth."

"I'm sorry," Kevin said.

"Go."

Kevin stumbled out of the room, slamming the door behind him.

Rakim's eyes burned red with fury. He screamed, baring his fangs. He went to bite him. Todd pushed his arms out, causing Rakim to lose his grip. As he fell forward, Todd leaned to one side. Rakim missed his mark and, instead, exposed his own neck. Todd's face contorted into the demon. He bit into Rakim's neck. He clamped down until blood trickled out. He let go.

Todd put his hands under Rakim and pushed him up. He shifted out of the way before Rakim crashed down onto the floor. Todd stood. He punched him in the back, picked him up, and threw him across the room with brutal force. Rakim hit the wall and slid to the floor.

"I never suspected you would turn on me." Todd crossed the room. "If this is the path you've chosen, then I see no point in keeping you around. And besides. I can always make more of you once I reach the coven."

Rakim pushed himself to a standing position. With lightning speed, he punched Todd in the jaw. It broke. Todd stumbled back. Rakim swung again. Todd tried to block them with his hands. Rakim caught one of Todd's hands and snapped it back. The sickening crack of bone-breaking filled the air. He didn't scream.

His eyes blazed like the fires of hell. With his good hand, he latched onto Rakim's throat. He pushed his thumb into Rakim's esophagus and punctured his skin. Blood sprayed across Todd's face as Rakim choked on his own blood filling his throat. Todd jerked his hand from the wound and slapped them on both sides of Rakim's head. With a sharp twist, he broke his neck.

Rakim dropped to the floor. Todd rushed to the broken crate, picked up a large, splintered piece, went back to Rakim's body, and staked him through the heart. Like an automaton on a mission, he went to the door. He flung it open and came face to face with the R.A.

"What the hell is going on down here?" David said.

Todd backhanded him so hard, David spun and struck the wall, knocking himself out cold.

The clouds overhead grew dark and covered the campus like a shadow.

CHAPTER SEVENTY-ONE

Students had filed into the lobby and stared up at the dark sky as Eric and Curtis pushed their way to the main staircase and collapsed onto the steps, wheezing to catch their breath. They waited for Carmen and Dayton to arrive, as they didn't know where to go to find the lab.

"Where's your weapon?" Eric said as he looked Curtis over.

Curtis glanced at his hand. "Damn it, I must have dropped it back at the dorm." He looked around. "They don't have a fire ax or something in this building?"

"Probably in one of the stairwells. One of these floors has one. Wait until Carmen gets here and once we know where we're going, you can go look."

Carmen and Dayton burst in, out of breath. Unable to speak, Carmen pointed to the left side of the building.

"That way?" Eric said.

Carmen nodded. "Fourth Floor. Down by the back stairwell."

"You guys go on ahead. I'll find you." Curtis took off through a set of double doors on the first floor.

"Let's go." Eric headed up the stairs.

Carmen and Dayton followed. Students made a run for it, trying to reach their destinations before the rain came. Carmen saw Kevin stumble toward the building.

"Dayton, go with Eric. I'm right behind you." She started for the doors.

"Where are you going?"

"Just go catch up to him," she said with urgency.

Dayton took off after Eric. Carmen helped Kevin inside.

"You'll want to summon Michelle and Savannah," he said.

"What happened?"

"Rakim is dead."

"You saw him kill him?"

"No, but that's not a natural storm brewing. Todd is coming. We need to hurry."

Carmen closed her eyes and summoned Michelle and Savannah, who appeared looking a little worse for wear.

"What did he hit us with?" Savannah said. "I feel funny."

"It's the demon's powers you're feeling," Kevin said.

Michelle looked around. "I know where we are."

"What's the lab number? You remember," Carmen said.

"I remember where it is on the fourth floor."

"C'mon. Take me there."

Michelle stepped inside Carmen. Savannah followed. Then Carmen started up the stairs, with Kevin hobbling behind.

By the time they got to the fourth floor, Kevin had improved. Eric and Dayton were looking in the windows of the labs, hoping to see another crate and Zeborah. Carmen shuffled past them.

"Over here." She walked up to the lab door with the blacked-out window. She tried the knob. Locked. "Zeborah, open the door!"

"Move." Kevin nudged her to the side, gripped the doorknob tight and turned it. The lock broke and the door opened. "Let's go."

Everyone rushed inside. Carmen gasped. Eric, Dayton, and Kevin stopped dead in their tracks.

Zeborah lay battered, bruised, and bloodied in the far corner, wheezing as he breathed. He looked like he had gone ten rounds in a prizefight without putting his guard up.

Kevin knocked tables out of the way as he rushed to aid him. Carmen let out a terrible scream, startling everyone. She crashed to the floor and wept.

"Babe, what's wrong?" Dayton said. He kneeled alongside her. He put his arm around her shoulder.

"It's not me," Carmen said through tears. "Go to him." She bent over and wailed again, then said, "Stop being stubborn and go to him."

Savannah stepped out of Carmen's body and rushed to Zeborah's side. Her wails of sorrow got his attention. He looked at her and forced a smile as he tried to touch her.

"There you are," he whispered. "A beautiful as I remembah you."

Savannah grasped his hand with hers and brought it to her heart. "Zeborah, darlin', what has he done to you?"

"I'm alright. Just a little sore." He tried to reassure her.

"Liar," she chuckled as she tried to stifle her grief. "I've missed you."

"I'm sorry I wasn't there to stop him. I never meant for anythang to 'appen to you."

"Stop talkin' and rest up." She looked at Kevin. "Can't you do somethin'?"

"He needs time to heal."

"I thought vampires could heal themselves fast," Dayton said.

"Minor cuts, yes. This, done by one of our own, for him to heal, he needs blood. My blood is tainted so I can't give him any.

And we can't afford to have him feed off anyone here. You'd be left too weak to even run." Kevin started to look around the room. His eyes fell on the crate. "We need to make a switch and put him in the crate. Eric, you and Carmen get it open."

"Kim's in there," Zeborah said.

"We know." Kevin pointed to Dayton. "I need you over here to help me move him. Get down by his feet."

"I'll stay with you," Savannah caressed Zeborah's face.

———

Eric and Carmen struggled to get the lid off with their hands, but it wouldn't budge. He then took the crowbar he'd been carrying, slid the flat end between the lid and the box, and pushed down hard. It gave way with a loud crack. Eric repeated the process at the front and rear, then put the crowbar on the floor and took hold of the lid.

"Get the front." Eric motioned with a nod of his head. Carmen took position and waited. "Hey, you okay?" Carmen nodded. "Okay, on three. One. Two. Three."

They lifted together and pushed the lid off. It struck the floor with a resounding thud that made them jump. They peered inside. Kim lay with her arms at her side. Her eyes were closed.

"Kim?" Eric called to her. She didn't respond. "Kim, it's me, Eric. Wake up!" Still no response. "Carmen, get her legs. We have to get her out of here."

"I don't think I can lift her."

"Okay, help me sit her up, then we can go from there." Eric walked around to the opposite side of the crate. He and Carmen took hold of her arms and sat her up. "Okay, shift her to me." He leaned over enough to wrap his arms around her waist. Carmen maneuvered Kim's body, so she slumped onto his shoulder. "Get behind me. Don't let me drop her."

Carmen put her hands against his back as he lifted Kim out of the crate and carried her over to a long lab table. Eric nodded at Kevin, who took hold of Zeborah and, along with Dayton, lifted and carried him to the crate. They hoisted him inside, then put the lid on.

Eric put his ear to Kim's chest and listened. "She's breathing." He stood and looked at Kevin as he approached them. "She can't be sleep. What's wrong with her?"

Kevin scanned her body. He checked her wrist, followed by her neck. He inspected her shoulder.

"He bit her, look."

"We're too late?" Dayton said.

"No, she's only incapacitated." He looked at the wound closer. "This is from the demon half of him. I don't know how to wake her from this."

"Let's get her out of her and to the graves. We can figure everything else out after we get there." Eric lifted Kim and hoisted her over his shoulder.

"Put her down." Todd commanded from across the room.

CHAPTER SEVENTY-TWO

Kevin, Dayton, and Carmen stood in front of Eric, forming a wall. Todd marched into the room.

"Give it up, cousin," Kevin said. "You're not getting this girl."

Todd advanced toward them. His crimson eyes and his face morphed into the goat creature.

"She's ours. You will not stop the ascension. None of you." Todd glanced in the corner where Zeborah had been laying. He stopped, looked at the crate, and smiled. "Whatever you think you can do to save Zeborah won't work. The soil is spoiled. It won't help him heal." He looked in Eric's direction. "Kim is mine now, Eric. Put her down and walk away. She doesn't even want to be with you, anyway. Leave her and I'll let you all live."

The lab door opened. Everyone's attention went straight to it. Curtis stepped in, holding a fire axe. He fixed his gaze on Todd while he crossed the room. Once aligned with him, he held the axe, cross body, in both hands.

"I saw him come in here from down the hall." Curtis' eyes widened as he got a good look at Todd's face. "So, what're we doin'?"

"We need to get out the door," Carmen said.

Curtis nodded and walked back to the door, blocking it. "You guy's c'mon then." He tipped the blade of the axe in Todd's direction. "You come near us, and I'll split you in half."

Todd's face returned to normal, then he charged across the room and shoved Kevin into the wall. He turned and punched Dayton in the gut. He immediately grasped Carmen's arm, dragged her close, and palmed her forehead. She began sweating and grimaced in pain as her abilities reacted negatively to the demon's touch. He let go of her and she collapsed on the floor. He then turned his attention to Eric.

"Put her down, now." He inched closer to Eric until he backed up with Kim still over his shoulder. "You're not getting out of this lab."

Todd closed the gap. Eric saw a clear path. He bolted around a table, straight to the far side of the room. Todd chased him, trying to stop him before he could reach the door. Curtis ran toward Eric.

"Go, Eric, get out of here!" Curtis said as he passed him.

He raised the ax. Todd stopped and jumped back as Curtis swung and missed. He shoved Curtis as Kevin pounced on him and brought him to the floor. Todd flipped Kevin over, leapt on top of him, and with lightning speed, took hold of his right arm and broke it in three places. Kevin howled in pain.

Todd then turned in time to see Dayton and Carmen creeping to the door.

"Go! I got him!" Curtis reassured them.

Curtis swung the axe. This time, Todd gripped it by the handle. He snatched it from Curtis' hands, forcing him to stumble forward. He spun Curtis around and pulled him into his body. He glanced at Dayton and Carmen as he brought his right arm across Curtis' face, placed his hand around to the back of his head, then violently broke Curtis' neck. He dropped him to the floor and rushed toward Dayton.

Dayton pushed Carmen as he yelled, "Run!"

Todd held him by his throat. As he began to apply pressure, Kevin landed on top of him. He bared his fangs and bit down into Todd's neck. Todd punched Dayton, knocking him out cold, then he toppled backward and tried to punch Kevin with his elbow to get him to let go. It failed. He got to his feet and began slamming him into the wall.

Kevin finally let go and he slid to the floor. Bleeding from the wound in his neck, Todd lifted him by his shirt's collar and pinned him to the wall.

Kevin made a weak smile.

"Rakim poisoned me with his bite. And now I've poisoned you with mine." Kevin coughed. "You can't ascend with tainted blood in your system."

"This bite is not going to stop me. I will ascend and get my revenge."

"The demon will reject you. You'll be lucky if it doesn't kill you while breaking its union with you." Kevin laughed. "I made a promise to stop you, and I have. You can go to hell, Todd."

Todd morphed into the demon, bit Kevin in his neck, then dropped him to the floor and let him bleed out. He returned to his normal state, surveyed the body count around him, and exited the room to find Carmen and Eric.

CHAPTER SEVENTY-THREE

Overhead, thunder boomed and lightning danced, clearing the campus of students. With everyone taking shelter indoors, no one noticed Eric, fueled by adrenaline, running with a passed-out Kim slung over his shoulder.

He could see the burial site in the distance. But with the soft ground beneath his feet combined with the weight of Kim on him, he started to find it hard to keep up the pace he had started with.

The path he took sloped, and he almost stumbled. He slowed down, then stopped briefly to catch his breath. He looked back at the science building and realized none of the others were behind him.

He resumed running. He didn't want to think of what may have happened after he fled the lab. He crossed a concrete walkway, which gave him the much-needed traction to help him regain his speed. But at the site, he stepped the wrong way, and his ankle twisted. He screamed and stumbled forward. He was going to fall. Fearing he would hurt Kim; he spun his body in the opposite direction and landed on his free side. Kim slid off his shoulder.

He lay on his side for a moment, catching his breath before getting onto his knees. He looked around at the flat marble markers with the names of the founders etched into them. He dragged Kim onto the top of one of them. He slumped over her and heavily breathed in the cool air.

"We're safe now," he whispered to her. "Everything's gonna be all right."

Eric kissed her on her forehead and stared up at the charcoal sky. He wanted to sleep. He closed his eyes for a brief moment, counted to ten, and sat up on his elbows. Carmen approached, walking fast and crying. He stood up, and she ran to him.

"What happened?" he said. "Where is everybody?"

Carmen threw her arms open, fell into him, and began wailing. Eric hugged her.

"H-H-He killed Curtis," she sobbed. "He b-b-broke his neck."

"What?"

"Then he went after Dayton. He pushed me out the room to save me." Carmen's body shook. "I ran. Aye Dios Mio, I left Dayton!" She started to turn to go back, but Eric caught her. "Let go of me."

"You go back there, and he'll get you, too. If we are the only ones left, then we're the ones who have to stop him."

"Then we have to go back."

"No, we don't."

"Why not?"

Eric pointed. "Because here he comes."

Carmen watched as Todd approached from a distance, taking his time, a lone figure on an empty campus. The lightning flashed, making him look like an imposing force with the darkened sky above.

"Watch Kim," Eric said.

"What?" Carmen turned to him. "Where are you going?"

"Over there." He pointed behind them. Carmen followed his

finger and saw a buildings and grounds pickup truck sitting dormant at the other end of the site. "We need to arm ourselves." Eric took off, hobbling toward the truck.

Carmen looked back at Todd. He was halfway to her. She heard Michelle in her head.

What's the plan?

"You're still with me?"

I never left.

Carmen closed her eyes. *Savannah? Do you hear me?*

I'm here, darlin'.

Can you check on Dayton for me? Is he alive?

There were seconds of silence, then Savannah responded. *He's breathin'.*

I need you here with me and Michelle. Carmen took a deep breath and calmed herself. "It's time to end Todd." She opened her eyes. Savannah stood before her. Then Michelle materialized. "We need to keep him from getting to Kim."

"Savannah?" Michelle waved to get her attention. "I'll strike first, you strike second. If we mix it up, it will make it hard for him to focus."

"We can't let him get hold of us or we'll be in trouble. The ground here should weaken him so we can do damage. But if he gets hold of me, I want you two to leave my body. Whatever demon it is, it has an effect on you."

Michelle looked in Todd's direction. "Savannah, inside!" She stepped into Carmen. Savannah followed.

Eric returned as Todd approached the edge of the site. He looked at Kim laying on the marker. His gaze shifted to Eric holding a long-handled spade used for digging holes.

"Interesting choice of weapon. You plan to bury me with it?" Todd laughed at his own pun. "Hope you're better at using that than your friend with the ax."

"I'm going to kill you," Eric sneered.

"You're going to try to. You're not going to succeed. And really, a gravesite. You really think this is going to keep me from getting to Kim?"

"Come on in and take her," Eric chided.

"This is a waste of time."

"Still don't see you moving to get her."

Todd stepped forward, abruptly stopped, looked up and down, surveying a partition. His expression went from smug to bewildered. As he extended his hand, a nauseated expression developed on his face and, unexpectedly, his body started swaying. He withdrew his hand to avoid fainting.

"It works." Carmen backed up. "This area affects you. You almost passed out."

"We'll see." Todd stepped across the threshold of the site. He appeared stable and unphased. "Hmm." Carmen shot behind Eric. "Step aside, I'm taking Kim."

Eric turned the handle to the flat side of the spade. He swung and struck Todd in the upper shoulder. Todd stumbled sideways. Carmen stepped up and struck him with a combo punch followed by a hard kick to the chest. He went stumbling across the threshold. He appeared shocked.

"Not so strong now, huh? What's wrong? The ground too blessed for you?"

Todd glanced at the ground. He repositioned himself. Eric gripped the spade and dug his sneakers into the earth. Carmen recognized what Todd was about to do and readied herself. Todd crouched, then ran across the site, grabbing Eric around the waist. But before he could get Eric out of the gravesite, he slowed down long enough for Carmen to body-check him. He let go of Eric as he lost his footing, tripped over one of the markers, and spun out beyond the site.

"How hard did you hit him?" Eric said.

"I have some extra help inside," Carmen said.

She and Eric returned to Kim and waited. Todd rose to his feet. He strode back to where they were standing.

"Thank you," Todd said. "Now I know who to give my attention to first."

Todd stepped back in fast enough to grab Carmen by her shirt and tossed her across the ground and followed until she slid to a stop. He kept a slight distance from her and watched as she got to her feet, staggering as she composed herself.

"So, the bullied now bullies others? You're a real class act, Todd. No wonder the only friend you have is a soul-sucking demon."

Todd didn't react. He continued to stare at her. After a moment he said, "Predictable" and he turned swiftly and, with an open palm, slapped Eric hard across the face as he tried to sneak up behind him. The blow came so fast and powerful it sent Eric to the ground. He turned back to Carmen and attacked her. His face morphed as he slapped both hands by her face.

Carmen thought it was her own screams she heard until she sensed Michelle being ripped out of her sideways. Next, Savannah tore out of the opposite side, screaming too. Now separated, Todd shoved Carmen to the ground as his face morphed back to normal.

Exhausted, she lay on her back listening to the ghosts wail next to her.

"The advantage of having a soul-sucking demon as a friend is even spirits can be ripped from a body." Todd tapped the side of her face. "You still have so much to learn, young medium. I think I'll let you live."

"Why?" Carmen whispered.

"Because I can."

Carmen watched Todd head back to the gravesite, but not before kicking Eric as he writhed in pain.

"Eric!" she called out. "He's going to get Kim."

Eric let out a frustrated scream, pounded the ground with the fist of his good hand, and did his best to get up.

Carmen pushed herself across the ground toward him. Eric used the spade as support to pull himself up. He held his side as he took several deep breaths. He staggered to Carmen and helped her up.

"I think I can get to him," Eric said.

"You're not going to be able to get the drop on him." Carmen straightened up. "But I think there is one more thing I can do." She turned in Todd's direction. "How much energy do you have to swing that thing?"

"Enough to kill him."

"You can't miss then. You won't get a second chance."

"Don't worry about me."

"Follow me. Soon as he starts screaming, you move in."

"What're you going to do?"

Carmen walked with purpose. Her body ached, but she fought against the pain and forced herself to keep moving. Thunder boomed, startling her. Lightning flashed. She picked up her pace. Todd was now on all fours at the edge of the gravesite. He leaned forward, pawing at Kim to get hold of her. Carmen hurried to close the gap between them. He got Kim's leg and started to drag her off the marker, towards him. With three big steps, Carmen dropped down and closed her eyes.

In the expanse of her mind, she saw a black glass slab before her. She could barely make out the shape behind it. She concentrated on trying to shatter it. It shook and began to crack. A loud boom resounded and within seconds, the slab disintegrated, and before her stood Todd. With the protective barrier between them gone, he was now exposed to her abilities.

CHAPTER SEVENTY-FOUR

Todd dragged Kim off the marker and slid her out beyond the gravesites' boundaries. He spun her by her feet and pushed her further away from the perimeter.

Once clear of the site, he knelt next to her and caressed her hair. He admired her for a moment before he stood up, gripped her ankles, and started to drag her some more.

Kim opened her eyes, but she didn't say anything. She looked at him as she sat up. He stopped dragging her.

"Where am I?" She looked around. "Where the hell are you taking me?"

"You're on campus," he reassured her. "You don't remember what happened? You passed out while we were taking a walk. I was taking you to the clinic."

"The clinic? Why are you dragging me? Wait, you did something to me." Kim touched the wounds on her shoulder. "You bit me. Oh, my God! Get off me! Help!"

Todd lifted her off the ground. "I'm done with the niceties. You're leaving here with me, whether you—"

Todd stopped. Intense pressure built in his skull. He shook his head to make it go away, but it only intensified. He let go of Kim, palmed the side of his head, and squeezed the area of pain with his fingertips. The pressure made his eyes bleed. He screamed so loud, Kim covered her ears and balled up on the ground. He smacked the sides of his head.

"What the hell?" He looked at Carmen. She knelt, her fingers on her temples. Her eyes were fixed on him. "Bitch!" He heard Kim gasp. He noticed her looking over his shoulder and he spun around. The sharp flat edge of Eric's spade came down toward his head.

———

The spade embedded itself deep into Todd's neck. Blood poured into the mouth of the head and down the long handle.

Eric struggled to remove it. As he did, it left a deep gash. Eric swung the spade back, prepared to swing again. Todd started convulsing. He glared at Eric and started to laugh.

Todd let his hands go limp and began panting like a dog. Saliva dripped from his mouth as his teeth grew into sharp fangs. His fingernails fell off one by one as horrible talons grew out in their place. His eyes turned a crimson red as his face cracked. His bones snapped as he lurched lower to the ground. His face morphed into a half-goat, half dog.

He rushed at Eric and Eric swung the spade as hard as he could. The metal head struck Todd across the face. He stumbled a little but kept coming. Eric shuffled out of the way as fast as he could and Todd tripped over his foot, sending him sailing to the ground. As he tried to get back on his feet, Eric brought the spade up over his head, then down with as much force as he could. The flat end struck Todd on the top of his head and sent him back down on the ground.

Eric didn't wait. With the little energy he had left, he stepped on Todd's back. He gripped the handle as tight as he could, lifted it straight up, and brought it down with enough power it went clean through Todd's neck.

Todd's body shuddered. Eric brought the spade back up again, and back down with a fierce blow, severing Todd's head from the body while planting the spade into the ground.

Blood splattered as Todd's decapitated head rolled across the ground and onto one of the markers. Eric stumbled off Todd's body, exhausted. As he crawled away from the horrible sight, Kim crawled to him and threw her arms around him.

"I told you I wouldn't let him take you from me." He threw his arms around her and began to sob.

Kim broke their embrace and kissed him. Eric looked across and saw Carmen lying on the ground. She wasn't moving.

"Shit, Carmen!" Eric scrambled to his feet and rushed to her aid. "No, no, no." He lifted her and cradled her in his arms. "Carmen, it's Eric." He shook her gently.

"Oh my God, Carmen?" Kim rushed to Eric's side.

She weakly opened her eyes and looked at him. "Did you get him?"

"We got him," he whispered. "He's dead."

"Good." She looked at Kim. "Hey, roomie."

She smiled, then closed her eyes and went limp in Eric's arms.

CHAPTER SEVENTY-FIVE

Carmen awoke in a hospital bed, the sound of a heart monitor machine beeping somewhere off to her right. An IV drip injected into the top of her hand. Everything hurt. Two bouquets of flowers sat on a table to her left. She wondered who they were from. She found the call button lying near her hand and pressed it twice.

A nurse rushed in. Her eyes and mouth widened at the same time, forming a surprised look.

"You're up," she said. "How are you feeling, Ms. Guerra?"

"I'm weak. And I'm thirsty."

The nurse picked up a pitcher and cup from an adjacent table and poured her a drink. Carmen downed it.

"I'll go let the doctor know you're up."

"How long have I been asleep?"

"The doctor will talk to you." The nurse left the room.

Carmen adjusted the bed to a sitting position. The door opened, and a person walked in dressed in a white coat with a chart in hand. She wasn't expecting to recognize the face.

"I'm glad you're doin' better, Carmen," Zeborah said.

"What're you doing here?" The heart rate machine started to beep faster. "Where's the doctor?"

"Easy. You gonna get'chor self in a frenzy. Calm down and I'll explain. I'm not here ta hurt you. The doctor is, well, indisposed for now." Zeborah locked the door. He went closer, then stopped. He took a step back as he touched the side of his head. "Sorry, I keep my distance."

As Carmen began to calm down, so did the beeping of the machine. "Where's Savannah?"

"I'm here." Savanah materialized next to Zeborah. Smiling, she crossed the room and embraced Carmen. "I'm glad to see you awake." She stood and fussed with Carmen's hair. "Gotta get your hair done, girl, when you get outta here."

"Uh, I know." Carmen looked around. "Where's Michelle?"

"Oh, you won't be seein' her anymore. Law enforcement found her body, and the families layin her to rest. If the body is at rest, the spirit is too, aint that right, hun? Police got an anonymous tip from someone and, well, her folks are happy now." Zeborah glanced at the floor. "I s'pose you could call to her bein' a medium and all."

"I really wish I could have thanked her."

"If I see her again, I tell her for you," Savannah said.

"I'm s'posed to catch you up on what happened that night and after," Zeborah said.

"How long have I been out?"

"Four days."

"Four days? How could I sleep for four days?"

"Got somethin' to do with how much power you put out in your fight with Todd. And as far as anyone knows, Todd was a paranoid schizophrenic who had been off his med for some time. I told tha police he snapped, and that's what led to tha death of ya friend and why your boyfriend got beat up."

"What about Eric? He killed Todd. What did they say about that?"

"Todd's not dead and Eric didn't kill him."

"But Eric —"

"Chased him off campus after he attacked you and Kim. No one's seen him since. Nobody knows where he is and tha chances of finding him are slim."

"He's telling you the story everyone's stickin' to," Savannah said.

"Oh, I see." Carmen nodded. She understood. "What about Kevin?"

"A vampire named LaChard has his body. He's also the one who helped us clean up Todd's thangs. That's all I can say at this point. There were no vampires, demons, or ghosts. The dead are at peace and our worlds are safe for now," Zeborah said.

"It never happened," Carmen said.

"Very good." He held out his hand to Savannah. "Time ta go."

Savannah kissed Carmen on the cheek. "I don't know how to thank you."

"And I don't know how to thank *you*. I guess that makes us even."

"You be good now, ya hear? You ever need me, call me. Take care, darlin'."

She watched as Savannah joined Zeborah and took his hand.

"Zeborah, wait. I have one more question."

"Ask it."

"How are you doing? How are you holding up after all this?"

Zeborah stared at her for a moment. He looked as though he were pondering the question. But he turned and headed for the door. He unlocked it, cracked it, then looked back at her.

"I've got my Savannah back. That's all that matters." He smiled, then left the room.

EPILOGUE

Three days after Todd's so-called disappearance and the bodies of Curtis and Michelle were found, the school held a vigil. Poster-size photos of Michelle and Curtis stood nearly side by side in the sanctuary of the school chapel as students and family came to pay their respects and grieve together. Both mothers of the slain students greeted everyone who stopped by and, later, gave moving speeches about their children on the quad.

Carmen, released in time to hear Curtis' mom speak, watched from her dorm window. She thought it best not to make an appearance since word had gotten out. She had also been one of Todd's victims. Her presence would be a distraction. The day belonged to the fallen.

Maria, who had come to Bruckner with the family after they heard Carmen had been attacked, sat with her during the event, puttering around the room cleaning it and mumbling her disapproval of how both girls were keeping house. She stumbled across the medium book, partly sticking out from under Carmen's bed, and she picked it up. She thumbed through it without comment, then put it away far back on the shelf of Carmen's closet. She said nothing about it. She continued to clean, then they sat and talked about her fond memories of Curtis. Neither brought up the incident with Todd or Zeborah.

They met up with her family and Dayton afterward for dinner at the diner where they finally got to meet her boyfriend. Maria said all of two words to him at first, but warmed up to him near the end of the meal.

In the parking lot, Maria guided Carmen to the side, away from the rest of the family.

"I like him, Carmensita. He seems like a good boy." She cupped Carmen's face, kissed her on the cheek, then caressed her. "I'm so relieved jou're okay."

"Thanks, Abuela. For everything." Carmen took Maria's hands in hers and gave them a gentle squeeze. "I'm glad you're better."

"I was never sick." She gave Carmen a side-eye. "It's still cloudy, but jour aunt and I have been working at unblocking whatever spell or curse was jused to cause my lapse." She hugged Carmen. "At least I know why."

Carmen broke the embrace. "What do you mean?"

"The book in jour room. I am familiar with it. Saw one once many jears ago. They're rare, which is why I did not suggest jou look for it. So, I will assume whoever gave it to jou . . . I'm happy whatever way jou handled everything, jou saw it through."

"I still need you, Abuela."

"I'll always be here for jou. Now go on back to school and finish out jour jear. Next time I come up here will be for graduation." She and Carmen kissed on the cheeks. Carmen started to walk away, but Maria tugged her back and smirked. "Behave with jour boyfriend."

"Abuela!" Carmen blushed.

They walked arm in arm back to the family, where she said her goodbyes. She and Dayton got in his car and started back to campus to meet Eric and Kim.

———

Eric sat alone on the library steps, waiting for Kim. He stared at the science building as memories of his valiant run to the gravesite played over in his head. Followed by the killing of Todd, then Carmen passing out in his arms.

As he scanned the campus looking for Kim, He spotted a campus police car driving by and he recalled the moments after Carmen's collapse.

The storm clouds had started to dissipate roughly thirty minutes after Carmen passed out. Neither Kim nor he had called for help, yet EMS arrived a good fifteen minutes after the clouds changed. They were followed by a state police cruiser. Neither vehicle had lights or sirens on, nor were they followed by campus police. But they came upon them, and all four individuals got to work.

While the paramedics tended to Carmen, the two troopers gathered up Todd's remains. One of them, a rather large African American man with piercing eyes, took Eric to the side.

"Don't ask any questions. Tell me what I need to know and as far as you're concerned, you and I never saw or spoke to one another. Nod if you understand." Eric nodded. "Where was Todd living?"

"Basement floor of Chambers Hall. Dorms over there. Go through the back way, it's quicker."

"Where is his lab?"

"Science building, fourth floor. Go through the back way." Eric pointed to the science building.

"Last question, who am I?"

"I have no idea what you're talkin' about."

The trooper turned to his partner and said, "basement of that building there. I'll meet you in fifteen."

The partner took off running to the dorm while the lead trooper got in his car and headed to the science building.

The paramedics put Carmen in the back of their bus and waited. Another fifteen minutes went by with no one talking.

"Why don't you take her to the hospital?" Eric said.

The paramedics turned their heads.

"Maybe we should get campus police," Kim said.

"For what?" one of the paramedics said.

Eric started to respond as Zeborah walked up. He looked well-rested and refreshed. He whispered something to the paramedics. One of them went to the cab, turned the lights on, then ran the siren for half a minute.

Campus police turned a corner with their siren on. Zeborah turned to Eric.

"Say nothin'. Let me do all the talkin'."

The campus police skidded to a stop, rushed from their car, and Zeborah met them. He told them about Todd's 'schizophrenic' behavior, that he attacked Carmen, and he took off. He claimed he called the paramedics because he couldn't find campus police to help. The nervous looks on their faces, hearing they may have screwed up, caused them to take quick advantage of trying to track Todd down.

As EMS drove away, Zeborah approached them and said, "They're takin' Carmen to tha hospital, compliments of Mr. LaChard. Everything else is bein' taken care of. It will be as though we were neva here, and no altercation ever took place. You will not see me or any of my kin again. We'll contact the families of tha deceased and injured."

Then Zeborah walked to the road that cut through campus. The state trooper drove up, he got in, and they drove away. With not so much as a goodbye.

"Hey." Kim's voice brought him out of his memories. "You okay?"

Eric stared a minute before saying, "Yeah. I was, you know, deep in thought.

He went to her. She gave him a halfhearted smile, and the two embraced.

"I guess they're running late?"

"They should be here soon. Wanna sit?"

"No, I feel like standing." Kim looked around. "Nice function today for Curtis and Michelle."

"Yeah." Eric nodded. "I'm gonna really miss him."

They shared an awkward silence.

Kim cleared her throat. "I have a bizarre question."

"I don't know where we go from here," Eric said. "That's what you wanted to know." He took a deep breath and exhaled. "I don't know how any of us are going to get along now."

"We need to be there for one another. Shouldn't we?"

"Being there for each other is important." Eric took her hand. Kim smiled.

"Yea," she said. She hung her head a little. "But do you think we'll ever get past this?"

Feeling Eric's gaze, Kim looked back at him. He touched her shoulder where she suffered the bite wound.

"I think we'll be okay," he said. "Time heals all wounds."

He closed his arms around her, and he held her tight. She put her head in his chest and both of them teared up. Dayton's car horn got their attention. Carmen, on the passenger side, waved.

"That's the Kim and Eric I want to see."

Hand in hand, they walked to the car. Carmen got out and raced to them. The three of them embraced one another. They headed for the car, but Carmen stopped. She stared at the library steps, smiled, and walked up to where Eric had been sitting. They watched as she nodded, put her hands to her mouth, then hugged the air. Then she stepped back, mouthed something, waved good-bye, and walked to the car.

"Let's go. We're going to be late. We won't get a lane if we are."

Eric and Kim got in. They looked back at the steps, and then at one another.

"Okay, let's get some bowling in," Dayton said.

They drove away from the library. Eric looked back at the building.

"I'm going to miss Curtis. I didn't even go to the memorial to say goodbye."

Carmen shifted in her seat, looked at Eric with teary eyes. "It's okay. I just said it to him from all of us."

ABOUT MARC L. ABBOTT

Marc L Abbott is an award-winning African American writer from Brooklyn, NY.

Growing up, Marc was often in trouble in school for writing short fiction in his notebooks instead of paying attention to lessons in class. But it was clear his love for writing would lead him down a literary path.

He self-published his first novel, *A Gamble of Faith*, in 2004, after a successful 3 year run of the play (which he wrote and directed for the New York City stage) of the same name. He would go on to publish the YA novel, *The Hooky Party*, in 2007 and then the children's book, *Etienne and the Star Dust Express* in 2012.

In 2013 Marc switched gears and turned to writing horror, a genre he's loved since being introduced to it by his father as a kid. The move paid off and since then, he has published numerous short stories which include "*Welcome to Brooklyn, Gabe*" which is featured in the Bram Stoker nominated anthology *New York State of Fright* and "*A Marked Man*" featured in the *Hell's Heart* horror anthology. In 2019 he co-authored *Hell at the Way Station*, which he won two African American Literary Awards (Best Anthology/Best Science Fiction). The sequel, *Hell at Brooklyn Tea*, was released in January 2021.

His goal as a writer is to evoke fear and dread through quality fiction featuring strong characters, plots, and terrifying premises. His writing will feature new and original monsters of his own design. Contributing to the genre new terrors for not only himself but for future horror writers to build on.

When he's not writing, this Moth Story Slam and Grand Slam winner can be found performing storytelling throughout the borough of Brooklyn and curating a monthly storytelling open mic called Maaan, You've Got To Hear This!

When someone with a pistol meets someone with a magic wand, the pistol loses.

From Nicole Givens Kurtz comes a collection of weird western short stories nestled in the often horrific American past and tucked into the parched future. Here are tales of talisman, magic, and the power of ancients wielded by those strong enough to endure the harsh new frontier. These rugged individuals brought not only their belongings but their eastern beliefs with them. They weren't ready for the west.

Are you?

Saddle up.

Escape to a West as weird and wonderful as one might imagine.

In the shadows of ancient Benin, a demonic presence stalks an innocent girl on the cusp of womanhood. Seduced by this sinister stranger's fatal charm, the girl's soul descends into eternal damnation as she becomes one of the undead – a vampire slave to the merciless Promise Keeper.

For centuries across continents, the Promise Keeper haunts his victim's every move, invading her mind with violent commands in an unholy pact sealed in blood. Just as she dares hope his reach cannot extend to the glamour of New York City, an ill-fated romance once again shackles the reluctant asiman to her merciless master's bidding.

Now the Promise Keeper's web of deceit and murder ensnares fresh prey as he compels his undead servant to act against her very nature. In the end, not even true love may be enough to keep this vampire from honoring her agreement with the dark force that owns her soul. Will his unspoken promise be fulfilled at last?

ABOUT MOCHA MEMOIRS PRESS

Established in July 2010, Mocha Memoirs Press's mission is to amplify marginalized voices in speculative fiction genres (science fiction, fantasy, horror). We publish bold, fearless fiction that pushes boundaries and smashes gatekeepers.

We invite you to review our catalog to review the diversity in our stories. You can access the catalog at https://www.mochamemoirs press.com. Join our newsletter **here.**

You can also find us online:

instagram.com/mochamemoirspress

tiktok.com/@mochamemoirspress

bsky.app/profile/mochamemoirspress.com

x.com/mochamemoirspress

facebook.com/MochaMemoirsPress